THE TOWER OF AETHERIUS

THE TOWER OF AETHERIUS

ODYSSEY OF THE ETHEREAL BOOK 1

Jamie Kojola

Podium

Podium

THE TOWER
OF AETHERIUS

CHAPTER 1

Waking Up Sucks

Aesca awoke. Reluctant to banish the darkness, she slowly opened her eyes. Her body felt charged like never before. Her pajamas were missing. No underwear, either, and this was unlike her. Aesca maintained a rigid nightly routine of getting into her pajamas after she finished her raiding in *Eldest Fantasy Wars Online*. What had been different about last night?

The World First boss kill? *Yeah, that's why I went to bed later than usual. Pete and Callie wanted to talk afterward, and I fell into bed, still dressed.*

That did not explain why she was naked. Tiny glimpses of memories and images flickered through her mind. Something about EMTs giving her CPR? How could she have watched someone give her CPR?

That isn't physically possible.

Aesca exhaled in a giant sigh and coughed loudly. Thick dust lay everywhere, choking her and making her throat feel hoarse. Her slow waking was hastened by a fit of coughing, which only disturbed the dust, making it swirl thickly in the air. A mystery beyond being naked scared her mind into rapidly processing her predicament.

Where the hell am I?

The building comprised only a single, expansive room. The exterior walls were taller than a person and curved upward into a dome. No other walls or pillars existed in the building. It made the room feel spacious. The stonework looked ancient, yet the building seemed stable.

It's like a giant circus tent. What's holding up the roof?

The sudden thought it would collapse on her wriggled through her mind like a sour taste she couldn't dispel. The very little she could see of the stone walls showed extremely faded murals. Maybe another building could reveal more about who once lived here.

Besides her and the thick dust, only two other things seemed notable in the building. Next to where she lay, a fire burned. The flames were blue. Two foot-long pieces of wood crossed each other, and a circle of stones surrounded it. Despite the blue flame burning the wood, it did not seem to consume it. The imprint of where she had lain in the dust made clear she had huddled beside the fire for warmth.

Cripes! I don't remember drinking before bed.

A large wooden chest stood at the edge of the light provided by the blue fire. It looked neither old nor new and had no dust on it. The trunk had a small metal plate on the front. Even with the help of the firelight, Aesca could not make out the writing. She stood and walked over to the chest, brushing at the dust that clung to her. It was futile with how omnipresent it was.

Aetheria. The chest had her *EFWO* character's name on it. She pinched herself. "Ow." She did not wake up.

"Mrrrrrr." Half groan, half curse at life. She pushed up the lid of the chest. It came up quickly. For a moment, she thought she saw a flicker of teal energy glow around the chest and then vanish. Aesca braced herself for incoming trap damage. Nothing happened. "Me and my overactive imagination while lucid dreaming."

There's an idea.

Aesca focused on the idea of the fire getting larger to provide a more intense light to the room. Nothing happened. She tried to will a hot dog into existence in her hands. That didn't work either. She pinched herself again. Nope.

"Get a grip, Aesca Lampi." Scolding herself in her best imitation of Sister Bethany, the nun at her Catholic elementary school, she squared her shoulders and set about seeing what was in the chest. Clothes! The cure to nakedness. Naked beggars couldn't be choosy beggars.

A few different outfits lay in the chest. Aesca found socks, underwear, a sports bra, black canvas-like pants, a sleeveless turtleneck, and a long red coat, really more a duster, that she immediately fell in love with. It all went on right away, along with the front-lace combat boots that matched the coat. Unlike the jacket, the boots' coloration was hard to discern in the dim firelight. *Black or dark red? Who cares? They fit nicely and could crush a lot of peanuts at Texas Roadhouse.*

She even gave the empty room a twirl or two. The perfect fit for each piece of clothing blew her mind. Every single piece appeared perfectly tailored to her. *Maybe it's magic?* Aesca twirled again, jumped, and stepped side to side. It was all perfect. The calf-length long coat somehow never got in her way. *I'm firmly convinced excellent tailoring is magic, and it is magic I can believe in. Man, I need magic bras in the real world.*

The side of the chest held a few belts and a knife. It even had a sheath for the blade, so the belt and sheath went on. The edge of the knife looked very sharp.

It must be magic too.

Aesca glimpsed her own eyes reflected on the metal, which showed two bright teal lights. Did her eyes glow now? It was the only thing that made sense to her.

The only other thing still in the chest was a scroll. Straight out of a video game and in a trunk before Aesca. *Ugh. I'm firing my subconscious. Tacky gold holder? Bitch, please. You know most scrolls didn't have a holder.*

Annoyed at historical inaccuracies within her dream, Aesca pulled the scroll out and unrolled it. For a moment, the characters on it danced through her mind. Strange glyphs and sigils she couldn't comprehend covered the scroll. An undecipherable divine script the mortal mind could not understand assaulted her brain. The world turned sideways. Her mind shot through a prism, refracted a million times, and infused with who knew what recombined in another prism with a drop of lemon, and the world turned right side up. Suddenly, the scroll she was looking at made perfect sense. Why did she feel a little dizzy? *Oh, well.*

Dearest Aetheria,
Welcome to the family. We believe in you. Good luck climbing the tower.
—Aetherius

Why was she getting a scroll from a god in the *Eldest Fantasy Wars Online?* Stupid. Never had Aesca experienced such a ridiculous dream, and she wanted to wake up now. If this dream had a manager, she would call him to her table and go full Karen on his ass. Why was the message addressed to her video game character?

Just because I have blue-green hair down to my hips, and it sparkles in the darkness with internal illumination, they go and call me Aetheria.

Wait a minute!

Aesca's hair was brown. Also, it was only shoulder length. It did not glow in the dark. At all. Ordinary people's hair did not glow in the dark. Not even in dreams.

"Damn. *EFWO* never really captured the dazzling hair. Good job by my imagination." Still, hair that long needed a manager. A quick search through the chest turned up some scrunchies. Her glowing hair was in a manageable high ponytail a few seconds later. *Magical scrunchies, hopefully.*

I wonder what enchantments a scrunchie could hold? Why don't video games have a scrunchie slot? Some jerks would whine about how men can't use them, completely ignoring they could if they had long hair, and then the devs would take it away because the loudest idiots get all the attention.

A feeling of sickness in her gut interrupted Aesca's internal monologue about the unfairness of game developers. Something terrible was about to happen. Uncertain of what it was or even how she knew, she dove back toward the fire and rolled into a fetal position, pulling her arms and hands over her head.

Crrrrrraaack.

A horrible sound filled the air. The earth shook. Rocks fell. Dust rose thickly. Suppose this was what a massive earthquake was like. Aesca felt awful for past jokes about California sinking into the ocean after a Big One. The few minor earthquakes she had experienced on vacations hadn't seemed so apocalyptic, so this enlightened her about the terror an earthquake produced.

The ground continued to heave. A malicious and suffocating intent fell upon Aesca. It seemed directed at her and everything within a few miles of her. The intensity of the anger and its indiscriminate spread were irrational. No one in her life had ever directed so much spite, hate, and disdain at her. The earth shook. Rocks split and fell around her, and weird sounds like tectonic plates smashing against each other in terrible groans continuously assaulted her ears. Dust and debris fell like rain.

Then something hit the domed ceiling from the outside, and large roof pieces fell. One crashed down onto her legs. She thought she screamed before blackness took her into unconsciousness.

She awoke. It marked the second time she blinked to consciousness, and it sucked far more than the first time. Pain shot through her entire left leg. Aesca could not feel much there, and the massive rock over her leg looked like it weighed thousands of pounds. She struggled to push the large boulder, and in doing so noted a difference in her hand size and arm thickness, a new slenderness she hadn't possessed. *Where the hell am I?*

Appearances aside, it seemed like her strength had increased in this dream more than in the real world. She pushed, pulled, prodded, and even kicked with her still-freed right leg. Aesca's struggle with the rock seemed to take hours; in reality, she freed herself within five minutes.

Another aftershock shook the ground, and a terrible sound, like something breaking, echoed through the foundation of the building. Things quickly went from bad to worse as the earth went from a comfortable horizontal position to teetering violently. The floor stabilized at a sharp incline. The boulder she'd finally got off her leg tumbled down the floor and smashed through the stone wall. The wood of the fire followed.

Acting before thinking, she threw her hand out to catch the logs. Somehow, she grabbed a piece of wood and balanced the other against it, saving the fire. Of course, her hand was in the blue fire now. A rush of excruciating pain and heat flared in her hand, and then the room descended into darkness. No more fire. No more wood either. Had she dropped it in the assault of pain?

In shock, she failed to stabilize herself on the incline and tumbled down to crash into the wall. Her right knee smashed into the rock with an impact that sounded like breaking bones. As if that weren't bad enough, another series of aftershocks occurred. The chest came tumbling down. It smashed into her torso, rebounded a little, hit her head, then fell to rest against the wall beside her. Flashing lights filled her vision, and pain consumed her.

At length, the tide of pain and flashing lights before her eyes receded. The fire was gone, but with streams of light through the holes in the roof and the dim glow of her hair, she could see. Her left leg no longer hurt. Checking it left her stunned. She had no injuries. Even her clothes had mended. *How?*

Moving both legs revealed that neither was hurt. The pain had gone entirely. Not even a scratch remained from the giant rock that had crushed her leg. Not even a discolored bruise marked where she'd broken a knee against the wall. Her hands came away with no blood when she ran them over where the chest had impacted her head. No blood remained on the ground. *I didn't imagine getting hit in the head.*

"H-e-double hockey sticks. What in the world is going on?" Aesca cringed at how Minnesotan, the polite version of hell, she sounded in her mind.

Now, Aesca, your father was in the Navy. Don't you go swearing like he does, young lady.

"Fuck off, Mom," Aesca snarled at the voice that lectured her in her head.

One word kept dancing around in her mind. A dangerous word. One full of wonder and disdain simultaneously. It was a term that encompassed whole genres of media.

"I got isekai'd," Aesca said out loud. It sounded more confident than she felt.

The world had something to say in response to this declaration. Another aftershock, packed with intense malice, hit the area—another awful sound of some deep rock beneath her breaking. The floor tilted more.

"Jeez. I get it. You're mad at me, whoever you are. I need to get the hell out of here." Beyond the broken walls, she could see a ruined city. A subterranean metropolis. Rocks still fell from the ceiling high above. The angle of the ground increased slightly whenever another aftershock struck.

Aesca did not want to die inside the antediluvian ruins of a subterranean city. The erratic beams of sunlight from above revealed a wonderful place. Spires appeared to flow as water and rose high into the sky, refracting streams of colored light in a glorious revelation of their crystalline construction. Large domes glistened with a mysterious azure light from within. *Now isn't the time to gawk.*

She needed to move.

CHAPTER 2

Crossing the City

Oh, my god.

It was hard to quell the sense of awe in her chest. Aesca had made it a few steps—she climbed out of the hole in the domed building and ascended the roof. The view of the city she was in proved to be educational. They had built the sprawling metropolis on a plate or plateau. Each direction past what she could see revealed only the abyss of darkness. Whoever had made this fantastic place had not been human, or even a fictional race, like elves.

Some buildings only had sky entrances. Whoever had lived here had flown with so little effort, they'd built it into their architecture. Every curving wall and flowing window seemed to align with the buildings in a revelatory manner. The design spoke of an attunement with not nature, technology, or magic but with existence itself. This long-abandoned city spoke to her in subtle nuances, no matter where she looked. Aesca felt that whoever had lived here had been different on some fundamental level.

Each moment she spent in the city was another minuscule increase to the tilt of the plate the metropolis sprawled across. If this were *EFWO*, a countdown timer would tell her how long she had before something explosive happened. She had no timer.

"Menu?" she asked half expectantly. No user interface appeared. "Status. Status! Character sheet. Inventory. Menu. Help. Logout. Hearth. Return. Teleport. Attributes. Stats. Class. Backslash help."

While she tried many MMO and gaming commands, Aesca traversed the urban jungle. Light broke through the cavern in rays that pointed to what she thought was north, illuminating a sharp cliff. It looked like she could jump onto the ridge as the tilt increased. From there, she just hoped there was a way to the surface. The beams of sunlight proved there would be.

Her first jump off the curved roof of the building she had sheltered in gave her flashbacks of a particular web-slinging superhero. Her three-step lead-up run and jump were superhuman. Aesca had played softball as a teenager and wasn't wholly unathletic. But when one booted foot cracked stone as she leaped into the air, she knew more than just her hair had changed. Arms and legs comically flailing, she landed on the next building twenty feet away with an undignified crash.

"Oh, jeez." She stood and dusted herself off. Her center of gravity had changed significantly. Her legs were longer than she remembered, and her entire build had become more willowy. If she *was* Aetheria, this all made sense. Aesca had put the height slider to the maximum for Aetheria when she made her a decade ago. The aqua-haired cleric had been tall, lithe, and eye-catching. *You don't pick blue-green hair if you want to be subtle.* More than one of her guild mates had teased her about the choice.

Still, Aetheria had been a cleric based on healing, not a combatant. She couldn't jump twenty feet in *EFWO. Maybe I'm Aetheria, but not a cleric?*

Testing her new strength, dexterity, and agility was ridiculously fun. Every leap and dash Aesca made was revelatory about the capabilities of this new isekai'd body of hers. It was absurd how quickly she adapted to running, leaping, landing, and repeating the process. Caught up in the sheer thrill and awesomeness of her new capabilities, Aesca had crossed half the metropolis before she even noticed.

The other shoe inevitably dropped. It happened suddenly when a surge of glowing water struck Aesca in midair and startled her so much that she botched her landing, hit a wall, and fell thirty feet to the ground. Her landing was hard. There was a sickening snap, and something pierced through her clothing and chest, but at least her head didn't bounce off the ground, costing her precious time with a blackout.

"Cripes." Aesca gurgled the word, and blood accompanied it. Pain hit her like a truck, backed over her, then ran her over again for good measure. Groping blindly, she found a piece of metal piercing her chest. She pulled it out. Breathing with a wounded lung was an exciting new experience for her. The world spun and her vision swam, but Aesca clenched her jaw and focused. The pain subsided. Before long, she could even breathe again.

"Uffda." After coughing up a few more splatters of blood, she could breathe without issue. The hole in her shirt had already mended itself. Her skin underneath had also fully healed. "So, super regeneration. Guess I went from the Model-T human to Veyron human."

She realized she could see in this courtyard between buildings. A fountain filled the square. It infused the water with a glimmering aqua radiance. Aesca had never seen such ethereal-looking water in her life.

Unable to resist, she tossed the strange metal decorative fence piece that had impaled her to the side and walked over to sniff the water. It smelled like kiwi fruit. Touching a finger to the basin told her the water was warm and had no ill effects from contact. Aesca licked the droplets off her fingertip, which sent jolts of pleasure across her tongue. The taste was sweet and robust, and defied any words she tried to use to label the flavor.

Aesca scooped handfuls of the strange water and downed it. Like a woman dying from thirst, she drank with wild abandon. She only belatedly noticed the entire front of her shirt had become soaking wet. Odd. She usually had impeccable impulse control. As she drank again and again, warmth flowed through her. It felt like she grew with each swallow. Not in height, but in some weird sense of being she previously did not know. With each swallow, she gained a better understanding of her surroundings.

Oh, snap. Is this mana water? Is that why it's so refreshing and restoring? I wish I had a canteen.

No matter how much she drank, her stomach didn't seem to fill or even slosh. Yet she was on a timetable. When another aftershock hit the city, Aesca reluctantly stuck her head into the pool, took as many deep gulps as she could, then turned and jumped up the building she'd fallen from earlier. The mana water had reinvigorated her.

The next few leaps made her feel a surge of pride. With each jump, she went just a little higher, just a little farther. Before she knew it, she was clearing spans between three and four car lengths in a single jump. *Oh shit, oh shit, oh shit,* she screamed in her head as she leaped across what looked like impossible distances.

Aesca neared the towers closest to the cliffs. In her father's words, she was making good time. He had proudly said it after every trip up or down I-35 to the Twin Cities. Lacking a car hood to pat with those words, she patted her chest. *Hmm. Those are nice. Smaller now, but better for parkour.*

The best way to get off the ancient city and onto the cliff seemed to be one of the soaring, crystalline spires. It had a ground-floor entrance and was the tallest thing around. Abandoning the rooftops, she strolled in the front door.

Unlike the few other structures she had been inside, this one had no dust. The foyer was a sweeping, open-concept sphere surrounding spiral stairs rising to the next level. The walls showed a series of progressive images: a blue man and a black woman coming together to have children. The multicolored children then spread out across the world, a diaspora of self-interest. Images reflected the breadth of their pursuits. That was all the story the ground floor seemed to tell.

Aesca stepped gingerly as she climbed the crystalline spiral stairs. Unnerving was an understatement. The delicate crystal material looked like it would shatter from a dropped pin, but the way it took the impact of her boots teased at a durability far beyond its appearance.

Her walk was too quiet. Were her boots enchanted? The way her clothes mended themselves from damage made her think they were. "Inventory? Properties? Inspect?" No user interface or information came with her commands.

The next level of the spire was just like the room below it. The story continued. The children mastered different things. Magic. Art. Technology. Aesca couldn't help but notice that not one scene depicted fighting. *How very inhuman. They grew bored and missed their aloof parents.*

I always sucked at interpreting art. How am I feeling these things so clearly?

A unique hand did every panel or section of the scenes. Or maybe the same hand, but in different styles. As a librarian, Aesca couldn't identify cynical realism, Renaissance, Romantic, or Gothic styles with certainty. All she could say for sure was that someone had exquisitely rendered each panel in styles she had never seen before, but the true mastery was in the sensations and feelings the work invoked in her.

The third floor followed the same pattern.

The children wanted to be with their creators. The other races of this world held no interest for the children. Dragons, elves, humans, dwarves, orcs, strange mantis-people—none of them entertained or delighted the children. All the other races shared failings they did not. The destructive violence of the flawed races saw the children isolate themselves from the world, where they built monuments to their progenitors and begged to join them and be free of this tormented world. At the edge of many of these panels, a cruel-looking human woman glared at them.

The fourth floor was oversized compared to those below. The scenes showed the cruel human woman much more. She came among them and talked to them. Finally, she convinced each to leave this place. She would help them join their parents. The scenes were much less informative here, as it seemed from the hundreds of depictions that every child had a dedication in the murals. No names came to Aesca, nor could she discern any hidden languages.

The fifth floor was the last room of this type. The children had made a spire to commemorate their love for their parents. At the top of the spire, each one stepped through a glowing door and vanished. The last panel was in a peculiar style. It radiated triumph. There was a depiction of a dark-haired woman smiling in victory. It gave Aesca goosebumps. The woman's eyes were pure evil. They also seemed to watch her.

Aesca had no time to delay. She ran out the leftward of the two exits. Spiraling stairs went up on each side of the room. They formed a glorious climbing lattice that went up hundreds of feet more, where one last room remained. From there, she wanted to jump to the cliff. Every few minutes, the spire shifted perilously closer to the rock face.

Running up spiral stairs differed from the pseudo-parkour she had employed to cross the city. The higher she climbed, the more she could see of the sprawling metropolis of the reclusive people. It was a shame they had all left. Any world would benefit from a race that had shunned violence and mastered so many subjects in what the depictions made her think had been a reasonably short period. To show disdain for dragons, elves, and other fantastic races not found on Earth, they must have been amazing. It wasn't as if this world's races were influenced by Earth mythology, though.

Maybe actual dragons are just massive dicks?

Her climb ended in the last room. The bare walls screamed silently at her, and sorrow seemed to permeate the room. Two altars, one black and one aqua, stood touching, and the stone between them eddied into mixtures of blue-green and black. Upon each altar sat a glowing gem.

The ground shook.

Don't do it, don't do it, don't do—yep, I did it.

She grabbed both. Pain and delight danced in her; a drug-like euphoria filled her. Both gems puffed out of her hands. After the aqua gem vanished, it left a slight mist that reminded her of the smell of rain, plants growing, and the satisfaction of ice cream on a hot summer day. The black orb left a miasma that smelled of dark places, death, and elderly people's houses.

The ground shook again. Laughing like an idiot, Aesca moved as far from the cliff as possible. From there, she ran. It turned out her previous speeds had not been her maximum. Like Usain Bolt, Aesca crossed the top of the spire and leaped off, toward the sun-dappled cliff.

CHAPTER 3

Climbing to the Sun

Aesca grasped the cliff face with strong fingers, and her booted feet found a small ledge to situate herself on. She had made it! She had escaped from the tilting underground city before it plunged into the depths.

As if fate had a dramatic sense of timing, one last terrible groan accompanied yet another aftershock. The city tilted further on its plate, until some magic or unseen support broke, and the whole metropolis fell into the abyss. How was there such a vast abyss underground? *Are there different laws of physics in this place? Dimensional overlap? I can jump amazingly far.*

A deep sadness filled her. It was a shame such a beautiful and remarkable city was now lost. The things one could have learned from whatever the ancient pacifists left behind were undoubtedly amazing.

Aesca had landed on the cliff with about thirty feet of stone underneath her still. Not a significant margin of error, but the daunting part was looking up. Daylight peeked through the top of what looked like a crevasse. It seemed exceptionally far away, and the cliffs were uneven. The walls at the climbing gym felt like a meager amount of preparation for this.

The rock face looked worst nearest her—the higher areas looked much more even. *People had to have a way to get down to their subterranean city. Unless they just used magic or flew. Stupid flying. I wish I could fly.*

With a seemingly bottomless abyss beneath her that had eaten an entire city, Aesca was not feeling enthusiastic about trying to swing and jump her way up the cliff. That left doing this the old-fashioned way. The few extra inches of arm length she'd gained in her new body were handy, but not nearly as convenient as her increased physical strength. *This must be how Olympic athletes feel about minor workouts.*

Climbing proved more terrifying than problematic. Aesca had done a few pull-ups in her life, but since she'd awoken here, her strength had increased enough to enable her to pull herself up one-handed from handhold to handhold. Without a rope, she was erring on the side of caution, trying to keep each hand in a different spot as frequently as possible in case the rock gave way.

She swore under her breath as rocks scraped and cut her hands to hell, but her wounds healed before blood could be smeared onto the stone, a minor problem prevented before it became an issue. Her new regenerative capabilities also seemed to keep her from getting too tired.

Aesca had no way to keep track of time, but the climb seemed to pass quickly, and soon she felt it wouldn't be long before she reached the sunlight at the top of the crevasse. When she hit the section that appeared to be worked stone, the climb went faster—until it didn't.

The shock came as she pulled herself up using one of the holes in the stone, and an eel shot out and bit her hand. More eels shot out of other holes, landing on her and viciously nibbling her arms, legs, torso, and face. Aesca lost her hold on the cliff and fell.

Oh, fuck!

Nausea struck immediately. Panic and rushing endorphins surged through Aesca as she scrambled to get a hold as the cliff flew past her. Her first three grabs at extended ledges and outcroppings missed, but miraculously her fingers closed around the fourth, and then she braced for impact as her momentum shifted, slamming her into the side of the cliff. She lost her grip on the outcropping, but it didn't matter—she was tumbling down a long hallway.

I'll take luck over falling into the abyss.

Aesca lay on her back, panting, staring at a perfectly smooth tunnel. She would have been even more amazed to find out her limbs had extended in impossible ways for her to reach this place. It had been no lucky grab. The tunnel's floor, wall, and curved ceiling were all of the same perfectly smooth material. It appeared to be glassy obsidian. Under the surface, thousands of thin lines ran. Some looked like trees, others mosaics, suns, and stars. There didn't seem to be any rhyme or reason to the patterns. Yet, the longer she lay there, the more the lines seemed to come alive, and she could feel energy emanating from the tunnel.

The power came in waves and flowed like an invisible ocean that Aesca could sense but not see. Light shone dimly inside all the tunnel surfaces. Suddenly, the entire tunnel became a place of radiant beauty. The artistry stole Aesca's breath.

"Damn." The word echoed down the tunnel oddly, proving even the acoustics had a hint of the magical.

Aesca stood. The tunnel depicted an island around her. At its center rose a massive glowing tower. Beyond lay perfect nature. No humans, no elves, nothing. She began walking down the passageway, not wanting to try a hand at the cliff again if she had other options. If nothing else, she wanted to witness the artistry that the forgotten people of a lost city had left behind, before having to deal with the eels again. Her wounds had healed, but her clothes had not fully knitted back together.

Voices whispered as she walked along the passageway.

"Welcome, human. Please enjoy the works of art we have inscribed in the entry to Nova Azura. Nova Azura remains a beacon of hope and beauty for a world of strife. Though we Aetherials have left this world, we hope your lot in the cosmos improves. Nova Azura contains all the knowledge we have gathered during our time on Grief. We bequeath

this knowledge to you, the first visitor to arrive since our departure 153,792,948.7 years ago. We hope that the world of our birth prospers."

Aesca rolled her eyes. They cared so much, they had abandoned the place. But the time that had passed since they left made her step back and stumble into the wall.

"Cripes. No one found this place for *153 million years*? Jeez, did you leave the guard dogs out or something?"

The chorus-like voice did not answer her. It did not come back at all. That was the extent of the Aetherials' care about this world. A brief note and a city with all they knew.

"Aw, shit."

It was all gone now.

The incline of the tunnel increased, hopefully leading her toward the surface. The vivid scenes on the walls changed as she walked. Among the locations was a depiction of the world of Grief from space. It appeared to be a larger planet than Earth, but Aesca couldn't quite understand why she felt that way. Grief had eight significant continents. Too bad she couldn't zoom in, or she might know where Nova Azura was. The other scenes she walked past were beautiful, but seemed to be predominantly the Aetherials bragging about their fancy art, science, and knowledge. *How bad had this world gotten that such an advanced race would leave?*

After a while, the light show began to taper off, and the end of the tunnel came into view. Aesca stepped out of the passageway, looking out at the same cliff she had fallen from, only now she was much higher. Taking in the scenery, she laughed.

"It would've saved me a lot of trouble if I had found this tunnel initially." The oddness of the cliff made sense now. The tunnel was part of the entrance to Nova Azura, and from here, there were remnants of stairs leading to the surface. After a hundred million years, the stairs down into the city and to the surface had deteriorated significantly. *Something probably destroyed the entrance from the tunnel to the metropolis: earthquakes, erosion, or that evil lady in the pictures.*

The holes with the eels were a fair distance from the partly intact path to the surface. *Does the construction repel them somehow, or are they a defense mechanism? There can't be much that comes or goes around here if I'm the first person in millions of years.*

Deciding that the eels were a trap, she poked at the remnants of the stairs because the Aetherials had been nothing but trouble so far. Some risers were perfectly solid, some were missing, and the rest ranged anywhere in between. But Aesca's ascent was ultimately anti-climactic. With moderate caution, she walked right up, having to jump only a few gaps.

The top of the steps ended at another small tunnel into the cliff. It had collapsed ages ago, and the rubble was too much to clear.

"Guess that's why you didn't get any visitors, Nova Azura." The cliff continued rising to the crevasse at the surface. With only twenty feet of climbing, Aesca laughed, jumped to the top of the crack, and landed on solid ground. *Victory!*

Aesca landed in a clearing. Lush, vibrant grasses, flowers, and shrubs she couldn't identify filled her vision. A forest surrounded the clearing. Based on the tunnel, she had already been expecting it, but it was indeed a tropical forest. Untamed and untrampled by the feet of sentient races, it was a lot to take in. Towering trees, massive canopies, and the overwhelming sound of insects and animal life overwhelmed sight and sound. It all hit Aesca like a punch to the gut. The sensations she felt were overwhelming. There were so many things touching and shifting the unseen tides of mana. Could other people sense her in mana the way she seemed to feel things?

The most substantial presence was the massive tower in the island's center. The tower never seemed to end; it just went out of view. *Does it go into space?* It had a visible glow and radiated a challenge to all who beheld it. It called to her without a word. A siren song of provocation and the promise of rewards beyond measure lulled her into gawking. Catching sight of a massive figure flying around the tower pulled her out of the spell.

Aesca watched a dragon circle the tower and then fly off to the south. "Holy fuck. Dragons. Towers. Ancient cities. Healing like comic characters. Glowing blue hair. Self-mending clothes. I got isekai'd into a real fantasy world." She laughed like a madwoman. "I'm in a fantasy world, with magic, dragons, mana..." Endorphins flooded her body, and the anxiety and joy of this revelation made her physically shake. "So that's the tower from the letter. I'm going to climb you."

But first, she needed to get a basic grasp of everything. Fighting. Some food. More gear. Could she learn magic? Aesca needed to figure out how to *use* mana, not just sense it. Even if she couldn't cast spells, many games and books were rife with people using mana for a myriad of effects.

"I can do this."

She rolled her shoulders and built up her resolve. Growls from the forest answered Aesca's declaration. The sensation of dark mana filled her. At least two things were charging through the foliage at the edge of the clearing.

"I can do this," Aesca reiterated, and drew her knife.

CHAPTER 4

The First Fight

As Aesca watched, two strange creatures approached her. They seemed to be some sort of hybrid animal—a powerful, graceful jaguar combined with the scales and claws of a reptile. Yet, there was something more to them, some otherworldly quality that set them apart from any natural beast. Aesca struggled to find the words to describe them, and in the absence of better options, came up with the word "Jagrepts."

I am the most creative person ever.

The two Jagrepts were roughly the size of a jungle cat, and they seemed to emanate darkness, devouring the light around them. They were covered in matte black scales, but also a strange energy that radiated out and almost took physical form, like fur. Each of the monster's four feet ended in five vicious claws. Behind each Jagrept, a long, black barbed tail twitched, controlling the monsters' movements.

They approached her swiftly, each almost flanking her. Then everything turned dark. *Oh, yeah, of course they can make clouds of darkness. Why wouldn't the first monsters I find be able to do that?*

Aesca was so distracted by the pitch darkness, she didn't realize she could still sense the two Jagrepts until they were biting at her. Her new body's massively increased reaction time allowed her to swing her arm around immediately and stab her knife into the hard scales of the Jagrept on her right. The scales blunted her thrust, but the sliding blade tip found purchase between two scales, and with her new strength, she plunged the blade deep into the creature's throat. After falling to the ground, the Jagrept bled out.

The Jagrept on the left made contact. A third Jagrept simultaneously leaped out of the shadows behind her. The sharp teeth of the flanking monster viciously mauled her left thigh while the ambushing Jagrept shredded her back with repeated slashes of its claws. When she had her knife again, both creatures retreated into the pitch-black void.

Aesca could feel them circling. Their presence carried a miasmatic sensation that conflicted with the regular flow of mana she sensed. She waited, the wounds on her back and thigh already burning and itching as her skin knitted itself back together. Noticing the diminishing scent of blood in the air, the Jagrepts snarled, attacking simultaneously once more.

One came at her head-on, and she aimed at its skull with her knife. She missed, her elbow connecting with its head instead, and the creature took a massive bite out of her soft left side. Its tail arced and stabbed through her left shoulder. Unlike the visceral pain of tearing flesh, that wound had a throbbing quality. *Poison? Of course they're poisonous. Why wouldn't this darkness-creating jaguar/reptile hybrid be full of poison?*

The pain was overwhelming her mind. She contorted in agony, luckily avoiding the flanking Jagrept's teeth going for her throat. Aesca doubled down on anger to get her through the pain and violently punched the incoming Jagrept in the snout. Fury gave her strength she'd never dreamed of, and the Jagrept's skull shattered near its eyes. So did most of the bones in her hand.

Her victory was short-lived. As the Jagrept fell to the ground to die, its still-moving tail whipped around and stabbed her in the throat. Again, poison started coursing through Aesca's veins. Her regeneration ability was already working overtime to heal her first toxic exposure and previous injuries.

The sole remaining Jagrept chose that moment to ambush her. Pain wracked Aesca too severely for her to have even a chance of following the miasmatic presence with her senses. It made no warning sounds before it slashed at the backs of her heels and calves. Just like that, her mobility became nonexistent.

The final predator circled a few times—precious seconds for her healing to purge the poison from her throat and heal her carotid artery. Just as the creature attacked, Aesca spit out bile, blood, and strange black stuff at it, taking it by surprise. The giant predator's claws missed her face by millimeters.

Her life flashed before her eyes. *Not again. I will not die again!* Knifepoint found purchase against the scales, and she stabbed. She kept stabbing until the sensation of wrongness dissipated as it had when the other two creatures had died. Once she could feel nothing else in the mana flows, she fought the temptation to let the pain cause her to collapse. This new world seemed brutal, and she couldn't take even a minute to rest. She needed to stand up and be ready for the next threat.

Her body rebelled against her desires. Couldn't she just lie there for a bit? A minute?

Get. Up. Now.

Aesca made the mistake of putting pressure on her still-healing shattered hand to stand up. She fought through the pain and stood up. She straightened, tall, and glared at the darkness.

"Oh, jeez, just fuck off already."

Aesca drew a deep, full breath, then started sputtering and coughing. The air tasted and smelled like what she assumed miasmatic energy would taste and smell like. Damp and rotting things. Death. Like foul dirt that left an oily taste and sensation in her mouth, even though she had eaten nothing. Had she?

The rays of the beautiful, glorious sun hit her again as the darkness finally dissipated, and the warmth felt good on her skin. The corpses of the Jagrepts were gone. Not a single scale, piece of fur, or even tooth remained to show for the battle she had with them. No pools of her blood covered anything, not even her clothes. *What the fuck?*

Her clothing had already restored itself. The only evidence of her fight with the Jagrepts were the knicks and imperfections left on her knife from dealing with the scaled bastards.

"So, no loot? Worst isekai world ever." Aesca glared at the tower rising into the sky. If the forest was full of crap like these Jagrepts, she needed to get better at fighting, on the double. *I've read and watched way too many light novels and comics. Relying on tanking damage, out-healing damage, and slowly wearing enemies down is a shitty strategy. I need more weapons. Even some damn rocks to throw could help. What can I make with a knife? Find a club, maybe, and trim a few branches into shitty spears.*

One thing is for sure: I can't stay here. Fighting blindly around a giant hole in the ground is a terrible idea. There's nothing down in the tunnel to make retreating there worthwhile. I need to improvise some weapons as I go. Maybe I can avoid most bad things by sticking to the forest canopy. I'm ridiculously agile now.

Not waiting to find out whether it was a good idea, Aesca committed to the climb. Climbing the cliff had made climbing trees a joke in comparison. *Just how much do I weigh now? The limbs should bend more than this, right?*

Admittedly, Aesca had never gone jumping and running through trees like a crazy Tarzan or a mad person on *Survivor*, but when in Rome, right? She could run down branches without them breaking under her and jump off to land on another. When she consciously thought about it, branches bent more, so she tried not to. *Aw shit, now I can't stop thinking about it.*

After jumping and jogging in circles for the better part of five minutes, Aesca wrote off the decreased weight effect as something to do with her boots. *Is that true? Are you a pair of magic jungle jumping boots? I don't know, but if we think that way, it'll keep me from falling forty feet to the jungle floor.*

Native animals, even predatory ones like insects and canopy-dwelling ambushers, left her alone. All these creatures felt ordinary with her mana sense. None had the miasmal taint of the Jagrepts. *Do they leave me alone because they're unfamiliar with humans, so they don't recognize me as prey, or is it something related to the mana flows around me?*

Aesca assumed, possibly wrongly, that all life on this planet had a mana sense of some variety. *Are there animals out there that see by mana? I bet that'd be more accurate than relying on refracted light. Maybe they can sense intent through it? I'm getting ahead of myself, though. I need to work more on perceiving mana. The large flows are still hard to follow, and living things seem minuscule.*

Something about that felt wrong or off about her assumptions and reasoning, but Aesca couldn't pinpoint what. Experimenting and learning as she went was the best she could plausibly hope for.

Near the edges of her mana sense, she sensed the occasional flicker of corruption and darkness. More monsters hunting across the island? For now, she shifted course toward the scent of salt on the breeze. She could check the perimeter for manufactured structures if this were an island.

She did not make it to the beach before something caught her attention. To the east, she saw a small valley wreathed in fog, but in front of her, a strange pillar of stone rising amid the canopy caused her to stop. Looking closer, she saw it was not actually what she thought. Somehow, a strange grouping of trees had petrified. While not the first group of petrified trees she had seen, it was the first to have what looked like an artificial structure. If she were to imagine an elven tree-shaped house, it would look exactly like this. Strangely, it still had a functional stone door.

"Freaky. Did the original occupants live here when it was a tree? Did they grow it and turn it to stone, or did the petrification happen naturally?" Talking to herself might be a bad habit, but Aesca felt she might be lonely in this world, so she needed to get used to being alone. Not alone in the fashion she had grown used to on Earth, where she had voice and text chats to talk to people while she played video games.

The interior of the tree house was mostly empty. The furniture had petrified along with the house. Open stone cabinets, an eating nook with a window, and the platform for a mattress in one of the side rooms stood as testaments to the skills of the architect of this strange building. With the ever-lowering of the sun, Aesca decided to camp out in the tree house for the night. It had already been a very exhausting day. She shut the door.

Through the window, Aesca watched as three moons rose—one blue, one that looked like Earth's, and an eerie red moon. *Charting the oceans for this planet must be hell. Mrs. Jones could have told me how three moons might affect the tides.* Aesca herself had no idea. So much of the knowledge about Earth had always been at hand. She had adopted a dangerous reliance on technology to allow for fast reference. Here, she knew so little of where she was. But it seemed she would have a lot of opportunities to find out.

I should have watched those reality competition shows with Gordon Ramsay. I bet I could have learned something valuable. Maybe. Or it could've just been him screaming, 'Drink your pee, you donkey!' at the cameraman.

Aesca fell asleep dreaming of Gordon Ramsay.

CHAPTER 5

Not-So-Sweet Dreams

O h, Gordon, the spatula is for the frosting, you devil!" Aesca said coyly.

The dream of Mr. Ramsay faded, into one of herself at the top of an impossibly tall building. An older man sat at the fire, making himself s'mores. Next to the man, a very familiar woman sat, hunched. She was tall with broad shoulders and wide hips, brown hair, and hazel eyes. Aesca Lampi.

The older man had eyes the color of the sky, and his hair wasn't white as she'd initially thought, but a whitish blue that hinted at sky and clouds. He radiated a powerful aura. Somehow, the slouching woman was completely ignoring the imposing power of the man, as if she were blind to it.

Neither of the figures acknowledged Aesca's presence, although she could swear the old man looked straight at her for a fraction of a second and winked.

Pay attention. I'm only going to remind you once. Another voice spoke in her mind. It sounded feminine and far away, and it did not speak again.

"So, you're an actual god, not just one in *EFWO*?" the slouching woman asked the man.

"Yes. We've gone over this already. You, Aesca, are dead, and I, Aetherius, am a god, like in your MMO. I'm offering you a second chance, *as you*, otherwise it is back into the Samsara for you."

"So, I get to keep being me instead of returning to whatever the Samsara is?" Observing Aesca clucked her tongue at her dream self; after all, she had gone through comparative religion, and she damn well knew what the Samsara was. Although, the slump, the loss, something about the other woman's posture made her get goosebumps and feel sick to her stomach.

"On a basic level, yes. You keep your consciousness if you want to. We will reincarnate you in an adult-like body, a new body. There may be a few quirks to adjust to. In return, you try to save a world. How does that sound, Aesca?" Aetherius seemed very familiar. Well, no, his voice was very similar to Pete's. Of course, a god would sound like the most challenging raid team member.

"I've always hated the name Aesca. I wanted to be an Ashley, Amanda, Jennifer, or Jessica." Again, the old her, the woman on the couch, was acting out of character, morose, in shock, babbling.

"Is that why you only went by your character name online, even in chat? You could always take that on as your name and appearance. By taking on our essence, you will change. The Samsara will lose its hold on you, a rare thing for one born human. You'll walk the path to becoming a true Ethereal being." Something in the man's tone made it sound like an arduous path.

"I can be Aetheria?" A spark of hope filled the brown-haired woman's eyes. *Watching yourself is weird.*

"If that is what you want. Accepting our Flame won't make you an Aetherial. You'll still be human, but I will enhance your body and soul. You'll become something new, spiritually. Something on the Path to the Ethereal. It happens on worlds more advanced in the spiritual paths than Earth."

"Flame? Do I get fire powers?" Old Aesca laughed.

"What abilities you gain will depend on the path you walk and build for yourself. The possibilities are infinite. We can influence some of what you will start with to give you the best possibility of success."

"Why me?"

"We watch a lot of worlds. It goes with being nearly omniscient, you know. A few of us found your culture amusing, especially the video games. When some developer made a pantheon that resembled us, well, we investigated it. We'd been searching for a leader with a strong, stubborn streak for years when we stumbled across you. Recent negotiations by the Trickster have allowed for unprecedented possibilities here on Grief."

"What's so special about Grief, and what's wrong with it? Also: Who names a planet Grief?" The old Aesca was still sulking, but she seemed to pay more attention than before.

"It is an old world—one of the few I sent my children to when it was young. Grief had the misfortune of drawing Oizys as the lead god. Every god gets at least one planet they are the lead on, and Grief drew Oizys, to its eternal regret."

"But you are a god. Just beat her up and take her planet." It seemed far more straightforward than needing mortal intermediaries.

"Forbidden. No direct conflict between gods. The towers are how we may contest a planet's leadership. Every god may elect one Challenger they empower to take on the towers of a world. Beat ten, and you may unseat a god. Until recently, I was the only god with a Challenger left on Grief."

"That's stupid. Why can't you have a council vote or deal with it yourselves? It's inhumane to make those with less strength suffer, perish, and strive for something that is out of their reach."

"I agree, but it is the method we must work with." Aetherius's annoyance was nearly a physical thing. It was that strong.

"Who makes you do anything? A bigger god?" Aesca laughed a little.

"Yes. The Overgod. There are only a few scenarios in which we gods may war with one another. While the system of the towers is cruel, it is what we are bound to. Thus, mortals, too, are bound. The towers have other uses as well. They allow for planar travel and are among Creation's best training grounds."

Aetherius smiled, and it was the smile of a car salesman about to give her the absolute best price to stop her from walking off the lot.

"Thanks to the Trickster, we can give you the best odds any Challenger has ever had on Grief."

"So, it'll be easy?" The old Aesca was dubious.

Laughter met her question. "No. Not even slightly. I said you'll have the best odds anyone has ever had. It will still be tough. You'll reincarnate into a new body. Even with all your advantages, you will start as weak as a newborn kitten."

"Lead me through it. I become a Challenger. I climb some towers, boot Oizys off the high chair, and then?"

"What do you want?"

"Could I go back to Earth? See other planets?"

"You could. By the time you've beaten the ten towers, you'll be capable of doing almost anything you want under your power. Every tower conquered will confer significant gifts. That is why they are so popular, despite being incredibly difficult to climb. It is rare for non-Challengers to beat a tower."

Stars shone in Aesca's eyes until all the god's words settled in. "It's rare to beat one, and I have to beat ten? You're a terrible salesman."

"I did mention advantages. You will have the gift of rapid regeneration." The car salesman-like smile came back.

"Like Deadpool? Oh man, this will be a real shitshow, right?"

Observing Aesca saw her dream self grimace, and she remembered all the comics, light novels, and movies in which the fast-healing person got completely demolished in every fight.

A shudder shifted through her dream self. "Ugh. Do I get cheat powers?"

"All new challenges come with growing pains. Expect a lot of growing pains, like you did with each new raid. After all, you don't even know how to sense or touch mana. As far as cheats go, I can't give you any hints, I'm afraid. Rules are rules. I can only explain the situation and offer you reincarnation and a chance to climb the heavens." Aetherius winked.

"So, do I sign a contract with you? How does it work?" The old Aesca had decided.

"No contracts, no. You agree, and we start. Quite simple. Prior reincarnations have shown the process to be a painful one. Adding in our Flames is going to make it even more painful. I can't ease the side effects, but they are short term. Just power through the best you can."

"Alright, then, Aetherius, let's do this. You picked me because my character's name is Aetheria, didn't you?" The woman on the couch smirked at the question before adding another. "Why is your voice so familiar?"

"I'll admit a fondness for your name, but your character is why I chose you."

Aesca noticed amusement the god had not shown previously.

"You have my vote of confidence on using Aetheria as your name in your new life. After all, you're absorbing a flicker of my Flame in this process. Welcome to the family."

As kindly as those words were, the force of power that descended upon the soul of Aesca, that literally ripped her into stray spiritual particles and reassembled her spiritually and physically, was not at all kind. The dream faded.

Aetheria jerked awake. Sweat covered her forehead. The long red coat had been her blanket, not because the weather required one but because the stone bed was hard. It was a tropical island. It was hot.

"Cripes. How the hell did I forget about that? 'Uncomfortable' must be the understatement of the millennia. It was so painful I blocked out how I reincarnated. Why did he keep talking about Flames?"

Aesca had died. It flickered through her memory.

"I watched the EMTs giving me CPR. Right..." She could see it now. She'd had a brain aneurysm in her sleep and died. And as Aetheria, she had watched it all occur with Aetherius.

Unsheathing the knife on her belt, she tried to study her face in its reflection. The three moons provided adequate light. Her hair sparkled and glowed. A pale face looked back at her with eyes that shared the same aqua glow as her hair. She looked exactly like the Aetheria she had built in the *EFWO* character builder long ago.

"Would've been nice if he hadn't just dumped me naked in an abandoned subterranean city with just some clothes and a note. Guess that must have been his kids' city, then. You better not blame me for it falling into the abyss! Shoddy craftsmanship?" Laughing, Aetheria looked up at the sky as if she were meeting eyes with Aetherius.

Her laughter betrayed the slightest tinge of hysteria. She threw the coat back on and walked to the window to look out at the island.

Aetheria stared at the massive tower. It had already been her ultimate destination, but now she had even more reason to head there. It also reinforced her plans to explore the island, resupply, and gain some practical experience before tackling the most dreadful thing on the island. Aetherius had hinted at more cheat abilities than regeneration. Exploration was necessary.

Realization dawned on her, and more laughter came. "Oh, jeez. I'm a god-chosen isekai heroine. Sister Bethany always said God loved me. I wonder how monotheism works if there are whole pantheons out there. Aetherius mentioned an Overgod?" Aetheria didn't ponder that for long, and it didn't matter now. She had so many more problems than theology. "Anime hair, regeneration, maybe more cheat powers, and I'm an isekai heroine. Niiiiiice."

She laughed again. At least she found herself humorous. That joke would have slayed in her guild's discord. *Who cares? They would just be pity laughs because I'm a raid leader. Huh. I wonder who took over for me? It better not have been Callie.*

Another important takeaway: Aetherius had confirmed she would have to learn to use mana.

Can I breathe it in and use it? It can't be that easy, can it?

CHAPTER 6

Breathing Causes So Many Problems

Morning sun covered the island, but only a fraction of its rays broke through the canopy of the tropical forest to the forest floor. The ever-present breeze carried the inescapable scent of the ocean. Standing at the base of the petrified tree house, Aetheria was psyching herself up to test what would happen if she breathed in mana.

I can do this. I can control mana. Magic will be mine.

Aetheria closed her eyes and repeated the mantra, focusing all her attention on the energy flowing through the natural world. She could feel the unseen tide of power surrounding her, and she inhaled deeply, trying to draw it into her body. It was as if she were chugging a can of 5-hour ENERGY in one go, the surging energy overwhelming her senses and pushing against her attempts to harness and control it. She desired to wield this power to become more, but she had not expected resistance from the energy. Mana wasn't supposed to be sentient. Yet, it fought her control and longed to remain free and untamed. A battle of wills between them continued, each attempting to assert dominance over the other.

The books, games, anime, and every other story Aetheria had read had failed to convey the sheer difficulty of containing mana. Sweat broke across her brow, and she exhaled the energy.

You win round one. Now I know how tough of an opponent you are, though.

The surrounding jungle had grown louder with insects and small animals. A strange-colored exotic-looking bird sat on a branch. The bird chirped at Aetheria between eating insects that had gathered to watch the human.

"What? I'm not a Disney princess. I don't speak Bird. At least, I don't *think* I speak Bird, do I?" The continued nonsensical chirping reassured her she did not. *Maybe it just doesn't talk human.*

Round two.

Aetheria was ready for the battle this time. She took a deep, slow breath, trying to draw only a tiny amount of mana into her body. The intense struggle was much more manageable when she tried to control less energy, and being prepared for the fight from the beginning also helped. The energy flowed through her body on its own, spreading out from her lungs to her limbs. She tried to visualize a firebolt and shouted, "Firebolt!" but nothing happened.

The mana in her body did not respond to her commands. It simply flowed through her and then escaped into the air, returning to the invisible tides of energy that flowed through the natural world.

"Okay. That was a total failure. Maybe this is one of those worlds where you need spell circles? Incantations? I need to find a settlement. Even a hedge wizard would be helpful. A wise old wizard would be best..."

Waving the dissipating energy away from her, she turned to face the direction of the ocean. "Whatever. I'll try again tonight." It was time to check out the island. She needed to find supplies and prepare for whatever ordeal awaited her in the tower. *The Tower of Druaga* had been one of a good deal of anime shows she had watched, and it seemed the towers here were probably much worse than those she had seen in that show.

An annoyed clucking sound marked the beginning of her walk to the beach. But her annoyance rapidly gave way to wonder. Even on the forest floor, there was a bounty of biodiversity she had never seen. The real problem came down to not knowing what was safe to eat. While many of the berries and fruits looked tantalizing, they all had bright colors that left her dubious.

Temptation overtook wariness when she found what looked exactly like an apple. A quick cut with her knife revealed it smelled like an apple. Throwing caution to the wind, she took a bite, and it tasted amazing. The fruit was ripe, sweet, just a touch tart, and carried the warmth and energy of mana. And this time, it didn't try to escape from her body. The power settled in with the other lingering energy she had swallowed.

It had been a day since she had last eaten. Ravenous hunger emerged now that her tongue and stomach had tasted food. After her fourth apple, Aetheria forced herself to stop. She needed to keep moving to the beach, and there was still a chance that the apples were poisonous. She recognized another food source as the jungle gave way to sparser trees. Palm trees. Coconuts wouldn't be deadly.

With her improved physicality, she quickly cracked a coconut against a rock. After she drank the milk, she ripped the coconut apart to help herself to the meat within.

Was this supposed to be an island paradise for the Aetherials? Abundant food, tropical climate, their giant magic tower to gather resources from, a sea to protect them from other races? Way to give your kids all the advantages, Aetherius. I bet they probably didn't even have to deal with jaguar-reptile monsters.

Thinking about the monsters seemed to jinx her. Even as she thought about it, a roar of annoyance came from the area back by her tree house.

"Uh-oh. Someone's having a bad day. They must've run out of coffee. Coffee is a tropical plant, isn't it?" Another roar followed the first. The canopy shuddered as something colossal approached her. Dimly, she could feel the dark presence of the monster. This one held a much more concentrated miasma than the Jagrepts had. Aetheria knew she couldn't hide from something that could shake the canopies of the forest. Her only option was to fight and hope she could kill whatever was coming faster than it could overcome her regenerative abilities.

Aetheria turned and stood her ground. Her only weapon was a knife. Questions about her decision-making process arose when the monster charged into view. It stood at least twice her height and had to be at least ten car lengths long. The massive reptile's pitch-black scales pulled the dim light of the jungle floor in and darkened its surroundings. Its thick hide looked exceptionally dense. When the colossal lizard carelessly brushed against trees, the trees took damage. Black scales gleamed with the promise of pain to come.

Oh, great, a giant monitor lizard with shadow powers. What's up with this island and shadow powers? Isn't Aetherius supposed to be about the sky? Cripes, this is going to suck.

The monster charged her. In the last few seconds, as Aetheria prepared to dodge, the lizard sped up in a blurring motion of shadow, and Aetheria heard a *crunch*. It had moved so fast she hadn't been able to even dodge. Its massive maw had swallowed her entirely, and its giant teeth snapped the tree at her back in half. Fragments of bark and wood exploded like shrapnel behind her as she attempted to stay on her feet.

Guess you're the whale, and I'm Geppetto. Bad news for you, asshole. I'm not a nice old man!

In the mouth of the monster, the tongue underneath her rolled, pushing her toward the sharp teeth, pulling her back to the esophagus. But those were not the only threats. Aetheria smelled decay, rot, and corrosion. The latter predominantly came from the esophagus, where digestion would promise a slow, painful death, but the monster's saliva was also corrosive. As it covered her clothes, a severe caustic burn of pain started slowly and quickly built up.

Her regeneration worked on her wounds, but it did nothing for the cause. She was almost swimming in the reptile's saliva, with no obvious solution to escape it immediately visible.

An eight-inch knife blade was not much to work with, but it was all she had. Aetheria pushed the pain down. *Fear is the mind-killer, right?* But fear wasn't the problem she had to deal with right now. Her pain was the problem, but she could overcome it. She compartmentalized the agony, then ran roughshod over it through sheer force of will.

The first few swings of her knife at the tongue felt like taking a hatchet to a redwood. Aesca had always hated getting wood for campfires. Aetheria was superior to Aesca, though. Swing after swing left gaping wounds that sent the monster into a frenzy. She was supposed to die quietly, like a good little snack. Did nothing on this island fight back against these monsters? Driven by spite and survival instinct, Aetheria lunged, hacked, and sliced until she had bisected the esophageal tissue. A strange roar erupted from the reptile's lungs, and its mouth opened.

She was immediately stunned. *Bullshit! NERF stun locks! Overpowered bullshit!* For a fraction of a second, she was back to raging internally over being stun locked in a duel or PvP before she remembered this was real life now. Released, she flew out of the jaws, and her back slammed against a tree with a loud series of crunches and cracks. Based on the impact, she had snapped a tree trunk, continued to strike another, and then fell limply to the ground.

The agony of acid corroding her skin had not abated, and now she had a broken back, and who knew how many shattered and fractured bones. Immediately, the pain of regeneration kicked in on the new wounds. Her vision swam and tears leaked down her face. Aetheria had held onto her knife throughout and worked up to her feet through sheer willpower.

The colossal monitor lizard monster hissed at her as she stood. At least, she thought it was hissing, until she realized it was spitting acid at her. All she could do was grimace and fight through the pain until her body was mobile again. *I never wanted to know what having my spine realigned from the inside felt like. I miss not knowing that.*

Mobility returned to her. Aetheria charged toward the reptile. It stopped spitting acid as she darted forward. This time, she was the one who closed the distance and started attacking before it knew what had happened. Unfortunately, she didn't have the overwhelming attack power the monster had. Her knife just lacked the piercing capability to bypass the scales. She stabbed the blade fully into one of the lizard's massive eyes before it reacted to her. The monster used its whole maw like a club to bat her back.

As she fell, the giant lizard's tail struck her, and she felt a sinking sensation in her stomach. The tail was a baseball bat and she was a ball. Worse, the reptile was great at hitting home runs. Her frail human body crashed into rocks, trees, roots, and dirt as she bounced and rolled. The terrifying ride finally stopped when she hit a boulder and came to a halt. Despite the pain, Aetheria kept her eyes open and pushed herself up. Her limbs ached intensely, and she vomited as she struggled to stand, but she got to her feet.

I'm never going to get used to bones resetting themselves. Although, at this rate, I might be there by the end of the day.

"Oh, gross." She had made the mistake of looking down only to see the lizard's corrosive saliva still working away at her skin, and her forearm going from bent at a sharp angle to straight over a few seconds. She vomited again.

Wiping her mouth clean with the back of her left hand, Aetheria looked for the monster. She couldn't see it, but it was still near. The miasmic energy of its essence was close. Extremely close. It was right under her. *Oh, fuck.*

The ground broke apart as the lizard emerged from beneath her. In shadowy, lightning-fast motion, its open maw snapped around her.

CHAPTER 7

Not Geppetto

For the second time that day, Aetheria found herself in the giant lizard's mouth. The fight was not going at all as she had hoped. Initially, she thought she could trade blows with the monster and come out the victor via the power of regeneration. Instead, she was getting beaten to a pulp and inflicting only minor wounds between blows from the monster that would otherwise have killed or crippled her original body.

It was time to go with battle plan B: make shit up as she went along. *I'm fighting monsters, vastly under-equipped and underpowered. Fighting them as if I am on even footing is stupid. Aetherius gave me my cheat power, so let's embrace the pain.*

The tongue she had hacked at earlier tried to bat at her and toss her toward the sharp teeth. Aetheria embraced gravity, dodged the forked tongue, and fell straight toward the monster's esophagus. The monster's throat opened wide to swallow her whole even as she stabbed the blade into its fleshy throat and let gravity and her body weight pull the sharp knife down with her. Terrible black blood filled the monster's throat as she fell into its stomach.

The entire world twisted as the lizard went from shooting up from the ground vertically to landing horizontally on the earth. As expected, it created another vibratory growl that stunned her. In those precious seconds, she fell into the acidic liquids sloshing in the monster's stomach. Corrosive liquid covered her entirely. Aetheria fought against the pain, but it was not the only thing that assaulted her. The scents that tortured her nose were beyond description. It didn't help that she knew some of that smell was her hair, clothing, and flesh melting.

As Aetheria looked around in the darkness of the monster's stomach, she noticed that the dim, flickering illumination cast by her hair was the only light source in the otherwise pitch-black environment. Besides this glow were the sparks of illumination created when her hair regenerated. Despite the dimness of the light, it was enough for her to use to navigate the beast's stomach.

As soon as the creature was lying horizontally and Aetheria regained her balance, she sprang out of the pool of acidic liquid. She landed on the soft flesh of the higher stomach lining, her feet sinking slightly into the surface as she looked around for a way to escape. Despite the pain and nausea that the corrosive liquid was causing, she was determined to find a way out of the beast's stomach and back to safety.

When she impacted the stomach wall, she hacked at the lining with all her strength. Despite the terrible textural feeling sending shivers into her soul, she savagely gripped the disgusting lining of the stomach wall with her left hand while hacking through it with the knife in her right hand.

This all makes total sense. I'm being eaten alive, skin dissolving, seeing by the light of my sparkly hair, and I've got the creeps from monster innards. Grief is a good name for this world, after all.

Empowered by self-deprecation, she cut through the stomach lining and began hacking through the lizard's flesh. From there, it became a blur to her. It was just muscle, fat, and the occasional organ that she sliced and stabbed. Occasional wooziness and blackness surrounded her. She wasn't sure if it was all the damage her body was working on healing or the lack of oxygen as she performed interior surgery. All Aetheria knew was that eventually she stabbed a big, beating organ that looked like a heart embedded with crystals, and then, a few minutes later, she lay on the forest floor.

"That's bullshit! I deserve some loot after killing that thing! Where's my reward?" Aetheria's voice boomed through the forest as her body shook with exhaustion and adrenaline. She convulsed as if she had a high fever, and the terrible smell and taste that filled her nostrils and mouth were unbearable. No matter how much she tried to get rid of it, the taste of death and decay lingered, and even biting into an apple did nothing to ease it. She knew that only time would make the sensation fade away.

Aetheria was still fuming about the lack of loot when the vile smells and tastes finally stopped assaulting her. She helped herself to two more apples. The lovely warm, energized feeling she had from eating them helped shake off her considerable exposure to the miasmatic energies.

"Clothes all restored. Skin back to normal. No more internal pain." It did not matter if she looked like a crazy person as she poked at her body and clothing. No one was around to judge her, and if they were, what kind of person would piss off someone who had just butchered their way out of a giant lizard from the inside?

"I need more weapons. Stabbers, you are a good little boy, but I'd like to avoid repeating what we just did."

Aetheria made another sweep of the area and then a third. A low growl emitted from her throat, and she kicked a broken limb across the jungle floor when she failed to turn up so much as even a black scale.

"This is bullshit. No menu, no experience, no loot." Bitching at the air did no good, and she muttered tirades about how this was the worst isekai ever until she got to the beach.

The ocean waves were massive, but what quieted her were the various sea monsters she could see offshore. Some fought with each other, and others just prowled, looking for an easy dinner. They were too far away for her to sense the miasma, or they were actual beasts based on the sensations she perceived via mana. All ignored her as she scratched out an enormous mark on the beach and then built a pile of rubble.

"X marks the spot, straight-ish line to the tree house."

Aetheria walked along the beach. She hoped to find a dock, ruins, or an active settlement. The order of the day, however, was a disappointment. The sun had gone from early morning—Aetheria guessed 7 a.m.—to high noon by the time she had finished circling the entire island at a fast jog. Without GPS, she could only estimate distances. She assumed that her run—which would have been faster than Aesca's full-speed run—had been somewhere around fifteen miles per hour. Based on what she guessed had been five hours of running, the island had seventy-five miles of shoreline.

Disappointment gave way to curiosity when she returned to the petrified tree house. Mist and fog still obscured the small valley not far away. With the sun riding high in the sky, Aetheria decided that settling down for the night this early would be wasteful. She walked into the fog. Sound ceased within the mist, and a heavy layer of condensation formed on her skin and beaded in her hair as she walked through the gloom. A strange sensation tingled at the back of her mind, like a sixth sense, warning her something was investigating her.

The tingle vanished, and she broke through the fog into the valley, where a small stream ran down the middle. Arranged along the sheer rock cliffs, eight giant stone obelisks marked all sides of the valley except the one spot where she had entered. Each obelisk had strange glowing scripts and four symbols, in the same order, inscribed into the stone by the same hand. They resembled nothing Aetheria had ever come across before. They were like glyphs or logograms.

As interesting as the obelisks were, she had no means to learn anything about them, so she left them alone. Much more interesting were five houses and what looked to be a communal building or lodge. Aetheria dubbed the architectural style "rustic elven." The houses were all made in the image of nature. Each had a full-grown adult tree that towered above the house. Aetheria was certain that the buildings had sprouted up from the ground. Rustic-looking or not, each was a work of art that someone had guided the growth of with precision and grace. The small, abandoned area felt tranquil, with only the sounds of the babbling stream and the soft breeze caressing the large house trees.

After a circuit of the exterior of the six buildings, she found a seventh structure. They had excavated a cave into the rocky cliff, and a large, heavy iron door ominously blocked passage into whatever lay secured behind it. The door's mysterious creator had embedded symbols of other metals into the iron door. Some glowed, others looked mundane, and Aetheria surmised that a mix of magic and faith lay before her. Some symbols were like the script on the obelisks, while others gave her a religious vibe.

"Oh, yeah, this door is *so* trapped. You are getting left for last."

The first house Aetheria entered was genuinely gorgeous. Someone had carved the interior walls from the wood's natural grain, creating a beautiful, shining effect she had never seen before. It reminded her of wood-resin furniture on Earth. Only it seemed unlikely that power tools had been in use here. For a moment, Aetheria allowed herself to wonder if elves had inhabited this place. Still, she quickly suppressed her excitement and reminded herself to be cautious—she did not want to walk into any traps.

As she explored the house's main room, it struck Aetheria that it resembled more an armory than a living room. Whoever had lived here had lined two walls with various spears, each with a unique blade design. There were leaf-shaped blades, barbed blades, diamond-shaped blades, winged blades, and even some with a foot-long sword blade. Aetheria felt a twinge of guilt for not being able to name each type of spear.

"Oh, well. It isn't like I'm a historian. I'm a librarian. I *was* a librarian. Cut yourself some slack, woman."

The first spear she picked up and examined appeared to be a well-maintained weapon. A faint residue of some kind of oil clung to the blade. The carvings along the haft were intricate, and the spear felt balanced. She was about to practice a few thrusts in the air with it when it vanished from her hands in a *poof*.

"Um . . ." Aetheria blinked in surprise.

Curious, she repeated the process with another spear, thrusting it into the air. She was thinking about proper posture when this one also went *poof*.

"What in the h-e-double hockey sticks is going on here?" Now that she thought about it, quite a few things had vanished from her hands since she had woken up on the island. *Where are they going? Am I consuming them to generate magic? Is that what fueled my regeneration?*

Determined to find answers, she picked up a third spear. This one she just stared at. She waited. Nothing happened. After a couple of minutes, her mind wandered. She was thinking about how she would carry any of this loot when the third spear disappeared from her hand.

This time, she caught some of the process. The spear became energy that flowed into her skin and then deeper into her. Not deeper into her body, but into the spiritual her. Aetheria lost track of the flow at that point, but she still had fifty or more spears on the walls to test out.

It took her ten more before she could follow the items' route. It turned out she didn't even have to touch anything, but she did need to be within at least six inches of an item to trigger its disappearance. Once activated, the object became energy and flowed into the nearest point of her body—into her soul?—through a mysterious aperture, and then materialized inside what she called the Vault. Having read more than her share of cultivation stories, she was convinced the strange opening between her heart (physical) and soul (ephemeral) was a soul aperture, or the fabled cornerstone of spiritual cultivation.

CHAPTER 8

The Vault

Aetheria believed the Vault was another dimension connected to her essence or soul. Within its bounds lay various objects, including the clothing she had previously absorbed, trinkets gained in Nova Azura, two radiant Ethereal crystals in energy harmony, and four black crystals that exuded a toxic aura. It was easy to identify that toxic aura as the dark mana she had taken to calling miasma.

I've got an inventory. Or at least something like an inventory.

Aetheria made several attempts to retrieve a spear from the Vault. She learned the key was first to identify the desired object, then pull it through the "soul aperture" using the power of her being. Once this became second nature, the last step of guided conjuration proved to be the most challenging. Summoning required careful direction of the appearance of the called object, deciding such details as orientation and angle of emergence. She discovered that the only restrictions on this process were that the thing could not appear within the confines of another object.

Seriously, a tutorial would've been nice. Who would know to hoover things up and spit them back out instinctively? So, I have all the knowledge of the Aetherials, but no way to read it. The black crystals must be the equivalent of monster cores. Three Jagrepts and one monitor lizard—four crystals—it adds up.

The Vault also offered a total sense and knowledge of an item. Mentally, she could run her hand down the haft of a spear in the Vault and know what it felt like, heft it and know its weight and balance. Unlike the simple stow-and-retrieve process, these mental sensations were complex and challenging to access. Unfortunately, there was no user interface for any of this. Not even any numbers!

"Rustic and... personal. Yeah, personal. Not at all basic and lacking." She smirked. "Seriously, though, this is sweet. Instant retrieval and stowing of weapons. If I build a big enough armory, I could be like that badass in *Fairy Tail*."

Aetheria tried to imagine herself as an equipment-based wizard but couldn't do it. Having an inventory didn't give her any of the redheaded heroine's other powers or skills, so it would just have to be a lame joke for now. Plus, she only had spears, not swords, unless one of the other houses was full of bladed weaponry.

You are stalling. Quit being ridiculous, young lady. Aetheria could almost feel the rap of the ruler across her fingers that accompanied the voice of Sister Bethany.

Her subconscious mind was right. She was stalling. The ability to stow and retrieve objects inside her soul felt like a power that went beyond typical fantasy. The series she had read did not address game item management outside brief references to bottomless bags or backpacks. It was usually just waved away as part of some grand system or advantage to being a reincarnated or portal isekai hero. This form of storage was one she could understand conceptually.

Still, I'd like to get the rundown on how I innately knew to "eat" things with my soul. Something tied up with the Flames Aetherius gave me?

Aetheria was venturing into unknown territory. Her familiarity with fantasy literature would be of little help to her now. She breathed deeply for a minute, and then naturally, before spending five minutes carefully storing the fifty-eight spears that adorned the walls. The Vault appeared limitless and had no problem accommodating the chairs and coffee table she tossed inside.

"Oh, man, this is going to be *Skyrim* all over again. Twenty thousand cheese wheels sliding down a mountain to kill my enemies. Maybe one of these houses will have a cheese cellar." The first house only had three rooms, a living area, and two bunk rooms. Each bunk room had four bunks, which she immediately hoarded in the Vault.

The second house had a similar layout. The two bedrooms, however, had actual beds instead of cots. She hoovered up everything. Rustic but exceptionally well-made clothing for men, mattresses, blankets, two walking staffs, an armoire, a nightstand, a couple of horn-handled knives, and a couch all went into the Vault. Overall, a disappointment, but compared to what she had entered the valley with, she was already wealthy. Assuming she ever found people to trade with.

The third house provided something new: books! Three books lay carelessly atop a nightstand in the first bedroom she entered. The bindings and covers were pristine. If Aetheria hadn't known better, she would have said they were brand new. The language was a mystery to her. Staring at the books as she had Aetherius's letter accomplished nothing—she couldn't decipher any words. The closet revealed women's clothes, tailored, sadly, for someone taller than Aetheria. The only personal effect in the house was a decorative hairpin.

House number four was the worst. It had no weapons, clothes, or furniture; just carved stone trinkets. She hoovered it all up and still wasn't approaching any limitations on her Vault.

Number five was different in multiple ways. It was a larger home with a primary bedroom, a servant's room, and a second main bedroom. Books lay scattered across the entire house, some old, some new. There were even scrolls lying around, with notations she couldn't read. Someone had been trying to accomplish a research project here. The primary bedroom had a stash of wine bottles near the bed. A third of the bottles lay opened and empty. Books, scrolls, and wine all went into the Vault.

If that's poison, I will kill whoever left it here.

The closet of the main bedroom contained clothing. It was all laces and silks, entirely in contrast to the other houses' rustic armor and utilitarian hunting clothes. Whoever had stayed here gave her the impression of the stereotypical foppish noble.

Above the mantle of the main room hung a captivating portrait of a red-haired elven woman. The elf's green eyes seemed to pierce into Aetheria, judging her. Aetheria stole the portrait too.

Try judging me from my dimensional Vault, ha! Hopefully, the picture isn't haunted.

She left the beds in the fifth house. For now, it seemed like the best house to operate out of, and it was much more comfortable than her stone tree house.

Aetheria felt creeped out upon entering the communal hall at the center of the cluster of houses. Whoever had lived in the valley had adorned the walls with the preserved heads of exotic animals she could not identify. One, with red scales, resembled a wyvern, while another, with a fierce, reptilian countenance, looked like a tyrannosaurus. Despite having no immediate use for them, Aetheria stored the animal heads in her Vault, thinking they might have value as trade items in the future. Tables, chairs, utensils, and cooking tools were all thrown into the Vault too.

"Behold my secret ninja technique: falling table!" Aetheria jumped into the rafters from the floor with ease. When her hand touched the wooden beams, a large table appeared out of nowhere beneath her. It hung in the air much like all tables do, which is to say, not at all. A loud crash echoed through the hunting lodge, and Aetheria's cheeks flushed bright red.

"Cripes, that works. Alright, I feel justified in becoming a hoarder now."

The residents had stocked the bar with exquisite bottles full of enticingly glowing liquors. She took them all. She swept through the bar like a black hole and almost squealed in delight when she found a cellar door. Wine racks, kegs, waxed canvas packets of sealed provisions—weird bread—and basic supplies such as rope, knives, shovels, packs, and caltrops all got stored in the Vault.

Aetheria moved on, whistling a merry tune, and ended up in front of the cave door.

That's a mausoleum or something like it. Crypt?

Instinct whispered to her that she would get hurt if she touched the door. She touched the door anyway and pushed it open.

Light flared, her hair stood up along her neck, and a lightning bolt struck her.

"Uffda." She coughed and began patting herself to assess any damage. She concluded that she was fine. The pain had already receded.

"Aetheria gains +1 to tanking traps." Her words were flat, but she couldn't hide her smirk. If there wasn't a system to keep track of her achievements, she would do it herself. "Note to self: trap detection and trap dismantling are worth investigating if I ever get a chance."

The open door revealed stairs descending into the cliff. Dim light sources hung periodically on the wall; if worse came to worst, she could see by the light of her sparkly hair.

I'm a superheroine, not a My Little Pony!

Aetheria didn't want to dwell on the fact she was a sparkle princess and instead tromped down the stairs. She came to an oval-shaped room, with five passages branching off from it: two on each side and one behind a stone altar at the opposite end of the entrance. As she entered, she noticed an elf lying on the crypt floor, dressed in elaborate robes similar in cut to those in the primary bedroom of the fifth house. The elf was deceased. A fancy staff and an open book lay near their outstretched hands. Seeing no one else present, Aetheria looted the body, taking everything simultaneously.

Having half-expected the corpse to jump up and attack her, she released a sigh she didn't know she'd been holding when nothing happened.

Cough. Cough.

Startled, Aetheria scanned the room again. This time, she noticed the spectral figure of an elven man sitting on the altar. She was sure he had not been there before.

The specter was not the man she had just looted. This one had purple hair, an amazingly handsome face, and a sparkle of sarcasm in his cold, dead eyes. Instinctually, Aetheria liked him. Pity he was dead. She'd always had a thing for hot elven men. At least, she had when they were just fictional.

"Hi." *Smooth. Real smooth, girl.*

The specter spoke. Aetheria couldn't understand a word. He tried another, harsher language. Still, she didn't understand.

After moments of staring at each other, the specter seemed to shrug. He began to chant softly. Suddenly, a blue crystal lattice of energy appeared, and after several verses of chanting, it solidified into a physical object that floated toward her. The specter gestured for her to do something with it, and when he saw that she didn't understand, he mimed holding the object to his forehead.

"This better not be a trick."

Aetheria held the sparkling crystal to her forehead, and as the dim light enveloped her, she felt a rush of knowledge enter her mind. Unlike the traumatic experience of learning her current language, which had left her mind refracted and with a drop of lemon added, this time the process was smooth and painless. The crystal imbued her with a deep understanding of not one but two languages: a beautiful, melodic tongue that seemed almost like a bird song given human syllables, and a rough, guttural language that she was unsurprised to discover was Orcish.

"Can you understand me now, Great One?" The elf specter asked with a tone reserved for one's social superior.

"I can. What language is this?"

"That one you just looted called it Ancient Elven. It predates us. Our Creator taught us elves to speak it in our infancy. It is the language of nature and seasons, Primeval Sylvan."

"Sounds fancy."

CHAPTER 9

The Elf Ghost

Aetheria savored the tea that the ghost had conjured with magic. It was invigorating, laced with the most delectable honey she had ever tasted, and provided the caffeine boost she desperately craved.

"This may be the finest tea I have ever tasted," she exclaimed. "You're proving to be a much more gracious host than I expected, for a deceased individual. Especially with the corpse on the floor."

"Well, he was here to loot the tomb and challenge the Trial to become the next Lord Amaryllis. All of his preparation was for naught, though. Whoever led him here lied to him about his genealogy. He was no Amaryllis, but a cursed Narine. No doubt Oizys sent him to his death for her amusement."

"Oizys? Goddess of Misery?"

"Yes, the same, Great One. It was Oizys who orchestrated my downfall. I am Werylin. I was a minstrel once, but my house demanded I take over when my father passed. So, I traded flute for spell and blade and gained renown and greatness. The Council was on the cusp of announcing my rise as the next Imperator when the orc hordes rose for the sixth great Green Tide. My rival, House Narine, betrayed our mutual defense of the border to allow the Tides to sweep into our lands. Through luck, we held off the Green Tide because of a traveling Paladin of the Sun.

"With the butcher's bill paid, House Narine called for us to help them. The Tide had split and broke around our territory like a river. Even the orcs were afraid of the strange paladin. The paladin made for the capital to aid our clergy there and bid me help our allies. But I was bitter. The Narine filth had attempted to kill us all, and if not for the paladin, they would have succeeded. They dared pretend innocence and cry for help.

"I did not aid them as my oaths, vows, and the laws of elvenkind required. Out of spite, I betrayed my honor, and we saved another house. They made me the Imperator for a time. Yet when the sixth Green Tide ended a century later, my sins came calling, and we heard the grievances of the few surviving Narine. The laughter of Oizys has haunted me every day since."

"That's rough. Do you regret your choices?"

"In my folly, I allowed my emotions to cloud my judgment and committed a grave error. Instead of upholding justice and protecting the innocent citizens of Narine, I betrayed

a rival lord. It is a decision I deeply regret. I should have known better and controlled my desires, for anger has only ever led to sorrow and remorse."

"Eloquent."

"I was a minstrel, Great One."

"Why do you keep calling me 'Great One?'"

"You are on the path of the ancients, Great Aetherial. Surely, with your eyes, Aetherius himself has blessed you?"

"Well, you could say that. Aetherius called me family and sent me as his Challenger for the Tow—"

The ghost prostrated himself over the altar. Aetheria stopped talking. *Awkward.*

Silence reigned until the specter looked at her again and noticed her frown. He did not speak.

"Jeepers, man, just talk. We had a pleasant enough conversation going before. What's going on?"

Werylin looked appalled. *"I'm but a failed noble of a long-gone kingdom, unfit to bask in the glory of not only a Challenger sent by the Lord of the Sky, but one declared his own family. No, no. Daring to speak to you brings me even greater shame."*

"Relax, Werylin. I'm just a human with some extra-cool friends. I don't know anything about this world beyond that Oizys sucks, there used to be an Aetherial city on this island before she tricked them away, and Nova Azura is gone forever. All those earthquakes? Yeah, I was stuck down there and escaped just before the abyss swallowed the city."

"We searched for Nova Azura on this island for years, using every magical technique. Despite our efforts, it remained elusive, leading some scholars to dismiss the legend of the children of Aetherius as nothing more than a myth. It is a shame that Nova Azura is now gone. Unsurprisingly, Oizys played a role in the people's departure, as she has a history of tempting the elder races away from this world or crushing those who oppose her rule. Over the ages, many of the Elder races have vanished, leaving only the lesser races behind."

"Classy lady, Oizys. So, you got locked down here as punishment? How long ago? Can I free you somehow?" The minstrel seemed a likable sort. If it were in her power to help him, she would.

"No, Great One. Though you walk a great path, you are not yet strong enough to break the bonds that bind me. Should you return in a few centuries, I am sure you could manage it then. As for how long, I stopped counting after my thirtieth century."

"Stop calling me 'Great One'. Just call me Aetheria." Was this ghost over three thousand years old for real? Holy. Shit. The number was so high that she forgot to take offense, assuming he'd beat her handily.

"Of course, Gr-Aetheria. Your name is quite close to the Lord of the Sky."

"Yeah, that's part of why he likes me so much. Always rely on narcissists to love themselves, even in others."

The ghost chuckled nervously. Werylin didn't say she was committing blasphemy, but it was writ plain on his features.

You're not in Minnesota anymore, girl. Any atheist and blasphemy jokes are liable to get you strung up here. Yay, fantasy gods? "Anyway... do you know anything about the tower on the island? I'm supposed to climb it. Well, ten of them."

The ghost laughed as if she'd told a great joke, until he realized she was being serious.

"You truly are a Challenger, then? Would you defy heavenly rule? Cast Oizys from the Throne of Grief and let another ascend in her stead? I thought that was in jest..." Werylin seemed to wander off into his thoughts for a time, only to be drawn back when Aetheria coughed a few times to get his attention.

"It is the Tower of Aetherius, one of the most difficult towers. Supposedly, Aetherius designed it to be a training field for his children more than a test for other races, and thus any who cannot cope with the overwhelming flows of Aether will perish. Even we elves, with our racial links to magic and nature, cannot tolerate the Aether long enough to consider climbing this tower. Instead, we used the island for hunting the monsters drawn by the Aether flows of the tower."

"Oh, yeah, lots of monsters. I've been fighting a few already. Annoying how they disappear when I kill them, and they don't leave any loot. Is that normal? What is Aether?" Aetheria felt like it should not have worked that way.

"No, Aetheria, that is not normal. Perhaps you dispersed their corrupted energies with the potency of your Aether energy. It is quite strong. Aether is the divine element, the breath of the gods, divinity itself. It stands opposite to Nether, the element of darkness and the underworld."

"Makes sense with my whole situation. So, you haven't climbed the Tower of Aetherius? Have you ever climbed any of the others?" Her quest was to beat ten of them, so all knowledge was valuable.

"In my youth as a minstrel, I climbed to the fifteenth floor of the Tower of Gaea. In this, all the towers are the same: the fifteenth floors of the towers are city and trade zones. They seem to be linked and shared by all the towers. Not just the towers on Grief, either. Some in my day traveled to other worlds through the strange nature of the fifteenth floors. On rare occasions, one can even meet a Challenger from other worlds in the cities. It's quite an ordeal when one of you shows up. Bells ring, and the Dwellers hold feasts in their honor. Some citizens are Climbers, but most are Dwellers."

"I'm going to get a parade. Awkward. What's a Dweller?"

"Those who have joined life in the tower, either permanently or for a contracted amount of time. It comes with certain duties to the tower, but Dwellers aren't allowed to discuss it with outsiders. Worlds that are poor and dangerous and short-lived races regularly make deals like this. Aging is strange within the towers. Even elder elves have taken on such contracts to get a chance at fulfilling their life's work before it is time to join the gods."

"That's interesting. So, the tower has instanced cities?" Aetheria waved her hand before he could ask. "Don't worry about it. So, it must have been boring being down here for three thousand years alone. Is there anything I can do to help you for now? Want some of that dead guy's books to learn the new language from? It will probably take me quite a while to climb the tower and return." She had nothing else to give him, and he'd provided much helpful knowledge.

"I would appreciate that, Lady Aetheria. The dead one before you came was the first to visit in a very long time. I had wondered if the wards around the lodge had failed and time had swallowed the encampment. In return for your thoughtful gift, there is a secret passage in the lodge. Next to the stairs going down is a piece of molded wood, a pressure plate. Also, press the triangular grain at head height in the wall. I leave whatever treasure remains of House Amaryllis to you, Shining One."

Aetheria materialized a stack of books for the ghost. His last honorific surprised her. "'Shining One?'"

"Your aura burns with clear Aether. Your eyes shine like fonts of power. To a specter such as I, you are exquisite to behold, great lady. Your soul will buoy you against even the most powerful of the undead."

"Cool. Thanks for the information, Werylin. I'll keep that in mind. Any chance you could teach me magic?"

The ghost looked disappointed. *"I am afraid not. My method of magic was that of Spellsong, a rare and distinctive art that is difficult to master by those of other races. I know of no aetheric spellsingers, though I may be unaware of their existence. If you encounter someone who can teach you the ways of Spellsong, I advise caution in choosing this path. It's difficult to alter one's magical path once you walk it."*

"Path?"

"The Pathway to Power. Sorcery, martial, mental, eldritch, divine. The paths are unlimited, as are the perils upon the paths. At the end? Some say immortality, others godhood. All I know is the deeper one journeys on the path, the worse the consequences. Rare are those with straight paths. They are called the Winding Ways for a reason." The spectral ghost gestured at its tomb.

"Right." She didn't understand, but that was fine.

"Thanks for all your help, Werylin. I'll visit again after I've conquered the tower. Peace out." Aetheria waved her hand at him and turned back toward the surface. If anything were down in the tomb, she wouldn't fight Werylin over it. He'd been too helpful.

"Safe travels under sun and moons, Aetherial One."

One last wave and Aetheria exited the crypt. First, she sorted through the Vault and summoned a small hand mirror she'd looted earlier. The face that looked back at her was gorgeous. She'd spent a long time in character creation with Aetheria, and every graphics update had brought cosmetic options to upgrade her even more. The most stunning aspect of her appearance was her eyes. The colors constantly shifted between blue and green, the colors of the Mediterranean. Behind that lurked a burning flame she could sense but not see. In her mind, she pictured the blue flame that had warmed her when she awoke on Grief.

That's where the fire went. She must have absorbed it. "Cool. Cool, cool, cool." She laughed as she headed back for the lodge.

She had a secret door to find.

CHAPTER 10

The Haul

The secret-door mechanism was exactly where Werylin had said it would be. Aetheria pursued the sound of the opening door into the basement. She promptly whistled—the door was wide and tall enough for a car to go through.

"Cripes! How the heck did they hide that so easily? How did I miss a giant hidden door? I need to bump my perception stat. Oh, wait, I don't have stats. Where are those 'goggles of secret door finding' when I need th—" She stopped abruptly as she walked into the hidden room.

The amount of loot surprised her.

"Werylin, you glorious bastard. If I figure out how to get you a body again, I'll kiss you." She would, too.

Aetheria stood in a secret room that was about ten feet by twenty feet. Shelves and hooks lined the walls, and magical spheres provided a soft ambient light among the shelves. She took everything as she walked up and down the rows of equipment. She wasn't just a hoarder, she reasoned. It would simply be foolish not to take advantage of the opportunity to see the upper limit of her inventory, if there even was one.

Of the items on the first set of shelves, she was most interested in a collection of leather gauntlets and boots, some silk clothing, an assortment of travel rations that looked like bread, and various forms of money. There was a selection of potions that she assumed were for healing and mana, and a sack that was bigger on the inside. She was thrilled when she could store this last item, which she surmised held either a chef's spice collection or an alchemist's stockpile. The second row of shelves contained more mundane but handy tools such as a pickax, spade, rope, pitons, hammers, axe, and hatchet, which she also added to her inventory.

The last row of shelves in the secret room held a vast assortment of knives, including throwing, hunting, skinning, and even some strange hooked knives that Aetheria guessed were for scaling creatures. The metal of these knives differed from all the others. Aetheria added over a hundred of them to her inventory.

The remaining wall featured two large vertical shelves and an ornate wooden case with hazy glass that obscured its contents. Gemstones filled the vertical shelves, which Aetheria happily added to her inventory. She did not spend time considering what kind of jewelry, accessories, or charms she could make with them if she ever met a crafter. *Do crafters even exist like that? Why not? Almost all games have an accessory slot. A magic scrunchie will be mine.*

As Aetheria opened the wooden case, she let out a whistle of surprise at what she found inside. There lay an ornate bow crafted from ashen wood. Its curved limbs were inscribed with strange glyphs, and its string sparkled as if woven from something Ethereal and fae. Holding the stunning bow made Aetheria long to shoot arrows at everything in sight. It had been almost fifteen years since she had last shot a bow. She missed her carefree teenage years at her parents' cabin on the lake.

"Why are there no arrows?" she asked aloud, noting the absence of any quiver. She had looted every other item in the room except for the light orbs, which she proceeded to do. What was the point of infinite storage if she didn't try to fill it up? The room descended into darkness, and she stumbled like a fool back into the sunlit first level. She was eager to test the bow in the courtyard, hoping she might have overlooked some arrows in one of the houses.

As she crossed the courtyard, she tested the strength of the bow's draw and was pleased to find that everything worked perfectly. The draw was firm but not strenuous. As she drew back the string, an arrow of glowing blue energy manifested itself. Letting out another whistle, Aetheria aimed at one of the rocks in the courtyard. The bow drew a minuscule amount of power from her to imbue the arrow, and when she released it, the effect was like a high-powered sniper rifle going off.

The explosion of sound was akin to that of an M-80. Azure mists dissipated as rock fragments shot out, and soil clumps rained down from the sky a second later. The destructive power of the magical arrow left Aetheria slack-jawed with awe.

"Best bow ever!" she exclaimed, giddy with excitement. She practiced with the bow until she could hit the general target, thrilled to have a ranged attack option besides her knives and spears.

Exhilarated but ready to slow her pace, Aetheria set herself up in the fifth house, where she had left the beds and found the noble's clothing. The first order of business was to compare the clothing Aetherius had given her in the chest with the armor she'd found in the elves' storage. While the shimmering items provided by the god looked mundane, they repaired themselves and seemed to blunt a regular knife far better than the elven leather armor. The self-repair alone would have sealed the deal for her, but that it was comparable or even slightly better was beyond her expectations.

That took care of one decision: armor versus clothing. Now she had a more critical decision: Which clothing?

The red leather duster was staying. It remained cool against Aetheria's skin even in the jungle, and the style made her happy. She swapped to a pair of red leather pants that matched the dark red, almost black, ankle boots. With the coat providing much coverage, she opted for a black tank top. She felt perfectly comfortable wearing both pieces of clothing, and the magical sports bra was almost invisible underneath. She finished the outfit with a dark teal scarf and a pair of black, fingerless gloves.

"I apologize in advance for all the times you are going to get melted, burned, stabbed, and who knows what else." Before her skin, it seemed much better that the cloth should suffer damage first.

After looking in the hand mirror, Aetheria whistled.

"Damn. If every fifteenth floor is a town, or if I ever reach a proper town in this world, I will be anything but inconspicuous," Aetheria mused to herself. Without a yardstick or other measuring tools, she estimated she was six feet tall, possibly an inch or two taller. Despite her slender build, she now possessed incredible strength. She guessed she appeared to be in her twenties again, with the most striking features being her glowing hair and eyes. Others in this world of magic might sense her "Aether energy," as Werylin had called it.

"I guess blending in is out of the question anyway if they ring bells and have a Challenger parade for me every time I pop up on a fifteen multiple. Maybe I can find a wig before then. No. I need to be so badass no one wants to screw with me. Training montage, go!"

Refreshed from her fashion review, Aetheria returned to the courtyard of the little hunting hamlet. She spent the rest of the day training there, fighting imaginary foes with her new spears, practicing summoning them into her hands to strike or throw with, making practice thrusts, and trying to learn how to fight effectively. A seasoned fighter likely would have mocked her attempts, but she hoped that by becoming comfortable with the weapons, she could at least achieve a basic level of competence to let her regeneration carry her through a fight.

Besides training with her spears, Aetheria worked on her skills with the bow and throwing knives. She spent hours practicing her aim, trying to get a feel for the right amount of force and timing when releasing an arrow or throwing a knife. As the sun set, she switched her focus to the blades, honing her technique for close combat. She lunged and parried while she imagined herself facing off against a skilled opponent.

By the time dusk fell, Aetheria was exhausted. She had made progress in all areas of her training and was confident that she could hold her own in a fight better than she had been capable of that morning. She retired to the communal hall, where she lit a fire in the fireplace and tended to her weapons, sharpening and oiling them until they gleamed in the firelight. She knew there would be more challenges ahead, but she was ready to face them with all the weapons and (paltry) skills at her disposal.

Finally, Aetheria made her way back to the noble's house and lay on one of the beds. She stared out at the strange constellations. Not even one was remotely similar to the night sky she had grown up with. She blinked away moisture from her eyes and thought about home.

How were her parents? Losing a daughter would not be easy for them. They had doted on her for the last thirty-five years. Questionable naming tastes aside, they had been extraordinary parents. They wouldn't have grandchildren now. No son or daughter-in-law. Although her dad had given up on that when he realized how into

EFWO she was. Her mother, though, had continued to set her up with people's sons and nephews, and she even tried to arrange a date with Emma's daughter.

"I'm sorry, Mom and Dad. Maybe if I'd had a different life, I might have reached forty. Look after them for me, please, Aetherius?" It had been a long time since she had prayed. It was awkward.

"And monitor Pete and Callie for me, too. All the idiots in the Knights of Academia don't know what to do without me. Walking into walls, bringing the wrong potions and flasks to raids, dancing into the fire instead of out of it."

Partial poems filled her mind, but none genuinely fit her mood. Instead, Aetheria just blew a kiss at the night sky, then settled under the blankets for sleep. By some miracle, she found rest quickly, and night passed into morning. She was unaware that the bursts of aetheric energy her training had created had caused the island's monsters to go into a frenzy. Thick mists blocked out the sounds, and the warding runes hid the village.

In the morning, Aetheria availed herself of some of the elven provisions. The food was stale but light. She had definitely had worse during camping trips. Afterward, she psyched herself up and walked toward the fog. *Tower time.*

"Thanks for the gifts, Werylin," she called out, blowing a kiss toward the tomb.

The thick band of mist was about twenty feet wide, and as she approached it, she heard frustrated monsters snarling at each other from within.

"Yeah, no." Aetheria sighed. So much for it being a quick jaunt to the tower.

Aetheria stood and listened to the dampened sounds of multiple monsters raging on the other side of the fog. She thought she could hear them fighting each other, but that was probably too much to hope for.

Well, I do not know what I'm about to walk into. First encounter attempt, that's all. Improvise.

She stepped into the fog.

CHAPTER 11

To the Tower

The sounds of enraged creatures fighting one another grew louder as she progressed through the fog. Finally, she took the last step into the jungle, breaking free of concealment. No longer blocked by the mist, her mana sense came back online. The number of miasmatic concentrations she could feel in the vicinity was high, and more lurked at the edges of her senses. What had drawn them all?

At a glance, Aetheria identified what looked like a gang of velociraptors, a pack of dark wolves, a T-Rex, a cow-sized porcupine whose spines glowed with darkness, and a hideous moss-covered, sloth-like creature with razor-sharp claws and large canine teeth. They had destroyed the nearest trees in their fierce disagreements.

Aetheria summoned her bow and it appeared in her hands. Swiftly, she let the first arrow fly at the porcupine monster. Bits of quills and flesh flew everywhere, but that was the only arrow Aetheria could get off before the raptors were upon her. The bow disappeared, replaced by one of the sharp metal spears. Practicing with imaginary targets was a lot different from trying to block with the butt of the spear and thrust with the point against multiple live targets.

The sharp hooked claws of the raptors gouged holes in her divine clothing and flesh alike, even as she killed the first raptor with a spear in the eye. Aetheria blocked one raptor's attacks with the butt of the spear, stabbed another in the throat, and then readjusted to stab another with a hard thrust in what she thought was the heart.

Her wounds quickly accumulated as she went blow for blow with the remaining three raptors. Her injuries were visibly healing, while the monsters' wounds did not. She leaped onto a raptor's back, letting her spear go to her inventory for a pure wood one. There, she broke its neck with her most brutal kick. Promptly, she jumped, using the flex of the spear to vault up into the canopy.

Aetheria wrapped her legs around a branch and hung upside down. She summoned the bow to her hands and quickly fired two mana arrows. While her aim was not precise, the nature of the magic arrows obliterated the two remaining raptors in sprays of flesh, just as it had done the porcupine. It felt more like a gun or crossbow than a bow with the insanely fast velocity of the energy arrows.

Miasma flickered at her senses momentarily as a dark form appeared in the tree next to her. The evil sloth-like monster had somehow teleported up into the tree and, in a very un-sloth-like motion, slashed at her with shocking speed, its vicious claws shredding her flesh and the branch she clung to. As she plummeted to the jungle floor, she stowed the bow before it got destroyed. She did not land gracefully when her boots hit the ground, but she landed on her feet, which in the end was a mistake—her leg broke, and the pain that shot through her now was a familiar, if unwelcome, companion.

Once again, Aetheria felt the flickering sensation of miasma, and the sloth creature appeared. A spear appeared in her hand. Fiercely, she thrust its metal tip through the sloth's throat more than once, and then shoved the weapon in further a couple of times, to be safe.

Its corpse was already dematerializing when Aetheria's leg healed and could hold weight without hurting. She had the nagging sensation of someone watching her, and she turned to see a burst of fire light up the jungle. The T-Rex and a pack of five wolves had been fighting, but the dinosaur monster had finally noticed her. The flames seemed to be a large enough warning for the wolves. When one of their pack was incinerated, they retreated into the brush.

Fire breath. Great. Hopefully, my clothes are fire-resistant.

The enormous eyes of the predator tracked her, and the T-Rex raised its head and roared. Her body stopped responding to her commands. *Paralysis? Why the heck does everything on this island have stuns and paralysis?!*

The dinosaur lowered its body and charged right toward her.

I can move. I can move. I. CAN. MOVE!

Had she overpowered the force of paralysis on her, or had it worn off just in time? She had no way to tell. There was no combat log. No debuff icons. There was nothing to give her any insight into anything beyond how her body felt. She believed she powered through it. As the massive dinosaur's teeth snapped through the air, Aetheria gracefully dodged to the side. She had narrowly avoided the deadly attack. She contorted and rolled before jumping into the canopy again. The action bought her a few precious seconds to pull the bow back out and fire an arrow into the snout of the T-Rex as it looked up at her.

I don't know why I expected anything more.

Raptors, porcupines, and rocks had all fallen after a single shot of the bow. But the T-Rex's defenses proved greater than all the other monsters she had fought. A few scales broke off, others charred, and a roar of pain arose from what she assumed was annoyance at the damage near its nostrils, but as far as actual damage done to the massive monster? Almost none.

It inhaled.

Aetheria dropped from branch to branch until she reached the ground. The T-Rex's enormous head followed her. The monster opened its jaws, and heat and flame filled the forest. Aetheria stepped quickly away before leaping back into the branches. Flames licked at her shoes. The cries and yelps of the wolf pack she'd sensed in the brush told her they had not expected her to perceive them or turn the T-Rex on them. Two small miasmatic concentrations further fled the battle, and the rest of the wolves perished in the fire.

After looping around a tree, she found her gaze matched by the T-Rex's.

"It is too bad you can't just be my friend, Rexy. You could cook meals for me, eat all my enemies, and I could ride you. It would be a perfect match."

The dinosaur seemed to think she had taunted it. It roared another mental attack. This time, she resisted the assault. She did not even slow down, and when it charged, she closed the gap and leaped onto the creature's neck. There, a wicked spear appeared in her hands, which she thrust down past its thick scales into flesh. Furiously, the monster shook its neck, attempting to throw Aetheria off. Pushing down with all her strength, she ran down its back, dragging the embedded spearhead after her. Infuriated by the growing wound, the T-Rex threw itself backward to the ground.

Aetheria's new agility allowed her to jump off the creature into the treetops. Before the monster could get back up, she dropped from the canopy heights again like a crazy dragoon. Her feet braced the cross-shaped upper portion of the spear and she drove the blade straight into the T-Rex's softer underbelly and vital organs.

Silence ruled the forest floor after the death of the giant T-Rex.

"Note to self: buy enchanted leg braces or something for falling damage." Aetheria's clothing and body regenerated. Monsters turned to haze. Their cores appeared in the Vault—she still missed how that process worked. Maybe if she could get a few monsters alone, she could follow the process the way she had learned to store things.

Unfortunately, there were many more monsters. Dimly, Aetheria could feel their miasmatic energy. As she saw it, she had three choices. She could fight them all, or retreat into the elven lodge, or make haste for the tower. If the monsters gave her experience, it might be tempting to farm them, but they didn't. The miasma crystals or cores were of unknown usefulness to her yet. Werylin had warned that the monsters could breach the protections around the lodge, so Aetheria felt that option was terrible. She didn't know the requirements to spawn a monster. Was it a day/night thing? A time-related thing? X quantity of miasma coalescing? She had absolutely no idea.

Tentatively, she headed for the tower, but when she looked up through a clearing in the jungle canopy, her decision suddenly felt forced. Massive figures flew in circles midway up the tower. Dragons. Two dragons who were so colossal, she could make them out from this distance.

The monsters in the jungle with her seemed like footnotes next to the two enormous dragons. Centipedes, hydras, more wolves. What were they compared to the giant forms circling the tower? They made her tentative decision final, and instead of a measured pace that let her pick off and kill monsters that got in her way, she fell into a sprint. The jungle turned into green flashes around her. Dreadful creatures fell behind, unable to maintain pace with her hectic run. Even the sleek jungle predators could not keep up with her.

The ever-imposing tower grew taller and more prominent in the sky above her, until finally she vaulted up the broken steps toward the entrance. Only after making it halfway up the steps did she realize no monsters were following her. Behind her, at the base of the steps, a shimmering, almost transparent field of energy circled the lower tower. Safety?

The dragons seemed to have roosted on the tower. Aetheria's panic settled down momentarily, and she caught her breath. *Safe zone mechanic? Magical ward? I guess it's the same difference. Not that I want to test it and find out.*

As she ascended the steps, Aetheria could sense the swarm of monsters that had gathered at the base. Despite their efforts, none seemed able to breach the magical field that interposed between them.

Well, then, I suppose it's tower time. She hummed the tune to "U Can't Touch This" while she climbed the remaining steps and approached the mysterious door at the tower's base.

Upon closer inspection, Aetheria noticed a series of glyphs inscribed around the door, written in a language she could decipher. "Son of Time, Brother of Chaos, Lord of the Upper Heavens," the inscription read. "The Tower of Aetherius welcomes those who can withstand its flows. If you are strong, reach the top of the Tower of Aetherius, and one wish will be yours."

Hmm, a wish. I don't recall anyone mentioning that. I should have asked Werylin how many levels there were in total.

The dragons were still nesting on the tower, but Aetheria could feel their gaze on her, or thought she could. *They are gosh-darned dragons. How would that not make someone nervous?*

Aetheria summoned a spear into her hand. *Just in case I need to stab something immediately.*

"Ready check." She looked down at her clothing. All the damage caused in the fights had long since been mended. None of the physical damage she had taken remained. She was as ready as she could be.

"Ready."

With a deep breath, she stepped through the portal and into the Tower of Aetherius.

CHAPTER 12

The First Floor

Teleportation is a strange experience. *If MMO characters were real, would that be what walking into an instance feels like?*

Wherever the real Tower of Aetherius was, it wasn't on Grief. Existing as nothing but molecules held together by some outside power while hurtling through space in some equivalent to warp travel was an impossibly unique sensation. Aetheria compared it to a bad acid trip, where all the weird feelings were real. Before materializing, she could feel other tower destinations. There were far more than ten. Were there just ten per world? Did every god everywhere have a tower? Maybe the towers were a type of nexus hub for the servants of gods to fast travel to worlds they had dominion in?

It doesn't matter. Please stop it.

Aetheria appeared in a room. The floor was loose gravel. Brown walls rose to a ceiling the same color and material as the walls. She could almost touch the ceiling on her tiptoes. She rapped her knuckles against the wall, revealing it to be sturdier than it appeared, with a density bordering on concrete. A sizable cylindrical pillar in the middle of the room went up through the ceiling, though she couldn't see what was in the room above. Wooden spokes around the pillar emerged at ninety degrees at ground level, giving it an almost turnstile look.

The heavy concentration of mana in the air was unsettling. The energy swirled around Aetheria with far greater intensity than anything she had experienced on the island. It was a heady, almost intoxicating sensation, and she basked in the tingle of invisible power coursing through her.

The only thing to do in the room was push the turnstile, so Aetheria set to work. Using the spokes to leverage her strength, she applied pressure to the mechanism, which felt like pushing against a wall. Undeterred, Aetheria pulled out a knife and marked an "X" on the floor at her start position so that she could keep track of her progress. Changing the direction, she pushed the apparatus. It moved.

With each push, the resistance increased, and it wasn't until her fifth rotation that Aetheria saw any visible results. A sigil showing the number five in the strange language Aetherius's letter had taught her glowed on the wall. Each complete cycle of five added another glyph to the wall, and the force required to turn the lever grew with every rotation. When Aetheria reached twenty cycles, the loose gravel beneath her feet began to shift and grind.

On the twenty-fifth cycle, stone pillars emerged about a foot from the ground. With every cycle after that, more of the posts rose into the air. The ceiling shifted in the same way on the thirtieth cycle. The pillars had risen halfway to the top by the hundredth cycle. Counter-pressure on the lever had ballooned. The effort it required on her part per circle increased in a non-linear fashion, and at one hundred, she had exceeded regular human limitations. At this rate, she would be straining at a hundred and fifty.

Well, don't I feel dumb? It's a spiral staircase. Okay, so I raise the pillar steps from out of the ground. The ceiling reshapes going up to the next floor. How many floors like this are there? I can barely see another lever on the pillar on the next floor.

Stolen glimpses of the room above her were not that educational. The second floor appeared to have the same bland brown construction on all sides, the same obnoxious ever-present light, and the same script glowed on the walls.

Her stomach growled. Luckily, Aetheria had already considered how she would eat while forced to labor. A quick spin and her back held the counter-pressure of the bar she had been pushing, and she plodded backward while elven rations appeared in her hands. The progress was slow, but the few times she had tested stopping, she learned the counterweight significantly increased without applying pressure.

"If I understand this right, there are two possibilities when I get to the end of pushing the post. It will lock into place, or I need to haul ass as it starts the spin down to no stairs. Since this is a challenge, I doubt they were nice enough for it just to lock in place and let me leisurely walk to the top. So, I'll assume it will turn to shit, and I'll have to leg it. Oh, son of a gun, I don't have any water provisions. Just booze."

"While I'm talking to myself, is anyone listening? Aetherius? Trial Master? Tower Butler? Anyone? Oh, maybe there's a system in here? Menu? Stats. Help. Character. Crud." Dissatisfied with the results, Aetheria spun around and pushed harder. By the one hundred and fiftieth cycle, she thought the counter-pressure might be enough to damage even the most extraordinary human athletes on Earth. By one hundred and sixty, the only description she could give to the effort was herculean.

The gap between floors had shrunk, and she could easily make the run and jump as it was. What stopped her from going? She couldn't tell how many levels above her there were. It seemed like a physical test, but also one of patience and planning.

Reaching one hundred and ninety rotations, Aetheria had surpassed what she thought would exhaust a horse. She had used this strength to snap a coconut in half with her bare hands and break a dinosaur's neck with a well-placed kick. It was the strength one might expect from a superhero. How was an average person supposed to manage this? Aetheria realized that ordinary people probably weren't meant to. Towers, dungeons, and quests to take down a goddess were not ordinary mortals' domain. She needed to stop thinking of herself as Aesca the librarian and embrace her true potential as Aetheria.

Sweat streamed down her forehead as she reached one hundred and ninety-seven rotations. She had resorted to drawing in mana and air with each breath to sustain her flagging strength. The infusion of energy seemed to restore her vigor, clear her fatigue, and give her an extra boost with each inhalation. So, she kept at it. She took in bigger and bigger breaths of mana to fuel her struggling body. Had there been mana on Earth that she had been ignorant of? It certainly was a possibility.

At two hundred rotations, the lever sounded like it hit something solid as it reached the starting point. Aetheria could feel the counterforce building and knew this was a timed event. "Poop taco," she cursed under her breath.

All the writing on the walls changed with a new inscription: *Risk-free or Rewarding.*

Aetheria literally steamed with exertion. She let go of the lever and sprinted up the spiral stairs. The lever was vibrating but had not yet started backward.

The room above the first was identical, with steps already raised and leading to the third level. She gave it a cursory glance before dashing up the stairs. The lever in each room began to turn counterclockwise, and the stairs lowered. Aetheria refused to give in to panic. She raced to the fourth room, checked that it was empty, and ran up the stairs to the fifth room. There, she faced a decision: there was a chest along one wall.

She hated being greedy but ran to touch the chest and send it into her inventory. Every advantage could be vital when you started a new game. She quickly changed direction and climbed the already half-lowered stairs to jump into the sixth room. She landed with a roll and bumped into another chest.

Only now, after all the running, did Aetheria take a few seconds to frown at the fact that she was emitting steam. It rose off her forearms and escaped through the cuffs of her coat. When she touched her forehead, it felt warm, but not enough to create steam. She wondered if it represented excess mana. It made sense that there might be a limit on how much mana her body could contain. If mana had flows like the air had currents, it would follow that unbound mana would return to those currents, especially if not used or bound to a specific purpose. But how did one tie it to a goal? The way Aetheria used it seemed inefficient, but no superior alternatives came to mind.

The sixth room had no lever. It was a large, circular chamber filled with identical chests, each marked with a number. Aetheria counted one hundred trunks in total. For fun, she checked the chest from the fifth floor and found it contained a torch and flint. If she had missed the jump to the sixth room, she would have been furious—a torch and flint weren't worth all that effort. In the future, this might be a lesson to remember: greed does not always merit a reward. She had flint in her inventory already, and while she had no torches, she had the magic glowing orbs from the elves. Had something created this challenge specifically for her, or was it meant to be a group effort? She had questions.

Whoever designed this wanted her to choose a chest. A decision was required: six floors, one hundred chests, two hundred rotations. Not ready to decide, Aetheria lit the torch and carried it around the room. She hoped the light would reveal something. After making several circuits of the room, she noticed that the torch's light shimmered when it hit the metal bindings of the thirty-third chest.

Aetheria groaned. Two hundred divided by six was thirty-three, with an extra third. Was that the solution? It felt wrong to her. She touched the chest, but nothing happened. She didn't try to open it, instead just shunting it into her inventory. Still, nothing happened. She recalled the chest and dropped it back on the ground. She flipped its lid open. Inside the trunk lay a canteen of water, cool to the touch. It appeared to be aluminum. Inscribed on the canteen were two words in the language of Aetherius: cool and water. It went into the Vault.

Then she walked around and shoved the rest of the chests into the Vault. If nothing else, she could use them to drop on enemies or sell them for cheap. She hoovered up all the chests smoothly enough until suddenly, two chests opened their lids and lashed sharp tongues at her.

Awesome. Mimics. Aetheria dodged the tongues, but one mimic bit down hard on her right hand, its sharp, painful teeth ripping at her flesh and clothing. A spear appeared in her left hand, and she stabbed at the monster furiously. The strength of her assault surprised the pretender. Empowered by rage, Aetheria vastly exceeded the force needed to slay the mimic. She felt confident she had grown more muscular than she was the day before.

Is it the Aether in here? What is Aether, anyway? Just mana? Was this whole "trial" just a strength-building exercise?

OW!

She had momentarily forgotten the second mimic. It wrapped its tongue around her upper body, bound her arms to her torso, and left her spear flopping uselessly in her hand. The mouth of the chest opened wider until it looked like it would quickly eat her in one bite.

From her inventory, she conjured an armoire and dropped it onto the mimic. The tongue lost its grip on her. Aetheria pierced it repeatedly with a spear. The monster failed to land another attack on her before she killed it.

The mimics did not immediately turn to miasma and, instead, remained there. There were five colored spheres of energy. Each was the same color as Aetheria's hair, and when she picked them up, the power inside transferred into her body. It was pleasant and almost sensual. As she picked up the spheres, the mimics turned into miasmic mist, which she inhaled by mistake. The fog didn't hurt, but it was a pleasant cold, like stepping into air conditioning after being outside on a humid summer day. Goosebumps rose on her arms as a cool sensation spread through her body, smoothing out the heat generated by the aqua energy that had preceded the miasma.

Interesting. She could absorb the miasma, which didn't feel evil, destructive, or harmful. This time, at least. Should she keep doing that? She had no answer to that question for now.

A light glimmered out of nowhere and formed a doorway labeled "Floor 2."

"Well, that answers that," Aetheria muttered to herself. Each "floor" was likely to be its own dimension or world, with no actual relation to the height climbed in the tower. A small part of her had hoped that climbing upward meant she was now on Floor 6. She shook her head and took a deep breath to clear her mind.

"No way back, only forward. I can do this. I'm super awesome. I can rip coconuts in half barehanded." She summoned a stored coconut, drank the milk, and ate some meat. "So, Floor Two, is anyone going to give me instructions? Say hello. Do I get a name tag? A tutorial? Your tower needs tutorials, Aetherius!" she shouted at the uncaring walls.

Before anything else, Aetheria explored the contents of the chests she had placed in her inventory. Ninety of them were empty. One held a sack of gold coins, another held a set of fur armor that looked atrocious, two stored stacks of arrows, three were full of what appeared to be containers of Spam, one was full of marbles, another had ball bearings, and the final chest contained a single blue rose. Perhaps it was helpful in alchemy?

While not the massive haul she had hoped for, Aetheria now had ninety-eight chests she could use as weapons or distractions.

"Ready check." She said to herself. "Ready."

Aetheria stepped through the doorway. The scent of salt and the odor of five unwashed men who had her surrounded assaulted her nose.

CHAPTER 13

The First Quest

She was suddenly atop a windswept cliff. The wind carried the overpowering smell of salt, detritus, and storms on the far horizon. The five men arrayed in a rough circle around her looked shocked to have a woman randomly appear, and one smelled so strongly of body odor it seemed to mute all other smells.

Standing opposite and facing her stood a man wearing long robes and grasping a staff. She dubbed him Magey. To Magey's left was a man, a few inches shorter than her, wearing stylish clothes with chain armor mostly hidden beneath. A dagger and rapier upon his hip made her decide he was a duelist. To Magey's right was a rugged man. He had long black hair, an unkempt beard, well-fitting but not stylish leather and hide armor, a scimitar upon his hip, and a quiver and bow upon his back. Aetheria named him Rangerdanger, because he had all the sex appeal of a lumberjack and eyes that smoldered.

To the left of the duelist was a man in rags. Rags that concealed all the black leather armor, knives, pouches, and who knew what? At least she assumed they had previously covered the armor and weapons. It looked as if he had recently lost a good bit of cloth. She was undecided if he was a rogue or an assassin, but his sinister eyes and the curved daggers upon his hip made her think he was a killer. She dubbed him Assy. Assy was short, nearly a head shorter than she was. She thought she might already be the target of malice because of the way he stroked the hilt of his dagger.

The last was a great wall of a man. Taller than she was and as broad-shouldered as two of her together. He wore pieces of plate armor that were not an entire set. The armor appeared haphazardly cobbled together. The warrior had lost his codpiece and had no helm, nor did he have pauldrons. Unlike the others, he had already lifted a very large flail while shouting at her in a language she didn't understand.

Oh, great, here we go again. Why isn't there just a common language?

"Look, I don't want a fight if we don't need to have one. Hello? Hello? Hello? Of course, none of you understand me. Well, I will not feel bad about taking out some guys who think surrounding and threatening a lady five-on-one is fair." Aetheria tried all three languages she knew with hello. None got any reaction, although the ranger's eyes twitched a little at the Sylvan.

Prison movies, anime, TV shows, light novels, and every RPG she had ever played often had scenarios like this. *Be proactive or reactive. Be the proactive one; assert yourself. They all look like they've had a bit of an altercation recently, so maybe they aren't that good.*

Each of the men spoke to her and each other in a language she couldn't understand. They moved for their weapons, and the man with the flail started waving it. Aetheria moved at full speed. She became a blur, and another blur crashed into where she had been. A thrown knife vibrated in the ground after it passed through where she had stood previously.

In her mind, Aetheria saw her move: an awesome dash, slide, then pulling a Van Damme and punching the plate-wearing man in the crotch. It went precisely to her plan—initially. The sprint went fine, and the tumble and roll were mainly okay. When she punched upward, she maybe didn't hold back enough. Whatever impromptu nut-cup armor the man had in his breeches provided the same resistance as paper, and a total power punch from Aetheria inflicted maximum damage. The giant oaf released a horrifying scream of pain and fell forward onto the ground, where he held his crotch and cried.

Aetheria botched her recovery slightly, unprepared for the ridiculous scenario, before she caught a foot against a rock and leveraged a jump to a standing position. Her bow and a mana arrow aimed at Magey's torso appeared in her hand. Again, someone threw a knife, and while it missed her, it went right through the string of her bow. Fortunately, the energy bow remained utterly unaffected.

All four other men stared at her, open-mouthed. Magey dropped his staff and raised his hands in surrender. The duelist, who looked quite pale, did the same. Assy unsheathed his blades and yelled harshly at her, but he stopped and resheathed his daggers to go to the downed thug. The ranger gave her bow an appraising look and gave her a new once-over, reassessing the threat.

"I wasn't trying to end that guy's chances at having kids, but you should know better than threatening a woman with weapons, especially when she's talking gibberish at you and you can't understand her either." Why was she even trying? "Which one of you asshats threw the knives?"

"Please. No. Hurt," the mage begged in a language sort of close to Sylvan. He struggled with the language. It sounded wrong to her. The pronunciation was off, but at least there were words she understood. The rogue tended to the injuries of the big man, offering him a vial of pungent-smelling liquid. Now that Aetheria was really seeing them, they all looked as though they had lost a recent fight. Especially the one she had struck.

"Why did you shout and get ready to attack me?" Aetheria kept the bow trained on the mage. The mage relayed what she said to his party. They talked, but she still couldn't pick up any familiar words.

"Scary dark colors. Dark Lord soldiers. Mistake." The mage gestured at her outfit. She was wearing a decent amount of black and red, which maybe looked a little menacing.

"What kind of Dark Lord has minions with aqua-blue hair, a radiant smile, and glowing blue eyes?" Uncertain if sarcasm would carry through how dim their communication method was, she arched a brow at him.

As he relayed her words to his party, the mage looked amused. Assy muttered rude words, the ranger stayed quiet, and the noble-looking duelist looked apologetically at her. She thought they could resolve this situation peacefully when the freshly healed big man stood up. He was tall. Aetheria assumed she was around six feet now, maybe taller, and he had a solid foot on her.

Aetheria didn't deny she felt a little intimidated as the colossal warrior stood fully erect, but then he bowed his head to her. More words she didn't understand. The rogue seemed angry that the big man apologized and glared murder at Aetheria.

"Magic? Make talk easy." The mage gestured at his staff on the ground.

"Go ahead." Aetheria let the bow vanish from her hands, although she casually summoned a spear to lean on in what she hoped was a lighthearted way. All five men watched closely at how her weapons appeared and disappeared. That ability wasn't common in these parts, it seemed, wherever the heck these parts were. Was the tower just a giant interstellar collection of planets and dimensions cobbled together, or was it its own realm? Were these people real, or were they the equivalent of non-player characters?

They certainly seemed to have emotions. Assy and the big man appeared to have a bit of a thing for one another, if she was reading the subtext behind the rogue's anger correctly. The mage had very expressive eyes, and when he chanted and formed magic, Aetheria could barely feel the mana respond to him. The effect of his spell on the surrounding currents seemed minuscule, and the spell model he formed with it felt very hollow. Her mana sense felt very basic, but she could tell he built a geometric shape with sigils and runes that provided meaning, and the words he chanted seemed to be a focus rather than a primary component.

It was very different spell casting from what they had employed in *EFWO*, where the character just chanted two or three words, glowed a bunch, then flung a spell. When the mage finished the spell, each of the six people glowed briefly, and Aetheria had to hide a smile. *I just experienced my first proper spell!*

"Let's see if this works now. Greetings, fair lady." The nobleman was the first to speak.

"Of course it is going to work, Benedict. Has Albert ever had a language spell go wrong before?" Assy hissed at the duelist. Understanding people and seeing that Assy was a dick to everyone was so lovely that Aetheria laughed.

"Hi. Sorry about breaking your testicles, big guy, but you sort of deserved it for menacing a woman surrounded by five strange men all brandishing weapons and shouting nonsense at her." What should she introduce herself to these people as? Aetheria had apparent connections to Aetherius, and this was his tower. The ghost elf had treated her practically like a divine figure.

The large man grunted. "You are right. The sage sent us out to find a wandering demigod to save the keep, and then we prepared to attack her when she appeared. I'm Dylan. Real sorry about that..." Dylan trailed off after he realized he didn't know how to address her.

"Aetheria." If they thought she was a demigod, why not fuel it? It could come in handy. "You can call me Ria, though."

The mage immediately went to a knee, lowering his head in subservience. The others gaped a little, then mimicked him. The rogue still glared at her with hostility.

"Are you perchance descended from the great Aetherius, Lady Aetheria?" Albert, the mage, got straight to the point.

"Aetherius calls me one of his children," Aetheria answered softly. Was he her father? No. She had a father, essence, spark, Flame, or whatever else aside. He was in Minnesota and had been the one to get her a librarian job after she graduated from the U of M. He had even helped her buy her house. Aetherius might call her his child, and he might take on a fatherly role. But she had a dad already.

"The forces of the Dark Lord besiege our keep, Most Esteemed Daughter of the Sky. We beg for your aid against the forces of darkness." Benedict, the noble duelist, requested this with an earnestness that warred with the glimmer of amusement in his eyes. Aetheria enjoyed her first experience of being asked to go on a quest like the thousands she'd done in *EFWO*, in real life.

"Yeah, sure. You betcha." Aetheria coughed, trying to act casual. "I would be happy to help in whatever way I can."

"The people of Othain will know freedom from the darkness once more! We should hurry to the keep. The siege began as the great sage Baldonoff sent us to find you. Breaking through even the back lines left us beaten." Benedict sounded ashamed.

"Alright, lead the way. It's nice to be working with you all." Despite her smile and agreement to help them with no mercenary bartering, Assy still scowled at her. *Maybe he is just naturally an unpleasant person. Or he will be all grudge-y forever because I hurt his boyfriend. Or he's the one who threw the knives.*

"By the way, how long will this spell last? And what language do you all speak?" she inquired as she moved to walk alongside Albert.

"We speak the human language of Allyerian, which spread across the continent during the rise of the ancient Allyerian empire. Their language, laws, and ruins are all we have to commemorate them anymore. The spell will last for two days. If we get low on time, I'll recast it. What language is it you speak, Lady Aetheria? My pendant helps me with elven languages, but it could barely process whatever tongue you speak." Albert's thirst for knowledge was an equal match for his love of dispensing knowledge. Or maybe he just really wanted to talk to their "demigod."

"Ancient empire? Sounds fantastic. Maybe if I have time, I could see some of these ruins. The common name for my language is Primeval Sylvan." The authority and confidence she answered the question with were utterly fake. She did not know what language she spoke. *What kind of god changes your primary language and doesn't even tell you the new language's name? Jerkbutt.*

As the others prepared for the trek, Benedict pulled out a post that he shoved into the ground. From there, the noble closed his eyes and offered a brief prayer or incantation under his breath. Each ring on the post glowed, and spectral horses formed, connected to ropes on a bar.

"Mount up. We'll hit Baldonoff's Keep within an hour if we make haste. Hopefully, the outer walls haven't fallen yet."

Thus, Aetheria got to ride her first summoned mount. The trek to the keep was full of questions, answers, and unending glares from Assy, whose name she still hadn't learned.

It turned out that her expectation of a minor assault was wrong. The Dark Lord's army looked truly daunting when they neared the keep. *So much for a small starter quest; this is more of a Helm's Deep scenario than a problem you throw a single hero at. Stupid me and my big, stupid mouth.*

CHAPTER 14

Baldonoff's Keep

The composition of the Dark Lord's army only slightly comforted Aetheria. While over a thousand figures made up the tide of bodies assaulting the keep, few were imposing. The most common enemy was goblins, which comprised at least two-thirds of the force. Even her untrained eye could tell they were no ordinary goblins but zombies.

I thought goblins would be ugly, but zombified goblins are hideous. Ew. Are those orcs?

Scattered among the tide of "zomblins" were the occasional much taller zombie orcs. Whoever had animated the undead horde apparently had a more challenging time gaining orc corpses than goblins, unless there was a difference in difficulty in raising orcs versus goblins. The army radiated a dark miasma like monsters did, although on a lesser scale and of a distinct flavor. If the monsters Aetheria fought on the island were a red pinot noir, these undead were a watered-down red blend.

Towering above the undead zombies were four massive figures. Each one looked like they had been made from the same pattern. The only differences came from the materials used to build them. With corpse golems, that material was corpses—mostly goblin corpses, but there were a few recognizably human components to the large abominations. Each massive creature pulled siege weapons closer to the keep while the zombies tried to swarm and break the doors.

The keep itself still stood. The tides of zombies had proven ill-equipped to break through heavy stone outer fortifications. The zombies trampled and destroyed all the outlying buildings in the pressing wave of rotting flesh. The stalemate would not last once the siege weapons opened the fortifications to the lesser horde.

The five men and Aetheria sat upon spectral horses, viewing the state of the siege from a nearby hill.

"I'll handle the army. You guys go take a nap." She couldn't resist falling back on the sarcasm in the face of a real-life zombie horde. Her brightest, most sugary smile was enough to counteract the sarcasm. She thought.

"Okay," Assy, who she had learned was Bernard, immediately piped up.

"We shall assist you, my lady." Benedict, the duelist, immediately refuted the rogue.

"I can best assist you from the walls." Albert the mage informed the group.

"I love smashing goblins. They say if you fight a Dark Lord, there's a chance you'll become a hero in this life or your next. I'd be a great hero." Fully recovered from his nearly becoming a eunuch, Dylan hefted his flail to show his eagerness.

Rangerdanger, whose name she still had not learned, ran a hand through his greasy hair. Proximity to his awful odor and poor hygiene had killed any attraction Aetheria had initially felt toward him. *Does being a ranger prevent bathing? Maybe they take an oath to foreswear all the benefits of society, like soap.*

"I shall join Albert on the wall. The flags show the sage and his apprentices are about to join the fray. I'll trust the demigods back to you, Dylan, Benedict, and Bernard. Bring great honor to Othain."

Oh gods, his breath is worse than his B.O. Rangerdanger could teach a dragon a thing or two about breath weapons.

Never split the party! That was the tabletop gaming mantra to avoid party wipes. Video games went the other way, constantly breaking the party to compartmentalize plot progression and tell multiple stories simultaneously. Fictional characters enjoyed the protection of plot armor. Aetheria enjoyed ridiculously awesome regeneration powers, but she was a little dubious if any of the three joining her on the field would last. That played into some of her ignorance about the tower.

Were these men real? Were they just NPCs generated by the power of a god? Without knowledge, Aetheria decided she would treat this world and its problems like a factual reality, full of real people with actual problems. Thus, she would try to stick to the most significant thing she learned from dying and reincarnating: life is sacred.

"I don't suppose you can get us to the front of the gate? It'd be nice to have something against our backs."

Albert nodded and formed a spell construct. "Blessings of Aetherius upon you, radiant lady." Albert offered the prayer as his spell finished. A shimmering doorway appeared before them. Dylan charged through, laughing. Benedict followed, and Bernard brought up the rear of the three.

"We'll have to get some drinks after this, yeah?"

Aetheria vanished through the door, instantly appearing in front of the enormous gates to the keep. Dylan was already clearing the ground with large sweeps of his flail. The big thug might not stand a chance against someone as fast as Aetheria, but he destroyed the zombies with no issue. Benedict fought behind and to the side of Dylan, providing flank protection. The duelist precisely dismembered enemies weakened by the giant flail. Bernard was nowhere to be seen.

Stealth? I want stealth. Maybe he'll teach me to hide in plain sight if I give him some shinies.

Not one to wait, Aetheria leaped onto a small ledge on the wall and summoned her bow. Her plan wouldn't work with a standard bow, but she didn't have a standard bow. Her initial targets were going to be the four flesh golems. They were the most potent source of miasma she could sense in the army. Still, teamwork was essential, so she released a few quick shots into clumps of undead right at the front line, to soften them up for the boys.

The large blast radius and mystical power in her arrows seemed incredibly potent against the undead. Was all magic effective against zombies? If so, why would a keep with mages like Albert and some great sage with apprentices need protecting? Dylan's open-mouthed stare at the effects of her arrows said she was beyond the range of ordinary magic for this place.

The first corpse golem took four arrows to kill.

My bow feels a little cheat-like. It shoots more like a gun and has an area-of-effect explosion. Still, four shots to kill will get me targeted sooner rather than later. Can I up the oomph?

In the next shot, Aetheria tried to guide some of her mana into the bow. The arrow took on a vivid aqua color, and when it hit the corpse golem, wild blue flames shot out as stars. Stars that incinerated and atomized everything in a fifty-foot radius. The mystical stars annihilated the siege weapon, corpse golem, hundreds of goblins, and dozens of orcs.

"Oh, jeez." *Overkill, sure, but impressive.*

She infused the next arrow she nocked in the same way, and when it struck the corpse golem, it exploded into a twenty-foot vortex of energy and then collapsed like a gravity well. The destruction was not as massive as the first time, but the idea that she might have almost caused a black hole was scary.

She infused a little extra mana into the last arrow.

Halfway to the target, the arrow became a dragon made of blue fire that ate everything it passed. The dragon demolished golems, goblins, orcs, vegetation, structures, land, stone, and farms. Everywhere it passed, it left smoking ruin behind.

"Good way to break a bow, overloading it with power. One more, and that one's about to explode in your face." The voice was Bernard's. Aetheria couldn't pick up where it came from. He had to be very close.

"Shit. You are right. Thanks for the warning." *Well, I'm an idiot.*

The bow's fine engravings looked worn, the Ethereal bowstring faded, and the inscribed sigils and runes that gave it magic were dimmer. It looked like even one more regular shot would consign the bow to destruction by a careless owner.

Oops. So, I'm a badass with mana. Or is my mana unique somehow? Aspected? Does this mean I'm intense?

Aetheria sighed. That was her only ranged weapon. She had many throwing knives, but her accuracy was pretty trash with them, and they created nowhere near the bow's destructive power. Maybe she could overload regular weapons with mana as a means of offense?

Waves of miasma crashed into the field from the back lines of the undead horde. The enemy did not seem to take the counterassault lying down. Dark clouds drifted through the army, each zombie they passed growing slightly and its concentration of miasma increasing. Aetheria knew a buff spell when she saw one. In her mind, they had just shifted up a phase in this encounter.

A massive fireball distracted Aetheria from plotting her next move. It sailed from the keep walls through the air, arcing, and then fell on a large concentration of the undead. The fireball exploded when it hit an orc, and a thirty-foot sphere of fiery destruction immediately expanded. When the heat waves settled, it became evident that very few undead had escaped destruction. Those who survived drifted out of the area of impact, but most didn't make it before they fell as piles of ash.

A volley of five more fireballs flew through the air and struck down clumps of the undead. These spells were all noticeably weaker than the first, barely reaching a fifteen-foot radius, and while they killed the goblins on impact, the orcs survived it and made it out of the blast location, still able to fight.

They had artillery now. Aetheria summoned a spear and waved to get the attention of Dylan and Benedict.

"Let's go find their leader. With the siege weapons down, they aren't getting past the gates. Maybe we can end this before they retreat." The duelist looked slightly dubious, but the look quickly vanished from his face.

"I'm at your command, my lady." Benedict bowed, then shouted to Dylan. "We'll go through where Lady Aetheria's blue dragon arrow passed! The divine energies seem to repulse the undead still!"

Divine energies? It was just mana, my dude. But sure, keep thinking about that. All I did was almost break my bow. Maybe broke it. Fuck. It will be a bitch to find someone who can fix unique elven bows, right?

"You got it, boss!" Dylan grunted. He took the lead and charged through the unorganized horde, and for ten minutes they fought to reach the area where the destruction of the dragon arrow had started. There, they were able to breathe— Benedict had been right about the glowing area keeping the undead repelled.

The relatively short but intense fights were a grim reminder to Aetheria about the survivability she enjoyed with regeneration. Each minor wound on Dylan and Benedict would add up, and while they had a few healing potions, Aetheria did not know how many, or how effective they were against extreme injuries.

Their trek down the damaged path was short-lived. Two massive oak trees stomped toward them, a figure clad in black and green perched in the first tree. The closer they came, the easier it became to discern the features of the person. It was an elven woman, and if she wasn't a druid, Aetheria would eat her own hair. Green robes, flowers, and leaves decorated the tree rider's blond hair. She held a gnarly looking staff.

Definitely a druid. Wait, when did that guy get there?

A second figure, male, rode the other tree, clad in black with pallid skin, and carrying a scythe. He didn't hold a sign that said, "Hi, I'm a necromancer," but he might as well have. The pale, dark magician was an elf.

"Great. Looks like we found your 'Dark Lord.' Why are you fighting elves?" Aetheria frowned at Benedict.

"Not elves, m'lady. Terrorists. They hunt any who enter the forests, barring the expansion of the keep, and deny any negotiations."

Aetheria took a deep breath and prepared herself for what was to come.

CHAPTER 15

Traitor

Oh, sure, you didn't tell me the Dark Lord was attacking you because—" Aetheria did not finish the sentence, mostly because she took an arrow in the throat. It was a blow that would incapacitate most people, but Aetheria wasn't most people. She fell to the ground and began to convulse.

Should I be playing dead? Playing dead is always hard. This might be a new level of difficulty, though. Seriously, how am I supposed to not flop around like a fish out of the water while I can feel my muscles pushing the arrow back out of my throat? Ew. This power is so nasty. Throat wounds aren't an instant kill, so playing dead is unnecessary. Yay, flopping like a fish.

"I've got you now, traitor." The voice was Bernard's, but Aetheria did not know where it had come from. *Stealth is overpowered. NERF rogues!*

The faint twang of a bowstring sounded, and Benedict went down with an arrow deep in his eye. No healing was going to save him unless someone possessed resurrection magic. Whoever shot at them was a genuinely superb archer. *Ohhh. Damn.*

"Traitor!" Big Dylan charged backward, but vines rose from the ground to trap him. Despite his size, he failed in his struggles against the thick vines. An arrow took him in the neck. Not an instant kill, but death by bleeding out was a valid concern for those without Aetheria's regeneration.

A familiar voice screamed out in pain. The sound of daggers meeting flesh, and then the clash of metal. Aetheria growled—her inaction was directly contributing to the assailants moving to secondary targets. She rose and darted over to Benedict. He was already cooling. He did, however, have a healing potion, which she opened and poured into Dylan's mouth. All the while, she kept an eye on what was happening behind them.

Bernard and the ranger were fighting, and it was not going well for the ranger. Bernard had cut the archer's Achilles tendons using stealth and inflicted a nasty blow across his gut.

The healing potion went to work on Dylan while Aetheria cut the vines off him.

"Help Bernard with the ranger, then get back to the keep. I think he did some terrible things before coming after us." Aetheria had one eye on the fight, the other on the elves who approached. When the big man hesitated, she shoved him forward, and walked toward the elves who advanced in their trees.

The most eye-catching of all her spears appeared in her hand. It was a gold-colored spear. Yellow flames danced along its triple head. It had a beautiful phoenix motif and felt appropriate for fighting a druid and a necromancer.

"Hail and well met," Aetheria said in a loud and confident voice to the tree-bound elves in Primeval Sylvan.

The tree elementals stopped moving. The druid and the necromancer looked shocked to hear a human speaking Primeval Sylvan. They moved to each other to talk in quiet whispers. Aetheria was in no hurry, though, and their talking allowed her to take a much better look at the two of them. For elves, they looked younger than she would expect for a pair waging war on human encroachment.

"Who are you?" the druid finally demanded. "The elementals refuse to go any closer to you. Why? How did you learn to speak Primeval Sylvan?"

"My name is Aetheria, daughter of Aetherius, and I am a Challenger for the world of Grief." The elves' facial expressions immediately confirmed one of Aetheria's suspicions: they were siblings. Or were they just elves, and she was racist in thinking they looked alike? "As for why the elementals don't want to play with me, I'd go back to the whole being Aetheria, daughter of Aetherius thing. Apparently, the old man is a real big deal."

Both elves looked shocked to be face-to-face with a demigod. Or god. Or something in between. Not that Aetheria felt like a demigod. She felt like a human who'd just had an arrow pushed out of her throat by her own vocal cords. Not much about that felt divine.

"Oh, and I learned Primeval Sylvan from a lovely specter. I think you probably know him. Werylin Amaryllis? Minstrel, bad decision maker, guardian of a tomb?"

"How...?" The male elf silenced himself.

"She is a demigod," the druid hissed to her sibling.

"So, I'm out of the loop here. Let's catch me up. Humans ignored old pacts and started coming for your sacred elven forests. Your elders didn't want to do anything. You took it in your own hands to scare off the humans, using an undead army, working with the terribly smelly ranger back there. Am I about right?" Aetheria was about to pat herself on the back, but the druid laughed.

"Well, sort of. That's scarily accurate. But no, we didn't work with the ranger."

"Uh, actually..." The necromancer brother cleared his throat. "I had a deal with him to assassinate the leader of the keep. He was one of those skulkers always on the edge of the domain, so I turned him to our purposes. You nature lovers are always so fanatical. He and a few others were too eager to become traitors if it meant gaining a tree house in our forests."

Aetheria glanced over her shoulder to see Bernard and Dylan wipe the blood off their weapons on the ranger's limp body.

"Get back to the keep. Things are probably bad there," Aetheria commanded the two humans, but her eyes never left the necromancer and the druid.

"So, how are we going to do this? Werylin did me a favor, so I don't want to wipe out the survivors of his house living in the tower." Aetheria wasn't sure about that guess, but the widened eyes and literal gasp that escaped the druid made her laugh. *I've still got it.*

"Well, the humans must stay out of our woods. They signed treaties to that effect two hundred years ago. They can't ignore treaties because it was a few generations for them, or there's no point in any race making treaties with them."

"You killed quite a few of them with the undead horde. Ruined a lot of farmland and houses, too."

"They killed six of our kin while encroaching into the forests, and hundreds of trees."

"Is there a peaceful solution? Maybe a border village where humans have to obey elven law? Regular contact with humans might keep them reminded of their treaties. Isolationism sure didn't keep them aware of their obligations. Was your treaty even with these humans?" It was odd, but obvious questions sometimes needed to be asked.

"I..." Both elves frowned at one another. They didn't know.

Let's see. If this were Star Trek, *this is where Captain Kirk would have a bare-chested duel with some badass, emerge victorious, then get drunk and sleep with all the pretty elf women. I'm up for all that but the topless part.*

"So, do I challenge you two or one of your elders for the right to decide the outcome of this whole human/elf problem?"

"You can fight us, both of us," the siblings answered simultaneously.

Oh, fuck me, I didn't even notice they were twins. Stupid fraternal siblings. Do twins have telepathy in the magical world? Maybe. Do elves? Be calm, be cool. I can beat up two kids.

"Fine. Any rules?"

"No killing. We fight until you or we yield."

"Alright. Get down here, and let's fight then," Aetheria declared with a lot more bravado than she felt. She was not above using a little psychological warfare, though, and took in deep breaths of mana. By the time the twins jumped to the ground, the air around Aetheria was already steaming, but she kept drawing ever more mana to her.

The twins looked at her like something was wrong with the situation, but they took a fighting stance and bowed to her.

Aetheria slightly bowed her head and said, "Go," at the same time as the twins.

Aetheria moved far faster than either of the elves could. Her boots slammed into the ground, and shockwaves and dirt exploded behind her. The distance between her and the necromancer closed instantly. She kicked him in the crotch, recovered her posture, and slammed the butt of her spear into his gut. Then she took a deep breath. Shockingly, what looked like tiny black wisps got sucked out of the necromancer into her lungs. The familiar coolness of the miasma filled her.

He slumped to the ground, unconscious.

"What?!" the druid shouted in shock. From her perception, the human had teleported in front of her brother, struck him in a blur, and then drained his essence. All before she could even cast a spell, the mana fields in the area were going insane in reaction to whatever the human was doing. Humans did not act like this. Perhaps being related to Aetherius had not been a lie?

"Well, that was overkill." Aetheria looked at the crumpled elf and walked toward the druid. Her walk felt sped up, and the surrounding air alternated with black and aqua energy pulses. She was almost touching the elf before the druid snapped out of whatever reverie she had been in and chanted weird words. Two large hands of dirt reached up from the earth itself to grasp Aetheria.

"Oh, magic. Nice. You're my first." Aetheria winked at the druid and wondered why she was laughing.

Is energy over-absorption like being on drugs? Laughing gas? I feel powerful. Giddy. Fast. Strong. Horny. Hungry. I suffer everything, really. I can almost see the mana now. Maybe I just wasn't taking in enough before?

She inhaled deeply. The earthen hands withered and fell to the ground as clumps of carbon with no magic.

"That's not possi—"

Aetheria interrupted the druid with a punch to the gut. When that didn't knock her out, she moved forward and was about to kick her when the female elf coughed out, "Yield," along with some blood.

"Oh. Okay. Sorry about the punch. I guess I'm still getting used to how strong I am." Aetheria smiled in what she thought was a comforting way. The elven woman looked more scared.

"Better check on your brother. I don't do any healing."

The giddiness was still wiggling around her brain like a worm. While the druid rushed to her brother's side to chant a healing spell, Aetheria looked in what she judged was the least populated direction and exhaled deeply, expelling the energy she no longer needed.

Sharp gusts of winds picked up, and a hurricane-like gale shot off into the distance. Dark storm clouds appeared in the sky. *Did I just make a hurricane for real?*

"What are you?" the druid asked, in awe.

"A human with a sugar daddy named Aetherius." The look of horror on the druid's face made it very hard for Aetheria to maintain a straight face. *I'm so going to get in trouble for blasphemy. I wonder if a mana high is an acceptable deflection of guilt? Or maybe he's my daddy, so I can say stuff like that in my defense? Ugh. I will buy into this stuff just to avoid responsibility for my tongue. Not.*

"So, are you Werylin's great-great-great-great-granddaughter? You look like him."

"No. I am Werylin's great-granddaughter. The best perk of being a Dweller are near immortality and agelessness. I'm only seventy. Ithyrra Amaryllis, at your service. Tamsin here is going to be unconscious for a while longer. So, you met Werylin? He's still bound to the tomb? Still sane?" Curiosity was a dangerous lure, and Ithyrra fell right into it.

"Yes. Werylin's still guarding the tomb. Perfectly sane. He taught me Primeval Sylvan and shared some great tea with me. I thought I'd try to give him a body back if I make it through here. So, I don't suppose I could get a vial of your blood just in case I figure out how to do that?"

CHAPTER 16

Talking Heads

Aetheria was not the biggest fan of meetings. She'd had to endure so few of them in her job as a librarian, until the state started regionalizing everything and demanding more cooperation. But of course, everything did not simply go away after she'd defeated the twin elves. Why would it?

Two days later, she was sitting at a large table in a tent halfway between Baldonoff's Keep and the forest. Ribbons and other decorations created a somber but festive environment for the negotiations.

Albert the mage was representing the keep. Apparently, he was the great sage's son and heir, and with the death of the sage and most of his senior apprentices at the hands of turncoat rangers and druids, he was now the lord of the keep. The elves were represented by Ithyrra and Tamsin's father.

Aetheria's role in proceedings was to sit as a nuclear warhead, ready to go off if either side tried to drift away from making a genuine effort at peace. Which, of course, meant there was steam coming off her in waves, although she was just sitting in her chair, breathing.

I am not addicted to the lovely feeling of being full of energy, she told herself. *It is nice, though, and people listen to me when I'm on the edge of going into full-out glow mode.*

"Ahem. Lady Aetheria?" Albert tried to drag her attention back to the matter at hand.

"What did I miss?"

"We have come to an agreement on a comanaged border settlement. With that, the treaty is ready for your review." Albert offered her a scroll to review.

The overall peace deal was relatively simple. The elves had negotiated such things frequently in the past; their problem was they were too isolationist. All Aetheria had suggested was a mixed-race town where elves and humans could mingle, reinforcing the pact between races through exposure and mutually beneficial trade.

Other details included exchanged ambassadors. They would charge a small group of humans and elves to foster positive relations with one another. To Aetheria, it sounded like a charity group. The elves seemed inclined to a steadfast commitment to peace through politics, but Ithyrra and her father were cagey about whether it was because Aetheria had kicked their asses or because it was their original intent.

Afterward, Aetheria mingled among the humans and elves, but she was searching for her four new friends. She found Albert first.

"Good luck running a kingdom. It doesn't look like an entertaining job, you know."

"It does not, does it? I thought there would be decades before I assumed the role of sage. My assistants found what you asked for. The topics on Aether and Nether are sketchy, but they well documented the other elements in the book. Nether's ties to necromancy, creation of monsters, and its other multifaceted evil powers make it something of a taboo topic. Similarly, the churches do not appreciate arcanists delving into the nature of divinity and Aether. It is the best I could do." Albert offered her a grimoire, thick and only slightly dusty. The humans and elves had each offered her rewards. This was what she had asked for from the humans.

"I'm sorry for your losses, Albert. I couldn't help Benedict."

"Our losses were largely at the hands of the maligned rangers. My father ignored the growing resentment as they complained about losing the wilds, the hostile relationship with the elves, and an ever-increasing agitation among the spirits." Albert seemed at peace with the events that had transpired, but his eyes gave away the sorrow and depression he had bottled up about the losses and betrayal by their friend, Vance, the ranger.

"I hope it gets better. I'll be leaving soon, and it's doubtful I'll ever return. Good luck." She squeezed his shoulder, and gave the slender mage a kiss on the cheek that left him blushing. The envious glances it earned the mage left Aetheria smirking as she went looking for the others.

She found Dylan and Bernard next. They had found a secluded corner where they could commiserate together and keep watch over Albert.

Her parting with the two was much quicker. She and Bernard exchanged nods, and she and Dylan fist-bumped.

"Sorry about the dick punch, Dylan."

"I wouldn't wish that upon my worst enemy, Lady Aetheria. Maybe go for people's kidneys going forward?" the big man suggested with a precarious grin. He wasn't quite ready to joke about the experience yet. Aetheria was unaware that a folk song was already being sung about Dylan the Wall having his manhood crushed. It would haunt the man for years.

"Stay alive, you two." She wished them well.

The last person she sought was Ithyrra's father. The older elf was sipping wine by himself, clearly waiting for her. Atop the table before him lay a series of crystals, the objects she had asked for from him.

"Preparing to sneak out and slip up to the next level?"

"That's the way it works, right? How are... they? About the mechanics of the tower?" Aetheria gestured at the humans.

"It is hard to tell. Discussions like that can get you in a recursive loop or trigger events to shift focus. Being a Dweller differs from being a Native. We can leave when our time is up. They can't or won't. Even with thousands of years to observe them, discerning the truth has eluded us. It can trigger events, usually unpleasant ones. We quickly learned not to press too hard."

That's convenient. Don't push the NPCs too much; we'll punish you with awful shit. Sounds like lazy tower management. I bet if I ask Aetherius about it, he'll also blame this on some rules by the Overgod.

"What did you get for me?"

The elf gestured at the three crystals.

"The human language, Gnomish, and Dwarven. Those were the only three languages for which we could find someone with mastery enough to cast the spell. You already speak Primeval Sylvan and Orcish. I'm surprised Grandfather shared our language with you, but you are quite... unique. I have a request for you, Lady Aetheria."

"Oh, what's that?" Aetheria absorbed the language crystals while Ismir talked.

"Would you speak with Tasmin before you depart? When you fought, something about him changed. Ithyrra claims you lifted the curse from him. If so, he will have a long path to walk to learn sorcery once again. The Nether affinity that forced him to become a necromancer is now gone, and our mystics claim the curse on the family cleansed."

"That's wonderful news, then. I'll check on Ithyrra and Tamsin before I leave. I can feel the Gateway this time. It's just waiting for me to summon it." Her displeasure, at last, lay open for any to hear.

I'm not a fan of just knowing things, somehow. How does that even work? Is it the same mental fuckery that happens to the natives and Dwellers to keep them on task for Climbers?

"Thanks for the crystals, Ismir. Oh, and thanks for the blood for Werylin, too. I won't do anything creepy with it, I promise."

The elf only looked a little worried. "The resurrection of Werylin would bode well for the elves still on Grief. If you succeed in your mission, we might leave the tower. Good luck, Lady Aetheria. You'll find my children in the white tent."

"Ope, let me sneak by ya, there." Even in Primeval Sylvan, she sounded Minnesotan. How was that fair?

Traveling through the party was not a challenge. While everyone was happy to smile at her, no one wanted to talk to her. Kicking the crap out of the twins had not left the elves with a great impression of her, and the humans just wanted her to convey their gratitude to Aetherius for sending his beautiful, unique, gracious, and fabulous daughter to help them.

I'm not an object! Thank me directly, assholes! I bet this is payback from Aetherius for the heresy. Learn to take a joke, "Dad."

The white tent was the one in which Ismir and his children were actually staying. Two elven guards stood at the entrance flap, but they did not hinder her. Aetheria breezed past them and from the main room of the flap back to the far-right partitioned room. Inside, Tasmin lay on a bed. Not unconscious any longer, but still weak.

"Lady Aetheria." He bowed his head, but the weakness in the man was still visible. Even moving that much seemed like a stretch for him.

"Tasmin. I hear you can't do necromancy anymore. Is that a good thing or a bad thing?" She had no reason to be anything other than direct.

"A good thing, I think? I never liked the Dark Arts, but it was my only affinity." The elf grimaced. Aetheria could just imagine how *not* fun being a necromancer was. *All the body parts. Ew.*

"Have they tested to see if you have a new affinity?"

"No. When I've rebuilt my strength, it is the first thing we will do, though."

Aetheria dropped her butt onto the bed next to the elf. She hovered her hand a foot or so from his chest. "May I?"

"Uh. Sure?" Wary approval.

She touched the skin above the low neckline of his recovery clothing. "Aetherius, please bless this man, Tasmin Amaryllis, with a boon to replace the power I took from him." She pushed a bit of her mana into her fingertips as she prayed.

Is this how clerics pray? I just clicked a button when playing EFWO. *It's been years since I visited a church.*

Some of the energy in her fingertips passed into the elf, and his eyes went wide and glowed azure for a few moments before fading to his regular blue.

"Well, I think you'll be just fine now. Good luck learning magic all over again. Your dad said it'd be a rough road."

The elf stammered to thank her.

"Just say thank you, brother," Ithyrra said from behind Aetheria.

"Thank you, Lady Aetheria."

"Not a problem. Glad to help. Take care of yourself." Aetheria blew him a kiss, and the elf turned red.

"Got a few minutes, Ithyrra? I wanted to talk before I leave."

"I'll be back in a while, brother. Let's talk outside?" Ithyrra led the way.

Dusk was no hindrance to navigating the camp or the surrounding woods. Ithyrra didn't take them too far into the woods, but far enough to give them some privacy. A slight grin played on the elf's lips.

"So the great human hero saves the day, then disappears at night. A legend for the natives to tell one another until the next Climber comes through. Want me to plant any stories about you among the humans?"

Ithyrra was a mischievous one, it turned out. Aetheria quickly discovered that she was not nearly as severe as she had expected. The blond elf was almost exactly what she imagined an elven druid should be: beautiful, centered, with a fleeting feeling of spirits surrounding her. The cleverly cut robes that showed off cleavage and legs might have helped, too.

"Hmm. You could always spread the story that I am a fabulous lover. Does that sound fun?"

"Yes. It sounds fantastic."

Ithyrra ran a solitary finger from Aetheria's temple, along the curve of her jaw, before the elf's finger pushed the human's chin up, and pressed her own lips against hers in an invitational kiss. Ithyrra then leaned forward, her warm breath tickling Aetheria's earlobe. "You can leave in the morning. Tonight is mine."

Later, Aetheria slipped out of the white tent in the dim light of dawn.

I can't tell if that's jealousy of me, Ithyrra, or both, in their eyes. Or are they annoyed that elves don't hide when they are having sex? No shame, I guess, and no volume control? Awkward.

The guards got a salute, and Aetheria walked away from the tents.

"Good luck, lass." Bernard's voice came from the shadows.

"Don't suppose you'll teach me stealth before I leave?"

"The sparkly hair would keep you from becoming unseen."

"The world isn't fair."

"Nope."

"Stay safe, Bernard. And keep Dylan out of trouble."

A shimmering door appeared before her, and she stepped through it.

She came out the other side in a place with rolling hills, mist covering the low ground between the peaks. She saw no signs of civilization.

Here we go. Floor Three.

CHAPTER 17

Foggy Banks

Visibility atop the hills was lacking. The world just turned into a foggy gray mix at approximately a quarter of a mile. The only sound was the slapping of water against the shore. *Is there a lake or ocean nearby?*

The air carried no scent of salt, so if there was an ocean or sea, it was fresh water. Of course, in a place like the tower, the body of liquid could just be purple acid or liquid mercury. Who knew what other strange and magical elements and materials existed in this place? Aetheria was not confident about her guesses regarding the purpose of this floor of the tower.

She summoned a chest from her inventory. Empty, of course. A kick of her boot sent the crate tumbling down the hillside. The thuds it made were reassuring as it passed into the thick fog, and then it stopped with a crash. The chest had collided with something.

Every hill she could see looked the same. There were no markings, distinctive grasses, or differences from what she could see. The only scent in the air was a muskiness that the fog partially concealed with its dank humidity. Aetheria summoned a spear and gouged a cross in the grass. She labeled the four sides N, E, S, and W.

I'm not finding out what is in the lowlands until I have to. Seems pretty apparent something terrible will be down there. Flesh-eating mist? Killer leeches? Tentacle monsters, definitely tentacle monsters.

With a running start, she leaped through the air across the lowland chasms to the next hill. Barely. Her impact with the next hill was a few feet above the dense fog. Something slithered down there, the sounds faint and possibly in her imagination. She went through the steps of making a cross again, this time denoting a star behind S to show her point of origin.

Her visibility did not seem to have extended any further. She made another run and jumped toward N. Again, she landed barely above the dense fog.

Is that a shadow moving in the fog? There's the slithering again.

Aetheria questioned the nature of this challenge. Was this a puzzle? A maze? Combat? Not knowing the fundamental basis of the challenge made learning what to do difficult. *This is a bit too much like the old hard-core games. Even* Morrowind *at least had a journal so you could remind yourself what quests you were on. Where's my quest log or journal?*

Muttering to herself, she recreated her cross and noted S with two stars.

Once more, she ran and leaped the chasm between hills. Mid-jump, she saw deeper shadows within the dense lowland fog and felt the slightest sensation of miasma. Startled but not shocked, she landed smoothly on the next hill. Once she had walked up the incline to the top, Aetheria frowned.

"Huh." The next hill in N direction was bisected by a wall of fog. "That explains why I never saw new hills."

So, I'm in a confined area. Either I'm meant to escape it via a puzzle somehow, or there are some beasties in the lowlands I'm expected to defeat. Maybe multiple solutions? This is supposed to be a learning environment for the Aetherial race, so there's a teachable lesson somewhere. Assuming people know jack about this tower. I could probably make a multipurpose series of contingency-level dungeons if I were a god. There's no way every person gets thrown onto the same floors anyway, or there would just be cheat books on how to deal with everything.

Do I go to look at the half-hill?

While Aetheria pondered which way to go, the sense of miasma gradually increased from the lowlands. A slow but constant buildup of power. As the energy built up, the fog rose slowly. When she noticed the rising mist, it had already gained a foot, putting her in dangerous territory of landing in the mist.

With no idea of her goal beyond the rapidly growing suspicion of trial by combat, she started sucking in mana. She was steaming already after ten breaths. The surrounding air crackled with aqua and black energy pulses at twenty breaths. By thirty breaths, Aetheria had an aura of aqua energy that occasionally crackled and popped with black miasma.

The more power she drew into herself, the more miasma stirred in the fog. As on the island, miasmatic monsters seemed drawn to her when she breathed in copious amounts of mana. The mist continued to rise while she drew in power, slowly at first, but higher and faster the more mana she drew. The mist rose until only the tops of the hills remained above it.

The first monster to strike from the fog moved like a lightning bolt—a lightning bolt of black scales, white fangs, and a forked tongue. Hyped up on mana, Aetheria moved even faster than the black viper. Mandibles snapped shut, missing her as she danced aside, repositioned, and unleashed a bare-fisted punch to the side of the snake's head.

Aetheria pushed mana into her fist and tried to imagine an explosion on impact. She got what she imagined: her right hand exploding into the same fragments of scale, bone, and flesh that the viper became. A blast of aqua power filled the world as roars and hisses came from the sea of fog. Aetheria's pained shouts rose above the rest of the noise.

"Oh, fucking shit! Poop taco! Oh, that's special." Words randomly poured out of Aetheria's mouth as the realization of what had happened sank in. She had utterly obliterated the black viper. Whatever energy she had unleashed had traveled through her hand, exploded, and kept on exploding inside the viper. It covered the scenic hilltops in splattered gore, and a feeding frenzy occurred inside the sea of fog as monsters ate monster, and bits of Aetheria's right hand, too.

"Oh. Jeez. *Cripes.*" The pain kicked in, and colors flashed before her eyes. The bones in her hand were regrowing, then the flesh. Aetheria vomited. "Uffda."

So. Disgusting. I hate biology.

Disgusted and enchanted by her new right hand, she failed to notice another viper striking from the fog. She dodged out of the way at the last minute, and the viper's fangs only penetrated and ripped her thigh before she was out of its bite. *Of course it's venomous. Why wouldn't it be?*

She moved through the pain. This time, she focused on imagining her fist as incredibly durable. She counterpunched the snake in the face. Her fist impacted with the black scales and then went through the snake's head matter until her arm was fully extended. She yanked her arm free and jumped back.

Ew. Ew. I just punched a snake in the brain.

Anxiety, pain, confusion, and the agony of her body neutralizing venom and reknitting her thigh—all of these required her to keep pulling in deep breaths of mana. Black miasma flowed from the dying form of the snake into her lungs, sending mixed sensations of hot mana and cold miasma through her extremities.

Energy manipulation is dangerous. Until I find a teacher, no more trying to make explosions. Being tough worked really well, though. I can use that.

The vanishing miasma of the two dead monsters filled Aetheria's lungs, and the fog's height dropped slightly. Shadows slithered in the fog, and monsters began launching themselves at her. There seemed to be only three variants: black vipers, writhing leeches, and centipedes.

The black vipers predominantly bit, relying on venomous fangs to deal with their prey. The leeches were the size of a golden retriever. They were slow, but they launched themselves like arrows to latch onto her once they were within ten feet. The vipers and leeches were not really much of a problem for Aetheria. With each kick and punch, she effortlessly destroyed them. Her focus on strength and durability with the mana seemed to pay off. The leeches exploded when she hit them, which was super disgusting, but when she sucked in mana and miasma in the same breath, all the blood and gore dematerialized into the miasma that she inhaled.

The centipedes were disgusting. Aetheria did not want to touch them, but punched them all the same. The first one she hit exploded into a cloud of acid that burned her face and hand until she breathed in the miasma and broke the monster into molecules. The centipedes had an acid spit. They rolled into balls and tried to run her over.

The sound of combat raged for over half an hour as Aetheria punched, kicked, headbutted, and stomped snakes, insects, and worms. Inevitably, she eventually stood alone, looking over a series of duplicate hills with no evidence of the monsters. She had turned them all into miasma and consumed them.

Still no door. Not done.

Spikes of miasma filled the air just moments before her ultimate challenge appeared. Each of the hills shuddered. Grass and dirt tore as something fought its way out of each slope.

"Oh, are you joshing me? *Snapping turtles?* For cripe's sake." Flashbacks to almost losing a hand as a child reared their ugly head in her mind.

A quick count showed she was facing approximately thirty snapping turtles, all opening their maws and breathing green mists that spread quickly. The mist made her skin feel like it was burning, her eyes like they were melting. Breathing was incredibly painful; her chest fell in sharp, erratic movements thanks to the burning sensations.

Close your eyes. Breathe deeply. I am powerful and indestructible. I'm untouchable and a super badass.

She walked into a turtle with her eyes closed.

Got you, asshole.

One punch obliterated much of the turtle's shell, and with her eyes closed, she started ripping organic material apart until she had weakened the turtle to the point of her being able to inhale its miasma.

Doing this with thirty turtles would take too long, especially if she walked into a mouth and had to regenerate limbs. *What happens if they bite my head off? Game over? What actually kills me? I should find that out at some point. Open your eyes. Work through the pain. Pain is transitory.*

Flicking her eyes open, Aetheria saw she was about to get bitten by another turtle. Sluggishly (apparently strengthening her whole body like this significantly slowed her down), she stepped into the attack and caught the monster's upper jaw. From there, many punches killed it, and it was yet more miasma for her to absorb.

With each monster killed, the next inhalation infused her with more power. Aetheria knew her regeneration was in overdrive. It healed her bites and the energy ravaging her body. The worse she got hurt, the more energy her regeneration consumed. So she was stuck in a semi-stable loop of how much damage the power caused her.

Finally, Aetheria stood alone on a flat plain and exhaled the energy into the distant fog borders. The power turned into a shooting star and flew into an unseen cosmos.

"Wow." She whistled and cracked her neck before frowning. A doorway appeared next to her.

It feels like I almost failed this one. I really think there was another solution, with directions or a puzzle. Some kind of intelligent solution to the problem other than just murdering dozens upon dozens of monsters that weren't even that difficult.

If the tower is for training, what path am I putting myself on by answering problems with brute force?

"I need more knowledge. Help a girl out?" Aetheria stepped through the door to Floor 4.

CHAPTER 18

The Village of Masters

Challenge: Receive Acknowledgment from at least four masters."

A large wooden post rose well above her height. Attached to the wood at chin height was a sign that gave her a challenge. Her first glance at the poster showed the text swirling, symbols changing to the written language Aetherius had taught her. No living being she had met could speak that language, so she was inclined to think it was divine. Thus, the tower had likely made the sign, rather than the village that lay down the road.

The post stood where three paths met and converged toward the village. Beyond the town, mountains rose into the clouds, and thick temperate forests lay in every other direction. The sort of forests that Aesca had grown up with all her life. A small comfort compared to the strange buildings that awaited her in the village.

Before Aetheria's eyes, the strange language faded to reveal a regular signpost. It simply read, "Solace," and pointed in the direction ahead of her. Three other pointers went in the other directions: "Kingsbrooke," "Olanberg," and "Castle of Dread." *Wow, the last one sounds pleasant. Maybe I'll vacation there.*

No one met Aetheria on the road as she strolled toward the village. A hip-high stone wall surrounded the entire town, although it was newer in some areas than others. They had moved the fence several times to accommodate the growing city. The most prominent building in town looked like a quintessential mage's tower. Spiraling up into the air, its upper-floor windows alight with strange effects, there was no doubt in her mind a wizard lived there.

When she passed the open gates into town, the wandering citizens on the streets all turned to look at her simultaneously. The expressions on their faces varied. Some looked annoyed, some looked put upon, and others looked eager.

This is going to be a town full of Dwellers, right? Some will get rewards for helping me, and some for derailing me? It wouldn't be a trial otherwise, would it? They have at least four masters, so they're probably almost all specialists in... something.

"Hello there, my lady." The first person to address her was an elf who spoke Primeval Sylvan. If Ismir had been Werylin's grandson, she had a feeling this might actually be Werylin's son himself. Tricky for the elf to sneak them all into the tower, away from mortal repercussions before his downfall.

"Hello, and aren't you the most handsome elf I've seen today? Your purple hair is lovely. Did you get it from your father, perchance?" The elf looked startled when she answered him in the same tongue. What had perhaps been an attempt at the humiliation of a newcomer quickly changed as gears turned in the elf's head.

"*Ahem.* I did not expect to meet a human so fluent in Sylvan. Tell me, how did you learn it, young lady?" The purple-haired elf smiled at her compliment but did not offer a name or return the compliment.

"Oh, this lovely purple-haired specter of an elf taught it to me; his name was Werylin Amaryllis. Lovely man. Quite lonely guarding a tomb, though." The reaction she was looking for was there. A tightening around the elf's eyes, a slight catch in his breath, losing perfect posture for a fraction of a moment.

"I see. What might be your name, and what brings you to Solace? Looking to learn something specific? I am the most esteemed Grand Bard-in-residence and Master Spellsinger; should that pique your interest?"

"You can call me Ria. Well, it's a pleasure to meet you, Grand Bard, but I think I'll look around your fine town. Good day." She smiled sparklingly at the elf before side-stepping around him, leaving him still slightly reeling at being dismissed so easily. Werylin had warned her about choosing the wrong path, and music wasn't really her thing.

No one style of architecture covered Solace. Each of the larger buildings had its own flair and style. Some had gargoyles on roofs, and others had flocks of birds watching everything. One even had a cow on the top for no reason she could see.

No one else approached her as she wandered the town. The people all seemed more than happy to watch her instead. Eventually, Aetheria found what looked to be an inn and walked inside. The tables and chairs showed excellent craftsmanship, and the bar top glistened with a relatively recent coat of lacquer. The man behind the bar might as well have had a floating sign above his head that said "bartender." He even had a slightly curled mustaches. Hopefully, he spoke a language she knew.

"Hello, I was wondering if you had any vacancies?" She tried the human language she had picked up first. The man looked human, after all.

"Sure, there are always vacancies. Few Climbers coming around old Aetherius's tower. It's been around thirty years since the last Climber made it to our domain. What level are we this time, anyway?" His eyes sparkled with humor, and he had an easygoing way about him. Aetheria instinctively wanted to talk with him and gossip, but put a tight rein on that. If this was the village of masters, was this the orator or something more nefarious?

"Fourth. I'm Ria. By the way, what do you teach?"

"That early? Someone must really want you to do well. Usually, Solace shows up in the thirties, after the second city. I'm Sam, master mixologist. Not the most popular of subspecialties of alchemy, but having a good mixologist in your city can put you ahead of a slew of bad things. Preventative brews, morale boosters, all the fun things. Room's free, by the by. We don't charge Challengers." The barkeep winked at her.

"Ah. So I guess my telepathic SOS told everyone a Challenger was here when I hit this floor?"

"Yes, ma'am. There'll be a few who will want to teach you, and some who won't want anything to do with you. More important than any of that, though, got any ideas on what you want to learn?" Sam grinned and didn't beat around the bush. Aetheria assumed no one was interested in his profession beyond the beer he served.

"Well, I need someone who can teach me to fight. Someone who can teach me about Aether, Nether, or both, and after that... I'm not sure I know enough to even think about the right things to learn." Aetheria went with blunt honesty, and the bartender seemed to respond well to it.

"Quite a few martial artists around the town. No one who does anything with Nether in town. Ascyn, the fox—man, well, actually, he's a Kitsune. Beastfolk types can be touchy about what you call their race, so be sure and call him a Kitsune. He's a martial artist who uses some Aether Arts. It might be your best bet. Few people can touch Aether," Sam noted with a hint of being impressed.

She desperately wanted to ask why that was or what Aether actually was, but she didn't want to give up the depths of her ignorance just yet.

"Ascyn, you say? Alright. Is there a village directory anywhere, or do I just wander around and meet people until I stumble on people I find intriguing?"

"There's a list in your room, lass. Why not freshen up, look it over, and come back for supper?"

"Thanks, Sam. I'll do that." Aetheria placed one of the elven liquor bottles she'd looted from the lodge, where she'd stayed after meeting Werylin, on the bar top. "Free or not, you deserve some recompense."

"I like your style, Ria." Sam tossed her a door key with a number on it.

It turned out her room was on the top floor, in the west corner of the building. It was a large room with a fireplace, bed, armoire, and an adjacent room. Initially, she assumed it would be a closet, but it was a bathroom. A wooden barrel-style tub had a spigot connected to a strange crystal, and she thought some magic was involved in the tub's drain, too. The sight of a magical (she assumed) toilet next to the barrel tub made her almost feel like she was in civilized society again.

I shouldn't be this excited about not having to shit in the woods like a bear, but here we are. Plus, a bath! Oh, maybe there's a candlemaker or perfumer in Solace. I deserve some aromatherapy after the last few days.

After a bath and nap, Aetheria looked through the small handwritten book next to the bed. It contained a list of masters and their general specialties. There were many: masters of martial arts, brawling, spellsinging, spellcraft, mana manipulation, alchemy, divining, and more. Given the list's size versus the town's size, all of Solace's citizens must be masters or part of a master's entourage.

A floral scent hung about her nicely from the soap she'd used in her bath. Her hair sparkled more after a wash than it usually did. Bathing in a proper bath felt liberating, humanizing, and just all-around fantastic. A few dips in a river with Ithyrra had been fun but came nowhere near the luxurious feeling of hot water and soap.

Am I used to this already?

Aetheria stood before a full-length mirror. Her skin showed no signs of the terrible injuries she had endured since her reincarnation. No blemishes at all marred her pale skin. Her musculature had improved slightly since her rebirth, too. Her willowy arms and legs had grown just a little. Like a villain, she could crush a man's head like a sparrow egg between her thighs now. Her stomach was smooth, but the form of abdominal muscles almost showed.

"Maybe I'll have a whole six-pack by Floor Twenty. Behold, I am all that is a woman." After flexing before the mirror a few times, she got embarrassed and knew it was time to get dressed.

Shockingly, her clothes all smelled fresh even after she'd been away from them. They were immaculate.

Self-mending, self-cleaning, perfect fitting... Dying would've been worth it just for these clothes.

No. That's a slight overstatement. Very slight.

She attired herself in her familiar dark red boots, red pants, the best magical sports bra in all Creation, a black and teal shirt, an aqua scarf, a red scrunchie, black fingerless gloves, and the long red coat, and felt herself. A small part of her mind wondered if she had bound herself to the clothes.

"I need to find someone who understands what the Vault is."

Interdimensional Master, or someone who at least understood spatial/soul stuff, would definitely be one of the four masters she would seek here in Solace. Something in her gut told her the Vault was far more than a convenient storage space. She just didn't know what else she could use it for.

"Let's prioritize here. I need to learn how to fight, about Aether, about the Vault, how to do magic, how to speak even more languages, and maybe how to do first aid. If I have to help others on a future floor, I'm not prepared for that right now. Oh, and buy all the stuff these guys will sell me. As masters, they should have excellent stuff. Maybe someone can repair my bow?" None of the elves on Floor 2 could manage that feat.

"Do I need the bow if I learn magic, though? Can't hurt to keep it." Shrugging, Aetheria set out of her room to find some teachers. The little handwritten book showed that Ascyn the fox-man lived just outside of town near the western wall. A bite to eat in the inn, and she'd set off to meet him.

Plans change, though. When Aetheria's feet hit the bottom of the stairs, an extremely full common room said, "Welcome to Solace!" simultaneously.

CHAPTER 19

Master Ascyn

The night went by in a flash. Strange individuals, after even more eccentric individuals, introduced themselves to Aetheria. She reassured herself by drinking with friendly people and eating excellent food. She could now say she had shared shots of whiskey with a praying mantis person.

It's only been a few days, and I was already forgetting the fantastic benefits of civilized society. I understand how some anime characters become total battle maniacs now. I need to remember this feeling going forward. Someday the climb will be done, and I'll have to at least partially fit back into whatever society I end up in.

Morning came with light spilling into her eyes from the window. She had forgotten to shut the curtains. She had expected to be hungover this morning, yet her regeneration pulled through again. Her mind was clear, with no hint of a headache. She had held her liquor last night far better than she had ever managed to in her life on Earth.

Do I attribute it strictly to the regeneration, or is the younger super-body also in play here?

With a wave at Sam, Aetheria wandered the streets of Solace on her journey to the western gate. She passed alchemists, blacksmiths, bread makers, a seedy-looking gambling parlor, a jeweler, and even a perfumer. Most common in Solace, however, were martial guilds or dojos. Ranging from plain to exquisitely ornate, these establishments seemed to be the domicile of incredible masters of various fighting styles.

If all these are so fancy, how awesome is an Aether Arts place going to be?

Whistling with anticipation, she wandered out the gate and followed the instructions Ascyn had given her the night before. Ten minutes later, she walked into a farmyard with a big red barn, a sprawling white farmhouse, three chicken coops, a large stable, and a couple of goats wandering around being assholes.

Did he give me the wrong directions?

Little fox-people children ran about the yard playing. A slightly older boy attempted to get the goats to behave. An older fox-woman peeked her head out of the farmhouse's porch and waved to her in greeting, beckoning her to come inside.

"Good morning! You must be Ria. Ascyn is out in the pasture, checking the fences. Have you had breakfast? Oh, silly me. I'm Zaira."

Inside the porch was a small table with a carafe of pleasant-smelling tea and a plate with a steaming muffin. Despite Aetheria's intentions to head out after Ascyn, she sat down, ate the muffin, and chit-chatted with Zaira. She learned very little in terms of practical knowledge, but she gained a familiarity with the names of the farm. When the muffin was done, Zaira explained how to find Ascyn, and off across the pasture Aetheria went.

The entire morning felt surreal. Besides the fox-people, the farm wouldn't have been out of place back home in Minnesota. Even the surrounding countryside could have been straight from Earth: mostly flat land with marginal hills, temperate deciduous forests with a healthy mix of conifers.

"You don't make a lot of noise, but your aura is as good as screaming at the top of your lungs that you are here and ready to fight." Ascyn greeted her with a wave, and the hound lazing at his feet gave a single bark as hello.

I'm screaming, huh? In comparison, he barely even makes a bleep to my mana senses.

"Sorry? I haven't had any real instruction on using mana or anything."

The fox-man laughed as if she'd just said the funniest thing in the world.

"Oh, lass, you aren't sensing mana. That's Aether. Breath of the gods. Mana is the barest shadow of Aether, the tool of mortals." Ascyn was still laughing a little but gave a slight, rueful shake.

"Oh. Well. That explains why my magic bow almost exploded when I pushed Aether into it, right?" Aetheria grinned sheepishly when Ascyn's eyes widened.

"You what? Well, you survived, so there's that. I wouldn't recommend doing that on the regular. Aether pushes mana-derived magics into extreme blowup-ness. Never know what random catastrophe you'll get."

That... would explain the dramatic explosions.

"Any other surprises I need to know before we start your training?" Slightly narrowed eyes fixated on her. Aetheria stood her ground with a smile, and her lack of squirming under his gaze made him smile even more.

"Well, if that's Aether, then I can also suck in and use Nether." The grimoire she'd been given by Ismir on Floor 2 had been educational, although she'd misidentified the tier of energy she was using. These revelations explained why her attempts at harnessing mana, as guided by the book, had failed spectacularly.

Ascyn whistled appreciatively. "No wonder you're a Challenger. We can't help you with the Nether, but we'll get you cycling Aether properly. Depending on if you are a quick study, we might even get you set up with an art."

"And fighting?"

Ascyn laughed again. "You need to learn to use your body before considering fighting with it. We'll get there."

"How long do people usually stay on this floor?" There seemed to be a lot to learn here, with people willing to teach it.

"The shortest was about six months. The longest was eight years. Depends on where you are at, what you can learn, and how much knowledge you want versus how quickly you want up the tower. Some never leave, becoming Dwellers here."

Aetheria blinked repeatedly.

"Eight years?"

"Eight years is the blink of an eye for many of us, Ria. I've been on the floor of the masters long enough. I gave up counting. After five years, the tower gets impatient with most Climbers."

She had overlooked that most of these instructors would be thousands of years old. It seemed it was the most significant selling point in becoming a Dweller. Near freedom from the ravages of time. Extra time to achieve a life's work, breakthrough to immortality, and do whatever the individual's obsession was. It made all too much sense to Aetheria that the gods probably had little difficulty getting people with the rewards that awaited the worthy.

"Give me a hand here with the fence posts, then we'll head back to the yard and test you. Find out where you stand and what your raw potential might be."

During the next half hour, Ascyn provided instructions on how to position a post, talking little. If Aetheria had thought herself strong, watching Ascyn shove poles barehanded into the soil without even a flex put her slightly in her place. Not that he was stronger than she was, but his use of force was perfect, and he did it all without damaging the posts. Not visibly, at least. If she did that, she'd shatter the post and become a splinter pincushion.

Their arrival at the farmyard didn't cause a stir. A few children running around waved at them. To her surprise, Ascyn led her into the barn. The fox-man looked amused by her surprise, and gestured to a radiant energy portal. Passing through it, they emerged in another place. The sky was blue, the clouds pink, and the training grounds were vast.

"Now we shall see what they make a Challenger out of. Lift the weights until you find one you cannot lift."

Aetheria progressed through a series of weights with the old fox-man as her guide.

"What unit of measure do you use for weight?"

"Meters for distance, grams for weight. Each increase by a hundred kilograms."

Oh, my god. Metric units won the measuring war in the fantasy worlds outside of Earth! Good thing I know my metric units well. Mostly.

The first three weights were no challenge to her. The first one wasn't a shock, the second made sense, but the third had Aetheria feeling different. Being strong in fights previously was one thing. It was in non-quantifiable situations. Now that she might know her limits, it was getting a little real. Already she was casually lifting over two hundred and seventy kilos.

The following weight was hard, but she managed. The fifth, she couldn't lift above her knees.

"Impressive." Aetheria caught a glimmer of Aether in Ascyn's eyes after she set down the last weight. Had he been monitoring her with some kind of mystical sense?

"Next, agility. Run five laps."

Again, the fox-man watched her with eyes that glowed with Aether. She found the starting demarcation, and when Ascyn said, "Go," her right foot pushed off with an explosive force that sent dirt billowing behind her. The track was significantly longer than the one she used to run in high school.

"Seven minutes. That's fast, even by Kitsune standards. You didn't even slow down and aren't drawing on Aether to fuel your endurance yet. You're going to be ridiculous, lass." Ascyn pointed toward another field, an obstacle course.

"Cross that. Time doesn't matter."

An hour later, the two were sitting on the farmhouse porch. Ascyn sipped an herbal tea, while Aetheria drank a lovely fruit punch that Zaira had provided.

"Your physical capabilities are all astounding. I'll give you that. You don't know how to apply the force you can generate yet. You don't need to destroy the surrounding environment every time you jump or speed up. You have incredible intuitive usage of Aether physiology, but that's what it is—intuitive."

"Strong and fast, that's me. What's Aether physiology, and why are you saying intuitive like it's a bad thing?"

"You are using Aether to adapt your body to what you're doing. Lengthening your arms, shortening your coat, increasing your density to take punches. You aren't doing it very well. If you were, you'd lift five or six times what you did today."

Aetheria stopped drinking punch mid-swallow and then coughed harshly.

"Excuse me, did I hear you just say 'lengthening my arms' and 'shortening my coat?'"

Ascyn gave a deep belly laugh, then got pegged on the side of his head with a muffin.

"Manners, dear!" Zaira chided from deeper in the farmhouse. Ascyn started eating the muffin, talking between bites.

"You heard right. You aren't a real shapeshifter or metamorph, but you will be. Rare to see someone instinctively lean that way with Aether manipulation. Most people's sense of identity and body image is too strong to allow subconscious alterations to their meat puppet."

Memories flickered at the edge of her awareness. "Luckily" catching a ledge while falling down the cliff, pulling out strength at just the right moments in fights, the crazy acrobatics she'd been doing since becoming Aetheria, the way she kept having to alter her sense of gravity and weight...

"Huh."

"Didn't think you were aware you were doing it. You've got a lot of potential. We'll see how much talent you have going forward. We'll start your training tomorrow. I'll take your mornings for a few weeks. You can pick another master for your afternoons, and we'll revise as we go. Once we've got you properly cycling Aether, how fast we progress will be all about you." The Kitsune winked.

"Alright, that sounds doable. Any recommendations on who else would synergize with your education best? My biggest mystery is an internal space I possess. I can store things in it and pull them out at will."

Ascyn's eyes got big. Huge. Then he almost fell out of his chair laughing.

"Are you kidding me, lass? You've got a spiritual plane in the gathering stage?" Ascyn shook his head as if it were the most ridiculous thing he'd ever heard.

CHAPTER 20

The Soul Witch

So, care to explain what a spiritual plane is? Are we talking inner-world equivalent?" Aetheria arched a brow at the still-guffawing Ascyn as he rolled around on the floor, entirely too amused. *I flex my light novel reading, and I get laughed at. Figures.*

"If you're going to dust the porch, dust the rest of the house too, dear." Zaira's chiding voice calmed the Aether Arts master, who quickly got off the floor.

Are these masters all going to be like this?

Ascyn coughed and brushed at his fur, trying to regain some dignity.

"Better to let the Soul Witch explain it to you. You'll want to make her your next stop."

"Soul Witch?" *That doesn't sound ominous at all.*

"Aoibhe. She's got the crystal tower on the north side of Solace. She's right about what you need, knows about inner worlds and spiritual planes, and is one of the few in town who knows something of the Paths of the Ethereal. No doubt about it, you're on the Path of the Ethereal, with Aether and Nether."

"Right. Aoibhe, north, crystal tower. Ethereal? Isn't that just the same thing as Aether? In my home world, Ethereal was an off-shoot of Aether."

Ascyn shook his head. "No, lass, no. Fire, water, wind, and earth make up the worldly elements besides two spiritual elements, Aether and Nether. Aether represents the heavens, celestial, and divine power. Nether symbolizes the dark, void, and death. If you combine the two, you get the Ethereal. The source of everything. Go talk to Aoibhe. We'll start our lessons for real in the morning."

Ascyn shooed her out, but Zaira gave her a ham and cheese sandwich for the road. The deliciousness of the smoked ham and the creaminess of the cheese soothed Aetheria's annoyance at being ushered out. The bread was crunchy on the outside and chewy on the inside, with a rich wheat flavor.

Note to self: buy a bunch of sandwiches off Zaira before I leave this floor.

People waved and said greetings as she meandered through Solace, but no one bothered her. While the benefits granted by the tower to those who helped Climbers were good, no one would get desperate in the first week or two that a new Climber was in town.

The crystalline tower of Aoibhe was hard to miss. One of the larger structures in Solace, the building sparkled in the noon sun. With each step Aetheria took, the refracted colors of light changed with her change in position.

Living near that thing must be like having a giant prism for a neighbor. That's gotta be rough.

A small path led from the street to the tower's main entrance, where a sizable crystalline door almost, but not entirely, blended into the rest of the structure. Next to it was a pull-lever, presumably some sort of chime. Aetheria pulled it. There was no immediate reaction, but after about half a minute, a young, dark-haired man opened the door. He wore black robes and looked like he hadn't slept for a few days.

"What is it? We don't want any." The mage attempted to shut the door again before Aetheria's boot stopped it from closing.

"I'm here to see Aoibhe. My name is Ria. Ascyn sent me." Maybe Master Ascyn's name would help with this guy?

"The Kitsune? Who cares what he... Wait, I don't know you. I know everyone in Solace."

"I'm new. How'd a Dweller fail to hear there's a Challenger in town?" She arched a single brow while inflecting her tone with true wonderment at how this could have happened.

"I... well, Lady Aoibhe will see you shortly, Challenger. If you are lying or wasting her time, you will regret it." With a warning look, the man gestured inside. Aetheria availed herself of a nice, big comfy reclining chair in their entry parlor while the man scurried off up a set of stairs.

Before any great witch appeared, the young man came back.

"This way, if you please, Lady Ria. It seems knowledge of your arrival has spread throughout the city while I experimented. My deepest apologies. If you could not mention it to Lady Aoibhe, I would be exceptionally grateful. My name is Edwin. I am Lady Aoibhe's second apprentice."

Ohh. Multiple apprentices. Ascyn just had a farm full of what I assume are his grandkids. Although the portal in his barn was unexpected. Are there glow portals in all these masters' places?

"Don't worry about it, Edwin. We all make mistakes when we're tired and hungry." Her friendly smile seemed to fly over the apprentice's head. The sleep-deprived mage's distrustful eyes still held an unpleasant look. *Must be the type who blames everyone else for his own failings. So, like half the people I've ever met.*

Their steps echoed quietly as they climbed floor after floor, until on the tenth floor, Edwin stopped and gestured toward the only thing ahead of them on the landing: a door.

"Lady Aoibhe awaits. Good day, Lady Ria."

"See you later, Ed." With a salute, Aetheria wandered to the door and gave it a light push. It was a pull door. Blushing, she pulled it open.

The suite that was contained behind the door was exceptionally grand. "Luxury" did not do the place justice at all. The floors were made of a dark crystal and covered with precisely laid-out rugs. A logic that Aetheria did not understand ran behind each rug's placement, color, and size. The puzzle gnawed at her brain like an annoying worm, but she had so much more to look at. The high walls and ceilings were all made of the same dark crystal as the floors. Crystal that occasionally offered you a glimpse of something else. Somewhere else? Somewhen else?

Now this is magic.

Aoibhe's parlor was the smallest of the other rooms she could see. An open arch led the way into a library full of grimoires and other tomes. Stack upon stacks of scrolls sat on displays. The librarian wanted to know how she had organized everything. The book lover in her wanted to just read everything in there. A faint cough distracted her from studying the library. Aetheria turned to see a woman walking through another archway into the parlor.

Some people are just the sort who steal attention when they enter the room. Aetheria assumed she was one now, with her sparkling hair, glowing eyes, and sharp style. Aoibhe stole Atheria's attention immediately, though. The witch was her height and wore a dress that incorporated armor pieces. Her colors seemed to be black and purple, while her hair and eyes were iridescent gold. The witch did not wear a cloak. Instead, she had a pair of orange-red angelic wings behind her. They settled over her shoulders like a mantle when she glided through the room.

With a gauntleted hand, Aoibhe gestured toward the sofa she also sat on.

"Hello, Aetheria. You're quite the sight. A first-stage Cultivator with a spiritual plane, a soul repository, and burning with Aether and Nether. You're even the adopted daughter of Aetherius an—" Aoibhe winced. A hand went to her temple. Something had clearly caused her a great deal of pain. The witch clicked her tongue in vexation while rubbing at her forehead.

The blond angelic beauty had an accent Aetheria could only describe as something akin to Ukrainian.

"Anyway, I'm glad you came. You want to learn from me?"

"Yes, that's exactly why I'm here. Ascyn seemed to think you were the only one in Solace with any grasp for the Ethereal Path that I'm apparently on. What's a soul repository?"

The sofa was comfortable. Obviously, *you don't decorate a tower like this with crap furniture. Maybe I can commission a bed while I'm here, pop it out, and nap on future floors.*

"You're young, exceptionally young, but then you aren't. Reincarnation. A soul repository is an early stage of an inner world. A proto-form. You can store things, yes, but you should be able to manipulate what you have placed inside of it. I knew a pyromancer who stored coals, flammables, and extinguishing chemicals in theirs. They could synergize with the items inside of them to bolster their fire abilities."

"That's really cool, but I haven't figured out how to do anything like that." Aetheria felt sheepish admitting that to someone she wanted to like.

"Just learning to use it is a feat. You must access your soul to do it, but your introspection and easy access likely coincide with the vast trauma you suffered in death and rebirth." A steel-covered finger tapped at her lip in thought. "I shall have to design a training regiment to uncover what uses your repository could offer."

"That would be great. Could you help me learn some magic, too?" Aetheria smiled hopefully.

"Unlikely." Aoibhe sighed. "You are at an exceptionally early stage in using Aether and Nether, and you have no ability with mana."

"Aetherius said I could learn to control mana."

Aoibhe's eyes widened slightly, then she tilted her head to the side, looking Aetheria up and down. "Did he now, or did he say something you took to mean that?"

"Um. Let's see. Aetherius said... I didn't even know how to see or touch mana." Aetheria laughed and nodded respectfully to Aoibhe. "My apologies."

"No need to apologize. I've been wrong before. Your control is too weak to learn magic now. We will work on your control. You are at a disadvantage. Usually, those who control Aether, Nether, or both have decades to grow used to the energies. That said, we can probably figure out some improvisational Aether releases into an art if Ascyn can't figure out how to teach you some."

"I feel like I'm back in kindergarten. By the way, why does everyone here speak Primeval Sylvan?" It was weird to her that everyone spoke the first language she had used on this floor.

"We don't. There's a translation field in effect over most of this floor. In some areas, they disable it for people to learn or practice other languages." Aoibhe gave Aetheria a look that her brain processed as, "You are so cute, I could just eat you."

It was a pleasant look. *Do. Not. Blush.*

"So, control and repository training. Sounds doable. Ascyn claimed my mornings. Do you want my afternoons, then? I'm staying at Sam's for now."

As if the witch could sense what Aetheria thought, Aoibhe gestured at the tower.

"Why don't you stay with me, dear? The tower is large enough, and only three live here. As for which hours of your day I get, I'll leave it to your discretion. I'm a greedy woman, liable to take them all." The intense, golden-eyed stare of the angelic woman made Aetheria's stomach flutter.

"Sure, I'll stay here." *In a crazy opulent palace made of crystal with a beautiful angelic witch.* "Is it rude of me to ask what race you are?"

"Slightly rude, but I'll forgive it. Nephilim are rare and, depending on which world you came from, nonexistent. My mother was a human, my father a fallen servant of the heavens. My heritage has allowed me to walk the Path of the Ethereal as far as I have."

"Well, if I'm going to be slightly rude, I'll keep asking questions. Tell me to stop, if you don't mind. How far have you reached on the Ethereal Path?"

"Impudent. I like it. I'm on the fifth stage of the Ethereal Path, a lady of the Ethereal. All masters in Solace are at least at the fourth stage of their paths. The better of us are on the fifth. Rumors circulate of one or two masters who are sixth-tier, but there are few reasons why a Tier Six Cultivator would remain in the tower."

"Huh. How come you stay in the tower?"

Aoibhe smirked. "That answer requires wine and the spilling of some of your secrets, daughter of Aetherius."

A bottle of elven wine appeared in Aetheria's hand. "Got glasses?"

CHAPTER 21

Training with the Masters

Weeks passed quickly. Aetheria learned the whole routine of cycling Aether, which theoretically was also like cycling Nether. She had already figured out the gathering process, but the mental techniques to push the energy through her body were another matter. On her sixth day of practice, she controlled Aether and its internal flow instead of allowing it to dissipate. The more she cycled the power, the more she could feel her being filling and keeping energy.

The growth was minuscule, which showed how early in her development she was. Yet each drop of an ocean contributed to the size of the whole. *Or so Ascyn says.*

Using that energy was proving to be more difficult. Aetheria's body and soul repository were greedy and loath to give up any power she locked down. It took her a month to recapture her previous success with controlling her density at will. It took her two months to bounce her density up or down to alternate strength versus speed. The results were ridiculous, though. She could throw a three-thousand-kilogram weight fifty meters at her highest density. She also could not move faster than a walk while she was doing it.

At her lightest, she broke 150 kilometers per hour. Ascyn assured her she would get faster but needed to work on her running form. Inconveniently, he didn't know how she needed to adjust her posture, just that she did. As with her most muscular alteration, her fastest was so weak she couldn't lift more than ten kilos.

Aetheria's progress with Ascyn was faster than with Aoibhe. Their first week together was just the exploration of the limitations and nature of her soul repository. In Aoibhe's defense, half of their lessons were also on understanding how to cycle Aether, and she was a much better teacher than Ascyn, who was more interested in the fighting aspects than the theory behind things. Shortly after the one-month mark, Aoibhe handed Aetheria a glowing crystal that radiated a terrible cold.

"Store it," the witch instructed simply.

Aetheria tossed it into her soul repository. From there, Aoibhe had her describe its nature, appearance, and feel from within storage. Once Aetheria could tell its awful chill, Aoibhe guided her to manifest its cold to radiate from her hand. With repeated practice, she performed small novelties like freezing water in a cup, chilling wine, and giving Edwin a bit of frostbite for leering at her and Aoibhe just a little too much when he thought they weren't looking.

"Why can't I shoot bolts of ice?"

"Inexperience. You'll get there, dear. Before throwing bolts and beams, it is probably more in your wheelhouse to imbue attacks with your fists or emit close-range pulse attacks. The ice crystal is the core of an ice elemental. Someone would eventually drain it of its power over time in normal magical use. My theory is that inside your repository, it will remain fully charged while allowing you to copy its ice attribute without draining it."

"Why would that work?"

"You are on the path to becoming a being of Ethereal nature. Your reincarnation left an indelible imprint upon your soul and essence. You come from a world with technology. The stories of your home world involved driving a vehicle you called a car with a combustion engine that ran on gasoline. Mana is the dirtiest and poorest grade of this gasoline. Mana that is aspected to elements is a slight improvement. The mana ignites Aether and/or Nether, sometimes singular, sometimes a combination, to create magic."

"The spellforms I sense mages making?"

"Are the mana constructions or the fuel they spend to stir the Aether or Nether?"

"So, I'm never going to need to learn spellforms since I manipulate them directly?"

"Yes, and no. You will need some form or system of impressing your will upon the energy. Some do this with chants, some with sigils and runes, and some through signing. I have even seen some do it through their sword's movements. The method needs to have *meaning* for the user. Spellsingers' techniques would be useless to me, just as my incantation would be useless to them. We find no meaning in each other's technique."

"So, impart meaning. Okay. How do I get to the stage of using Ethereal energy?"

"You wish to run before you walk. We all do. When you can combine the two energies without exploding, that is how you know you are ready to use Ethereal power."

"Exploding?"

"Like a sheep full of explosives. Kaboom."

"Do you often see sheep full of explosives, Aoibhe?"

"Yes, darling. They are the alchemist's favorite test for his new explosives. The children of Solace have taken to watching his experiments for entertainment. So, exploding sheep are no rarity here, dear."

Dragons of a Feather, Flocking Together

Time: Months ago
Place: Grief, Outside Tower of Aetherius

Two massive dragons soared above the island once called Nova Azura. On one, scales the color of the sky glistened in the sun and shimmered a bright blue. In contrast, the other dragon was so dark as to be a black hole, absorbing any light near it. They could not be more dissimilar in aspect. Yet, in size and immense magical power, neither held an edge over the other. They were opposite but equal.

It had been millions of years since either of the colossal beings had graced the skies of Nova Azura. Civilizations had fallen, mountains had risen and eroded away, and the light of hope had left a fledgling world. It had been a slow departure. Oizys's heel upon the world's throat had grown heavier every century. Elder race after elder race had fled the world of Grief for greener pastures, free of the tyranny of tragedy. The younger races never seemed to learn the lesson of sorrow as the Goddess of Misery struck them down one after another.

Perhaps for the short-lived races, a chance at glory was worth the risk of the inevitable fall. Like Icarus, they wished to fly near the sun in defiance of history, and like at most casinos, the Goddess of Misfortune rigged the game. They could not win, yet they played anyway. Thus, through suffering, they earned the pity of other gods.

+She did well with the spirit. If she frees him down the road, he could be a problem for Oizys.+ The immense blue dragon spoke into the mind of the black dragon. Other beings would find such a thing impossible. The alien minds of the draconic behemoths defied lesser beings' access, and if one breached their passive mental defenses, contact would drive most mortals irrevocably insane.

~The tower is full of its descendants. Arrange for it to happen, and I'll do my part.~
+What do you think of her combat so far?+
~Mediocre. We didn't bring her here for her ability to punch things. Thankfully.~
+She's not doing that badly.+

~Without regeneration, she would already be dead. Don't think I didn't notice she's already using Aether. You overdid her reincarnation, you old fool.~

+Oh, blame me? You were the one who decided who should lead the way in your specialty!+

~I never claimed the specialty of reincarnation.~

+Was that one of our daughters?+

~Son, but who really remembers anymore?~

+Do not let Thanatos hear that.+

~Bah. Oh, she's starting a mob train. Think she'll make it to the tower?~

+Of course she will. It might be in pieces, but she'll get there. She has the Flame of Aetherius.+

~If only the great god Aetherius weren't a doddering idiot who forgot his island over-flowed with Tier Two and Three monsters.~

+I didn't forget. I just had total faith in Aesca. I also knew you would give your Flame in such a slow process, so I wanted to compensate for your stinginess.+

~They're calling for Pete on Discord. It's raid time in ten minutes. And I already told you I went slow because you went overboard. It took twenty years for her to stop exploding in that out-of-time room! Someday you'll learn restraint.~

+Right, right? Let's leave these avatars here for now. We can review the footage when we reclaim them post-raid.+

~Agreed.~

Three months later, Aetheria, Ascyn, and Aoibhe stood near where Aetheria had initially appeared on Floor 4, near the crossroads outside of town.

"You will do well, my dear. Take this. Let us see how quickly you can master something new in the field." The Soul Witch handed over an elemental core, pulsating with raw power. Aetheria's reading in her library had given her the knowledge to identify it as a Grand Wind core from a powerful air elemental. It vanished into her repository.

Ascyn laughed.

"I don't have any shiny presents for you, lass. Just do what we worked on. Bring back some loot, too. The grandkids are all clamoring for some souvenirs from 'Auntie Ria.'" Ascyn rolled his eyes at how much the young had taken to Aetheria. "And don't forget that ridiculous asshole, Durgan, will buy nearly anything from the Dread Castle. Don't leave a nail behind."

"Any last-minute dire warnings from the two of you? How does this castle... actually, never mind." It was a dungeon in a tower. *Of course it's always populated by enemies. Might as well ask them how the tower itself works.*

Both shook their heads.

"A kiss for good luck?" Aetheria asked Aoibhe.

Before she could react, Ascyn was there, kissing her on the cheek.

"Thought you'd never ask, lass. Zaira says it's because my fur is turning silver. I keep telling her silver is sexy." Laughing hysterically, the Kitsune began the walk back toward town, giving the Soul Witch and the Challenger a moment alone.

"Ew. Ascyn licked my cheek."

Aoibhe laughed deeply before she stepped up to dip Aetheria back and give her a genuine kiss.

"There, now you don't have a reason to complain, and you have a good-luck kiss. Don't do anything too reckless, darling."

"I do too! I wanted to be the one to dip *you*," Aetheria pouted.

"Do well in your test, and maybe."

"See you in a few days, sexy." With a wink and a blown kiss, Aetheria vanished like the wind. Altering her density to almost nothing was nearly instant now. A sparkling aqua blur shot down the path toward the Castle of Dread.

Crossing miles in minutes was a ridiculous feeling. Exhilaration never failed to fill Aetheria's mind when she ran like this. The world seemed so slow around her compared to her speed. Falling leaves from trees seemed to descend slowly as she darted down the road. Ascyn had not timed her for a few weeks, but she was confident she could break 250 kilometers an hour now. The idea of outrunning sports cars brought a manic smile as she closed the distance from Solace to the Castle of Dread in twenty minutes.

Aoibhe had told her, in her adorable, Ukrainian-like accent, *"The exhilaration will fade with time. The recklessness, delusions of grandeur, hunger, and horniness never fade entirely. Not for me, anyway."*

So far, Aetheria had to agree with the Soul Witch. Channeling the power of Aether brought with it a lot of stimulation. She was not even sure she wanted those feelings to fade and just become a regular part of her life, but the recklessness and mood alterations were something she could do without. *"To control the Ethereal, you must first control yourself,"* Aoibhe had said.

The Castle of Dread was massive. Its exterior walls were in varying stages of solid to completely missing. Each destructed area looked like it told a tale of others like herself coming here for training. A story of combatants honing themselves against the forces of evil—or, at least, enemies the tower had decided were evil.

Aetheria shot through the shattered front gates of the castle, an aqua-red bolt of lightning darting through the many skeletons littering the courtyard, and skidded to a stop with her back to one of the still-standing exterior walls.

Each of the skeleton's eye sockets burned with a dark purple energy she knew to be a form of Nether. Their creator had given these undead a sheer hatred for the living that had nothing to do with the Nether. Purple flaming eyes locked upon her vibrant form, and the clattering and raising of weapons sounded across the open courtyard as all the skeletons swarmed at her. She guessed there were at least fifty. That was a lot of targets to test out her new arts and techniques on.

Step One: Gather them.

The air surrounding her crackled and pulsed with a powerful aqua-colored aura, and bolts of black static occasionally throbbed around her. Aetheria's aura had grown in strength and visibility when she was manifesting Aether. Ascyn had said as she grew stronger, it would only grow more concentrated.

Step Two: Ice Cascade.

Aetheria jumped approximately twelve meters high with only a slight arc. She held both hands above her head, forming a raging ball of Aether that she threw down before her. Piercing cold shot across the courtyard as the energy orb broke and cascaded in every direction. Wherever the torrent of power went, ice remained behind. The ice sheets were approximately ten centimeters high and locked all the skeletons touching the ground—which was all of them—in place.

Step Three: Crash!

Aetheria's destiny climbed as her jump was descending. When her feet hit the thick ice and ground beneath, it was as if a two-metric-ton object had smashed into the ground instead of a young woman.

Step Four: Aetherflame Nova.

It was unnecessary, but the gamer inside of her couldn't resist snapping her fingers as her aura expanded in a nova. All the aetheric ice fragments in the air exploded outward from her, while the ice clinging to the skeletons combusted into blue-green colored Aetherflame. Waves of Aetherflame blasted across the keep courtyard, consumed the simplistic undead skeletons, and left no traces of their bones behind. The Aetherflame finished the undead utterly. Their weapons and armor crashed to the ground.

Damn girl, damn. Too bad I didn't have a drone to record that. That had to have looked sweet as hell.

Aetheria appraised the results of the attack. Not a single skeleton remained. She could have easily wiped them out using Density Control alone, but she wanted to try some of the flashier things she'd worked with. Aetheric ice had been one trick she learned from Aoibhe, while Aetherflame Nova was the first art that Ascyn had taught her.

They combo together really nicely. I'm thinking Aetherflame Nova should combine well with just about anything.

Aetheria's aura pulsed with another infusion of Aether as she inhaled deeply, and she darted across the courtyard. She maneuvered her glowing form back and forth as she vacuumed every weapon, piece of armor, scrap of cloth, and shiny rock that looked valuable into her repository. As she finished, an explosion shattered the main gates to the inner keep, fragments of the wooden doors shredding the air. Even with a quick change in density, Aetheria could feel her regeneration pushing splinters out of her skin.

Standing in the open archway was a figure in black plate mail with two burning red eyes of hate.

Oh, man, Death Knights look so gosh-darn cool. Look at that tattered cape and the black sword trailing evil smoke in the shape of skulls!

CHAPTER 22

Castle of Dread

Silence reigned for a moment after the Death Knight had shattered the interior gates. Aetheria and the red-eyed dark-magic wielder stared at one another.

The Death Knight broke the silence, uttering a single word in a terrible language she did not speak. Aetheria assumed it had said, "*Die!*" because dark Nether energies assaulted her mind and soul—or tried to. The cocoon of Aether around her blunted the assault, and as Aetheria breathed in the Nether energy and took it for herself, the spell instantly broke apart, like a cookie in a toddler's hands. She inhaled deeply and waggled her finger at her unholy opponent.

"Opening with death spells is such a dick move, Death Knight."

A light pulse illuminated the area as Aetheria altered her density and, in a blur, was suddenly in front of the Death Knight. Her open palm slammed into its chest armor with a screeching sound. The armor dented, and the blow hurled the Death Knight back through the gates it had just blown apart. Aetheria was not smiling, though.

Damn, magic plate armor is hard. It was kind of dumb to think I could break a Death Knight's armor in one hit.

Ticks of regeneration mended the damage the blow had caused her, even at her densest. Open-handed melee against an armored opponent would not work. A surge of Nether energy made her turn as the Death Knight appeared behind her. It swung its dark, smoking blade for her neck. But the undead fighter was too slow. A cold pulse surrounded her left hand. She dodged the blade, then stepped in and delivered another punch. This time her hand radiated cold as it impacted the Death Knight's chest plate.

The Death Knight shot back and slammed against the damaged exterior walls, but the ice that built up on its plate did nothing to slow the Death Knight or damage the armor. Only the impact of her hand against the plate caused another dent in it.

Okay, cold against the undead isn't great. Good thing Aoibhe gave me a present.

With a gesture from the Death Knight, four skeletons rose from the ground behind Aetheria. While the Death Knight got back to its feet, she dismantled the four skeletons with vicious punches. Brute strength worked well on simple skeletons, and their Nether energy became hers.

A surge of Nether warned her another spell was incoming. A wave of black energy that reeked of death closed in on her. She could dodge it, but instead, Aetheria stood her ground. *This is going to hurt.*

She was here for live combat trials, to improvise and learn. The black wave crashed into her, simultaneously ripping at her flesh and soul. It found no purchase in attacking her soul, but ripped her skin to shreds. *My Nether energy now, cheese-head.*

Aetheria breathed it in. She had never done many drugs, but she imagined that snorting up a Death Knight's spell was comparable to a line of cocaine. Cold wracked her insides as she processed the deadly energies. Goosebumps covered her skin despite it being a warm day, and black sparks filled her aura temporarily.

The Death Knight wasn't impressed. While she showed off, it closed the distance and jabbed its sword through her gut.

"Not cool, dude," Aetheria groaned and kicked the Death Knight. The undead flew across the courtyard again, and an even deeper cold seeped through her stomach.

How do I breathe in the energy that's already inside of me? Sparkle Princess Aetheria defies logic! I hope...

Aetheria concluded that breathing was irrelevant to the process, and only a habit or focus on her part. She still breathed in physically, but mentally she imagined hoovering the necrotic curses eating her gut from the inside. Another flush of cold filled her, followed by the feeling of strength as she made the energies her own. More pain as her regeneration healed her side. The pain was the ever-constant companion to all fighting, it seemed.

The Death Knight was halfway back to her when she shook off the cold and pain.

Okay, no more screwing around. I'm pretty sure that sword can kill me.

Aetheria tried to psych herself up. She had not been holding back, but bravado and sarcasm were her main go-to in these situations.

The Death Knight reached a similar conclusion: its magic was pointless, but its sword was effective.

Aetheria talked to herself while dodging the cursed sword. "Let's see. Roses on your vambrace, and your sword has an eagle on the cross guard. That means you are Lycean. You don't understand me, because why would the translation field operate in a dungeon? Right."

"All the higher undead at the Dread Castle are Climbers who died in disgrace some-where in the tower. Some of the lower tiers are as well, but it is rarer. The Death Knights and liches were all Climbers who made poor decisions during the trials of the tower. Destroying their physical bodies will do nothing. The curse that made them will simply reform them in a day or two. You can only stop these undead by destroying their souls or redeeming them. Destruction of the soul is no easy feat, but it is often easier than redemption."

Aoibhe had explained the undead to her. It jived with the information she had gotten from reading fantasy on Earth. *Are there plane walkers or bored gods who write fantasy novels on non-magic worlds to prepare their inhabitants for isekai? Nah, that's crazy...*

The Death Knight was no mindless undead like the skeletons. Each time Aetheria dodged made the next strike that much harder to avoid. Ascyn had spent entire days stabbing spears and swords at her from point blank. Her ability to contort and flow around attacks was far more impressive than her speed-dodging was. When the Death Knight overextended, she twisted her torso around the attack, elbowed the sword down so the undead couldn't change his attack, and pulsed Aetherflame Nova in a spherical release around her.

To an outside spectator, it would have looked as though she had become the center of an enormous sphere of green-blue fireworks. To her, it looked like semi-transparent glitter, if glitter sought the Nether that fueled the Death Knight and then combusted it.

A terrible roar of pain erupted from the Death Knight as it burned _un_alive.

"But wait, there's more!" Aetheria chimed in her best Billy May voice.

Her fists took on a golden-flame effect, only slightly marred by the occasional pulse of an aqua-green flame. Aoibhe had let her borrow an item called a Soul Purifier. Incredibly expensive, exceptionally rare, and ridiculously powerful. It was an item that would not only purify the soul of the dead but also increase its chance of finding a better reincarnation in its journey through Samsara.

It's working.

Aetheria grinned as she cupped her hands together and drew in copious amounts of Aether, which she immediately channeled into the space between her hands. Golden-green-blue Aether coalesced and formed a sphere the size of her head. Just looking at the energy was intoxicating. It felt different from her usual Aether. Just like the aetheric ice she had created earlier, Aetheria aspected it as well.

The Death Knight's roars ended just as it took a giant glowing ball to the face.

A white and gold dagger appeared in Aetheria's hand, and she darted forward and stabbed it right between its red eyes of hate. The blade seemed to release the aspected holy energy into surging golden flames that engulfed the Death Knight.

"I release you to a better life, Lycean Greenwater. Forget your sins and find peace in the next life."

The asshole stabbed her in the gut even as he burned out of existence. The necromancer in Solace, Antara, had been the one to provide the names and brief histories on the current undead of the castle, Death Knight and above. Antara had not mentioned that Mr. Greenwater would stab her, even if he were still alive.

I can't decide if that makes Antara or Greenwater the real jerk.

"Uffda! Dick move, Lycean!" She collected the sword. Immediately her eyes widened at how much of a Nether source it was inside her repository. The armor and trinkets the Death Knight had left behind were minor treasures in comparison. The pain of the weapon vanishing, mixed with her regeneration kicking in simultaneously, left Aetheria imagining someone performing sub-zero icicle acupuncture on her innards.

What jerk decided healing should hurt?

The gate stood open before her.

One Death Knight down. Two more to go.

Aetheria released Adrian Lechner and Marie Daniel the same way, except she avoided their last-minute counterattacks with spells and weapons. Again, Antara the Necromancer had provided the knowledge for this hunt, and so far it'd been accurate since the souls were possibly saved. According to Aoibhe, without their true names, she wouldn't be able to prevent the Death Knights from self-resurrecting in a few days' time, no matter how much damage one might do to them. The blessed dagger and mimicry of the Soul Purifier worked perfectly to counteract the curse on the Death Knights, but Aetheria didn't feel very proud. Rare and expensive items had allowed her to defeat the Death Knights. Without them, the best she could do would be to force them to reform over a few days.

Three sets of Death Knight armor and weapons (sword, flail, and axe) should turn a tidy profit in Solace, she thought. Mixed with all the treasure she found walking the corridors of the Castle of Dread, her personal wealth was skyrocketing.

But after defeating the last Death Knight, the halls of the decrepit castle turned darker. A mist began rising from the floor. *Boss music would start about now if this were a video game.*

The only noise she could hear was her heart pounding as cold crept into her limbs.

"You took away my friends." The voice sounded akin to crumbling leather and whispers of the damned. It originated from all around her. The amount of Nether in the castle spiked through the roof, exceeding the Aether.

"I guess you'll have to be my new friend." From the mists rose a figure almost a head shorter than Aetheria. Black robes covered its skeletal remains, and its face was a glowing skull. The being had taken some time in its undead existence to decorate its skull with jewelry and gemstones, accentuating a sense of femininity that the lich had no other way to express. The skeleton was just different enough to confirm for Aetheria that this was an elf. That it spoke Primeval Sylvan gave it away.

"Alora Amaryllis."

"Above even the Death Knights, the elite of the undead are the liches. There are many paths to immortality, and lichdom is one of the worst. The sacrifices required are immense, and undeath is for the shortsighted and weak, too pathetic to make their way down another path of the Winding Way. There is no redemption for a lich. Destroy them, then destroy their phylactery. You do them and the living a favor." Aoibhe's words rang in Aetheria's mind.

With a gesture, the lich sent four green glowing spectral claws through the air to attack Aetheria.

At the very last moment, she triggered Aetherflame Nova in a condensed aura around her, igniting the Nether energies in the spell before she breathed them in. She smiled at the lich.

"Sorry, Alora. There's no redemption for you, just true death."

No fear showed in the flaming eye sockets of the lich's skull. A skeletal finger traced a symbol of death in the air.

The Nether energy Aetheria had consumed tried to fight against her, to rip at her living body from the inside. It became a battle of wills to stop the Nether and cycle it through her system the way she did with Aether. Only then did the energy refuse to answer the call of the lich. By then, the lich had prepared its next assault, though, and the hallway around Aetheria burst into a noxious cloud that sought to kill anything living.

Holding her breath did not help. The terrible spell tried to seep into her pores and melt her skin. Aetheria darted through the hall like a bolt of lightning and slammed the blessed dagger into one of the lich's flaming eye sockets. She did what Ascyn and Aoibhe had repeatedly warned her *not* to do—funnel Aether into items. The glowing dagger in the lich's skull shone like the sun before it exploded.

The blowback threw Aetheria so hard she hit the wall more forcefully than a NASCAR driver.

CHAPTER 23

Life is a Lich

Ohhh. Gosh darn, that hurt," she groaned as she dropped to the floor, leaving an Aetheria-sized dent in the stone wall behind her.

"It is the last thing you're going to feel," the lich growled from within the cascading explosions of holy energy. The chain reaction of power was slowly milling the undead's body to pieces—if all too slowly.

"This floor is usually far higher in the tower, my dear. You are not ready to fight a lich or Death Knight at their full power yet, but because this is level four, you have a chance. Powerful enemies in the lower levels of the tower are inhibited, unable to pull their full power unless you are near their tier. The details of how the towers scale is a mystery, but mostly anything you encounter is potentially beatable."

Aoibhe's words reassured Aetheria that she wasn't screwed. Death Knights and liches were the stuff of end-game legend, not beginner fodder. With debuffs in play on their power, she had a solid chance of killing (rekilling? final killing?) the lich.

"Meteor!" the lich shouted, skeletal finger wreathed in fire. The lich's body remained caught in the cascading explosions of holy Aether.

Aetheria kicked it into high gear, reversing her density to drop-kick the exploding lich through several walls, then following. *Hopefully, Meteor is more like a boring falling rock than an actual meteor?*

Aetheria's hopes were dashed when a meteor impacted the top towers of the castle, destroyed them, and crashed into the hallway they had occupied, causing another explosion.

It's the end of the world as we know it, and I don't feel fine!

Whole levels of the castle collapsed. Massive rocks fell. Aetheria pulsed Aetherflame Nova, but it didn't have the oomph to deal with strictly physical problems. Calling on a whole new level of desperation, she synergized with the Grand Wind core in her repository. With no time to experiment, she just tapped into the core, pulled as much Aether into her hands as she could, and released it.

Aetheria's vision filled with green energy. A massive vortex of aetheric wind had come into being around her, and it was atomizing the debris, the castle, and anything else in her vicinity without a care. Not a great power to call on if she had allies.

Damn. Now, where is the lich a... oh. Aetheria stared dumbly at her lower body. One of her legs was missing.

"If I don't find the old one, will my pants, socks, and boots still repair?" she inquired into the air while gritting her teeth. Her mouth became a thin-lipped snarl as the incredible pain of regenerating an entire leg descended like Texans on a barbecue. Stars danced before her eyes. The skull of the lich floated before her, holy explosions still working to destroy it, and now the vortex of aetheric wind was grinding away at the last of the lich like heavy grit sandpaper to joint compound.

"I removed the Nether infusion that gave your grandson necromancer affinities." Aetheria forced her words through gritted teeth. The pain of regeneration was blinding. "And I'm going to resurrect your father when I'm done with this tower. House Amaryllis didn't need necromancy to survive, you great big dummy." Aetheria locked eyes with the disintegrating skull. "I slept with your granddaughter, too."

The last of the lich's skull evaporated into the uncontrolled vortex.

Maybe I shouldn't have added the last part. That was kind of mean-spirited, but she dropped a meteor on me, which was definitely not cool. I don't even want to think about what that spell would do without restraints on her power.

Finally, the vortex of aetheric wind died and dispersed. Aetheria's leg had fully healed by then. Somehow, her boots and socks came back, too. *Not going to question it. Nope.*

The castle was in terrible condition. The first order of business was to find the lich's soul vessel, which, now that everything else was dead and destroyed, proved fairly easy as it was the largest source of the Nether left. A few jabs with the holy dagger, and then Aetheria crushed the hairpin between her hands.

"Rest in peace, Alora."

It took her two days to loot the rest of the castle. Cave-ins were less of a problem once she realized she could either repository them or just vortex them. Vortex had the nasty side effect of collateral damage, but the sheer joy of powerful wind throwing rubble revealed a primal love of destruction within her she hadn't known existed. Throwing big rocks and rubble into her repository had the advantage of being potential projectiles or a trap in the future. On the evening of her third day since leaving Solace, she wandered back into town and went straight to Durgan's.

From the outside, Durgan's looked like a store. The front actually was a store, manned by one of Durgan's children too "soft" to work the forges. Durgan himself was in the back, where a three-walled workshop let a faint breeze provide a brief reprieve from the ever-present heat.

Durgan was not a dwarf, as one might expect. He was a demi-human. If his race had a name, he didn't mention one. The man's skin glistened with an inner fire, and his hair and eyes were bright red. Overall, he was quite attractive, but a bit too muscular to be Aetheria's type.

"Well, you survived the Castle of Dread. Quite the meteor that hit it two days ago."

"Liches are sore losers. I've got an awful lot of loot to sell you, though. I'll cut you that discount Ascyn bargained for if you can repair my bow and teach me a few things."

"Fine, fine. How many Death Knight weapons did you get?"

"Three, but I'm keeping one. It's got an interesting resonance." The other two weapons, a flail and axe, appeared in her hands.

"Nice, very nice. It's a deal then, Ria. We'll work out the money. For now, you can start learning while I finish up this dagger."

Yay, blacksmithing!

Later that night...

Boo, blacksmithing!

Thanks to regeneration, her aches and pains all ebbed away on their own. But it did nothing for the mental fatigue of being in a sweltering environment doing precise hammering for hours on end. It was exceptionally tedious, and unlike in *EFWO*, she could not just keep clicking the Craft button until she was a master. Durgan had proved to be an excellent teacher, though, so she was determined to make him her third master acknowledgment. She felt a sense of accomplishment that clicking Craft couldn't scratch nearly as well.

In the morning, she found herself before a small cottage near the south wall. Sam, the bartender, had said if she wanted to learn alchemy and first aid, her best candidate lived here. When she rapped on the door, it opened to reveal a figure half her height. It had red scales and orange glittery eyes, and its snout twitched when it sniffed at seeing a human on its doorstep.

"What do you want, Challenger?"

Its voice was higher pitched than she had expected. Aoibhe had mentioned Regro was a master alchemist, herbalist, and skilled medical practitioner. She had not mentioned he was a kobold. *Minor details!*

"I'd like to learn from you. Ascyn and Sam recommended you as the healer I'd most likely be able to learn from."

"Ascyn is a dumb, smelly fox. But he is right about this. You have a powerful aura. I can teach you to do some things, but you must do something for me first." The little reptilian man looked exceptionally sinister in the moment, like he was going to ask for her to assassinate someone.

"And what do I have to do for you?"

"You must learn Aoibhe's munch-berry pie recipe, and bake me one for every lesson I give you."

"What's a munch-berry?"

"Is purple berry growing outside of town. Plentiful, tasty, helps focus and purify aura."

Sure, sure, I bet it does. It's totally not that you're just a gluttonous, sweet-toothed reptile.

"Fine. I'm sure I can sweet-talk Aoibhe. I'll be back with pies."

Aoibhe, of course, played hard to get. Luckily, Aetheria had things the Soul Witch wanted.

Thus, Aetheria's days alternated between work with Ascyn, Aoibhe, Durgan, and Regro. Days slipped by, and then months. Life in Solace was pleasant. Everyone wanted to help Aetheria, and she picked up a smattering of other skills from the various inhabitants. An ogre mage who styled himself a master polyglot taught her more languages, Zaira taught her cooking, Werylin's son, Corrin, taught her oration, a dark and sultry master named Selenthe taught her how to dance, and so on.

Three years passed this way. One night, after drinking heavily and making merry, Aetheria and Aoibhe stood atop the crystal tower.

"Are you going to miss me?"

"That is an unfair question, darling, and you know it. Of course I will. The last few years have been fantastic. If you were closer to my tier, I would come with you. You must grow more first. In fact, I have two going-away presents for you." The nephilim pulled out two crystals. One was glowing white; the other was transparent and had one of the red-orange feathers from Aoibhe's wings encased in it. Aetheria knew all too well the softness of the feathers, and how nice it felt to have those wings wrapped around her.

"What are these?"

"The white one will allow you to talk to me. It may only work a few times. Magic like that is unpredictable within the dimensional variance of the towers. It has no chance of working outside of the tower. Try to save it for a dire need, dear. The other is for when you have reached the rank of Ethereal Lady, preferably, but Ethereal Scion would be acceptable, too. By that point, my contract with the tower should be up, and if you infuse that with your essence, it will open the soul conduit between us. Using the conduit, I can travel to your side. Use it within a tower, any tower, and I shall come to you."

Aoibhe became blurry in her vision, and moisture trickled down Aetheria's cheeks. A deep, steadying breath helped her keep it together. Barely. *Oh. I'm crying a little. Tears of joy are okay, though.*

"Thank you. You're really going to leave the tower to join me?"

"That is what I said, sweetest. Not only do I love you, but you are on the same path as I. Together we could traverse the Winding Ways, if you want that?" Brave, ever confident, Aoibhe looked self-conscious now, and surely Aetheria had misheard the faint quiver in the last questioning words?

"I want that. That's the first time you've said you love me, you know. I love you, too. I'll do my best to get to the top of the tower and closer to your level. Won't you miss Solace and your crystal tower?"

"My tower can come with me; I am a Lady of the Ethereal, after all. As for Solace, it is an interesting place when you first arrive. After a century, it grows old.

Wanderlust rises in your heart, the desire to see new horizons and find new enemies. The tower allows us only short sojourns into the surroundings of this floor, and only one or two may take a sabbatical at a time. It is better than being trapped here, but it still wears upon the soul."

"Well, your presents are totally better than the one I got you."

"You got me a present?"

"Close your eyes."

Aetheria stepped up to Aoibhe when she had done as instructed and slipped a necklace around the witch's neck. Ria had smithed and enchanted the silver chain, one of the most obnoxious things she'd ever forged with Durgan. The pendant was a swirling yin-yang design that Aetheria had infused with copious amounts of Aether and Nether until the energies had crystallized into their present form. The crystalline energy carried her essence and would hopefully serve as a constant reminder of her to Aoibhe.

Rather than tell Aoibhe to open her eyes, Aetheria pressed her lips to the witch's.

Minutes later, the Soul Witch was lightly caressing the pendant between her fingers.

"Go now, Aetheria. You've said your goodbyes, and the longer you linger, the harder it will be for both of us." Aoibhe's voice held a brittleness and vulnerability she had never shown except in the privacy of her quarters. It filled Aetheria's heart with swimming emotions, but also a sharp pain that she was leaving her. She had an additional reason to climb this tower, and to do it fast.

"I know. Long goodbyes are in my nature, though. It's a Minnesotan thing."

"You will have to show me your Minnesota someday."

"Sure, after we topple ten towers, destroy a goddess, and walk the Hidden Paths."

Aetheria blew a kiss at her girlfriend and triggered the doorway to Floor 5. She had achieved acknowledgment from four masters during her first year. There had been no compelling reason to leave until the tower started to subtly "encourage" it by making life difficult around Solace until she finally packed her bags. She couldn't in good conscience risk a plague on Ascyn's grandkids just because she wanted to learn more or keep spending her nights in Aoibhe's feathered embrace.

"I love you, be a good witch!"

Aetheria turned and jumped through the door made of light and stepped out into a sweltering desert. Both women had kept up the facade of not crying until the other was out of sight.

The blistering heat evaporated her tears almost immediately.

CHAPTER 24

Ice Cascade

Ice Cascade!" A massive ball of aetheric energy slammed into the ground and shot outward while Aetheria jumped into the air. Even after three years of work, she lacked the fine control to prevent friendly fire even for herself. The solution was to fire off Ice Cascade only when she wasn't touching the ground. Aetheria nearly fell on her ass when she hit the icy ground. For twenty meters around her, a roughly meter-deep layer of ice coated the scorching desert sands. The heat and sand tried to melt the ice, but unlike regular ice, aetheric ice didn't respond to heat or fire.

As she gazed out across the region, sparkles of light caught her attention in the sky. Familiar script formed.

SURVIVE: 23 hours, 59 minutes

"Well, can't get much more straightforward than that."

The scorching sun was unpleasant, but thanks to the cooling effect of the aetheric ice, she was comfortable. *There's going to be monsters, obviously. Desert, so it's going to be sandworms, scorpions, a mummy, a sphinx, or maybe just sandstorms. Or some terrible horrors I've never conceived of. Either way, I doubt they'll just let me sit on my ice floor and wait out the timer.*

The emotional farewell with Aoibhe was still weighing on her, and the tedium of just waiting wasn't helping. Three years of memories tied her to Solace. Leaving had been a tough decision for her, even when the disasters around town happened. Aetheria was no longer as much of a helpless girl. Ascyn and the others had trained her well, or as well as they could in the brief time they had. *Three years sounds so long, but it just went so fast. I hope the kids on the farm are okay.* Memories floated to the surface of her mind.

Aoibhe in a sleek black and purple dress. Strapless and ankle-length, with a long slit up to her right thigh. Aoibhe was pale-skinned but had a touch of natural bronze that Aetheria did not, and it set off her blond hair and orange-red angelic wings beautifully. The powerful Soul Witch, though not wearing her usual armored dresses or her big purple and black hat, still looked spectacular. Aoibhe was the first person she had met, besides herself, who had glowing eyes, but hers glowed with a holy golden radiance, not the aetheric blue of Aetheria's.

"You do have other clothes, after all! I was wondering if the gods had stranded you with only one outfit." A playful tone touched upon the Soul Witch's voice, and her golden eyes were not bashful about meeting Aetheria's. In fact, the witch seemed disappointed anytime Aetheria looked away from her.

Aetheria was wearing a black leather skort, fishnet stockings, knee-high red-laced black leather boots, a white halter top, and her trench coat's little brother, a red biker jacket. Her aqua scarf and red scrunchie remained. She had declared them staples of her limited style. Aetheria presented a very different image from that of the Soul Witch, who looked like a fantasy goddess at a dinner party. *I look like a college freshman hoping to get lucky.*

Aoibhe's eyes fueled her feelings, and she would be lying to say she wasn't interested in her new mentor and housemate.

"Well, Aetherius gave me an entire chest full of clothes when I first appeared on Grief. Only I stored everything but the initial outfit in my soul repository without knowing what was going on. At least I didn't have to run around the island naked."

"Some people might pay good money for that, myself included." The witch winked and poured them both glasses of wine. The view from the master chambers of the crystal tower showed all of Solace laid out below them, with the occasional glimmers of colored light that the tower cast across the town. "Where did you reincarnate?"

"Oh, a subterranean city. It belonged to Aetherius's kids, the Aetherials. Nova Azura. It kind of fell into the abyss after a bunch of hate-quakes—err, *earthquakes*, struck. I barely made it out in time." Aetheria lightly nibbled her lower lip. Aoibhe seemed to be as interested in her as she was in the witch. In Aetheria's experience, sometimes messaging got mixed up, though. It was always a bit difficult to work up the courage to directly jump to a subject like sexual attraction and the potential of rejection. She didn't even know the prevalence of relationships between women in this place.

The witch was silent for a moment. She looked stunned.

"You... reincarnated in the lost city of Nova Azura? It is a legend across many planets, the city of the Aeth—" Aoibhe rubbed at her head, scowling at the heavens. "It's a unique place. Was it beautiful? It is said that the power of the Primordial Gods who created them blessed the Elder Races' Origination Point."

"It was amazing. Crystalline towers like yours were common. Domed buildings made of strange light-capturing materials. Fountains with water enriched by... you know, I don't even know. I thought it was mana, but it was even more potent than Aether. So much art and unique architecture. It's a shame it fell into the abyss. What's an Origination Point?"

Aoibhe hung on every word about Nova Azura. Obviously, it was more important than Aetheria had thought.

"Mm. Well. The Primordial gods stood only upon so many worlds before their children spread out across the cosmos. The Origination Points are the places these gods came, in the fullness of their power, and birthed a race. Sometimes alone, sometimes with other gods. There is only one for each of the Elder Races. These areas are sacred and defy many laws of the natural world. Only a god or devil has the power to destroy an Origination Point."

"So, not much doubt Oizys was the one with a hate-boner for me? Makes sense. Aetherius mentioned something about maneuvering and tricking her to get the final accommodations for my reincarnation."

Aoibhe snorted. *Even her snort is beautiful. Ugh. Get a hold of yourself, woman. You are too old to have a crush on a nephilim the moment you meet her. Wait, did I just think that? Someone should slap me. What kind of moron wouldn't have a crush on a busty magic bombshell with wings who is giving you the sexy eyes and has the most adorable snort ever?*

"What is a 'hate-boner'? The translation field made little sense of that."

"Uh... Let's skip that. What about you? Where are you from originally?"

"A world called Sorroklos. Ancient texts described Sorroklos as a haven for the celestial messengers of the gods, a nexus world from which they carried the Holy Word far and wide. Until the corruption spread. The few high-ranking human priests on Sorroklos found themselves the playthings for fallen celestials. My mother was one of them. By the time I was an adult, the corruption had taken the world, and Aetherius whispered into my mind... to flee into his tower, climb it, and find Destiny. After I beat his tower, he offered me a job. In the thirty years it took me to clear the tower, the gods smote Sorroklos to end the corruption." If the witch blamed the gods, Aetheria couldn't tell.

"You beat the tower? In thirty years? Is that fast or slow?"

"I can't tell you, darling."

"Boo. So you took a job here just because you didn't have anywhere else to go?"

"No. I was already an Ethereal Scion, fourth rank of the Ethereal Path, and needed resources and time to work. This tower was perfect for my needs, and it has led me to meeting the most interesting people." Aetheria felt Aoibhe's golden eyes burning into her soul. It felt nice, but also dangerous. *Whoa, my heart is going a mile a minute.*

SURVIVE: 23 hours, 20 minutes

"You're sure you want to show me your priceless artifacts purloined from the Origination Point of an Elder Race?" Aoibhe's sarcasm did little to hide her surprise at how easily Aetheria trusted her. Normally, titles like Soul Witch, Walker of the Ethereal Path, and "Damn Blond Bitch," as they knew her around Solace, deterred others from trusting her. But Aetheria had looked into Aoibhe's soul and decided she trusted Aoibhe, and that was that.

She's cute when she's shocked. I suppose as a former Climber from an apocalypse planet she hasn't had a lot of socialization.

"Yeah, it's just the collected knowledge of an entire civilization—no biggie, right?" The answering twitch of Aoibhe's eyes and slight throb of the vein near her temple almost took the grin off Aetheria's face.

"Sweet darling, you jest, but what you hold is priceless. There are beings who would decimate entire worlds for the knowledge of Aetherius's children."

Okay. I'll remember that. Also, how cute is she when she gets worried about bad people doing things to me for stupid reasons? We could just play with some other orbs...

"I get it. I'll tamp down the irreverence."

Aetheria walked around the table and settled on Aoibhe's lap. An orb appeared in each of her hands, one teaming with Aether, the other with Nether. For whatever reason, the gems had become orbs of extremely potent and condensed energy that wouldn't leave her hands. Wouldn't or couldn't.

Aoibhe was careful not to touch either of the energy vortexes while she studied them with narrowed eyes and presumably other, more esoteric senses as well. Aetheria just sat patiently holding the orbs, enjoying the feeling of Aoibhe pressed against her. *Oh, she's wearing a new perfume today. Is that bourbon and vanilla? Damn, that's sexy and elegant. I need to meet the perfumer in town again.*

"Ria, these are Ethereal Locked. Only the one to whom they are bound can open them." Aoibhe laughed, unbelieving.

"What's that mean?"

"Well, it means that only someone on the Ethereal Path can open them. Minimum of tier Four, and there are puzzles and trials built into them. Each of these orbs is a dimension unto itself."

"Really? Jeez, that's cool. I just thought they were shiny gems originally. No, no, I get it, but until I'm a super scion of superness, I can't do anything with them, now can I?"

"I suppose you are right, for now. Do not tell anyone else about those orbs."

"Sure, you betcha. Feel like some dinner? Nylan mentioned making us a fancy dinner in thanks to me for killing his sister and all."

"Yes, you did a good job. Even if you lost style points for telling the pathetic lich that you slept with her granddaughter."

"Not my highest point, but in my defense, she dropped a meteor on me."

"Do you intend to sleep with every beautiful woman you meet throughout the tower?" An arched brow warned Aetheria this was a dangerous question.

"Not if I find someone to be loyal to. I still don't know a lot about this tower, and how... real... it is. But I resolved to treat everyone and everything like it is real, and like they deserve some compassion. That's the idea, anyway. What do you think?"

"That seems a lovely way to think, darling."

SURVIVE: 22 hours, 23 minutes

Crack.

The ice under her shuddered as something slammed into it from beneath the sands. A hairline crack ran two meters through her ice. *Worms?*

No. It was not worms that attacked her sheets of ice from below. Scurrying out of the sand were thousands upon thousands of scarab beetles.

"I *hate* beetles! Ice Cascade! *Ice Cascade!*"

Surging waves of power shot out from Aetheria. Arctic pulses of energy crashed into the gathering waves of insects and froze them solid. Aetheria's cascading freeze left affected insects encased in aetheric ice.

Despite this, the swarm still emerged from the ground outside her ice domain. The air vibrated with the wings of thousands of insects. They were forming a massive figure... and melting together.

Aw, jeez, that's not fair.

CHAPTER 25

Tree and Rock

Oh, *hell* to the *no*, you are *not* turning into a giant beetle of evil!"

Even as Aetheria shouted those words at the condensing swarm, she slammed her open palms together. Three years ago, this would have just made a clapping sound, like when normal people did it. But now she could channel her energies into her hands. She pulsed out Aetherflame Nova, following the shockwaves that shattered her own aetheric ice in front of her. The expanding nova caught every scrap of broken and breaking ice. The aetheric ice, consumed by aetheric flames, became superheated energy, expanding ever outward from her. She was not willing to go with restrained attacks this time.

Aetheria breathed in deeply, and when she exhaled, three dust devils formed from the gust. They became vortexes of Aether that absorbed the aetheric flames and moved toward the mega-beetle.

I shall call you plasma devils!

Her mental control over the three was weak, but precision is unnecessary when your target is a mass of beetles the size of a bus. One after another, the plasma devils struck the mass of beetles, pulling insects into the vortex and grinding them into dust, and combusting those that made it into the eye of the vortex. But with every beetle killed, the devils lost a fraction of their rotational power and heat. They destroyed only a quarter of the beetles before petering out.

How many bugs are there in this shithole? Save me, Rico!

Since there were no space marines with explosives around, and the giant beetle mass was taking form with ever more scarabs flying out of the sand, she had to save herself.

Aetheria imagined a tree. *Stretch into the sky and steal the power of the heavens.* Frost emerged from her next few breaths. A thin layer of ice crystallized over her right hand as she gestured, and a tree of aetheric ice grew from the sand before her. Higher it climbed, until it reached sixty feet. The sand under her compressed with her hugely increased mass. She moved like molasses. Aetheria broke into the aetheric ice tree slightly with her bare hand and, grasping it like a club, she bashed the monstrous beetle that had formed out of the insect horde. The ice tree shattered against the hardening exoskeleton of the nascent behemoth.

Aetheria pulsed Aetherflame Nova from her palm as the tree exploded. The pieces of the crystallized Aether combusted, and as she lightened herself, while she boggled at the ease with which she could change her own density, she slashed her right hand through the air so fast it created gusts. She did this five times. Her hand glowed with the power of the synergized wind core. Five aetheric slashes with tiny dust devils trailing them shot through the combusted tree, sucking up the heat before cutting into the exoskeleton of the mega-beetle.

The lingering heat from the combustion nearby burned her skin severely, but the pain was transitory. *Endure it, suffer the extra pain of healing, and be as good as new. Still, it'd be great if I couldn't friendly* fire *myself. Hahaha. I'm hilarious. Ow!*

Her attacks shattered the thick exoskeleton on the giant beetle's right side, the wind blades and their absorbed heat massively damaging the monster's insides.

"No! Nooo!" Aetheria shouted in fury as the wounds on the beetle closed back up. She was not the only one with regeneration. Worse, the flow of beetles from under the sand had not slowed down at all.

The beetle bellowed in rage at the damage it had taken.

Shit. I didn't kill it before it activated. Dang it!

The beetle's mandibles clattered and then it spit a stream of smaller beetles at her.

Aetheria ran the hell out of there; it was the only sane reaction to witnessing an insect attack you with a stream of smaller versions of itself. At her lightest, she easily cruised above the ground. She created a massive cloud of sand to obscure the air behind her. Not that she went far. She circled around the giant beetle a few times, and when she was certain it had lost sight of her, she skidded to a stop and started gulping down Aether. The air surrounding her smoked. Her aura thickened, solidified, and became a tangible thing. She inhaled more Aether until she looked like a new aqua-colored sun.

The beetle flew into the air, her location given away by the massive energies. It dive-bombed her. Aetheria jumped directly at the creature, pushing synergized air into a spinning vortex around her so she became like a drill. The beetle could actually fly, but it was not fast enough to dodge her. She pierced through its head and insides and shot out its rear end, a blue-green drill of destruction.

Aetheria's forward momentum died as she dropped her air synergy. There was no snap of her fingers, but her Aetherflame Nova exploded behind her, igniting the vortex that still raged in the beetle. She did not look back at the explosion.

As much as Aetheria would have loved to land in a superhero pose, her velocity had shot her a lot higher into the air than she had expected. It was not out of a desire to be cool that she hadn't looked back. It was because as the beetle became an exploded carcass, she was falling from a great height.

Ascyn drilled this into your head. Stop staring at the ground, dumbo. Shift your density, find or make a momentum break, land without breaking an ankle.

Too bad my Air affinity is so crap.

Her density went as low as she could get it. Her coat shifted just slightly to billow out behind her. Velocity halved, she created a marble of aetheric ice that shot out of her hand to the sand below. A twisting circular slide of ice rose, and she hit it. The impact dislocated her shoulder, and, groaning, she flew down the rest of the ice like a human bobsled. The inevitable crash into the sand might have been fun if not for the fact that she went into it face first. Almost half of her body ended up buried in sand, like a 1970s lawn dart into a poorly supervised child.

A vortex of air dispersed the sand and freed Aetheria, and she huffed and puffed a little. Unintentionally, she pulled in all the Nether of the thousands of defeated beetles. The cold was a sharp contrast to the sweltering desert, the chill so soul-freezing it made sitting on her ice plate earlier seem warm in comparison.

She still didn't know how to use the Nether. She could absorb it, cycle it, and store it, but she had never actually used it for anything yet. *Aoibhe said it would come in time.*

When she stopped shivering through sheer willpower, Aetheria finally noticed she had a problem.

The large beetle had died, as had thousands of small ones. But small ones were still swarming out of the sand as if there were an infinite number of the little bastards down there. The tides of insects were forming into another of the massive beetles.

SURVIVE: 22 hours, 17 minutes

Aetheria's lips tightened into a disgusted frown. A fifth and sixth stream of beetles emerged from the sands. *More than one at a time soon, or just as much faster spawns? I need to kill them much faster.*

Within her soul repository, she synergized with a particular ring. With a vicious gleam in her eyes, Aetheria launched herself off the ground in an arc over the nearest forming mega-beetle. Over it, she condensed her Aether into a massive chunk of aetheric rock that fell and crushed the bug with a horrific squelching sound. *Ugh. This is just like when Adam would get annoyed at us for ruining his campaign and say, "Rocks fall, everyone dies." It is really effective, though.*

Unfortunately, Aetheria did not have a high Earth affinity. As with wind, she could use it, but it was more about raw power than precision and control. Control was relatively unimportant when creating giant boulders in the air and dropping them on stupid insects.

With every death of a mega-beetle and its flowing smaller beetles, Aetheria sucked down more and more soul-chilling Nether. Minutes turned into hours, hours turned into a dozen hours, with no end in sight.

SURVIVE: 9 hours, 2 minutes

The swirling vortex of power around Aetheria had become more black than blue. She ripped apart any of the smaller beetles that came into her vicinity, atomized them, and absorbed them into her ever darkening aura.

This doesn't seem ominous at all. Clearly, I'm a force for justice in a desert of doom.

Goosebumps had become a permanent thing hours ago. Occasionally, the chill became so intense that tears formed at the edges of her eyes. That the tears would then freeze was definitely comforting. Definitely.

The act of defeating the mega-beetles had become significantly less work. No longer was she jumping and dropping rocks on them. Now, she simply stayed in a low-density state, jumped from the back of beetle to beetle, and shoved an aetheric ice spear through the weak gap in the neck. A pulse of Aetherflame and the bug roasted to death from the inside out. Which would, of course, result in yet more Nether flowing into her.

As much as she tried to push the Nether into ice or fire, it didn't work. It didn't work like Aether at all. *Maybe it's the opposite? I can't even think straight anymore. I'm so damn cold! This is worse than the year back home, when we had an entire month of negative fifty degrees Fahrenheit with wind chill! Why can't you stupid bugs be the ones who are cold instead of me?*

Her internal rant made her dark black aura pulse outward. Like a light bulb being flipped on in her head, she suddenly saw a way to use Nether. She dispersed her aura outward to almost five meters. Everything but her immediately froze, its warmth and life drained into Aetheria. It was the first warmth she had felt in hours, and the corresponding vacuum of Nether energy from the beetle deaths didn't seem so bad.

"Okay, this could work. Totally not an evil power. I'm now able to make a giant aura of vampiric icy death. Suck it, Death Knights, I'm more Death-y than you." Sure, the Death Knights on Floor 4 could not access a lot of their higher-tier powers because of the tower itself limiting them, but a little smack-talk was good for her mental health.

Like a terrible reaper, she dashed between insects and harvested them for their warmth. When no more mega-beetles remained and the streams from under the sand were not forming new ones as fast as she'd like, Aetheria came up with an idea.

"Sandstorm, ho!" She inhaled as much air, Aether, and Nether as she could into her lungs. Where she blew it all out, massive gusts, dust devils, and a small tornado all shot forward. Aetheria threw sand and held the devils and tornado stationary through an intense effort of will. Eventually, they excavated the sand to reveal a series of caves beneath, which the streams of beetles had been using to come to the surface.

Aetheria dropped into the caverns and beheld her true enemy. Ten massive organic wombs disgorged a constant stream of the beetles, only now they weren't migrating to the surface. They came straight at her—and died pointlessly in her aura. Her thoughts were becoming more lucid now that she wasn't frozen inside.

This entire floor isn't about survival. It's about mastering the Nether, or coming to terms with a method to deal with it. These beetles have never posed a genuine threat to me this whole time, but they are full to the brim with juicy Nether energy. I should have seen it sooner, but I picked up a little too much hubris. Of course, I waded through the monsters like a grim reaper. They meant me to master Nether.

To her mystical senses, the ten vessels before her were each little more than a font of Nether energy made into organic form, spewing out power like a hose.

Dad always said you had to be careful when drinking from the hose.

Aetheria dashed to the first of the pulsing wombs and stabbed her bare hand into it. Just her proximity had already wilted the thing, but her direct contact lay waste to it. As the fleshy structure died and withered, the ley line of Nether connected to Aetheria instead.

Immediately, she started alternating between hot and cold flashes. Her vision of the enormous cavern spiked back and forth between normal and looking inverted. The life energy of the other nine wombs, and the constant beetles they spread, sang to her like a siren song.

One after another suffered the same fate as the first, until the cavern had only a single living thing in it: Aetheria herself, her aura ever darker with ten fonts of Nether pumped into her. The only aqua left in her aura was in the bolts of aetheric lightning at the edges. She had inverted her aura from Aether to Nether.

Can I balance them? Isn't that the whole point of walking the Ethereal Path? Bending both to your will to wield the Original Power behind everything?

"Now, Ria, when the time comes, you will know what to do. There are no lessons for me to teach you about this. The melding of Aether and Nether is unique to all who walk the Ethereal Path. Only gods have a method set in stone, and you are not a god. You are a human, albeit a god-touched one. Consider who you are, and what you want to do. Let that guide you into making your own path. Symbolism can be important. I symbolized my path with a cauldron. I don't even know alchemy, but it seemed very witchy, and my hat is all I have of my mother."

Aoibhe was a witch, with a cauldron symbolizing her path. What could symbolize Aetheria's path? Her lack of affinities with two of the base elements made her a poor mage type to begin with. She held little to no interest in weaponry. Punching things was a lot more fun than she ever would have thought back on Earth. Aetheria imagined two of herself: one with aqua hair and aqua eyes, and the other with red hair and red eyes. The redhead was much more gothic, with a black theme instead of Aetheria's current red clothes.

Now shake hands.

That was it. That was the symbol of her path. Two hands became a single. Her fist in the black fingerless gloves. Hands could push. Hands could pull. They could fix or destroy. What couldn't hands do? Eat things. *It's not perfect symbolism, maybe, but fuck it if it isn't mine.*

The cavern exploded in light. The whole fifth level she was on detonated as if a nuclear explosion had ripped it apart, and then imploded to become foodstuff for Aetheria.

In the back of her mind was the image of an open palm balancing two flames—the blue-green flame of Aether and the black flame of Nether.

You might not have been the Keeper of the Flame, Mr. Cornell, but it sure looks like I am. You can bet your ass I'm going to stand my ground.

The door to the sixth floor appeared.

CHAPTER 26

The Shadow Cat (Dragon)

Floor 6 of Aetherius's tower had high domed ceilings. From the center of each dome, a series of exquisite crystalline fixtures hung. Strangely shaped crystal formations bathed the rectangular room in copious rays of light. The walls were a heavily grained wood paneling, with windows that looked out onto a splendid garden with fountains and peacocks strutting their stuff. Songbirds chittered and provided the faintest of background noise in the large hall where Aetheria stood.

It took her a few minutes to get her aura under control. Eventually, she found a balancing point where the black and aqua energies intermingled without one dominating the other. The desperate hunger for warmth and life in her aura was gone. *I'm not sure I want that ability back until I figure out how to control it better. That's all I need—to go to bed in a town, have a bad dream, and wake up inside a building full of dead people because I ate their life force.*

Without further infusions of energy, or the need to manifest any of her internal power, she let her aura calm down so it was invisible to the naked eye.

The room held ten tables. Each table had a stack of four boxes on it. There were only four stools in the entire room. All four were identical to one another: plain wood, lightly lacquered, and slightly too tall for sitting comfortably at any of the tables.

Aetheria sat down and opened the first box. It was a jigsaw puzzle; the box showed a picture of dogs playing poker.

Ugh. Dogs.

The puzzle was not terribly hard, but it took her multiple hours to get near to finishing it. The last piece of the puzzle was missing. The space taunted her. The next puzzle was of a brightly colored fish. It, too, was missing the last piece. The third puzzle was of a cat, and Aetheria enjoyed putting this one together the most until it, too, failed to have the last piece. The tabby stared at her with judgment in its eyes, and she felt rebuffed by the unfinished puzzles. The pattern continued to the fourth table.

As far as trials went, this one allowed her mind to wander. *What is my witch doing now? How are the farm kids? I hope Tamsin learned new magic. Should I even be here? I'm terrible at magic. I've only made it this far because of my regeneration. It's easy to be brave and face things when you know you'll just heal from it. Even if I beat this floor, and the next, can I beat the whole tower? Aoibhe beat a tower and took a Dweller offer.*

Aetheria would have liked to blame the new purple-tinted black flame that blazed in her soul for the self-doubt and self-consciousness, but those things had always haunted her. Life had always meant being second or third best, until she found *EFWO*. She'd climbed the ranks of PvP and claimed several top ranks for multiple seasons. For a few years, she'd flipped between guilds, never quite finding a home, until she'd joined up with the Knights of Academia. When the old raid leader quit, she tried out the role and it stuck. It took them two years to become a force that snatched up the server first left and right. Seven years to get a World First.

Then she died. *EFWO* had been a pillar of her confidence and identity when she was Aesca. Who was Aetheria? A mouthy, sarcastic near-immortal who wandered around and punched things. Aesca's Earth life had diverged from her childhood dreams. Not the ones of fantasy and wonder, but to become an educator and distributor of knowledge. *EFWO* had replaced it with dopamine hits and an obsession with climbing higher in the ranks: PvP, PvE, Crafting. It didn't matter. That fire had been lit under her, and by the time she became a librarian, the job had lost any interest or meaning. She paid lip service to it, but it had been an empty thing.

Neither *EFWO* nor being a librarian held much relevance to her current life as Aetheria, a would-be heroine and savior of a world. How could one even look at the responsibility for a universe, and, worse, being told by a freaking god you were their last chance? Aetheria tried not to think about it too much. Instead, she imagined life afterward. Traveling to new worlds, unknown places. Something the tower also provided. Her daydreams had expanded to include Aoibhe over the last year. The Soul Witch was special to her.

More puzzles, more single pieces missing.

"If I fail, I fail, right? Aetherius said I'm free of the Samsara, so if I actually fail, somehow it's game over. At which point it won't really be my problem anymore. Sort of a shitty way to look at it. 'Sorry, universe, I tried.'" Aetheria's laughter echoed strangely in the game hall.

"No, no, that's not the way. Failure is off the table. I'm going to shove my stylish boots up Oizys's backside and then disappear into the great beyond with my sexy witch partner in crime."

The last box on the last table had no picture on it. It contained all the previously missing pieces of the puzzles she'd done. Aetheria groaned at the task of sorting them. *Is this entire trial just a reflection of the slow, monotonous grind that life is for so many people? A reminder that not everyone is out adventuring? Other than the whole "save the world" deal, I'm not carrying much responsibility.*

She put the last piece of the final puzzle in, and a door of light appeared.

How many hours had she been there? The outside garden hadn't changed, but she was fairly sure that was all an illusion. Days? It didn't matter.

Aetheria stepped onto the seventh floor and found herself in a cavern. It was a large, almost spherical room with only one exit tunnel. Someone had covered the walls with a myriad of crystals in all the hues of the rainbow. The air in the chamber was vibrating with different frequencies of energy that made Aetheria's skin itch. It felt like ants crawling across her.

At the center of the room were seven eggs—six were still intact. Each egg looked like it could fit an adult golden retriever inside of it. A meter-long insectoid resembling a lacewing had cracked the seventh open and was happily still gobbling the insides of the egg. It didn't even notice she was in the room before she appeared behind it and punched a hand through its brain. A pungent smell of pheromones secreted from the corpse, and she kicked it to the side.

"Sorry, egg, but blame the tower, not me." A deep feeling of sadness welled up in her for the loss of whatever creature had lived in such a pretty, prismatic egg.

Aetheria felt six presences, the remaining eggs. They were curious about her, but none seemed capable of communicating directly with her.

Chattering from the tunnel forced her to turn. More lacewings, and once in the room, they flew into the air and fired bolts of acid at her. *No, at the eggs!*

Quickly, Aetheria formed a dome of aetheric ice around the eggs, at the same time diving to intercept the acid attack. It hurt. A lot. A fast pulse of Aetherflame burned it off her. The sudden creation of a defense barrier around the eggs pushed the attention of the ever-growing number of lacewings onto her.

Well. If I'm correct about those eggs, it would only make sense to use this...

Aetheria inhaled air and exhaled blue jets of fire that crisped multiple lacewings and burned more volleys of acid on the way to her. When she ran out of oxygen, the flames died out, and she heaved in a deep breath to claim more Aether and the Nether of the defeated. *No using the death aura here, might hit the eggs. I wonder...*

The lacewings swarmed her, changing the fight from ranged to melee. Some tried to sneak around to attack the barrier surrounding the eggs. They were the first to take on Aetheria in close quarters. Her fists were a force of destruction.

Wherever she punched a lacewing, it withered and weakened. She didn't even need to up her density with Nether-augmented punches. She could stay near the fast end of her imaginary density slider and still deal ridiculous damage despite being actually weak. Laughter slipped out of her lips, and the poetry of close dodges buoyed her spirits. Attack after attack, swings of sharp claws, the bite of evil mandibles, and close-range acid spits added a little fire to her spirit. *I forgot how fun this is. Whenever Pete swapped into tank mode instead of DPS in EFWO, I thought dodge tanks looked super cool. Acting like one is amazing.*

By her fifth lacewing, she had worked it out to a three-blow system. Left punch, right punch, knee. Dead lacewing. Repeat. Unfortunately, close combat efficiency in this scenario was not optimal. More insectoids flew in from the tunnel every moment.

"Okay, screw you guys. Ow. Ow. Ow." An insect had spit acid into her mouth when she was swearing at them. *This is that time a pigeon shit in my hair all over again.*

Aetheria considered what Ascyn had told her when asked what his favorite art was.

"Ahh, after all my secrets, are we? Well, my favorite combat art is one I call the Chain. Other people call it Ascyn's Chain, of course. You take on an enhanced Aether physiology temporarily, cast out binding strands of Aether, and then squeeze everything to death. Gory and messy, but damn, if it doesn't work great. Just don't use it somewhere you can't take a bath afterward."

Aetheria focused and her aura intensified, aqua light filling the entire chamber. The lacewings hesitated for a strange moment that seemed to hang in time.

Chains are so edgelord-y.

Aetheria's long, sparkling aqua hair became suddenly radiant, and elongated strands of Aether shot from her hair to bind around each lacewing in the room, constricting until they cut the bugs to death. Insect blood and body parts went flying.

Ohh. If I focused on making them razor wire, it'd be even more effective. I'll try that next time.

The bountiful and freed Nether energies from the lacewing's deaths coalesced into a swirling ball of Netherflame above her hand, which she flung down the tunnel entrance. The black flames stuck to the tunnel walls and ceiling like napalm. The flames continued to burn. If the "sticky fire" was anything like the Aether fire version, it would last between five to twenty minutes. No more lacewings came down the tunnel.

Instead, something else came. Something much bigger, with scales. The black flame went out, snuffed by the aura of a powerful presence.

Aww, crap. Let's hope I don't have to fight. This one has got major raid boss energy.

"What are you doing here, human? Are you... an Aetherial human with Nether? Interesting." The being that had entered the tunnel was a dragon with the face of a cat. Its scales were blue, and ephemeral fur of purple and red ran over its scaled body. "Few humans walk the Ethereal Path."

"Uh. Hiya. Name's Aetheria. I arrived a bit too late to save all the eggs." She commanded the aetheric ice to melt, revealing six safe eggs besides the breached egg.

Moisture shone across the cat-like eyes. "Unfortunate. Three hundred years they have incubated, only to lose one at the last minute."

"Wait, wait. Your eggs incubate for *three hundred years?*" Aetheria was gobsmacked.

"Yes, well, we can't all have our young in a few days like you humans," the cat-dragon murmured, almost under its breath. "It takes concentrated elemental, aetheric, and Nether energy for our young to hatch. Hence the crystals on the walls. Although..."

The eggs began to shift.

"Apparently, your excessive energies work just as well. A year early, even. Do you know how to birth a dragon, Aetheria?"

"Nope."

A Market Date

Time: Second month in Solace, Floor 4

Ascyn and Aoibhe did not believe in giving students ample amounts of time to themselves unless a subject required time to sink in. It wasn't until the second month of studying under the masters that they agreed to give Aetheria a weekend off.

She was leaving the crystal tower when a flutter of wings accompanied someone landing and falling into step next to her. It was the Soul Witch herself, her purple witch hat tilted at a slight angle from her descent from the heights of the tower. Today, Aoibhe wore a purple variation of the armored dresses she wore day to day.

"Fancy a companion for your visit to the market?" It was an earnest question, Aetheria thought, and she appreciated it.

"That sounds absolutely wonderful. Do I get the guided tour?"

"Certainly, darling. Do you know what you want to look at first? The natives from other towns make their way here for sales on Saturdays, so you picked a good day. Finding Solace so early in your climb is quite rare and provides an amazing opportunity for you. Most who reach Solace are at least second tier, if not third. What we in Solace consider almost worthless should be valuable to you."

At almost the same height, it was easy for either to match the other's stride—no need to shorten steps or lengthen them. Occasional summer breezes whispered through the trees on the boulevards, ruffled blond and aqua hair, and jingled the plethora of wind chimes, knickknacks, and other various ornaments that hung from the homes and businesses of the masters of Solace.

"I'd like to see magical things. How do you figure out what magical items do? Is there a spell?" Aetheria looked down at her standard equipment with curiosity, then back at Aoibhe. The red trench coat, her gloves, boots, scarf, and otherwise default outfit had no real enchantments yet. Even the boots she'd once thought made her silent were just really well made. Someday, she'd have the materials to enchant them up properly.

"There is a spell. Normal magical items are going to be a danger around you until you've become better at control. As happened with your bow, even basic items will be overtuned by your Aether usage. If you actively infuse them, it will trigger a Chaos surge. Do not ask me what that means, it could be anything. You could conjure flowers, a whale, a fireball, lightning, a black hole, an angry god... anything."

There go my hopes and dreams of buying a +1 longsword and +2 armor. Guess this isn't that kind of world.

"I'm sorry about your apprentice's waffle iron. I didn't stop to think there'd be normal magical items in the kitchen of an Ethereal Lady."

Aoibhe laughed. It was a beautiful explosion of contagious well-being from the witch.

"It was fine. The only one injured was yourself. Edwin had never experienced a Chaos surge before. It is a valuable experience for apprentices to learn to deal with Chaos and probability distortions. I heard him muttering about it, taking him weeks to regrow his eyebrows while you had already regrown your hand."

Red colored Aetheria's cheeks. Aoibhe was so calm and composed about her setting off a Chaos surge and endangering her apprentice. *Honestly, I think the only thing keeping her from laughing was the potential danger to Edwin.*

"Do you know how many Chaos surges I created over the years in adapting more traditional magic into Ethereal magic? Thousands. Tens of thousands. I once destroyed an entire tower floor except ten feet around me." Aoibhe winced and then laughed. Aetheria reveled in it.

"Oh, what are those?" she asked the witch, pointing to a stand selling what looked suspiciously like tacos.

"Flatbread made by Paul the baker. The stand is managed by A'ton'i, Paul's apprentice. They vary the meat and mix it with a selection of vegetables." Aoibhe looked surprised she was explaining, as it was a staple of the market.

"Oh, and what's that stand?"

"Wands. For mages. You could try an ice wand. Ice is your strongest affinity, followed by Fire. Your Aether would burn it out eventually, but it would still shoot regular ice or fire. Until it explodes in a Chaos surge when you do the same thing every Tower Climber who learns overload does: use it to do something ill-advised instead of thinking just a little harder to find a better alternative to a solution than a Chaos surge."

Chaos surges are bad. Find better solutions if possible.

"I think I'll stick to your suggestion and not carry too many things to overload."

"That wasn't quite what my words intended, darling. You have a soul repository. Throw them in there when you aren't using them. You won't risk accidental Chaos surges that way, but could still make use of overload if you absolutely must."

"Oh? So you used overload too?" A light blush rose in Aoibhe's cheeks at the question.

"Yes. It's a risk, but when things get dangerous, sometimes it's a worthy gamble. As you gain experience with Chaos surges, it is even possible to have an influence on the chaotic energies. A side benefit of the Ethereal Way. Few paths outside of the Ethereal or Order resist Chaos."

"Ah. We seem to be an awful lot alike, Aoibhe." Aetheria met the Soul Witch's gold gaze for a few seconds too long, till they both blushed and looked away.

Ugh. I'm acting like I'm thirteen again and trying to get Dylan Young to notice me.

After several more booths, Aetheria found a merchant who bought some of her spears, chests, and other odds and ends. With currency in her soul repository, the opportunities of the market opened up wide.

"Try this on." Aetheria handed the Witch a purple and black scarf with delicate yellow threading. "Oh yeah, I love it." She handed coins to the shopkeeper. Aoibhe arched a brow and gave her a questioning look.

"To what do I owe getting such a thoughtful gift? The yellow matches my eyes, and it's even the right purple to go with my hat. I adore it." The nephilim left the scarf on as they walked. They ate snacks and looked at jewelry. Aetheria learned a little about how enchanting worked, and at the end, they climbed up over a small tower overlooking the market.

"Ascyn says you get twitchy about training on heights. Would you like to go up?" The witch's angelic wings spread to their full wingspan behind her. The orange-red-hued feathered wings were glorious in the dwindling sunlight. Aoibhe held one hand out for Aetheria, who took it. Aoibhe's arms wrapped around her and pulled her into a tight embrace.

Then they were in the air, those large wings easily holding their combined weight. *Just how physically strong is Aoibhe? She's a caster-melee hybrid, so she's probably weaker than I would be at her tier. As for apples to apples, I think she's stronger than I am right now.*

Up they went, hundreds of feet higher than the tallest structures in Solace, and there, a blue ledge of Aoibhe's Ethereal air hardened to hold their weight.

"Making air platforms is so flipping cool. I need to learn it. Double jumps and triple jumps could be my thing." This close to Aoibhe, Aetheria could feel the quickened heartbeat of the witch against her own chest, and now that they were stationary, the seraphic wings draped around the two women providing a bulwark of warmth against the cool winds.

"Are you interested in ladies, Ria?" Aoibhe beat straight to the point.

"Yep." Aetheria bit her lower lip as her stomach did flips about what questions would follow that one.

"And are you interested in other races? Are you interested in me?" Aoibhe's breath tickled Aetheria's face as the two locked eyes.

"Definitely am, for sure." *Lobster-red cheeks against blue-green hair must look ridiculous.*

"I am interested in you. What relationships does your culture have? Nothing too ridiculous?"

"Oh, Earth was full of stupid, ridiculous things. I'm not angling to get half your sheep, though, but I haven't had a relationship for a few years now." *Unless we count long distance, which we will not.*

"I see. If you have no need for predefined terminology for now, shall we see where we are tomorrow?" Aoibhe seemed full of confidence in this conversation, but Aetheria could feel her pulse, and it was as fast and erratic as her own.

"Yeah…"

A pair of teeth nipped her earlobe, and then a husky voice whispered into her ear.

"To make love to a Soul Witch is to bind our souls for a time. It leaves a permanent link. Still interested?"

Aetheria found her voice. "I am. I am so, so interested."

Aoibhe pressed her lips warmly against Aetheria's.

How do her lips taste like strawberry tarts? We didn't even eat any tarts at the fair! And she smells like vanilla. Life is so unfair.

CHAPTER 27

New Life

It turned out they had time to kill before the eggs actually hatched, and the dragon was screwing with her—the entire process just involved sitting back and watching. Which made sense with eggs, but when a dragon casually asks questions, you doubt yourself.

"Hey, um, what's your name, anyway? I'm Aetheria, like I said before."

"Cedhess'Shaldurri'Zarreras'Berry'Calhua—"

Aetheria interrupted the dragon, seeing no sign of it finishing soon. "That's a bit long for my ability to pronounce. Nickname?"

"You may call me Shal. I had forgotten you humans are incapable of dealing with the length of our names. Since you speak in Ath, I thought perhaps you had the patience to hear my full name. How does a human come to speak the First Language or wield the Aetherflame? Your Netherflame is impressive, but is not *the* Netherflame."

It's going to be one of those conversations, isn't it? It's strange how you can contextualize the differences between titles and nouns sometimes. I should've read more books on languages.

"Ath? That's the name of this language? Aetherius taught it to me when I got reincarnated. If I'm understanding your meaning, I think Aetherius shared his own Flame, or spark, or essence, whatever it was, with me. Does that sound right?"

"It does. Your Netherflame will continue to purify itself. Have you met the Lady of Night? Your Flame, while not pure, echoes her own."

"Who?"

"The Lady of Night. The story, as I have been told it, is that Chronos woke one day with a terrible hangover to a cacophony outside his dwelling. His drunken visions had created many dreams and nightmares. Among them, Aetherius, Nyx, Chaos, Erebus, Metis, and so forth, who were all having a loud party outside his dwelling. The aforementioned change their stories frequently, so who really knows the truth? My father insists the gods are forever changing their stories because they are figments of faith, and all the peoples of all the worlds are chaos with no united belief, so there can be no unity in the gods. The gods themselves are elusive on this subject, which is fair enough. I would be cranky if someone questioned my existence."

"My personal theory is that Chronos is a terrible alcoholic, and that's why reality is so fragile and the questions of Origination are so murky."

"That's... well, no. I never met Nyx."

You've forgotten me already, after all our time together?

A voice lingered in Aetheria's mind. Had she actually heard it? No further answer came.

"So, are there aftereffects of creating a Netherflame? Maybe a bit of mental confusion for a few days?"

"Oh, no. Quite the opposite. You should be in a state of heightened acuity for up to a week afterward. Your ties with the Nether will grow stronger, but the connection is most raw and primal in that first span of time. A real pity for us long-lived races. The inspirations we could eke out with that most primal of intimacy..." The cat-dragon stared into the distance.

"What happened with the insects outside, anyway?" Aetheria asked Shal.

"Oh. The little kittens' father is out there rampaging. We had noticed none of the smallest ones got around us until you started using your arts and drew my attention. Azrael'asuludar'a—"

"I see," Aetheria interrupted, although it was unnecessary, as the six eggs began to crack and wobble, the beings inside fighting their way out.

Squee! Cute!

Breaking free from the eggs were six adorable figures. The coloration of each was distinctive: red accented by yellow, white accented by blue, blue stressed by silver, green accentuated by copper, yellow accentuated by blue, and the final kitten was black accentuated by lavender blue.

Unlike freshly born kittens, these all looked fully aware of their surroundings and gazed at one another and Shal with intelligence. *Why do I feel like they are having a conversation without me?*

While the mother and her new hatchlings (*kittendragonlings?*) were nuzzling and cuddling one another, Aetheria sat on the floor and watched with a smile. The sight was impossible not to be charmed by and lasted for over a half hour, until something landed on Aetheria's shoulder. She turned to find a black cat face looking into her eyes from inches away.

"It seems my son wants to form a bond with you, human." A masculine booming voice filled the room. The kittens all cowered a little before their father. Azrael was at least thirteen meters long and radiated an immense power. His scales were silver, and ephemeral black fur covered his body and face. His big silver-blue eyes noticed everything around him.

The cat on Aetheria's shoulders had curled its tail around her and settled against her hair and neck. Shal watched the two of them.

"He has my blessing. What do you say?" the cat-dragon inquired of her mate.

"You black kittens are always the most daring. Very well, Arkaziel'aethiare'-anathemal'suriksyn'asuludar'—"

Shal coughed.

"Fine. I acknowledge the bond between Arkaziel and the human, Aetheria," Azrael proclaimed.

"I, to acknowledge the bond," Shal said with a little less pompousness.

"Uh?" Aetheria asked, dumbly.

"For saving him and his siblings, he wishes to travel with you and enter a bond of friendship. In time, he'll talk to you on his own."

The snort of derision from the cat curled around her neck was unmistakable. For emphasis, his tail thwacked her chin.

This is going to be Zeusy all over again. Am I going to get clawed to hell every time I sleep?

"You know I'm a Challenger, right? Danger? Tower? Gods?"

Arkaziel's parents looked dubious. "Oh, don't worry, human. The StarMane clan has been around since the beginning. Little Arkaziel there is already three hundred years old, with the racial combat memories of all his ancestors, and is a Tier Two..." Azrael frowned. "A Tier Two Ethereal Cultivator."

Shal also frowned.

"Anyone going to clue me into the eerie silence?"

"The insects failed to consume the essence of the seventh egg. Arkaziel seems to have absorbed it before the insects could and has joined you on the Path of the Ethereal." Azrael seemed both pleased and displeased.

Shal didn't speak, but the look she was giving the black kitten and Aetheria was suspicious. *She thinks it has something to do with me and my energies, and not some kind of egg-essence merger.*

Again, it felt as though there were multiple conversations occurring on a level higher than she could comprehend. *They are definitely telepathic and I'm left out in the cold.*

A cold nose nuzzled into her neck to make itself the center of attention. Aetheria reached a hand up to stroke him. Surprise! The ephemeral fur over the scales was real, despite its illusory look. The fur was soft and warm, and like a cat, it seemed the kitten began to purr as she scratched it.

"Why don't you stay with us for a few dozen decades, Aetheria? Kill some insects, bond with Arkaziel more, learn from us. While you follow a traditional Cultivation Path, we have the knowledge of our ancestors going all the way back to Chronos's blessed creation of our kind. Did you know a fully grown StarMane can eat a planet, or bat one into a black hole just as easily?"

Aetheria blinked. There were giant draconic cats that could eat worlds and knock them into black holes? *Oh man, that's just... what the hell, gods? More importantly, why did they suddenly start acting like car salespeople? They're trying to trick me.*

"Just how big do your kind get? Also, what are the odds of actually hitting a planet into a black hole? That's got to be, like, super hard."

"Oh, it takes about three million years for one of us to get that big. Someone usually hunts us down for our scales, or fur, or to be a hero before then. Retribution this, vengeance that, greater good that, you know how people are. Can't stand a few little jokes."

Do not ask. Do not ask. "Little jokes like what?"

"Well, my uncle got hunted down for his scales by some Tier Five adventurers. Dragon-scale armor is a big hit, especially with stylish hides like ours. He killed all but one, but the fight still killed him. Whereas my great-grandpa is one of the planet-eating cats. Ever since he ate a few religiously important planets, Aetherius has been sheltering some of us." Azrael was forthright.

"Honey, why don't we give her one of Great-Grandpa's scales if she helps us kill the hive queen? It'll be a wonderful experience for her and Arkaziel." Shal came in with helpful hints. *I can't even tell if I'm bumbling into floor quests or just stumbling into random shit anymore, and we're only on Floor Seven! Also, am I suddenly starring in a show shot at the Universal lot in the '50s?*

Which, of course, is how a few hours later Aetheria was jumping off Azrael's back once the cat-dragons had breached the hive walls of the lacewings. Shal was with the new kittens, except Arkaziel. The assault team had also been joined by one of Shal's uncles. Uruzuriel was over sixty meters long, and lightning crackled along most of his length. Any insects that went near him died immediately. A very impressive offense and defense.

"Kill the queen. We'll make sure no prospective queens escape." Azrael jaunted off back into the skies.

"Alright, so, I don't know what kind of teamwork you got, Ark, but I'll start with the 'punch things to death' strategy. You got anything that'll help?" The kitten purred and nuzzled her neck more. She got no answer otherwise. So she began her slaughter. The insects were individually weaker than her, and without the need to protect anything, she could dash between clumps of them, delivering fiery and icy aetheric death.

Arkaziel fell asleep on her shoulder, occasionally snoring as she went ham. Aetheria didn't really mind. The kitten was comfortable and offset the influx of miasma she was taking in, feeding it all into the Netherflame inside her.

It went smoothly for the first six chambers she cleared until she came to what Azrael had described as the antechamber to the queen. Three very different bugs stood guard at the royal door.

The one on the left exploded in a vortex of wind before any of the three had even noticed Aetheria was in the room. *Haha, crit hit!* Wind was one of her weaker affinities, so any ranged attack successes with it always felt like a triumph.

The other two hive guards immediately engaged. These things were no lacewing she had ever seen. They had six legs, six arms, multiple sets of wings, and a raised torso. *What kind of psychopath makes a bug-centaur-kali-monster?*

They were fast, but not faster than her. The problem was that to stay faster than them, Aetheria had to give up the strength to meet their blows directly. Weaving between the eerily coordinated attacks of the two guards was pushing her to her limits, and while she waited for one of them to use an energy-fueled power to disrupt with Aetherflame, it just didn't come. The guards operated only with physical prowess.

"I'm firing up Aether and Nether for real, Arkaziel." The StarMane snored through her warning.

One hand glowing black, the other glowing green-blue, Aetheria started delivering counterblows that left smoking wounds behind. Her Nether-infused strikes rotted exoskeleton and flesh alike, weakening the guard every time she struck. Her right hand and its aetheric ice infusion froze pieces of exoskeleton that she then shattered with follow-up attacks.

Objectively, Aetheria was an adequate fighter. Her form was sloppy, she had openings, and she took more hits than she needed to in exchange for delivering blows of her own. The luxury of her regenerative capabilities afforded her to take risks, a feeling she still had when filled with Aether or Nether. The reckless urges, power, life, death—the need to eat a superb burrito. The torrential power of Aether and Nether affected the mind, but it made little difference for Aetheria.

Within moments, the shattered remnants of the hive guards dispersed into miasma and became another core in her repository, while their energies were fuel for her Netherflame.

The hive queen's chambers lay beyond the doors. Aetheria kicked them open and off the wall into the chamber. Something, a lot of things, were squished on impact.

Aetheria groaned. The entire room's floor was a seething mass of lacewings, from the size of the ones she knew on Earth to the biggest bug she'd ever seen.

Arkaziel sneezed on her neck and resumed snoring. *Goddamn cats.*

CHAPTER 28

The Hive Queen

The cacophony of the massive doors being shot into the hive queen's chambers created chaos. Aetheria cast a wall of sticky Netherflame to cover the entrance she'd just come through, to keep chasers off. She took a deep breath and focused on conjuring Aether extensions for her hair once more. *Thinner. More like wire. Sharp wire.*

Aetheria dashed into the room, and the extensions to her hair lashed out. Each strand hunted down an insect, ensnared it, and then tightened. With the modifications to her visualization, the bisection of insects was almost a laughable thing to watch. Even in such a target-rich environment, dodging only provided momentary safety—Aetheria had a lot of hair. Only five insects in the whole chamber resisted the Aether strands. The queen simply ignored them; the facsimile hair could not pierce her dense exoskeleton.

The four remaining royal guards, with six legs and four arms, positioned themselves around the queen. Unlike the guards outside the door, these had the presence of a power beyond mere might. The farthest back rose three appendages, each holding a wand. Lightning bolts cascaded from each wand to form one stronger bolt of electricity. As fast as Aetheria was, she missed the timing and dodge on the lightning, and took the bolt straight to the chest.

Purrrr. Arkaziel opened his eyes while Aetheria smoked and healed.

Hssssss. Her kitten hissed at the insects, his tail tapping her on the top of her head. *If I didn't know any better, I'd swear he was telling me to watch this.*

The StarMane leaped into the air, dark wings casually flapping to keep him aloft. *Some kind of flight that isn't totally based on physics. Who needs physics when you have magic, right?*

In a classic move known to all draconic species, the kitten inhaled, sneezed cutely, and then formed a glowing orb of energy in his mouth. Aetheria expected a breath attack, or a fireball-like attack; instead, a beam of coruscating white and black energy closed the distance across the room as Arkaziel aimed the beam back and forth over the four royal guards. When the blinding light stopped, Ark settled back onto her shoulders and let out a little sigh. Within seconds, the cat-dragon was sleeping again.

Cripes. I have a laser cat!

The entire chamber shook with the anger of the hive queen. A large opening appeared across the queen's exoskeleton near the side, and a gaping mess of flesh shot out an additional guard before the thick exoskeleton closed again. Beyond the shrieks that clawed at Aetheria's mind, the queen didn't seem to have any other offense.

The newest royal guard looked like the others physically, but its exoskeleton was dense and gleamed with a metallic sheen the others had not. *Is the queen able to make adaptive soldiers?*

Aetheria rushed forward to engage it. The insect blocked her blows with its strangely colored exoskeleton. The damn thing was fast and strong. So much so that when she went full strength to test its defenses, she was bashed in the stomach and sent hurling across the room. *Hacks!*

"Look, lass. Sometimes your little trick isn't going to work. Altering your density is nice, but it's a basic Aether physiology technique. You should keep working on it, because basic doesn't mean bad, but sometimes you're going to need to step things up a bit. Once you've got control of density, you can work on the next phase: mass. Through mass you can control force, weight, density, kinetic energy, and even gravity to an extent."

"Well, then, why don't we focus on just that?"

"What's density?"

"Uh, literally? Mass divided by volume..."

"Exactly. You haven't touched volume at all yet. You aren't quite touching mass properly yet either, but we'll get you there. If you can control your mass and learn a few arts, you'll have a leg up on anyone under third tier."

"So what's the first step in mass control?"

"Enhancing your own mass with Aether."

Fueled by Ascyn's guidance, Aetheria's aura came alive, Aether and Nether flaring around her in brilliant cascades as she dropped her density to almost nothing for maximum speed to close the gap on the royal guard. At the last second, she let her density max out. She slammed a boot on the ground, shattering stone, and gave her velocity a massive shot in the arm.

The hive guard brought two arms together to block her incoming telegraphed blow, even while Aether converted into temporary mass, which also reinforced her density. She struck the royal guard with her right fist, shattering its exoskeleton, and her fist continued through it.

Aetherflame Nova. Aetheria shunted the Aether mass into the flames, the fastest way she'd found to drop excess energy mass.

Inside the royal guard, her hand exploded with Aether fire, cooking the bug from the inside out and disrupting any magical energies it possessed. *Ew.*

The queen was making more shrieking sounds, but when her birth canal opened again, Aetheria was there. No punching this time: she lobbed a ball of concentrated Nether absorbed from her kills at the spawning canal. The black energy shattered on contact and spread like napalm, black flames bursting to life before the exoskeleton could close up again. Not that lack of oxygen would affect the Netherflame.

A creature the size of the hive queen would suffer a slow death if Aetheria left the Netherflame as the only thing to do the job. Even though one of this creature's spawn had eaten an adorable dragon kitten, she didn't feel it warranted a slow, painful death. According to Shal, even the hive queen was barely as intelligent as a wolf. They were just driven by hunger and converted domiciles taken over from other species they ate.

Aetheria gestured and a circle of thin aetheric ice formed around the queen, then encroached on the immobile insect. The ice thickened, turning a mix of dark green and blue, until it reached a critical mass and roiling water shot up from the ice framework. Jets of water fountained over the queen, doing no damage against her thick exoskeleton. Until Aetheria clicked her tongue. From the framework circle inward, all the water froze back into aetheric ice.

From there, it was a simple matter to repeat the mass-driven attack that had obliterated the last royal guard, shattering the ice and, with it, the hive queen's exoskeleton. Aetheria snapped her fingers, generating a shower of sparks via Aetherflame Nova. Then she quickly crossed the room to escape before the Aetherflame ignited the aetheric ice and Netherflame. Arkaziel chose that moment to sink his claws into her shoulder, just a little, and then purr contentedly.

Ugh. Of course, my animal companion is more cat than dragon. Just keep telling yourself he's a laser cat, he's a laser cat, he can shoot lasers. He is only a day old, he's probably tired. Plus, look how cute he is. Oh my gosh, who's a pretty kitty? Who's a little sweetheart?

Realization could be a slow thing. She stood petting her animal companion for a solid three minutes while fire and explosions filled the room they had left behind. It wasn't even the realization that the mission was complete that pulled her from petting Arkaziel—it was the infusion of Nether from the hive queen's death. It was the single biggest infusion she had taken in yet, more than from even the lich, and it confused her. The fight had not been that difficult.

When she climbed out of the hive to meet Azrael, Arkaziel's father was eating an animal that looked suspiciously like a giant chicken.

"Howdy. Do those things lay eggs, and if so, can I get a few? I bet they'd make great omelets."

"They do, and they do!" Azrael replied before swallowing the bird.

"Wait, how would you make an omelet?" Aetheria looked at his paws suspiciously.

"Most Aether-infused beings have some metamorphic capabilities. We StarManes can start learning to shapeshift at about a century after hatching. Opposable thumbs are quite... handy."

Aetheria was about to groan when her dragon kitten briefly opened his eyes, looked at his father, then let out a long, unamused sigh at his sire before going back to sleep.

"Anyway, how come the hive queen was so easy to kill?"

Azrael blinked a few times.

"Her psychic attacks kill most weak Tier Four beings, and she's capable of spawning adaptive warriors to counter attacks she witnesses personally or through the hive mind. If it were not for the Aetherflame and Netherflame in your soul, your task would have been much more arduous."

"Wait, they do that? What else do they do?" It was news to Aetheria, although Werylin had mentioned she was resistant to possession.

"The Flames are not part of your path. They represent part of your anima, your soul, and rise from the irrational depths. A true master of at least seventh tier can impart sparks of their own Flames onto others, but if the Flame and soul do not align, then the results can be explosive." Azrael chuckled, no doubt imagining Cultivators exploding.

"How does that protect my mind?"

"Your Flames are of Aether, Divinity, and Nether, Dark Divinity. You may be human, but you have a leg up on the quest for immortality that Cultivators seek."

"Still don't see how Divine Flames make me immune to mind attacks."

Azrael guffawed mightily, almost knocking her over.

"Flames only form when someone reaches the height of affinity with an element. Your affinity with Aether cannot increase any further, and your Nether affinity is close behind. The Flames are like a second well of power to draw from—a magical font all your own. They suffuse your being with beneficial boons to boot. Strength, speed, easier control of using related element physiology, increased passive energy accumulation, and so on.

"You'll only know what boons you're getting through experimentation. As you've noticed, we StarManes communicate telepathically. Your mind was closed to us, so we knew you wouldn't have issues with the queen."

Well, that explains why that felt easy. The queen couldn't use any of her actual power on me. Now I feel like an asshole, but better a winning asshole than getting brain-melted.

"Any other good advice for a newbie?"

"You're on the cusp of Tier Two. With both Flames lit and your Nether purifying with each gathering, you are in a sound position. Already, you are alternating between powers or using them simultaneously, and the second tier of the Ethereal Path is to bridge Aether and Nether. On some paths, the second tier is long, and on some it is short. On the Ethereal Path, it is short. One milestone to reach Tier Three: connect the two powers into the Ethereal power."

"Short, but difficult? I'm still just learning them, and I've only just lit the Netherflame."

"Every floor of the Tower of Aetherius is a training ground for those like you, Aetheria. You just have to make sure you find the lesson before you leave the level."

"I'm seeing why you StarManes are in hiding."

"It is a heavy burden to bear the love of Chronos more than all other races. Beauty, immortality, vast cosmic power, the ability to eat delicious planets..."

"Delicious planets?"

"Grandpa always said so."

Chronos really must be a drunk if he dreamed of cats who can eat worlds into existence. Or mixed cats and dragons to begin with. Gee, let's take the two most arrogant races and just smash them together, and if they live long enough, they can eat planets. I hope there's a better creation myth on the next floor—this one sucks.

CHAPTER 29

Gleaming the (Ice) Cube

The requirement for the next floor to open took three days. Apparently, the formalization of the bond between Aetheria and Arkaziel was the trigger. Ten minutes after the ceremony conducted by Azrael and Shal concluded, and she and Ark found one another psychically, Aetheria felt the ability to summon the door to the next floor. She spent a final day trading with the StarManes for odds and ends. Azrael was keen on the surplus of ham sandwiches she'd gotten from Zaira, so she traded ten of them for a large shadow core.

All of their other trades were food-related. Azrael was quite the gourmand, and the tower allowed him to wander across several floors to sate his appetites.

I can see why Aetherius offered them sanctuary. They aren't a bad lot, just cats... who are dragons... who grow up to eat planets. Better for everyone if they stay in the tower. Ugh, am I going to have problems with this lazy schmuck around my neck?

Day 1

Aetheria and Ark materialized in the middle of a massive colosseum. The seats were empty, minus a few cardboard cutouts of people sporadically placed. The floor of the colosseum was sand, and next to a five-meter-square block of aetheric ice was a tiny house.

"Welcome to Floor Eight, a contest of wills, a battle of brawn, a timed trial sure to make you quake in your boots. Can you place yourself on the leaderboard? Top one hundred get a prize, top ten get a boon! You've pushed levers, you've dallied with masters, you met a cat, but now... the greatest challenge of all awaits you here, in ICE OFF. I'm your friendly neighborhood Tower Administrator, and you, my dear, are on my radar. Let's go over the rules!" The shock jock cadence was perfect, if perfect meant taking the unbearable level to 11/10. Aetheria immediately imagined this Tower Administrator as a bored man in a control booth eating cheese puffs, and she couldn't hold back an eye roll.

"RULE NUMBER ONE: THERE ARE NO RULES. Seriously, there aren't. Your aim, if you can manage, is to destroy the block of ice and prevent it from reforming. You have a hundred years! If you can't do it by then, we'll boot you out of the tower, and you get to restart. BUT FIRST, let's look at the top times."

A leaderboard materialized, mounted on poles. The first screen came up with names in red. Familiar names, quickly scrolling across, then vanishing. Aetherius: 1 minute. Nyx: 1 minute, 4 seconds. Erebus: 1 minute, 5 seconds.

"No one cares about those dodgy old Primordials! No, what we need here is the other list!"

The text shifted and alternative names appeared.

Odin: 1 year, 3 days
Zeus: 1 year, 5 days
Ra: 1 year, 10 days
Shiva: 1 year, 78 days
Quetzalcoatl: 1 year, 83 days
Anu: 1 year, 98 days

As the names continued scrolling, Aetheria recognized the thirty-seventh. Aoibhe. It wasn't at all disconcerting that the list seemed to be made up entirely of gods, angels, or nephilim. Not at all. *Ugh, this one's going to be hard. Not follow basic instructions while being mocked by the cheap shock jock knockoff difficult, but a make rocks levitate with your brain level of challenging, isn't it?*

Arkaziel lifted his head to look at the challenge before them, snorted, and flew off toward the tiny house.

"Don't get my pillow full of fur!"

"Look at the utter confidence her companion has in her, abandoning her to face this trial alone, while he sleeps in comfort," boomed the Tower Administrator. "That's one hell of a bond, isn't it? Say what you will about StarManes, but one thing people never say is they aren't dicks.

"Now, then, it's the main event time. On your mark. Get set. GO!"

A new screen appeared above the leaderboard. A countdown display. It hit ten seconds before Aetheria quit staring at it.

The block of ice was green-hued and emitted a shocking level of chill. Tapping it with her knuckles felt like she was touching metal, not ice. With a shrug, Aetheria gave herself some room and started her trial and error with a punch. Full velocity, maximum density, and a few tons of extra mass. When her fist hit the ice, it was the ice that gave way, but barely. Hairline fractures ran out from her blow, and chunks of ice fell off, but the damage was minimal.

Cripes! If I hadn't added mass and density, that would've broken my hand. How do I make ice like this?

As she prepared for her next attempt, the hairline fractures merged, and the damage she had caused filled back in.

Frick!

"Oooh, she's noticed it regenerates! Look at that face. The last time I saw such a sour expression was when Dionysus mixed a cocktail with fifteen mega-lemons."

Ignore him. Ignore him. His terrible commentary is part of the trial, right? To make me get worked up, angry, forget what I'm supposed to be focused on, and miss something obvious. If punching doesn't work, let's try burning.

Aetheria inhaled deeply and blew out blue flames over the hunk of ice. The ice deformed, but she'd barely melted a foot when she needed to stop to actually breathe. By the time she regained her breath, the ice had melded back to normal.

"Wow, what lung capacity. Maybe you should work on your blowing, Princess." Aetheria flipped off the sky.

Okay, so fire breath doesn't have the oomph. Sticky fire.

She conjured a ball of black fire in her hand and let it grow until it was the size of a beach ball. Casually, she tossed the Netherflame onto the cube of ice, and then frowned. The Netherflame wasn't melting the ice. In fact, the ice was putting her Netherflame out.

"Oh, you just hate to see it, sports fans. Looks like Sparkle Princess can't create an intense enough Netherflame to even damage the ice!"

Yep. He's definitely part of the trial. Doesn't make me hate him any less.

Day 4

"Oh, another loss for Team Shiny Hair. Will she mope with her cat? No, she's trying again!"

"Oh, bite me," Aetheria growled between her teeth, before shifting her focus to her newest attempt. "Fire Tornado!"

A massive vortex of wind spawned over the ice cube, a golden-green sun of flame forming in its center. The orb exploded, and the tornado became a mass of churning aetheric air and fire that worked to grind down the ice cube. It burned off a meter of ice before the block's regeneration outpaced incoming damage. Slowly, the tornado's energy dwindled, until it burned itself out of existence.

"Clearly, our heroine has been to the planet Araiy, where aetheric tornadoes frequently catch fire elementals and become unstoppable natural disasters. No? Well, I was trying to explain why she might try such a stupid idea, but I guess we're just back to her being an idiot."

Hssssss. Aetheria could feel the annoyance and anger projected by Arkaziel. Each day, their bond grew.

Day 65

The bed in the tiny house was comfortable, but it was lonely. Even with Arkaziel to cuddle every night, not having anyone to talk to was wearing on Aetheria. The StarMane looked at her with intelligence, as if he understood everything she said, but she never got a reply from the cat-dragon. The emotional connection between them had bloomed, though, and they could share their emotions in a rudimentary form of communication.

Aetheria's next plan for the ice cube was to try a physical blow to embed her hand in the cube, launch Aetherflame, and then create aetheric ice to block regeneration.

Day 93

The fridge in the tiny house served her and Ark fried chicken and mashed potatoes and gravy. Both ate multiple servings and slept in until noon before they approached the ice.

"Alright, on three: one, two... *three*." Aetheria leaped into the air before altering herself to have every bit of density and every bit of mass she could generate from Aether energy. Arkaziel unleashed his light and darkness energy beam at the center of the top side of the cube. The coruscating beam hit like a heat ray melting normal ice, creating a meter-deep hollow in the top. Falling from above, Aetheria aimed herself at the depression in the ice. Before impact, her entire aura turned into flames, and she collided like a meteor into the cube.

Massive fractures crisscrossed the whole cube. Arkaziel and Aetheria had destroyed half the ice, although neither felt overjoyed. Arkaziel flopped over on the sand, panting and spent. Aetheria crawled away from the cube as her regeneration repaired her body after the brutal impact.

"Uffda, Arky, we need a better strategy."

"No words were truer than those spoken by babies. Maybe this Challenger peaked at level five? She's got moxie, but does she have the strength, the willpower, the unbridled need to conquer to make it past this challenge?"

"Hey, can we get more fried chicken?"

Day 130

Aetheria sat before the massive cube on a platform made of her own aetheric ice. Eyes closed in meditation, she visualized the ice cube losing its binding strength. Over the last two weeks, she had discovered there were actually glyphs of the Ath language inside the ice. Undoubtedly, they controlled the regeneration of the cube or provided the energy distribution that allowed the cube to operate.

My finger is the quill. Aether is the ink. Smudge the crossing, add a slash, glyph becomes one for renumeration instead of regeneration. Numbers won't save you, stupid ice!

Aetheria willed her imagined changes to the glyph to take hold inside the ice. One glyph changed before an outside pressure restored it to normal.

"Aww, it's so sad when they try so hard, but are just too dumb to figure it out." The Tower Administrator's laughter filled her ears. The jerk hadn't given them any more fried chicken, either. Instead, every day had offered a new type of broiled who-knew-what that even Arkaziel was hesitant to eat. Her stash of sandwiches from Zaira was getting perilously low, but she still had other provisions to last for at least a year. Provisions that tasted like sadness and regret.

Day 185

Aetheria stared at the ice. She compared the block to her Aetherflame.

Azrael said the Aetherflame is a font of power. My Aetherflame Nova disrupts other energies. If it stores other energies for my use... can it just eat other energy sources? Like the glyphs powering the cube?

She imagined her Aetherflame forming inside the cube of ice, sucking all the energy from the construct the way Arkaziel sucked down beef jerky, and then... shattering it with a punch?

"Oh, what have we here?" The Administrator sounded *interested*.

A replica of the green-blue flame inside her mind appeared inside the cube. The flame glowed brighter, brighter, as it consumed all the energy inside the cube. Each pulse of light saw the ice look subtly different. With a hysterical laugh, Aetheria stood up and kicked the massive cube of ice.

It shattered.

Pieces began to liquify and try to flow back together, and she focused on strengthening the voracious hunger of her Aetherflame. All movement stopped.

"And she's done it! Victory! At six months, Aetheria is our new first-place winner. *If* you can call that winning, using a filthy Primordial Technique to win on the normal ladder. Unfortunately, it counts, but knows deep shame. The lowest time on the Primordial board is four days." *All he's missing is an annoyed harrumph.*

"Make your choice, Sparkle Girl."

A list of options appeared in her mind. She chose the seventh. The Administrator didn't comment on her cackling like a madwoman as she chose. He had the last laugh: his announcer booth appeared on the arena floor to reveal a man eating fried chicken. They stared flatly at one another. The Administrator smiled.

Aetheria triggered the door to Floor 9.

CHAPTER 30

There Can Be Only One

When Aetheria chose her boon, the black fingerless gloves she wore glowed as Ethereal power flowed into them from out of nowhere. A flash of knowledge filled her mind, a brief tale.

Once there was a monk named Zhang. Zhang loved to drink, but the drink did not love him. Whenever the monk enjoyed himself, he would become violent and lay waste to his surroundings with poorly controlled power. The Order warned Zhang that if he did not control his misdeeds, they would banish him, as behavior such as this was not becoming of a monk.

Zhang got drunk and died in a duel with the master of the temple. Even his unparalleled destruction when drunk was no match for the precision and wisdom of the ancient monk. While the name Zhang lives on, we lost the temple master's name to time. These gloves are now enchanted with that ancient, unnamed master's power.

Aetheria blew raspberries at the sky, annoyed that there was no description of what the new magic did. Like she wasn't going to choose an option with such a ridiculous name? Punch Drunk Punchers. *Although they were kind of all like that. Whatever.*

She and Arkaziel stepped through the door to Floor 9 after looting everything in the tiny house. Maybe she was being petty, but she even took roughly a ton of sand. Someday she'd need a sandstorm, right?

Aetheria and Arkaziel appeared on a small island surrounded by a lake on three sides. The fourth side was cliffs and waterfalls. Settled back against the cliff was a massive statue of a woman. *That looks like it's straight out of ancient Rome.*

The platform on which the statue stood was simple, with an epitaph etched in the stone: *She wished... to be forgotten...*

Fish jumped in and out of the lake, and Arkaziel's tail started batting at her back.

"Yep. Go eat, you stomach on wings. I'll do the Climber's work while you stuff your belly. Save me a fish." The StarMane purred and nuzzled her neck with his cheek before flying off after the tasty fish.

"That's quite the companion you've got there."

The words were so soft, Aetheria almost missed them. The spectral form of the woman depicted in the statue stood before her. It was hard to make out her features, as she flickered and faded at random and made no effort to step closer. *Maybe it's just hard to see a ghost in the daylight?*

"Thanks. We're still getting acquainted. Who might you be?"

"No one. Once I was someone."

"That's exceptionally cryptic. Well, my name is Aetheria. Nice to meet you, spirit."

The ghost's spectral face had reacted to her name. Surprise, shock, and then a fleeting smile.

"Who named you after a goddess, human?"

"Aetherius."

"Of course. It would be Dad, wouldn't it? Since you're human, have that name, and... oh my. I see. Well, then, Aetheria, it's nice to meet you. Sailors across all of Grief loved Aetheria, Goddess of Water and Storm."

Awkward. Naming your chosen one after a deceased daughter? REALLY, Aetherius?

"Why do you want to be forgotten, Aetheria?"

"Why don't more people wish to be forgotten? For gods, death is not the end, just a setback. Only when our followers have forgotten us are we truly able to die. For those who fight their fate, even that might not be enough."

"Why are you seeking finality?"

"Gods are the playthings of chance as much as anyone else. Oizys saw my popularity in her world as an insult and led my path into misfortune. I fell in love with a demigod hero raised as a Challenger by Helios. We wed after he conquered his third tower. He died on his way to the fourth. A demigod killed by a fall from a horse." The laughter that followed the words was bitter.

"So, brought low by love?"

"No. That was the start. My fallen husband arose anew, opting to become a servant of Death rather than be reborn. Since I am the goddess of love, storms, and water, we were now antithetical to one another, and in time the wretch became one of Oizys's playthings. Her cruelty only made the mortals cry and identify ever more with me, for they tasted her depredations daily."

"Minor victories in karma."

"Very minor. Somehow, Oizys corrupted one of my high priests. As my clergy withered from within, as they worked my powers and miracles with ever-growing malice and self-aggrandizing purposes, who I am came under assault. A hero arose, as heroes are wont to do. A mighty paladin cleansed the church of the corruption, and all was well in the world of Grief."

"I know sarcasm when I hear it. What actually happened?"

"The paladin killed the high priest and took his place. I descended as an avatar to bless my new high priest in person."

Aetheria grimaced at the coldness in the spirit's voice. The pain showed clearly what came next.

"As I blessed his rise, he stabbed me with a cursed dagger. Aetherius was furious and secreted me away to be healed. So filled with hate, malice, and unbridled jealousy was the curse, it took almost five hundred years for me to heal."

"You survived a cursed ambush and went back for more?"

"Yes. The people didn't deserve Oizys's attentions any more than I did. Someone destroyed my temples and blacklisted my name in my absence. So I conjured my Challenger. Somehow, my chosen one reignited my name, spread my name far and wide, and rekindled hope briefly on Grief. After he cleared his fifth tower, he stumbled across a demon spawn who ensnared his heart. The fool gave the succubus the amulet that protected him from mental tampering and the touch of the gods. For his stupidity, he died underneath her, and his doppelgänger undid all the work he'd done. My little paladin's name became that of a slaver, a master of war crimes, a force worse than those of Oizys's minor cruelties, and my name was blacklisted yet again."

"Did you give up, then?"

"I did, but that wasn't enough. I attempted to reclaim the soul of my paladin from the succubus and found myself the target of a band of godkillers fresh from Oizys's tower. I killed nearly all of them, but close wasn't good enough. The godkillers had a rare path on the Winding Way. They called him a solipsist, and he infected me with ennui that neither Father nor faith could overcome. My name was, of course, raised after my second death on Grief. They worship me as Goddess of Violent Storms there, a corrupted title, but with enough truth to bind me to this curse of existence still."

"Ouch. What a bitch."

"Indeed. Father built this tomb for me. Isolated in the tower, my essence slowly dissipates despite the threads of faith from Grief. Yet without a kind hand, even here I will linger for millennia more."

"So you want me to kill you? How would I do that, when even a big-time god couldn't?"

"You could feast upon me using your Flames. The Aetherflame could devour my divinity, while your Netherflame could devour the corruption and darkness forced on me by Oizys."

"You want me to *eat...*"

"Yes."

"So, that'd be the humane thing to do. Let you have your end and peace. Or I could displace Oizys, resurrect your faith, and let you flourish as the Goddess of Water and Storm again."

"Won't work. It will pull me back into my own fallen tower the moment I leave Dad's tower, and guess who waits there for me?"

"Had to pitch it." Aetheria stared at her namesake. It was a shame.

"What happens when a god dies?"

"Ultimately, a new one arises. Either a new version of the dead god or a new god entirely, or a Cultivator ascends to godhood. Sometimes the god's domains are just transferred to another god. We poorly understood the mechanics. Not a lot of gods die, or we wouldn't be gods."

"Why can my Aether and Nether Flames kill you? The StarManes didn't act too impressed by my Aetherflame."

The ghost goddess laughed so hard she couldn't talk for a couple of minutes. *"You realize StarManes are one of only three species more arrogant than gods, right?"*

Aetheria couldn't contain the sigh. "Okay, so... could you educate me on what the Aetherflame and Netherflame actually are?"

"Flames are perhaps not rare. When someone has achieved the highest level of affinity and the seventh level of their path, they can create these. They are exceptionally rare at your stage, but that is not what makes yours powerful. You have the Flames of Primordials, Aetheria. Within you now burns the life force of two of the Eldest. That is what will let you kill a god."

"Wait, two? Aetherius..." Aetheria frowned. She had heard a disembodied woman's voice twice.

"If I had to guess, Aetherius and Nyx. Your Netherflame is still rough and unfinished, but the closer to crystallization you get it, the more you'll find my guess to be true. Do you even know how to use Nether?"

"Uh, only a little. Self-taught there. I've figured out a death aura, the Netherflame, an—"

The ghost laughed again. *"Oh, sweetheart. Nether Fire isn't going to be much good for you. The properties of your Netherflame match Nyx. Cold would be your best elemental match for your Nether, or use pure Nether subspecialties like Darkness or Undeath. You'll have much better luck that way."*

"Oh. Well, thanks. I just had some failures with Nether Fire, so maybe that's why... What's my Aetherflame lean toward?"

"Ice is your strongest affinity by far. When you cross the bridge to Ethereal power, Ice will remain your best affinity."

"How does that work? I have the Aether and Nether Flames, and Ice is still my highest affinity?"

"Luckily, you're working with a path that can use any affinity to manifest itself, don't you think? Ethereal Ice is a rare path, especially for a brawler like yourself."

"You can sense all of my affinities? Could you tell me what they are?"

"That depends. Can we come to an accord? I help you, and you help me get what I want?"

"Other than undead, I haven't killed any sentient people yet. Go figure that the first one will be a good person. Way to lie down the mental anguish, ya know?"

"We have an accord, then?"

"Yeah, you betcha." Aetheria wasn't thrilled about it, but she agreed.

"Well, then. Your highest elemental affinity is Ice, followed by Fire, then Earth, and lastly Wind. Clearly, your Nether and Aether affinities are exceptionally high, but it does not incline you to sub-affinities such as Time. You are exceptionally young, though, and you can gain and improve affinities. Not that it matters. Once you have reached the third tier of Ethereal cultivation, Ice alone will be more than enough."

"That tracks with what the masters in Solace said. They didn't warn me about Fire and Nether, but my Netherflame hadn't manifested yet."

"I can teach you a thing or two about Water and Ice. Ironic that Aetherius and Hemera would produce a sea goddess, isn't it?" The goddess's sociability had increased with the promise of her greatest wish secured. *"I'll even pass my Flame on to you, child."*

"Hemera is Day, right? How does that even work? Day and Sky make Water? You mentioned Storms, too, right? I could see a path through weather to Water. Who am I kidding? I don't get it." Aetheria laughed. *The gods are Crazy. Capital C.*

"Awesome. I could really use some teaching. Will extra Flames hurt my path? I have to admit, I'm still a little iffy about the concept behind them. Are all Aetherflames the same, then? Ice? How did you know my Netherflame matched Nyx? Is that something you can teach me?"

CHAPTER 31

We Didn't Start the Fire... Promise.

The ghost goddess regarded her namesake with amusement.

"That's where you want to start? Flames represent the pinnacle of affinity, but naturally, they only form in those of great power. What most people don't know is there are three types of Flames: Mortal, Godly, and Primordial. Once formed, you cannot change the nature of your Flame without extinguishing and reforming it."

"Okay. Three Flames. With names like those for classifications, I'm guessing power and abilities vary a lot?"

"Astute guess. The weakest of the Flames are Mortal, but they have wider proficiency. Your Nether Fire attempts would work just fine if you had a Mortal Flame, but you have a Primordial Flame, the Flame of Nyx. Nyx is Night. Fire is anathema. If you had the Godly Flame of Hades, you would have no problem using both Nether Fire and Ice but couldn't touch light or life, while the Mortal could. Primordial Strength comes with a smattering of limitations. Said limitations do nothing to truly limit their power, though."

"So if Aetherius is the god of Aether and the sky, shouldn't I have a way better affinity with Air?"

"Aetherius is a Primordial, little girl! He isn't the god of Aether, he is Aether. The cold high sky, the bright shining light, the promise of the Ethereal. Even for the lowest of the low, the diluted light of his glory becomes mana to nourish them."

"Guess that'll teach me to make assumptions based on what he was a god of in my world's mythology, or in the game I used to play. So, Ice will work well until I can pick up Light?"

"Yes. Ice 'will work.' It has excellent synergy with both Aetherius and Nyx, and you can continue that strength onward when you manipulate the Ethereal. You don't need light or dark—unless you want to have them?"

"Um. Do you know many people who say, 'No, no, I don't want to manipulate even more awesome powers'? I don't. I know greed is a sin and all, but knowledge is awesome and I'll chase as much as I can."

"Throughout time, there have been many who have eschewed knowledge for the sake of dedication to a singular ideal. Masters of one specialty. Hardly a worthwhile path for those who are free from the ravages of time."

"So where do we start with Ice?"

"Show me what you can do with Ice, and then we'll go from there."

Day 4

Aetheria, Arkaziel, and the ghost goddess had fallen into a schedule. The StarMane spent his day fishing, gorging himself, and bringing a few choice catches back to camp for Aetheria to cook. The cat-dragon demanded half of what she cooked, too. The pair slept in a small tent she had purchased back in Solace, with a proper bed pulled from her soul repository. The lake provided food, bathing, and practice with ice and water.

I never thought I'd be doing the whole 'sitting topless under a waterfall' training montage. Aetheria sat on a ledge of solid aetheric ice she had molded in the waterfall above the tomb, before it split in two. The water fell with the rage of white water rapids but subtly flowed around her. Her wet hair and the beaded moisture on her skin showed she had failed in deflecting water the whole time, though.

"Your control is pathetic by the standards of gods, but for a novice, you aren't doing that badly. Without a domain to enforce your will further, contact control is the most efficient way of training your powers. Unfortunately, you won't be able to erect a domain until you cross the threshold into the next tier, so let us do that now."

"Now? I'm ready?"

"The Guardian I summoned yesterday provided you with more than enough Nether to crystallize the Primordial Flame of Nyx."

"How do people normally cross to the second tier without Flames?"

"By spending thousands of years working toward creating a successful method of using Ethereal energy, unless they were born into a race that has an innate connection to the Ethereal, such as your lover. A normal mortal would have to have a fortuitous encounter that let them touch the Ethereal, then maintain it."

"Okay, so count myself lucky I get to cheat. Guess that's why the Administrator acted like the Flame was a cheat."

"He's just jealous. Admins are usually demigods or minor gods working off a debt to higher beings. Recall what I said about Flames being set in their rank? A Divine Flame cannot become a Primordial Flame."

"Great. Fantastic. Wonderful. I always wanted to have gods jealous of me, but it was supposed to be for my acerbic wit."

"Enough dawdling. Let the waterfall hit you. Feel the cold water. Focus on it flowing past you. Let your Aether and Nether Flames flow past you. Imagine them flowing in a sphere of water, orbiting one another. Does the Nether chase the Aether, or does Aether chase Nether? Do they move equal, opposite, or neither?"

Aetheria focused on the words and instructions. Imagining as instructed, a large sphere of water held two bouncing Flames within it. "They both chase. Aether retreats when it almost catches Nether, then Nether goes on the hunt until Aether loses it and hunts again. Each iteration is different, but the same."

"That's because they are the same. Half of a whole. The separation of the Ethereal into powers that we can more safely wield without breaking reality. Aether and Nether are not opposites; they are complementary. They need each other, just as Darkness and Light only have meaning with the other. When they fit together, you come to the Origination of Power. Can you put them together?"

Aetheria wanted to snort and say something about how if it were that simple she wouldn't need a teacher. Yet she recalled how easy some past things were, in theory. Just breathing energy in had actually been a basic version of how to cultivate. There was a reason the ghost had her imagine the sphere of water. If it weren't important, she could have said a glass bottle, or a hot-air balloon, or plenty of other things.

Freeze. Forcefully, Aetheria willed the two energies' movements to fall into their natural inclinations of repulsion and attraction. Aether and Nether created their own replica of a swirling yin yang within the water sphere. The water allowed her to freeze some of the essence of each in physical place. It didn't make sense; it was all imagination and will, but the two energies merged under her control. The final catalyst came from a spark of the Flame of Aetherius. Aqua-green Aether and black-purple Nether merged and flourished into a crimson energy. Her mind exploded with wave after wave of red energy, and an awareness hit her and pulled her down through a hole in space-time.

Aetheria was in a place of pure energy. Pure Ethereal energy. She floated through it like a dozing kid in an inner tube on a lazy river. Gradually, she sensed a massive and powerful presence floating toward her, much faster than she could move in this strange, quasi-solid energy.

"A human?" Surprise filled the feminine voice.

Aetheria beheld a cosmic beauty. For a fraction of a second, anyway, before it changed. It changed again and again as she perceived it. It was headache-inducing to watch.

"Wow, can you maybe not do that changing thing? I'm going to puke."

"Probably. What's in it for me?"

"I'll be your friend?"

"Interesting proposition. Better offer than most make." The shifting stopped, and a large eyeball stared at her. Not a Beholder-type eye, just one giant eyeball. It blinked when it talked.

"Thank you. So, where is this?"

"Part of the Origin."

"Who are you?"

"Some call me the Gatekeeper. You may call me Themis, daughter of Gaia and Aetherius."

"Do all who try to reach the Ethereal meet you then, Themis?"

"Of course. To reach any great heights, one must pass trials. I am the Judge. Ethereal power has no inclination to good or evil. It is the culmination of Aether and Nether, Order and Chaos. To climb the heights and wield such power, one must be *worthy*."

Don't panic, I'm sure minor shoplifting from the Tower Administrator doesn't count against me.

Themis changed from eyeball to human woman. Her light brown hair was pinned away from her face. Simple white robes flowed around her figure, tugged this way and that by the Ethereal ocean.

"What would you do with this power, human?" Suddenly, Themis had a sword in her right hand, scales in the left. All she lacked was a blindfold.

"I promised to take on ten towers and rebalance the world of Grief. So, climbing towers is definitely on the docket. After that, well, skipping across worlds with my girlfriend is the only other long-term plan I have."

Silence reigned for a time.

"You will not build a sect? An empire? No dynasty?"

"What? Oh, heck, no. That all sounds terrible. I want to see things, get caught up in adventures, maybe right some wrongs. Corny, I know, since I'm sure most people who get here have a driving ambition to be the best, and... well, you know, I kind of have that, too. I want to be a powerful person, but I don't want it for the sake of lording over people. I want to make the places I see a little better than they were when I found them.

"Of course, if that means using that power to kick ass, I'm pretty happy to do it. I'm kind of coming to enjoy being a badass brawler, if we're being totally honest."

Themis smirked.

"You may cross the bridge, Aetheria Etherfrost."

"Title, last name, or...?"

Before Themis offered an answer, if she was even going to, a current of power picked up Aetheria and pulled her through the unlimited Ethereal energies, back through to reality, and to the waterfall where she apparently still sat topless in the cold froth of water.

The ghost was waiting. *"Congratulations. We should get you back to your tent before the feedback kicks in. You've got maybe three minutes."*

"That's it? I'm now an Ethereal Bridge?" The rank names seemed quite literal for this version of the Ethereal Path. Gathering was rank one, Bridge was rank two. Grasper was rank three. *If I understand things right, I'll hit rank three when I can pull Ethereal energy from that deep ocean, instead of bridging my Aether and Nether together to make Ethereal energy.*

"What do you mean, 'feedback?'"

"Hurry, you fool! To your tent!"

Aetheria burst out of the waterfall like a shot, lightening her density and conjuring pillars of ice from the ground to provide a safe landing. She landed next to the tent and ran inside; the pillars of ice crumbled on their own.

Was Aetheria just pulling my leg? I should have asked her about the title name thi—

She screamed as pain wracked her body. Red energy, Ethereal energy, ripped at her skin, broke her fingers, pulverized her knee, and exploded an eye. The pain delivery man had once again run Aetheria over with his big honking truck, and this time he brought an entire fleet of friends to run her over too, one after another.

Arkaziel burst through the tent to protect his friend, though there was no one to protect her from. With no enemies to fight, all the StarMane could do was support Aetheria through their psychic bond.

"Better not die yet, human. You just transitioned to a rank where talking to you won't bring me dishonor."

At the tomb, the ghost reflected on the events of the day.

"This is exactly the reason most informed sentient beings hate StarManes."

CHAPTER 32

Tier Two

To advance to rank two is to be reforged. The first rank is still within the bounds of innate and mundane physiology. When you bridge the gap to the power of the Ethereal, it will pulverize your body into a fine paste and remake you into something different. Aetherius himself fashioned your new form, so what kind of reaction stepping into the higher tiers will have on you is difficult to predict. My wings were originally much smaller, and black. Not the only change I've endured walking the Winding Way."

The alien power of the Ethereal ravaged Aetheria's body as Aoibhe's lecture came back to her. Cell after cell fell under the attention of the esoteric power. Destruction was not the only outcome: replication and evolution also occurred.

"The first evolution in most paths is brutal to those who come from races not already aligned with the path they walk. There is a race of aquatic elves who barely even change in evolution if they follow the Path of Water The Ethereal is a path of great pain. Embrace the pain, let it reforge you, but do not give it full control. You are the master: prove that you will be the one to control it, and your future tier-ups will be smoother."

Aoibhe's lesson on what to do in this situation provided Aetheria with a life raft to cling to. The blond's voice echoing in her mind was a focal point, a guide to navigate the maze of pain. Arkaziel's mental reassurance lead her back to reality like a beacon.

She ignored the pain. She ignored the pain all the time. It was something she had become exceptionally good at since her rebirth. She had lost limbs, endured stabbing and impalement, had acid thrown on her, tasted death auras, and more. In every scenario, she had ultimately been the master of her pain. Aetheria still was prone to reaction to grievous wounds, but once she got past the shock, she usually had no problem mastering her pain.

But this was different. The Ethereal power's endless cycle of sub-atomic alteration gave no time for relief, no chance to recover or rally. The Ethereal power ignited a chain reaction inside of her. Domino after domino placed by Aetherius fell, triggering the next.

Aetheria doubled down to manage the pain. Aetherius was not in control of her transition, nor was Themis, or whoever, controlling the evolution process.

The master of my body is me. I am a walker of the Ethereal Path. I am Aetheria, and you will answer to me.

On Earth, such thoughts would have been a mere pep talk. When she had lived on Earth, she did not have the powers of Aether, Nether, or the Ethereal. She had no powers. Now, however, she had all three. Power combined with intent could move mountains.

Aetheria stood and took control of her body, even as her hair fluttered between red, purple, aqua, and white.

"My hair is aqua." Her hair was, in fact, aqua.

"Your eyes are red now," Arkaziel told her. He floated lazily in the air, watching her warily.

"My eyes are red now," Aetheria agreed. She scowled at the StarMane.

"I uh... learned to talk? It's a miracle!"

Aetheria and Arkaziel stared flatly at one another until they both just laughed.

"You okay, Ria?"

"Yeah, Ark. I'm okay. You're a massive dick for not talking to me just because I was Tier One."

"It's a terrible thing to disrespect the cultural traditions of other species, Ria."

"My cultural tradition is to squirt cats in the face when they're assholes."

"You wouldn't!"

"I would. I'm stable now. Go get some more fish for dinner. I'm hungry." A sandwich appeared in her hand from her soul repository.

Alone again, Aetheria looked at the black fingerless gloves on her hands. She imagined her hands becoming claws. Her fingers elongated; her nails turned into claws.

"Well, Ascyn was right." Her hand became human again.

"Gaining your Ethereal physiology is a painful thing. You handled it with more grace than most." The ghost of the goddess didn't even knock. Not that the tent flap had a door to knock on.

"Yeah. So, I guess that was a success. What's next?"

"You take my Flame, kill me, conquer this tower, and then nine more. When you climb the top of the tenth tower and depose Oizys from Grief, kick her in the ass for me, and kill the shell of my lost love."

"So, no more lessons?"

"I'll give you ten days after I impart my Flame. After that, you'll need to learn the rest for yourself."

"Thank you." For someone who just wanted to be forgotten, the ghost goddess was more accommodating than Aetheria had expected, which was that she would demand an end to things immediately.

"So, what is your Flame, anyway?"

"The Primordial Flame of Thalassa."

"I thought your name was Aetheria?"

"One of my names was Aetheria."

"Right... Well. Let's get on with this."

It turned out receiving Primordial Flames was a painful process.

Why wouldn't it be?

Day 14

Aetheria bowed to the ghost.

"So, how is this going to work? I push my Flames out, you go *poof*?"

"Essentially. When my Essence dissipates, this floor of the tower will crumble. Exit quickly."

"Explains why you said to pack the tent up. Alright, Arkaziel, you ready to exit stage left when this goes down?"

"Wait, why do I have to help? You're the one who got training and a shiny new Flame. All I got was a lot of fish."

"Which I am storing in my soul repository for you."

The StarMane snorted. "Never trust a banker."

Aetheria couldn't disagree with the sentiment.

"Let's do this, then. Thanks for everything, Thalassa. Time to murder you."

"Thank you, friend."

Aetheria manifested four sets of the Primordial Flame of Aetherius and the Primordial Flame of Nyx, then gave them a mental shove so they circled the ghost of Thalassa.

"If your parents or anyone else have any last words, they should say them now."

"I've already shared my goodbyes." A tear was noticeable on the ghost's cheek.

"Rest, Aetheria, and be forgotten."

The Aetherflame flared to life first, creating a vortex of green-blue light as it consumed the divinity of the Primordial goddess. Simultaneously, the black and purple Netherflames ignited and consumed the corruption Oizys had forced upon Thalassa. With almost no resistance offered by Thalassa, the process went quickly. The draining Flames feasted, and the ghost became less visible by the second. At last, nothing remained of the goddess. The floor shook and its reality began to crack.

Near Aetheria and Arkaziel, the door opened, and they jumped through to the tenth floor.

Aetheria and Arkaziel emerged in a room with hundreds of unlit candles. Only she and the cat-dragon gave off any light. Well, and the massive energies of the departed Thalassa still cycling through Aetheria and lighting the room like a miniature sun.

"Why if it isn't our Sparkle Princess, fresh from cannibalizing a ghost for a third Flame? When they write your biography, I'm sure that's going to come across well— not at all villainous."

Aetheria ignored the Administrator and wiped the moisture from her cheeks. That bag of hot air could say whatever he wanted while she calmed her emotions.

Killing someone was new to her, and the energies coursing inside her made it worse. The amount of power she had drawn from the ghost of the goddess had been far greater than what she'd imagined a mere ghost could contain.

She directed the coursing power into her newest Flame, the still-growing Flame of Thalassa. The Flames of Nyx and Aetherius had both crystallized into a firmness that was their limitation at Tier One. Now that she was in the second tier, both could take more energy, but her newest Flame wasn't even at the Gathering tier cap yet. In her mind, the Flame of Thalassa was a pale blue, so light it was nearly white. Torrents of energy flowed to the Flame, its radiance burned brighter by the second. The intensity of its light filled her mind with a cold yet soothing sense of calmness.

The pale blue flame grew more and more intense until it crystallized, the sign of it crossing into Tier Two. Aetheria pushed the energy coursing inside her into the Flames simultaneously. All three crystalline Flames burst with heightened intensity and greedily feasted on every drop of energy, and when they had consumed everything, they ravenously yearned for more. She blocked their flow with an iron will.

"Look at that. The human has finished her Primordial Goddess dinner. What some of us wouldn't give for these opportunities! Guess it pays to be a friend of Aetherius. Not that I'd ever insinuate any unfair accusations against a Challenger, especially when I'm the Administrator of the tower she's in. Nope, not me. Oh, she's narrowing her eyes and her dragon is looking for me. Stupid cat. Anyway, welcome to Floor Ten. Your task is to light every candle in that hall with Ethereal power, one at a time. If you light more than one at a time, all lit candles will go out. If you explode any portion of the room, I'll add a candelabra with fifty candles each time it happens."

Arkaziel hissed at the disembodied voice. "We get it. You're a bored asshole! Unless you've got fried chicken for us, piss off."

Aetheria patted the StarMane on the head for telling off the Administrator.

"Are you going to do this? You aren't that good at making Ethereal energy yet."

"Gee, thanks Ark. I love you, too, and have total faith in your ability to ruin a moment."

"Instead of twitching, your whole left eye just sort of expands when you're mad now. You'd better get the shapeshifting under control before we hit Floor Fifteen. I won't have you embarrassing me in a bastion of culture. Oh, I hope we get Sorlil or Nornhold for our first city. They have so much good food."

"Oh, they do? What kind of food do they have?" Aetheria ignored the candles. She was curious to see if the Administrator would get annoyed at her for wasting time.

He did not, even after ten minutes of listening to the StarMane lecture about a sandwich he'd never actually eaten. *Genetic memories seem like cheating somehow.*

"Alright. So, here we go. Ethereal Fire."

Aetheria forced tiny threads of Aether and Nether to spin above her right pointer finger. The trick she'd used to break through to the second tier was still her primary activation method for Ether. She could not yet pull it from her surroundings. She had to make it through her own Aether and Nether, and the process was far from fast. It

took her a minute to light the first candle. *The one-at-a-time rule is bullshit. Although...
he didn't say I had to light them myself.*

To test her theory, Aetheria used the candle she had lit to light another candle.
It worked. No comments from the Administrator. Not until she got halfway through
the room, and then suddenly every flame extinguished.

"Clever. Not against the letter of the rules, but against the spirit. I could let you
do that—take the simple pass to the next floor. If that's what you want, you can open
the gate now. But this is a lesson you need to learn. Learn it in safety, instead of while
getting your head cut off by an axe."

Aetheria bit her lip in annoyance. *On the one hand, I was quite clever there. But I
need the practice. Stupid, responsible decisions. I never liked adulting.*

"Screw the lessons! Go find food!" the cat-dragon purred in her ear.

"What are you, the devil? No. Here, eat a fish. I'm not taking a pity win."

"I'm not just some random mongrel to be drawn in by a fish, let me tell you."
But the StarMane feasted.

CHAPTER 33

Tedium

Days melded together without a source of sunlight or a clock to keep track. The Administrator was all too happy to chime in periodically that Aetheria was taking far too long for such a simple job. If he had any respect for her decision to properly take on the trial, it wasn't showing. In fact, he seemed to be annoyed that she was tackling the floor's challenge by the book.

He was not the only one annoyed by her decision. Arkaziel kept whining about being bored. Bored cats get destructive. If not for his sabotage, she could have finished the task three times over by now. In the last incident, her anger had spiked so severely that the StarMane had wisely decided it was nap time, and he had been snoring loudly ever since.

It was on the last stretch that she had an epiphany. Underneath a dome of aetheric ice, away from as many candles as she could be, she tried out her theory. Aetheria started by weaving tiny threads of Aether and Nether together into a very short length. She then applied a touch of both the Flame of Aetherius and the Flame of Nyx at one end. The resulting sparks created a reaction that fused the two energies together, forming Ethereal strands of power, which she then bent to her Fire affinity to create the Ether Flame.

This process was roughly five times faster than using the initial freezing method that had allowed her to reach the second tier. *If I can get the weaving faster, with practice I could probably make this almost instantaneous. It'd be really weak, though. Does time take a scale of investment of energy?*

This demanded more trials. Trials that showed she could weave thick, powerful strands just as quickly as she could thin, weak ones. The problem came in precision control, or any control, really—it was much more difficult than mastery of Aether or Nether. *I don't have an Ether Flame, no energy bonuses, and my Fire affinity is so-so. Ice really is my only option. You can't make Aetheric Ether or Nether Ether.*

Etheric fire felt comparable to trying to control normal wind, one of her not-so-great affinities. Etheric ice was not a problem to wield. The Primordial Flame of Thalassa provided her with natural enhancements enough to overcome the disadvantages of working with the unfamiliar Ether.

She finished Floor 10 in short order, without making the room explode even once.

"It's a miracle! A human completes Floor Ten in the Tower of Aetherius. Betting will pick up at the casino soon. How high will she get? Can she beat the MegaUltraSuperBoss on Floor Fourteen? Can she make it to the Behemoth on Floor Twenty-five? The halfway point is where so many Climbers fall, Floor Fifty, with its amazing, nigh-unbeatable occupant. It sounds ridiculous when you consider it took this Challenger two weeks to light a room full of candles. How sad."

The door to Floor 11 opened, and the Administrator's annoying voice chased her through into a massive botanical garden, the center of which was a fantastic fountain. The amazing work of engineering sent bursts of water into the air, where ephemeral light caught the falling water, mixed with light, and created illusions of random animals and plants.

"Welcome to Floor Eleven. Your control on the last level was embarrassing! So here's a chance to redeem yourself with something simple. Create the perfect etheric ice statue of your companion to take the prize position here, above this fountain, in Aetherius's third favorite garden. There are some requirements! First: it has to be made from Ethereal power, not using aetheric or Nether ice. Second: it must be perfect and win the approval of the subject himself, Arkaziel'aethiare'anathemal'suriksyn'asuludar'irithyl, the mighty Ethereal StarMane. Third: it must have no duration limitations! We'll reveal the last requirement when you gain the approval of the cat."

Aetheria couldn't contain her sigh even as Arkaziel's chest puffed up with pride, oblivious to the fact the Administrator was playing the cat-dragon's ego against her. *This is going to take longer than Solace did, isn't it?*

"Oh, this is so exciting, Ria! How are you going to capture my majesty? What scale do you want to use? This garden is almost adequate enough to benefit from my grandeur, so I'm thinking maybe a five- or six-times scale? I want to tower over everything. Can you make your ice glow? Note the slight glow of my fur, the iridescence of my black scales, and the sheen of my fine mane. I know it's not as glorious as my Elders, but in another thousand years, my mane will glimmer with the power of the cosmos itself. Chronos was wise to imbue our race with such natural supremacy."

Aetheria glared at Arkaziel even as he went on and on. The rising irritation from her in the psychic bond went completely unheeded by the cat-dragon. Ignoring the feelings of others was an almost supreme skill for his species. Even when confronted with projected emotions from their bondmates, it was as if the bond didn't exist.

It wouldn't shock me if the bastards could turn it off. It's genius—make their partner aware of all their whims and fancies while turning off their side of the link. Alternative theory: the mixture of cats and dragons overcomes the bounds of narcissism and traverses into mega-narcissism.

"I don't like the way you're glaring and not appreciating my grandeur, Ria. Look! Should I pose like this, with my wings out and all puffed up? Doing my breath attack? Nibbling on a delicacy from the depths of the tower? Oh. I think I see some fruit trees. Oh, ambrosial peaches! Just think up some really great poses. I'll be right back. I'll, uh, save you one."

The StarMane flew off while Aetheria gnawed at her lower lip.

The Tower Administrator outmaneuvered me here. This is going to be a giant clusterfuck. Ark is right, though; the sculpting can wait until I try some of these fruits. This place smells divine.

Day 8

"Cripes, Ark, there wasn't even anything wrong with that one!"

"Yes, yes, there was. My left eye had a horizontal iris."

"So you had to destroy it with a breath attack?"

"Yes."

The cat-dragon lazily licked his paw, meeting Aetheria's red-eyed gaze evenly. She wanted to throttle him. It didn't help that she could feel the genuine annoyance from the StarMane through their psychic bond. She didn't doubt the dumb thing was lamenting that it had been stuck with some stupid human incapable of capturing his grand beauty in ice.

Her creation of Ethereal power continued to increase in efficiency every day. Something more than just the practice seemed in effect, though. *Are the fruits from the garden some kind of cultivation tool? My Flames have been growing without me directly increasing them. Arkaziel has grown almost a foot longer while we've been here, too.*

"Have you at least decided on the size you want?" Aetheria tried to keep defeat out of her tone.

"Oh, about double the last one."

"That one was fifteen meters tall! The platform isn't long enough for a thirty-meter-tall Arkaziel."

"So make the platform bigger."

"It would make too much shade and the plums wouldn't grow anymore."

"Mmm. Plums. Fine, sure. Mmm." Arkaziel licked his face, eying the large fruit on the trees. "Fine. Fifteen meters is adequate. Barely." A burst of air accompanied the StarMane, taking off to go raid more fruit.

At least StarManes are omnivores.

Day 139

"What do you mean you didn't like the positioning of your wings? It's exactly how you told me to do it!"

"Well, sure, but it just felt wrong, and there was a flaw in your ice creation. Didn't you see that awful red tint to it? Just horrendous. I did you a favor. This statue will remain for all of time, celebrating my glory. We can't have an inferior creation, Aetheria!"

The cat-dragon fled.

"And look at that. The artist scares off her subject once again. Her temper is so severe she can't even maintain her hair or eye color. The problems of being a shapeshifter. Ready to call it quits yet, Sparkle Princess? You're only on Floor Eleven—redoing the first ten floors wouldn't take you that long, would it? Of course, I'll just put this trial up front again. How nice of me to help you better yourself!"

The Administrator's laughter echoed through the garden, but the serene Flame of Thalassa helped Aetheria regain control of her temper.

I'm never going to make that damned cat happy unless I bribe him, and I still don't even know what final condition the Administrator is going to pull out of his hat to screw me over.

Day 163

"Wow, your eyes look amazing in this one."

"Yeah, they do. You really captured my primal savagery," Arkaziel murmured appreciatively as he ate a steak from Aetheria's soul repository.

"Indeed! And look at the subtle sparkle of glory in the mane. That's just like what you asked for: masculine draconic glory."

"Of course! All dragons should display their greatest traits so that their lessers know how to worship them properly."

"We'll definitely need to get a few passes to the garden, so any cults that form around you on our journeys can come and worship you here... unless I make more statues like this whenever we find people who want to worship you?"

"Oh, that's a great idea, Ria! Now you're really, really using your head. I was afraid you were kind of slow-witted, even for a human, but I really underestimated you. We are definitely going to meet an awful lot of people who want to worship me." Arkaziel practically purred with the words.

"So you approve?"

"I do! It has captured my majestic beauty for all to see!"

"Well, now, that took less time than expected."

Aetheria cringed at the return of the Tower Administrator.

"The final challenge: animate it. Make it get up, walk around, fly a course over the garden, then settle back down for a nap."

"Oh, yes! That's a fantastic idea! I didn't know you knew how to do those things, Ria! You're almost as amazing as a StarMane! Do it! Make ice-me fly! I want to ride it!"

If she weren't a shapeshifter and incapable of doing it anymore, Aetheria would've cracked her neck. Instead, she compressed her lips into a thin line as she dropped the surrounding temperature. Arkaziel was completely oblivious and had already climbed on top of the fifteen-meter-tall statue of himself.

"Get down here, Ark. I'm not going to go straight into trying to animate the perfect sculpture of you. It'd be quite the boneheaded move, wouldn't it?"

Reluctantly, the cat-dragon flew back to perch on her shoulder. How did he land on her shoulder without forcing her to her knees? She assumed he had some method of mass storage when he shifted his size between house cat and terrifying dragon-cat. "So, what do we do?"

"Do you know how to animate things?"

"Oh, yeah. It's part of the path to learning intent. One of my uncles has an army of Earth golems that he likes to send after this village of faeries that steal his honey all the time. Just picture it moving, what you want it to do, and imbue that into it with some energy."

Aetheria doubted it was as simple as the StarMane said. However, she'd been wrong before. A lot of these techniques seemed to prioritize her ability to imagine results, and a strong will.

Day 169

"Stop it! Stop!" Arkaziel was being chased across the garden by a swarm of ice wasps that Aetheria had created and imbued with intent to harass the StarMane.

"You're such a grandiose StarMane! Surely you don't need the help of someone you wouldn't even talk to not so long ago." It was hard to keep the smirk off her lips. She managed somehow. Not that it really mattered—the StarMane could sense her emotions through their bond if he really wanted to.

"I'm sorry I stole your sandwich! Happy now? Make them go away, or I'll breathe on them. It'd be a shame if I blew up the sculpture! I'm so pretty!"

Aetheria groaned, but the wasps melted to water and evaporated.

"Should we loot the fruit trees one more time?" The StarMane gave her a dirty look before he turned to actual business.

"I already looted all the good stuff while you were playing with my wasps. Ready for the grand finale?"

"*Yes!* I'm going to ride myself!" Wasps forgotten, the StarMane hopped onto the etheric ice sculpture, ten times his size. Its head turned to look at Arkaziel, who chirped happily. "You already finished it?"

"Yes, sir. Enjoy your flight around the garden. It's time for Floor Twelve."

Aetheria watched Arkaziel ride the ice version of himself around the garden. The sight was worth all the hard work. *No, no, it wasn't. Almost six months... but all the fruit we ate, and that I stashed, might have been worth it.*

The StarMane had let slip that this was an ambrosial garden. Some of these fruits would probably be worth an awful lot in trade when they made it to a city. If she didn't eat them all before then—they tasted *divine*.

CHAPTER 34

Stand Your Ground

Floor 12 appeared to be an endless grassy plain dotted with copses of trees and bushes. As far as Aetheria could see in any direction, it looked the same. Despite the environment's blandness, the air was heavy with Aether and the ground was dense with concentrated flows of Nether. *This will be a combat trial; I can feel it.*

Arkaziel seemed to come to the same conclusion. The StarMane perched on her shoulder and watched the prairie grasses like a predator looking for prey.

"That's right, sports fans, it's time for some fighting. Our intrepid Sparkle Princess has been taking it easy for the last few levels. Does she even know her own strength anymore? Let's see just what she can do. The rules for this floor are simple: No moving your feet, not one step. Stand your ground against three waves and you're on to Floor Thirteen. Take a step and we restart that wave. As for you, Cat, you have the opposite rules. You aren't allowed to land or hover. Stay on the move."

The StarMane let out a derisive snort. His body tensed on her shoulder as he stifled his anger at a mere Tower Administrator telling him what to do.

"That's no problem: Arkaziel's the best flier the StarManes have seen in the last few generations. Isn't that right, buddy?" Aetheria scratched under his chin, and the cat-dragon puffed up.

"I'll show you, you overly daring bureaucratic minion."

"Go!" the Tower Administrator boomed.

Aetheria shifted into a defensive stance, and Ark zipped off. He became a black and purple blur, looking for things to murder.

She had to admit she was curious. None of the past few levels had provided an opportunity to test out just what her Tier Two capabilities were. *All those weights and measured tracks Ascyn had were nice for documenting precise physical growth.*

The first enemies to appear came from beneath the plain. Small bursts of Arkaziel's beam attack drew her attention to the Nether manifestations of monsters. Her maximum range for sensing Aether and Nether had expanded. She could sense them clearly at two kilometers. Arkaziel appeared to be enjoying the challenge of murdering monsters, because it felt like ages before any of a growing swarm actually made it to within twenty meters of her.

Ants? I suppose it makes sense for a swarm creature. I'm not allowed to move, so let's see how many I can wipe out with ranged attacks.

Energy coalesced into an orb above her right hand. Aiming at her enemies with her mind, Aetheria shot out spikes of etheric ice from the orb. With each spike she launched, the orb shrank fractionally. Both had a strange red tint. The etheric ice pierced through the exoskeletons of the ants without slowing. *That looks strong, but I don't know how powerful these ants are individually. If this is a wave scenario, you almost always start out with the small fries and work your way up to the bigger opponents.*

Cripes, my accuracy isn't great. Aetheria missed with three spears in a row before noticing this monster varied from its swarm mates—its color was a dark red instead of matte black. A fourth spear missed the ant as it crossed into five-meter range. A fifth spear missed, and the red ant closed in. It tried to, anyway, but the ground around Aetheria was slick ice and the ant immediately started skidding.

Mine now, Mr. Dodger-Ant. Spikes of aetheric ice shot up out of the frozen ground. The evasive red ant died, impaled.

Guess that was overkill. So the red ones dodge ranged attacks, and ice spikes from underneath count as not ranged, or at least when they're skidding around like that.

Flashes of Arkaziel's breath attack came from a different direction. It was about a half hour before another ant made it within Aetheria's personal space, and it died the same way as the first. *Anticlimactic. How long are each of these waves?*

It took another hour and ten more red ants before a new type of enemy showed up. Blue ants traveled with the red ones, but unlike the red, they could walk on the ice just fine. *They can't perform acrobatic maneuvers to dodge the ice spears, though, so ultimately they're just more orb-fodder... the hell?!*

"Obviously, the blue ones are immune to ice. It is as if this girl never even considered there might be a relationship between affinities and colors." The Administrator mocked her as two blue ants the size of cows closed in on her. Cold radiated from them.

Aetheria gave a slow, frightful smile. The surrounding daylight dimmed. Wisps of Nether seeped up out of the ice beneath her, clawing at the life force of the blue ants. Once even a single claw had a hold of the life-stuff of the insects, more and more dark tangles of Nether rose from the ever-blackening area around her.

"Not all types of cold are ice, you arrogant twit." The death aura she had first learned from the Death Knights on Floor 4 looked different now. All around her, ice darkened as gloom clawed from the ground at the air. The Primordial Flame of Nyx made the daylight retreat.

"There are a few huge ants coming this way. I'll finish the south side," Arkaziel warned as he flew by, giving the aura around Aetheria a wide berth. The StarMane looked bigger than she remembered. If he stood like a human, he'd almost be her height now.

"Okay. Don't tire yourself out. This is still the first wave!" He was gone. *Did he even hear me?*

Aetheria tossed up a frozen orb. It stopped and hung in the air, rotating lazily. As the next batch of ants got within fifteen meters, ice spears flew from the orb at Aetheria's mental commands. *Oh, fuck yeah, I've got turrets! Can I do two at once?*

Merging more etheric energy, she tossed up another red frozen orb, where it, too, hung in the air. Both turned at roughly the same speed, and when the next ant stepped into the kill field, both turret orbs fired spears of ice at it. *Hmmm. It's really hard to fire only one at a time. Maybe a single bigger orb is better than multiples? What if I drop the projectile size down to spikes instead of spears?*

This was no spell. Aetheria controlled the ice via the Flame of Thalassa, amplifying basic arts she had developed with Ascyn and on her own, with a dash of nascent intent. Changing her technique didn't require a recast. Instead, she focused on restructuring the visualization of the frozen orbs and then "reset" them. *Flash the bios on my etheric techniques—I am the EtherQueen.*

Smaller projectiles of red ice shot from each orb. Instead of firing them at once, Aetheria fell into alternating fire between the two. Against the ants, the smaller projectiles seemed to have no problem, and anything that made it into her death aura died gruesomely. Until the final three ant behemoths made it. The ant in the rear was largest, with energy tendrils connecting the other two to it. The front two both had exoskeletons that looked like obsidian, while the rear ant seemed to be prismatic.

The two obsidian warrior ants stalked through the death aura and were unaffected by the life leech or the ice on the ground.

"What will our hero do now? Immune to her death-trickery, cold, ineffective, with two behemoth royal guards coming into physical combat. Will she move and have to start the wave over?"

"Hey, know what else is part of the ice?"

The glowing red of her eyes was replaced with the blue of the waters, and a single radiant flame appeared between the two joined ants. Streams of water started leaking from their exoskeletons toward the Flame of Thalassa. *Damn it. Not an instant-kill. The tether?*

"Leave this to the professionals, Ria," Arkaziel bragged as he flew past once more, straight to the back-line ant. The StarMane's claws glittered with red Ethereal power as he flew past the large ant like a blur, leaving gaping cuts across the exoskeleton of the colony queen. Arkaziel made a sweeping turn and doubled back, and as he flew alongside his prior slashes, he inhaled and then exhaled the coruscating light and darkness beam attack along the cut. The energy blasted the armor to pieces. The beam then cut into the soft innards of the queen ant with a brutality that only a cat could unleash.

Wow. That's a lot more disturbing when you can feel Arkaziel's giddy happiness at killing things. I should have thought more about accepting a bond with a cat.

The constant stream of water from the two royal warriors was slowing them down, but they had not stopped entirely. Pillar after pillar of ice rose from the ground to intercept their attacks on Aetheria, while the Flame of Thalassa and the etheric frozen orbs kept attacking. The tides turned dramatically when the colony queen went down, though, and without the strange bond between the ants, the two warriors died quickly to the dehydration attack.

"Good job, Ark."

"The Sparkle Death Princess has cleared Wave One. You have five minutes before the next wave. You can move until it starts. Pee now, or may your bladder rest in peace."

Why does he sound unsettled? Normally, he's snarky or insulting. He barely made any effort there.

Six hours later, she and Arkaziel had completed the second wave.

"Wave Two complete. You've got ten minutes."

Something is definitely going on with the Administrator. Hmm.

All around Aetheria, the carcasses of beetles were being converted to Nether and fed to the Flame of Nyx. The second round had gone just like the first, only with beetles instead of ants. She and Arkaziel had made quick work of them, making her wonder during the entire fight when the other shoe was going to drop. It never did, though—even the boss fight at the end went as smoothly as the first.

Arkaziel radiated smugness and self-satisfaction. This was exactly the way the StarMane felt all trials should go. *Maybe he's being watched now? Or are we over-performing? Did he not factor in us eating all of Aetherius's ambrosial garden? What set of Climbers wouldn't eat all the magic fruit?*

Aetheria felt annoyed.

"Alright, one minute. Fair warning, kiddos, the first two rounds were just warm-ups. You know how much stronger you've become, and if you don't, you really wasted the first two rounds. Pass this one and you are on to the lovely thirteenth floor. Are you prepared? You aren't, but I am. I've got popcorn, chicken, and ambrosia fruit punch. I'm even broadcasting this to my mom—hi, Mom! This is the Sparkle Princess I told you about. Isn't she stupid looking?"

"Oh, hi, human! Oh, darling, I told you to stop showing me your tower antics. I'm not supposed to know what's happening in Aetherius's tower, just like he isn't supposed to peek into mine. I'm afraid that's going to add another thousand years to your contract with him, sweetheart."

Aetheria held in her laughter. The woman's voice was not old, but if this was the mother of a demigod or lesser god with their own tower, they were a real deal. Not necessarily relevant to anything Aetheria was doing, depending on if they were a god on Grief or not.

"Good luck showing up my son, Challenger. I look forward to when you come to the Tower of Earth." When no further words came, it was clear the goddess had left.

"That was Gaia," Arkaziel said conversationally.

"I figured, from the Tower of Earth comment."

"Guess the Administrator is at least a minor god, then. Primordials don't make demigods."

"Who cares? This round is probably going to be crazy. Help me not have to move if things get bad."

"You'll be fine." The StarMane's grin showed a lot of very sharp fangs.

"How'd you get so big, so fast?"

"Ancient StarMane secret."

"Hmm." She stared at Arkaziel flatly.

"Take your positions. Ready... Murder Hornets, go!" The Administrator's voice was thick with satisfaction and pleasure. The sky was also growing thick with swarms of flying insects.

"I hate hornets," Arkaziel hissed.

CHAPTER 35

Murder Hornets

Hornets were easy to hate. These were exceptionally detestable. With five-inch-long stingers, bladed protrusions on their fore and hind legs, glowing yellow eyes, and a spike on their foreheads, these were not hornets with which Aetheria was familiar. Everything about them screamed incoming pain. With a hiss, Arkaziel launched himself into the air so as not to violate the keep moving rule.

"I've had this idea lately about an Ethereal technique, since all of mine are Aether or Nether." Aetheria expanded her aura outward to five meters, the blue and black Aether and Nether mixing in psychedelic ways before a spark of Aetherflame triggered the conversion to blazing red Ethereal power. The red energy condensed and clung to her as if it were an ooze instead of energy.

But her icy death aura revolved around some contact with ice. The hornets were airborne and fast; they were nearly upon her. Auras were great, but they were instant death only for the very weak. Therefore, an aura of power was out of play.

She could release Ether Vortexes, but barely controlled destruction felt like the wrong answer. Arkaziel was out there flying around, and she didn't want to catch the StarMane inside one of her attacks. No, this was where she could fall back on what she had learned in the garden.

With her Ethereal energy, Aetheria formed three dragonflies, each a meter long. The hornets themselves were approximately half a meter. The red etheric ice creatures immediately darted toward the oncoming swarm and feasted. Aetheria pushed the rest of the energy into a storm of icicles that would rend apart anything trying to get near her.

It was not one brutal attack to wipe out all her enemies, but it was safe and continuous progress. It ripped every hornet that tried to get into the surrounding storm to shreds by ice, and the fallen enemies' deaths became Aetheria's strength. In the end, only she, Arkaziel, and the three dragonflies remained. She hadn't moved.

The Administrator didn't taunt her. In fact, he didn't say anything. The door to Floor 13 appeared. Aetheria ruffled Ark's furry head.

"Good job."

The StarMane purred and nuzzled her hand. "Obviously, no mere hornet can beat the greatest StarMane in generations!"

Aetheria and Ark appeared at the entrance of a large cave. Outside was a world of white storms. Inside, the cave was a little better, with drifts of snow and ice layered over rock. Their breath condensed in the chilly air, and after a small shiver, Aetheria summoned a ball of Aether fire to provide some warmth.

"Any idea on what we've got going on this time, Ark?"

"Mm. There's something old here. Old and fairly powerful. Maybe you'll get to eat another god ghost. I'm still jealous. I don't get to eat any gods."

"We'll find one to feed you eventually, I'm sure, buddy." Aetheria smiled reassuringly and ruffled his fur. Arkaziel leaned into it until he saw her smirking. He glared at her and hopped into the air—mostly hovering over the Aetherflame, she noted.

They came to a large chamber where apparitions worked. Three men, alike in familial appearance, were engaged in macabre labor. One fashioned bones into mountains. Another fashioned blood into oceans. The third fashioned brains into clouds. They ignored the living, going about their gruesome spectral labor. When one brother turned a skull into the sky, Aetheria growled under her breath and sent a wave of crystallized aetheric ice to purge the chamber of occupants.

With the specters gone, the room was barren and old. Maybe there was something underneath the countless layers of ice, but neither she nor Ark sensed anything worth excavating for.

The cave went deeper. With every step farther in, the chill of ice grew more severe. Oddly, it didn't bother Aetheria that much, but Arkaziel started to shiver and chitter, so she created a series of Aetherflames to circle around the StarMane and keep him warm.

The next chamber showed the three brothers again. This time, they were forming a planet out of eyebrows. *Cripes, really? Who even thinks of this stuff? This is Floor Thirteen. Is this some kind of horror bullshit?*

She didn't even try to interact with them, just passed through the chamber. The spectral brothers paid no attention to the interlopers.

The third large chamber was unlike the first two. Here, beneath the layers of built-up ice, Aetheria could see the carnage of the brothers' butchery. Blood, bits of flesh, hair, and other unmentionables remained frozen solid underneath layers of ice. The brothers did not work in this room; instead, they drank merrily and ate heartily at a table made of bones.

"That's Odin," Arkaziel murmured into her ear, pointing at the eldest brother.

"Oh, really? I know his name was on the leaderboard, but why's he got a ghost here in the tower?"

"It's not a ghost. Those are memories, and not Odin's. The flavor is all wrong for a god. It's something older, maybe memories from the being they butchered?"

Aetheria's enthusiasm for this floor rapidly waned.

The next chamber was much larger than the previous rooms. A massive figure covered in layers of ice and snow filled almost the whole cavern. The creature made very little noise, except every few minutes, when it unleashed a large snore. The snore seemed to be timed with drops of a strange, powerful feeling as liquid dripped from a hole in the roof into the giant's throat. The giant's skin had a naturally pallid blue cast to it and seemed to be androgynous.

"What do you think, Arka—you stupid cat!"

Arkaziel had flown up to the giant's face, then rapped the giant with a paw to the nose.

The giant coughed, and Arkaziel barely dodged the giant's hand, rubbing at its nose.

"Murph. Someone wants something? Better not be to hack me up again." The voice was masculine and disgruntled. The air that carried the words froze all water from the air near the giant's mouth. A nearly popsicle-like Arkaziel returned to hide in the Aetherflame heating circle Aetheria maintained.

"Howdy. I didn't mean to wake you up. My companion is a StarMane, and you know how they are," Aetheria apologized, casting her voice as loud as she could for the giant.

"StarManes? With a human? Strange times. I must have finally reached my goal of getting as drunk as Chronos." The giant roared at his joke. Icicles on the roof of the cavern shook dangerously.

"I'm Ria. This is Arkaziel. Who do we have the honor of addressing?" *Please don't turn into a fight. I'm not sure how well Arkaziel would thaw. Maybe it'd change his color.*

"Some call me Aurgelmir, but most know me as Ymir." The giant's expression changed from a grin to a frown when the StarMane looked nonplussed and the blue-haired human appeared confused.

"*Ymir.* Of whom those insufferable children of Bor make all the realms? First giant? Primordial being? Drank milk from a cow? Sired all the giants, and a lot of gods are half-breeds of my descent?"

"Sorry, I'm not that well versed in history. I was told they created the universe when Chronos got drunk and dreamed of a party outside his cave," Aetheria offered apologetically. She was intrigued. *Maybe this is a chance to figure out some real cosmological Origination stuff?*

"Bah, Chronos is such a blowhard. The Primordial Void itself spawned me. How could he come before me if he already had a cave? Huh? He couldn't, that's how! Just because time is the enemy of all mortals doesn't make Chronos any better than me," the giant muttered unhappily. "My flesh was used to create your worlds, so they should praise me left and right."

"Why are you in the Tower of Aetherius, oh great Ymir?" Aetheria hoped a smile and question would sidetrack the rising ire of the giant.

"Oh. We went drinking a few millennia ago, and I've been sleeping off the alcohol since. That's the best part about being Ymir, first in Creation. Lots of avatars.

Downside is that most of them get butchered into forming new planets by those obnoxious kids."

"Uh. So that's literal? They chop you up and fashion new planets?"

"Well, they chop me up, that part's for sure. New planets, maybe. Hard to tell when you die."

"But you don't die, you're right here."

"And I'm there, getting killed and turned into mountains and worlds."

"This conversation is making my head hurt."

"Eh," Ymir grunted a noncommittal noise. "So why does a human have three Primordial Flames? I sense Aetherius, Nyx, and Thalassa on you."

"I got elected to be a Challenger for the world of Grief, if you're at all familiar?"

"That shithole hasn't been pity-killed yet? That's what happens when you let one of Nyx and Erebus's kids be in charge of a planet. Nothing good comes of it. Even Khaos ruled her worlds better than most of those kids."

"Chaos? I thought Chaos was a man?"

"Khaos. Chaos. Man, woman, toaster. It's all the same. Change isn't as threatening to you mortals as it is to the gods. They really hate her. She's a great drinking partner, though, if you can avoid falling into her baiting you into amusing her."

"I'll keep that in mind."

"Do. She's insufferable about getting reactions out of people. How'd you get Nyx's Flame if Aetherius chose you as a Challenger?"

"No idea. My memory of that meeting seems to be damaged by the reincarnation process."

"Eh. Aetherius was never very good at that kind of thing. Flighty like the upper sky, and has about as much substance, too. Still, pretty excellent host." Ymir slipped out his tongue to catch a drop of the strangely powerful liquid dropping from the ceiling.

"I'll be sure to pass on the compliment when I see him next," Aetheria said, deadpan.

Ymir laughed, a great booming sound that filled the freezing cave with life.

"I like you, human. Since you seem to collect Flames, what would you trade me for a fragment of the Flame of Ymir, first in all Creation?"

Wasn't expecting that. Still, trade? Damn it. Everyone else gave me theirs for free or made me do a task. I guess I'd rather pay than owe someone something.

"How do you feel about ambrosial fruit?"

"I'm more of a meat and cheese snacker," Ymir noted with disinterest.

"Then have I got something for you! I was saving this for myself, but..." Aetheria summoned multiple large chests from her soul repository. Three of them were repurposed from earlier levels of the tower, and two larger ones she'd purchased in Solace.

Ymir and Arkaziel both sniffed the air in interest.

"Cured and smoked Aether-ellos, from the Solace level. Succulent, tender, some of the best eating I've had in the tower."

"You'd better be keeping some for me! You've been holding out on me, Ria!" Arkaziel hissed at her.

"You have a deal, human." The chests vanished in a poof, reappearing in Ymir's massive hands. He emptied an entire chest into his mouth, and emitted groans of flavor-induced pleasure.

"Brace yourself. Little StarMane, retreat into the circle of fire for your own protection."

Aetheria slipped Arkaziel a piece of jerky as he flew to the safety of a circle of fire.

"Uh, am I going to be okay?"

"Of course, of course. You survived the implantation of Nyx's Flame. Mine will only be a little worse."

She nodded. The room grew colder and colder. Hoarfrost accumulated on her skin. Her hair froze. In her mind, a new presence was manifesting—a flame of ice ignited. It burned blood red and radiated absolute zero. Her body temperature dropped moment by moment. Pain cascaded through her limbs and all sense of her extremities faded.

Pain is nothing. I am greater than my pain. I am Aetheria, Keeper of the Flames of Nyx, Aetherius, Thalassa, and Ymir. From the cold of Ymir came life, and like his corpse refashioned, this Flame will now be mine! She repeated her mantra for an indeterminate amount of time as cold ravaged her body and soul.

"Yes, that's it, little one. Embrace the cold."

CHAPTER 36

Ignorance is Bliss

Waves of pain, torment, and torture continued. Eventually, even Aetheria's high tolerance for suffering failed her, and she blissfully sank into unconsciousness. When she woke, it was to more pain, but this time, it was her body regenerating. She had apparently taken on a form similar to Ymir's while unconscious. With effort, she forced the excess mass and volume that made up her temporary "mini-giant" shape back into the repository.

"You survived, little one! Never has Ymir witnessed a mortal claim a Primordial Flame for their own, suffer the backlash, and reach equilibrium. Most mortals' heads just explode!"

Aetheria grimaced and rubbed at the side of her head.

Arkaziel emerged from his heat ring to sit on her shoulders. "Your head exploded," the StarMane said flatly.

"Only twice, and not all the way," Ymir countered.

"Where I come from, any head exploding is both lethal and horrifying. What happened?"

Ymir looked confused by her question, as if she were a dolt or drunkard.

"You're a Tier Two with three, now four Primordial Flames. The human soul is inviolable, more so than any other race, but the human body is among the weakest. Flames affect body and soul. Your soul adapted quickly; your body struggled. Your head exploded a few times, and your body froze and shattered. Your limbs regrew quickly. The show alone was worth giving you a fragment of my Flame. Not worth losing the bet. Aetherius cheated."

Aetheria paled. "Is there a limit on the number of Flames you can have?"

Ymir laughed. A deep, full amusement filled the cold cave. "That's a troublesome question. Your Flame does not define you mortals. You can bear them, you can make them, but they are not integral to your identity—that's what your soul is for. Yet each Flame will stress your body and soul. Head explosions might not stop you, but they stop most mortals from straying into the territory of us higher beings."

"Wait, you don't have a soul?"

"Not as you would understand it." Ymir waved that conversation away. "You are resilient, your restorative abilities are top-tier. You could probably hold two more Mortal Flames."

"What about on your or Nyx's level?"

Ymir laughed. She half expected the giant to say Nyx wasn't on his level, but he said nothing of the sort.

"In your present condition? You might not escape the cycle of exploding heads with another high Primordial Flame. The higher the tier you achieve, the more you can contain. Your meat-puppet body is your limitation. Human souls are inviolable, the flesh not so much. Aetherius, the cheater, augmented yours, but even that has limitations. I would not absorb another Flame unless you encounter Chaos, Chronos, or Brahma. At higher tiers, you can merge Flames."

"Isn't my body pretty far from a normal human?"

"Aetherius changed much. The underpinnings *were* still human. Your ascension to possess an Ethereal physiology has given you a much better vessel for containing your powers. You must explore this. Your flesh has become powerful, and you have removed many of your limitations. Shapeshifting is only one facet of the Art of Fleshcraft. Even if you do not take on the flesh of others, you can manipulate your own to great effect." Ymir's gigantic eyes narrowed and Aetheria felt herself being sized up on multiple levels.

"Do you know what the Flames of Nyx, Aetherius, Thalassa, and Ymir have in common?" Ymir waited, but Aetheria just shook her head. Flames didn't come with instruction manuals.

"No. I know almost nothing about what the Flames can do, except that Aetherius's and Nyx's both allow for strong Aether and Nether absorption."

Ymir groaned. "Shapeshifting. Shapeshifting is what all four have in common. Combined with your physiology, your ability to change your flesh should be beyond reproach. Now learn to live up to that.

"You are no mage. Your destiny is to break bones in your hand, crush skulls under your foot, and walk over your enemies' corpses. We aptly named the Winding Ways the view of what is close and far changing frequently. Your body is your greatest weapon, and the Primordial Flame of Ymir will strengthen you. All who alter self must ask: 'Do I forge my form, or do I allow others to forge me?'"

"That sounds very self-helpy, Ymir."

"It does, doesn't it? Hahaha." The cave shook with the giant's laughter. "I like you, little one. If you leave your little world and venture to one with my tower, then come visit Ymir. We will feast, and even your little StarMane companion is welcome as long as he doesn't try to eat my heart, like his grandfather did."

Arkaziel, in house cat form wrapped around her neck, bristled a little.

"You're going to get us blacklisted from so many places, aren't you?" Aetheria sighed, but couldn't she be too annoyed as Ark nuzzled her neck and purred. Her cat, Zeusy, had always acted like that after he'd destroyed something Aesca loved.

"You've been helpful, Ymir. I don't suppose you'd be willing to teach me any arts?" Aetheria tried her best smile on the giant.

Again, the cavern shook with the giant's laughter. "You are incorrigible. No. I do not use arts. Find your own path."

"Damn it, Arkaziel! Did you really have to take a bite out of his toe as we were leaving?" Aetheria scolded her companion. The door from the last floor closed.

The two had appeared on a large rock plateau so high it was nearly in the lower clouds. The ground far below glowed with the light of lava, and plumes of smoke rose occasionally as something burned down in the lower elevations. *Oh, cripes, the Administrator has heard of the Devil's Tower and added lava? Jerk.*

"I got a good mouthful. Primordials are delicious! Besides, Ymir knew it was coming, and it was just a bite of his toe. No one would ever blame me or hold it against me."

"I do. I'm blaming you."

"Well, that's really unfair, Ria. Just because Ymir gives you his Flame and compliments you on how amusing your head exploding was, you can't side with an evil ice giant over your trusted, handsome, genius, amazing in every way, and occasionally just a little hungry StarMane companion."

Aetheria conjured a small ball of water above her right hand and threw it at Arkaziel when he wasn't expecting it. The StarMane hissed at her and tried to brush water off his face with his paws.

"I never!"

"I told you we squirt cats in the face where I come from. No eating people who are being nice to us, even if they're Primordials."

"But Ria, that's how we StarManes evolve. We need to taste the rainbow of existence, gnaw the flesh of gods, dine on Primordial hearts, and really everything else. That's why I've gotten so big lately. All those monsters, and I, uh, maybe ate Thalassa's corpse when you weren't looking. She totally consented to it, though, and you ate her spirit, so you can't judge me!"

Only one thing shared the top of the tower of rock with them. A ten-meter-long squirrel with red and black eyes and fur that flamed. *Jeez. Fire versus ice: a tale as old as time.* Aetheria stretched her neck out and walked toward the squirrel. "You're on artillery, Ark. We'll talk about your diet later."

Power flared around her, the Aether and Nether energies of her aura swirling and dropping an oppressive weight on the entire area. The surrounding air chilled and her breath showed as steam. Possessing an Ethereal physiology had changed her. No longer was there a slider in her mind for density. She could change her mass and volume at will via shapeshifting fueled by energy or by borrowing from her soul repository and the items therein. Plus, her body could now take on much more helpful forms: extra width to provide greater force transference; extra muscles to generate even more power; claws to slice. Fleshcrafting, as Ymir had called it, was a facet of her evolution she had not taken full advantage of yet.

On her third step, her calf swelled, and Aetheria suddenly shot across the intervening distance between her and the squirrel, her right fist going straight for the massive monster's head. The damn thing actually dodged her punch. It leaped straight into the air.

"Bad idea." Aetheria's aura condensed and then expanded back out. In the ten meters around her, the world froze. Ice covered the stone underfoot. Large icicles formed in the air and spun around her. With a snap of her finger, her aura changed. Aether and Nether fused into Ether when her Aetherflame Nova provided the conversion spark. She bound the etheric energy to the Primordial Flame of Ymir.

Spikes of ice shot up like spears from the frozen ground as the squirrel fell. The vermin dodged spear after spear by the narrowest margin despite falling with no ability to dodge beyond contortion. Yet the monster came back down to the ground, Aetheria waiting. Her right hand slammed forward, her strength augmented by alterations, and her fist pulsed with the power of Ymir. The nimble rodent almost avoided her punch, but she was faster, and the chill of her aura slowed the monster's reflexes just enough.

The blow shattered several bones in the monster's face, but that wasn't the end of the damage with this attack. When Aetheria's fist made contact, she pulsed out her Ethereal power into the squirrel, condensing it into etheric ice. Dozens of small needle-like shards of nearly unbreakable ice pushed into the face of the monster with enough force to enter its brain.

The Flames of Aetherius and Nyx appeared, flanking her, and she commanded them to eat the squirrel. The monster never regained its footing—the energy drain and ice attack killed it before it had a chance.

Aetheria frowned. "If there's more, want me to save one for you to eat?"

"Sure, but... maybe not. There's another one coming up the mountain, but it's stinky. I have such delicate sensibilities, I could only force myself to eat four or five of the things."

"Are there more below?"

"Lots."

Another giant squirrel leaped onto the plateau. This one was almost half as large as the last, had many more streaks of red energy to its fur, and pushed waves of heat out from it to battle the icy aura around Aetheria.

"Demonic giant squirrels. I don't know how to feel about this."

The monster did not answer Aetheria's banter. Instead, it suddenly launched itself at her. Multiple afterimages shot forward at her to obfuscate the genuine attack. It was faster than she was.

Shit. Cheater. Teleported behind me.

One of the squirrel's claws pierced her chest and tried to push heat and burning into her. Instead, its arm froze solid and shattered when she casually tapped it with a hand.

"Way to be an asshole, Squirrel. What, you grow up in Wisconsin? Not even an 'Ope, let me sneak by ya there'?"

The demon squirrel roared in rage at the loss of its arm. Flames burst to life. The monster popped and sizzled. It seemed to be burning its own life force to amplify its attacks enough to have a chance of resisting her freezing aura.

"That teleport was nice, though. I need to figure out how to do that myself."

The squirrel raged and attacked again. Its remaining arm made it only halfway to her. A black and white coruscating beam of Ethereal energy bisected the squirrel, then refocused to annihilate its head.

"Nice sniping, Ark."

"Yep, I'm amazing. Three more coming up the cliff. Looks like we've got about seven more to deal with before their daddy or mommy comes to say hi."

CHAPTER 37

Burning Vermin

The next batch of fire squirrels made it up to the top of the plateau as a group of three. Four more and a very large one followed behind.

"Kill as many as you can before they get up here." Aetheria grimaced and fell into a defensive stance. The three enemies ignored the flying cat and faced her.

Before she could even count to two, they were on her. The first squirrel appeared behind her with a burst of flames. It lashed at her back with its claws. The attack shredded her coat and back even as the other two engaged her from the front.

Aetheria altered her aura, concentrating on the Nether, pulling streams of energy from the enemies to her. Using the extra life force, she regenerated almost instantaneously, which came in handy because she could only dodge one of the two front attacks, and took more painful clawed hits.

With the near-instant regeneration, she went on the offensive. Constantly draining the life from her enemies would keep her fighting. She chose the squirrel that had ambushed her as her first target, and when it came in for another attack, she bent her right arm in ways a human arm and shoulder could not bend, to stab an elongated finger-claw into its eye. Pain flared up her limb from the flames and scalding blood pouring out of the monster's wound. She weathered the heat and burns to pulse Nether tendrils through its brain. It fell lifeless, and she shifted her shape back to normal.

The two remaining squirrels moved to better flank her now that their companion was dead. Her Nether aura was still sapping life from her enemies, but neither acted pressed for time. They circled her until one suddenly hissed, formed a giant ball of fire with its tail, and threw it at her. Aetheria immediately rose a wall of ice from the ground to block the fire, and the other squirrel ambushed her, which she had expected.

What she hadn't expected was that the other one would run right up to her and detonate itself. The force of the explosion slammed her into her own ice wall, burning and pain engulfing her world. The ice wall shattered when she hit it, and the fireball attack crashed into her. Something about the kamikaze attack of the squirrel made the flames sticky and refuse to go out. Aetheria conjured the Aetherflame and consumed the flames that kept burning her. As they finally died out, the last squirrel shot forward and tried to plow her off the mountain.

When the squirrel crashed into her, it found a much heavier human than expected. Using its momentum, she reached out and snapped the monster's neck with elongated hands.

"Cripes. Self-exploding, trying to push me off the mountain. These things play by any means necessary to win." Aetheria gathered her breath, which drew the energy left behind by the monsters. The Flame of Ymir wasn't at its Tier One cap yet, and at this rate, it would take a few more hours of squirrel killing to get it there.

Two more squirrels leaped over the ledge of the plateau and charged straight at her. She raised a wall of ice behind her moments before what she had estimated to be the maximum range of the teleport attack. The squirrels hissed in frustration, but neither slowed their headlong rush.

Just before they closed the final few meters, pillars of aetheric ice rose underneath Aetheria, tossing her into the air. With a snap of her finger, sparks of Nether shot out to catch the pillars she left behind, igniting the aetheric ice so it became Ethereal in a cascade reaction down the pillars. When the base of the pillars lit up, red spears and shards of red ice shot in every direction. One squirrel took the brunt of the attack, but one down was better than none.

Survivor's guilt seemed to play upon the remaining monster for a moment. It changed its stance, then shot up into the air to attack Aetheria directly as she descended. Just before the squirrel hit her, she altered her mass suddenly, her coat flaring out like a parachute, and then transformed back to normal as she landed on the squirrel. She got a firm grip on its fur with one hand. The fur burned her, but she held on anyway. She transformed her other hand's fingers into elongated claws, which she shoved into the squirrel's neck, pulsing Nyx's Flame to steal its life.

Her boots touched down on the ground just as the largest squirrel demon yet appeared, climbing over the ledge, Arkaziel's energy beam scoring hits across its body. The damage looked trivial, though, and fixed itself as they watched. This monster's aura was heavier than Aetheria's, its concentration of energy extremely dense, and its mere presence scorched the air of the plateau. *Ice, theoretically, is Fire's counter. Unless the source of the fire is at least a whole tier higher than you.*

"This one is like fighting you, Ria! All the damage it takes just heals! Plus, it's made of lava, so I can't even get in there and hit it." Arkaziel sounded offended. He couldn't just kill the squirrel. The giant lava monstrosity was clearly the boss of the level, but even that didn't diminish Arkaziel's ego.

"I'm going to charge my Super Mega Ultimate Attack. You handle it until I finish." Most people would have been sheepish or beaten around the bush before they declared they intended to kill steal. Not Arkaziel.

This has to be part of the test. Being put up against fire as ice should be a curb stomp for me, but that thing is at least Tier Three, debuffed or not. There's got to be a lesson here, right?

The lava squirrel didn't rush in the way its little minions had. It slowly crossed the plateau in a leisurely stroll, its tail batting back and forth as it walked.

Why is the tail fli... aw, fuck!

The tail formed large balls of lava, which it flung in shots of three at Aetheria. She condensed her ice aura to only a meter around her, throwing up pillars of ice from the ground to block the blobs of lava. Speed alone let her dodge, but she wasn't sure how to tackle this problem. Lava would seriously screw her up, and not only was the squirrel able to fling it, but it also sure looked like actual lava. *No punching.*

Worse, when lava and ice collided, the results were explosive. *Ice might not be the best bet against lava.* Aetheria gestured and formed a series of increasingly large spears of ice. When there were ten spears, she launched them all at the lava squirrel, still slowly walking toward her, with a flick of her hand. The monster flung more lava bombs. This time, she just dodged the bombs with as wide a berth as possible so she could observe the impact of the spears against the monster.

Only the largest of the ten spears made contact with the lava squirrel. The resulting explosion looked impressive, but it did almost no damage to the monster. A very tiny area of its lava skin darkened but returned to superheated within seconds.

Damn it. So it heals wounds because it's lava. Even if you cool one section, it'll reheat pretty dang quickly.

The fight fell into a pattern. Aetheria launched ranged attacks that failed to do anything of significance. The boss kept slowly approaching. After running the squirrel in a circle around the plateau, another problem became apparent. Its slow strides were superheating the rock of the plateau, and when it passed an area a second time, the stone melted and lava geysers formed.

The Primordial Flame of Aetherius was her first answer to the problem. She imagined a replica of the Flame above the geyser, sucking in all of its power. The energy powering the geyser was still active under the control of the giant monster, and her attempt to steal the power required a contest of wills that slowed the process down so much that her energy theft was taking more of her power than it generated.

With her energy senses active, Aetheria saw her strategy wasn't going to work. The lava squirrel was pushing its own energy into everywhere it walked, and thousands of strands of power connected the beast to where it was passing. If she kept running, they would turn the whole plateau into a caldera before long.

So how do you stop lava? C'mon, nature documentaries, remind me. Water?

Aetheria projected the Primordial Flames of Aetherius and Thalassa into the sky, and visualized dark storm clouds forming and torrential rain. With each second, the clouds darkened and gathered from nowhere. For the first time, she felt an actual draw on her personal energies that wasn't just a trickle. The generation of frozen orbs, ice spears, ice pillars, her auras—none of that really had a noticeable impact on her internal energy reserves. The sky filled with colossal cumulonimbus clouds, and over half of her internal energy was gone.

"Ack! Rain! I'm getting wet! *Helllp*!" Arkaziel screeched and hissed from his flight over the tower sides, where he kept the small fries away and waited to kill steal.

Torrential rain fell from the still darkening sky. Aetheria increased her mass so as not to be thrown around by the strong winds across the top of the plateau. The hiss of steam and strong winds deafened all other sounds until a chorus of howls emerged from the thousands of demon squirrels still around the tower. The boss lava squirrel took up the howl as well, hissing and chittering at the sky. Its previously glowing body was now a dull black. Each second, it lost a little more luster.

Aetheria projected the Flame of Ymir into the sky. Instantly, instead of rain, projectiles of aetheric ice shot down like homing missiles. Hundreds and hundreds of tiny pieces of icy death concentrated on not just the lava squirrel but also all of its minions below the tower.

"Noooooo, that was supposed to be my kill!" Arkaziel cried in angst at the sight of the lava-squirrel and the thousands of projectiles. Cats did not like frozen food.

"Oh, I might have overdone that." Aetheria rubbed at the bridge of her nose. She felt like she had run five kilometers in a desert with a backpack full of weights and no water to drink. She sucked down the ever-present tides of Aether to replenish her lost power, and with it came tides of Nether from the monsters who were being mercilessly slaughtered by the blizzard.

Arkaziel appeared before her, chewing on something he'd gained on his way over.

"Did you stop to eat the lava heart?"

"Definitely not. I, uh, had some jerky."

"Whatever. You were excellent support today, Ark. Thank you. You've got a little lava juice on your chin."

"Yeah, it's kind of spicy. Got any milk in your repository?"

Aetheria rolled her eyes but conjured a saucer of milk from her repository for the cat-dragon.

She could open the door to Floor 15 in her mind, but she didn't immediately do it.

First, she was still controlling the flower of gathered energies, most of which she pushed into the Flame of Ymir to get it to the Tier One cap. The rest she let fill her body, to banish the exhaustion that filled her.

"Could you stop the blizzard? It's cold."

"Oh, right." Aetheria held up a hand and used the Flame of Aetherius to steal her power back from the sky. The drain efficiency was terrible. It returned roughly ten percent of what she had spent to create the storm. The clouds broke apart slowly.

"You ready for some civilization, Ria?"

"You know it, little buddy. Give me a little time to meditate, though. I want to perfect that on a smaller scale for next time, and a big city is a terrible place to work on making storms."

Arkaziel pouted, but perked up when their large tent appeared for him to nap inside.

CHAPTER 38

Nidhogg's Bane

Three months. That had been Aetheria's limit for enduring Arkaziel's incessant bitching about going back to civilization. During this time, though, she had made several breakthroughs in manipulating the weather and controlling her shapeshifting. She would have liked to spend more time mastering shapeshifting, but her StarMane companion had become simply unbearable. Even squirting the bastard with water did nothing to discourage his obnoxious behavior.

"Ohhh, I don't recognize this one!" Ark was excited to be the first of his clan to explore Floor 15. Aetheria and her companion had appeared sitting inside of a small seagoing vessel, a bireme. They were alone. All the empty seats near the oars felt peculiar. Stranger was the fact that they were not on the water—instead, magical chains secured their vessel, lifting them up to an elevated dock. Other vessels were also going up to the sky pier; some were descending to the ocean. The sky pier itself was sprawled over many square kilometers, but made up only a fraction of the whole city vessel in the sky. The rough ocean prevented Aetheria from getting an actual glimpse of what parts of the vessel went into the water, but she had no shortage of things to gape at when they reached the pier.

A bored-looking man with a clipboard, fur armor, facial tattoos, and a two-handed axe strapped to his back waited on the dock, his boot tapping impatiently as a plank joined the dock and the now secured bireme.

"Tax man," Arkaziel hissed to her.

The moment Aetheria's foot hit the plank, the world exploded with a peal of what sounded like massive melodic bells. These were followed by ominous melodies played by unseen pipe organs. All along the pier, people sought the source of the commotion. Natives all looked directly at Aetheria. No need to scan the pier. Dwellers seemed to have to look around to find her by description, instead of immediately knowing who and where she was. Then there were the other Climbers, who simply looked baffled by the sudden chaos.

The tax man had put his clipboard away, and bowed deeply before Aetheria and Arkaziel. She could see now that he was a guard.

"Welcome to Nidhogg's Bane, Lady Challenger. The Voice of Odin has waved your docking fees. Here's the docking slip. Some of you adventurers end up going out in the open ocean, some leave via the Rune Gates. The whole of Nidhogg's Bane is open to you. If you seek quarters, the finest inn worthy of your business is the Hanging Tree off the main courtyard. Anyone'll be able to direct you. Drottning Brünnhilde would no doubt welcome you to her palace, if you would rather be a state guest."

The guard spoke in one of the human languages Aetheria had learned previously. She was fairly certain that it wasn't a translation field effect—things like a translation field were difficult to tell when you were under the effect of one. The Native guard seemed eager for her to move on, though, as if displeasing her might bring some great wrath upon his head.

"Thank you. I guess I'll just explore for a bit. My companion won't be an issue?" Aetheria had half expected the guard to tell her StarManes weren't allowed in civilized society, or to charge her an entrance fee. Far too many people were still staring at her, gaping.

"Your flying cat, my lady? Nothing on the books against flying cats."

Aetheria blinked before looking down at Arkaziel perched on her shoulder. He looked almost entirely like a cat with fairy wings now, instead of the half dragon, half cat that he actually was. Through their bond, she could feel how pleased with himself Arkaziel was. The smirking cat purred as he rubbed his head against her neck.

He can shapeshift already? They said he wouldn't do that until he was almost a hundred. He has been eating some pretty enormous meals, though.

"Right, thanks." With a wave of her hand, Aetheria picked a direction that appeared to lead from the pier to higher levels. A long line of people stood before heavy gates with menacing guards who controlled the flow of people from the strange pier into Nidhogg's Bane proper. There seemed to be separate gates for citizens of the massive vessel of a city, while the slow-moving line serviced new arrivals, adventurers, and foreign merchants. She fell into the end of the line behind a group of two women and three men—Climbers, by the look of them.

"First time in one of the tower cities?" a short, pink-haired woman who dressed in the fashion of a rogue asked her while giving her a once-over.

"Yeah, just hit Floor Fifteen. You?"

"We just hit Floor Thirty in the Tower of Ares. I'm T'riss, this is Cynda, that's Sam, Jongar, and Tim. You're a Challenger and a solo Climber?" T'riss didn't beat around the bush.

"Uh, yeah. That's me, Challenger Lady. I'm hardly solo, though. I've got my trusty friend here." Aetheria scratched Arkaziel under the chin, and he put on a show of purring and being cute.

"Still, you must follow a really strong path or have a lot of powerful gear to be a solo Climber." T'riss sounded friendly, but there was no missing the longing for better gear that glittered in the eyes of her companions. She would need to remain on guard about what she revealed.

"No gear, sorry. As for paths, I suppose it's a pretty strong path. What path do you follow? I'm Ria, by the way."

"I follow the Path of Elusive Shadows. The weakest combatant in my party, but I've got a lot of other skills. Cynda follows the Path of Aquamarine Depths, Sam's something with a Bear, Jongar is on the Steel Skirmisher Path, and Tim there is an Enchanter."

"Quite the party. I'm on a Path of Frost." Aetheria smiled lightly, but she had no reason to reveal any more than that, especially with how vague T'riss was being about their own party, if not outright being deceptive.

The officer of the gate interrupted their chat. He walked along the line and stopped next to Aetheria.

"Lady Challenger? There's no need for you to wait in line like a common adventurer. The All-Father would not insult Aetherius so." The intense curiosity of the adventurers in line ahead and behind her, mixed with reactions to the name of her patron, told her that remaining in line, as was her first instinct, would only bring her an awful lot of questions now.

"Why, thank you... captain? Lead on. Good luck with the rest of your climb, T'riss." Aetheria offered a smile and wave and followed the captain toward the gate, skipping the line. Murmurs of "Aetherius" and "Challenger" followed her.

"Why's she get to skip the line?" A very large brute of a man in the company of three other large men all glared daggers at her.

"When you are a Challenger, you can skip the line, too. Now shut it, or I'll banish you from Nidhogg's Bane," the captain gruffly answered with definitive scorn. The threat of banishment quickly quelled obvious discontent. Aetheria kept her face blank and followed the captain through the security checkpoint.

"Enjoy your stay on the Bane, Challenger." The captain saluted her as she walked free of the pier and up the stairs to the main floor of Nidhogg's Bane.

The Bane was massive. Kilometers wide and almost twice as long, it looked like an island more than a human-constructed vessel. They had brought Earth aboard and pines, crops, and grasses grew everywhere. The residential areas looked densely packed, and a quick count revealed they averaged eight stories. A large palace was not the biggest landmark on the vessel that belonged to a strange half-dome covered in vines.

First things first. Aetheria ducked down an alley—and never emerged from it. Not as her normal self, anyway. Instead, she had shifted her sparkling blue-green hair to a red pixie cut, her aqua eyes to green, and her clothing to an armored dress in Aoibhe's style.

"Oh, due caution. I like it. Those adventurers had greedy eyes for you, which is hilarious. Everything of any value is in the repository. You enchanted your gloves, but the rest of your clothes aren't even stealable since they're part of you now."

It felt strange for the cat to be supportive. Something was bound to upend his new leaf.

"So what do we even do in these towns? Are there trainers? Obviously, merchants... We'll figure it out, I guess. Nothing says we have to stay here very long. I'll be going by the name Sarka while we're here."

After walking only three blocks, she observed that her plan seemed of dubious effectiveness. Natives were obvious, because every single one of them stopped to look at her before returning to their tasks. This made the Dwellers also take notice of her, as well as the occasional Climbers. Yet she made it fifteen blocks to the central courtyard of Nidhogg's Bane without incident.

A large, impressive inn with a sign showing a man hanging from a tree caught her eye. *The Hanging Tree, no doubt. I might as well see what amenities the best inn has. I can always go somewhere else if they don't have a room or are too expensive.*

The common room of the inn was warmly lit. A mix of large long tables and more intimate smaller tables, and even some elevated booths for privacy, filled the space. The bartender waved her over.

"Lady Challenger, interested in a room?" A slight smile played on the man's face. He appeared to be in his forties, had blond hair and blue eyes. When he walked down the bar toward her, she saw he was missing his left leg from the knee down.

"Please, just call me Sarka. How much for a nice, private room?"

"The well-wishes of Odin be upon you, Sarka. You can have the corner room on the second floor, room number seven." The bartender handed a key over to her.

"What do I owe you?"

"Room's complimentary, Lady Sarka. Meals too. Drinks be on your own coin, though, most Challengers mention their title loudly and drink mightily on others' coins."

"How long since the last Challenger was through here?"

"Before my time: eighty-one years. Only reason I know is because one of the Odinites was here when the bells went off announcing your arrival, and he mentioned nine worlds and nine days did Odin hang from the world tree, and it was an auspicious sign for a Challenger to arrive now."

"Is there a temple around here?"

"Next court down the road is the Holy Court. All the temples are there."

"Thanks, uh... I didn't catch your name?"

"Lief, Lady Sarka."

"Alright, thanks, Lief. I'm going to check out my room and take my leisure around town for a bit."

Intent declared, she checked her room. It consisted of a parlor with a desk, a private bathroom, and an opulent bedroom. All three rooms had interesting Magitech lighting. The Magitech system powered more than just the lighting. Interesting glyph-covered crystals set in pipes also provided the warm or cold water, and there was even a wind crystal to dry herself off with.

"I'm taking a nap here. Have the bartender send me some fish! Lots of fish." Ark curled up on the bed.

"Right—you stay here, keep out of trouble. I'll be back before too long."

Aetheria had no trouble leaving the Hanging Tree unbothered. This early in the afternoon, but after lunch, the place was relatively empty. True to Lief's instructions, the courtyard full of temples proved easy to find. Odin's temple stood largest in the square, the entrance flanked by statues of two massive ravens. She felt as if the birds were watching her as she crossed the threshold into the temple.

Only it was no temple she walked into. She stood in a cozy study lit by fire. An old man with an eyepatch sat in a comfortable-looking chair. A book in one hand, a mug of mead in the other, Odin focused on her with his sole eye.

"Why, hello, record-breaker."

CHAPTER 39

You've Got a Quest

O h, come on, you seriously aren't grumpy about me breaking your record, are you?" Aetheria asked the All-Father incredulously.

"No. I have a quest for you, Challenger. Remain in Nidhogg's Bane for a year and take part in the expedition to ward off Nidhogg from Yggdrasil."

"Fight an enormous dragon away from a world tree? You don't go small, do you, All-Father?" Aetheria fancied the idea she looked pixie-ish with her best impish grin and the bright red, sweetly short hair.

"Worthy tasks for worthy Challengers. Few are the Challengers who merit a quest in the safehold. Slaying this incarnation of Nidhogg will allow you to bring all of your Flames to your current capacity and allow your StarMane bandmate to reach his next growth milestone."

"Nice. I'll do it. The city seems worth saving."

"No bargaining for greater rewards? No holding out for a sweetened pot? An altruistic outlook?" Odin seemed shocked, and a little disappointed. *He must have had a sales pitch all ready.*

"It can't be that uncommon for people to be decent."

"Can be and is."

"Be the change you want to see?" Aetheria laughed.

"My temple will provide you with a private villa for the duration of your stay. That should cut down on your need for subterfuge."

"How very kind of you. I don't suppose there's a library full of wonderful knowledge in this private villa?" Aetheria tried altering her voice. The result was high-pitched and saccharine. The old god grimaced at it.

"You'll need to work on that. Have the priests bring you whatever literature you need, within reason and their capabilities."

"Sure. Do you need me to do anything else while I'm there?"

"You could give me some of that honey you stole from Aetherius's garden, with a few of the fruits, too."

Aetheria considered. A pot brimming with honey appeared in one hand, and a sack of fruit in the other. She handed both over to the god.

Odin offered her a scroll covered in runes. "You cannot *bridge* the gap to the Origin without first mastering conversion. It has been ages since we brewed ambrosial mead of the highest quality."

Reality shifted around her, pushed her out of Odin's study, and Aetheria, in the guise of Sarka, stared blankly at the door to the temple. A low-ranking novitiate stood before her patiently.

"I am to show you the way to your villa, Lady Challenger."

"Okay, let's stop at the Hanging Tree. I need to pick up my cat."

The villa was only six long blocks away from the holy courtyard full of temples. They had built a series of villas and estates with trees and bushes cleverly planted to give each stylish property an illusion of privacy. Land on a vessel such as the Bane had to be a big commodity. *It'd take some pretty ingenious engineering to make a ship like this any bigger, especially when at sea. I'll have to see what their engineers are capable of, if they let me near them. They must put so much magic into it.*

The first day of her stay at the villa was anticlimactic. Both Aetheria and Arkaziel availed themselves of the baths, kitchen, and beds, and reveled in the luxury. No matter how nice of a tent she had in storage, it was still just a tent. It didn't compare with a posh log villa surrounded by trees.

"You have my list?" Arkaziel stretched lazily, showing his fangs, while repositioning into the extra fluffy animal bed the temple had provided.

"Yes, I have your list. Digest your awful smelling troll heart while I'm gone, and eat some mint grass or something. Your breath smells absolutely *terrible*."

Arkaziel hissed at her. "I don't judge your smell."

"I smell like jasmine, and I know it."

"You're a shapeshifter on the Ethereal Path, and you settle for something as mundane as jasmine?"

"I'm not having this conversation right now. I'm going to the market." Aetheria scratched behind Arkaziel's ears until his leg twitched, and she smiled sweetly and blew a kiss to the cat. Her steps were practically a skip. It felt like decades since she'd been among other humanoids, let alone other humans. It was over a year since she left Solace already. Aoibhe's absence gnawed at her heart, but the connection between their souls strengthened by the day even still. Occasionally, in the depths of her soul, Aetheria felt warm pulses of love from the nephilim. They were infrequent and short, but they felt like being bathed in rainbows and sunshine on the inside. They were the only thing that had kept Aetheria from strangling Arkaziel on more than a few occasions already. *Living with a cat in a house is bad enough. Adventuring with one was a terrible idea. It's better than being totally alone, though.*

The blocks took her a minute or two longer than she was used to. The few inches of height difference she had given up as Sarka had left her strides a little shorter. Her body instinctively dealt with the differentials of shapeshifting, but the incongruities still occasionally stood out to her mind.

A sign reading "The Wyrd Works" led her to the first shop she found interesting. Inside, an old woman sat behind a dusty counter, fiddling with knitting needles, while a young man in his late teens or early twenties worked on copying a tome. He looked up.

"A customer? Welcome to The Wyrd Works. We specialize in arcane secrets. Is there something I can help you with? I'm Wulf, and I'd be happy to assist you."

Dang, even the shop boys are all Viking good-looking. Down, girl—you're taken. Still, remember you're Sarka for now. Smile cutely, bat your eyelashes, and see what this place sells.

"Arcane secrets? Fascinating. How about beyond arcane? Do you delve into Aether, Nether, or the Ethereal? Oh, I'm Sarka." From the young man's expression, she didn't screw up her attempt at giving him doe eyes. Arkaziel mercilessly mocked her when she messed up her shapeshifting. The old lady behind the counter gave Aetheria the side-eye, though, especially when she fake-blushed at giving her current alias.

They didn't call me Lady Challenger. They're Dwellers.

"We don't have anything like that, I'm afraid." Wulf sounded disappointed.

"I'll help this one. Why don't you scamper along to the training hall, boy?" The old woman's voice was raspy and experienced. Wulf looked shocked to be interrupted by the old woman, but muttered a "Yes, ma'am" and beat feet quickly. The youth even forgot to say a parting word to Aetheria.

"You've got quite the aura hidden there, girl. Are you even human?" Old or not, the woman's eyes pierced the soul. *It makes sense a peddler of secrets would also be an acquirer of secrets.*

"Yes, I'm human. Just adopted into some powerful families. So, do you have anything like I asked about?"

"Are you here for the upcoming Hunt?"

The old woman did not seem like someone she should lie to. Aetheria was feeling vibes similar to those the masters in Solace had given off. She had to be at least Tier Four on whatever path she walked.

"Odin requested I remain for a year and take part in the next Hunt, yes. I didn't catch your name."

"Amalia."

Silence reigned between the two for a solid minute, with neither woman backing down from the flat stares they gave each other. Amalia smiled. Aetheria smiled back.

"I've got a journal from a Tier Three on the Aetheric Ice Path, poetry from a self-proclaimed Ethereal lord, and a treatise on the chaotic properties of Nether and how to capitalize on them."

"How much for all three?" The idea made Aetheria's heart beat faster.

"We don't deal in coin, dear."

Aetheria rubbed her chin. *If it was good enough for Odin...* A single gleaming peach appeared in her hand.

The old lady's eyes lit up. "Deal. I'll throw in a journal from an Ice Path Challenger dating a few centuries back. They had the touch of Ymir too."

"I overpaid by that much?"

"You're offering a bounty from the gods, girl. For an old lady like me, that can and will restore me to my youth." Amalia gave an honest smile.

"If you get any new treasures along my inquiry lines, I'm staying in the villa owned by the Temple of Odin."

"Got it. I'll keep that in mind. Thank you, Sarka."

The old lady didn't look that surprised when the items vanished as soon as she handed them over to Aetheria.

"Is there anyone on the Bane who could help me work on manifesting a domain? I'm stuck somewhere halfway between aura and domain."

Amalia considered this.

"There's a Climber staying at the Bronze Longhouse. Muscle-bound elf, believe it or not. He has been going through all the training grounds, challenging anyone with a domain to contests of Assertive Dominance. Gossip says he hasn't lost yet and has made a pretty penny on the bets."

"Contests of Assertive Dominance?"

"A mental duel. You put your will, aura, domain, or intent up against someone else's. No actual fighting. Not a popular pastime on the Bane because of the lack of actual combat, but some want to prove themselves any way they can. They set victory terms at the start of the match and vary based on the abilities of the contestants."

"Thanks, Amalia." Aetheria offered the old woman a parting smile and left.

A few inquiries along the way got her to the nearest training area. The Natives still all instinctively knew she was a Challenger and were exceptionally polite to her. This training area had little in the way of amenities. There were nine sunken rings in which people could spar, and a dirt track. *The better ones are probably private or charge an entrance fee. I never even asked if there were any guilds in town.*

Pairs of men who looked like locals occupied three of the pits. Two of the pairs went back and forth only with martial prowess and weapons, while the third pair exchanged blows intermingled with the arts. Their raw combat power was incomparable to those who only used weapon technique. It was apples to oranges.

Aetheria found studying the men using arts difficult. Her senses of Aether, Nether, and Ether had increased by leaps and bounds, yet her senses for mana and other energies remained unrefined. Not that it was relevant in this practice, as both men were only using basic arts activated through their weapons. Arts on that level were for true novices who had not learned to finesse their abilities into much more versatile arts.

Aetheria was about to head to one of the other training grounds when a well-built elf walked over to the pit, accompanying one of the Bane's local warriors. Even from thirty feet away, she could hear the two ragging on one another and boasting.

She approached the sunken pit, where people were placing wagers.

"What's the rundown on these two?" One Native's eyes widened when she spoke to them, before he bowed his head to her.

"The elf is a Climber, Lady Challenger. He walks the Path of Denial and counters his opponents' domains with his own. The perfect path to control the Contest of

Dominance. Until he runs up against someone unhindered by mana and anima." The Native's eyes seemed to sparkle with a glint of hidden knowledge.

As he had predicted, the exchange was one-sided. The local activated a Domain of Axes, semitransparent axes appeared to cut the surrounding air. The elf's domain was simply a transparent bubble that pushed the axe domain back. Slowly, then inevitably, the axe domain fell and then crumpled.

"Anyone else want to take me on? Whatever aura, domain, or intent you throw my way, I'll crush it," the elf bragged. The Native gave Aetheria an unnecessary nudge as she vaulted into the pit.

"I'll give it a shot."

CHAPTER 40

Domains

The elf's eyes narrowed at her. In her current form, Aetheria was a head shorter than him, and her aura remained tightly contained to hide as much of her power as possible. The elf laughed mockingly.

"What do you think you're going to do in this contest, little girl? Can you even manifest an aura, let alone a domain?"

In answer, a weight dropped on the whole training ground. Black and purple energy erupted from Aetheria's pores, manifesting into a pure Nether aura. The whole training ground grew darker from her proximity, and the indistinct qualities of night seemed to lie heavy on Nidhogg's Bane for blocks around the training ground.

"Umm. Odds are one to one!" the sly man who'd been taking bets cried out, and a few onlookers descended to place bets. The Natives favored Aetheria, while the Dwellers and Climbers favored the Elf.

"Impressive, but still only an aura. No matter how much it speaks of night or how much power you shove into your aura, it is no match for me. For I am Eldarion De'ala'ar, The Denier." The muscular elf summoned his domain. The transparent bubble appeared around him. Aetheria noticed he had put more effort into this version than the last domain he had conjured. Bravado or not, Eldarion was taking her seriously.

"I was going to seek you out to learn more about domains, but you're kind of an arrogant dick." Aetheria smiled sweetly with the words, and ice spread from her feet across the floor of the arena. With it spread her aura as a proto-domain.

The ice and aura met the bubble of Denial. The bubble slowly pushed backward. The elf's eyes narrowed, his lips pressing together in a grimace.

"How?"

"You tell me."

The elf focused on his domain. Yet even when the veins on his forehead pulsed with effort, the bubble continued to lose ground to Aetheria's Nether aura. In less than two minutes, the elf's domain had receded to half a meter, and the rate of lost ground only sped up.

"Do you yield, or shall I end this?" The saccharine voice she had tried on Odin came out much better this time around. *Who'd have thought changing your voice would be so hard?*

The elf's eyes carried curse words Aetheria didn't even know in them. He did not answer her, instead grunting and pushing a pulse of his own aura at her. Eldarion meant to distract her, but his aura didn't even make it past the perimeter of her own. Theoretically, what Eldarion had just done was the traditional employment of an aura. Usually, they were only used to intimidate or stun, not be mini-domains like Aetheria's now was.

She shrugged, and the black and purple aura around her took on a new depth. The Flame of Nyx spread through her aura and consumed the rest of the elf's bubble of Denial in one quick surge. The elf fell to the ground from the rebound and stared at her with a new look: hope. The onlookers who had bet on the elf grumbled, while those who had bet on Aetheria cheered heartily.

"At the end there, you used a Flame to strengthen your aura?" Eldarion asked, although it was rhetorical.

"Yes."

"How does a Climber I've never heard of have such a powerful Flame?"

"Well, I've got stuff to do. Have a nice day." Aetheria waved and vaulted out of the ring.

"Wait! I'll teach you to use a domain properly if you tell me what Flame that was and how you gained it. You're the Challenger who's in town, aren't you?"

"That's all you want to know?" She arched a fine red brow at Eldarion.

"The origin of Flames often reveals much about one's past," the elf clarified. "People don't just hand out Flames willy-nilly! It takes decades to repair the loss of fragmentation, and gods never share of themselves with mortals."

"Fine, but you're also buying me lunch."

They journeyed to the Hanging Tree for a private table. Lunch turned out to be fish stew. *I suppose since this is a boat, most of their protein is going to be fish.*

"So, Lady Challenger, I should introduce myself properly. I am Eldarion The Denier, and I climb with a group based out of Eloiuisa."

"You can just call me Sarka. I'm climbing out of Grief."

The elf laughed. "Grief? That ancient hellhole driven to ruin by a Goddess of Misery?"

"Yeah."

"Oh. I, uh... My apologies. Grief is one of the ancient planets, yet it has no climbing teams worth anything, unlike other ancient worlds. I didn't know there were any Challengers left to take on that hell world."

"I'm the last, it turns out. So, you wanted to know what Flame I used and who gave it to me?"

"That was the deal."

"I used the Primordial Flame of Nyx and gained it from the aforementioned Nyx."

Silence reigned over their table.

"I thought it was too powerful to have been a Mortal Flame. Sometimes old monsters in the last tiers give their personal Flames to a promising disciple or descendant before they attempt to ascend. A legacy of sorts. For the right price, some masters will part with a sliver more."

"Doubt Nyx'll be willing to part with any more. Besides, I've been informed most people's heads explode when exposed to Primordial Flames."

"Yours didn't."

"I have testimonials that say mine did, more than once."

"You are still alive..."

"That does not mean my head didn't explode. It just precludes my head having stayed in an exploded state." Smiling sweetly had grown on Aetheria. Maybe "Sarka" would remain one of her forms. It was certainly interesting being a different height, if nothing else. *I miss my trench coat, though.*

"That explains the ease and strength of your Nether manipulation. You know, it's considered poor form to flex in such a way."

"The same poor form that it would be for you to flex over people who you beat just as easily?"

"Touché."

"Since those answers don't help you, I'll answer one other question for you, I guess."

"What tower are you climbing currently?"

"The Tower of Aetherius."

"How? I suppose a Nether Cultivator would have the skills to deal with the enhanced Aether density."

"That's true. Where there's Aether, there's also Nether." This time, her sweet smile got a wary look from the elf. "So, tell me about domains."

"You're close, I think. Instead of manifesting ice across the ground as you do, or expanding your aura, you expand your internalized energy. Let it suffuse the area until it becomes a field under your control. You'll need to start small, and I don't mean a meter wide. I mean a centimeter. Once you stabilize a domain, you can increase its size by expending energy. Bigger is not always better. The energy expenditure goes up the larger the area, but the intensity of the effect stays constant."

Aetheria frowned. *That doesn't sound right. Or do Flames break rules? Obviously, they break rules. That's why my aura is more powerful than his domain. If it takes someone in the highest tiers to make a Flame naturally and they only get imparted into prime disciples, the general knowledge of most Climbers is going to be pretty useless to me.*

"How do you control what your domain does?"

The elf blinked at her repeatedly. "It just... does?"

"What if you make use of more than one discipline?"

"You'd have two domains. If you were on a Fire and Ice Path, you could manifest a Fire or an Ice domain, or combine them into a Frozen Flame domain." The elf shrugged, leaving it uncertain whether the answer was guesswork or factual.

Ugh. Is this like those xianxia stories, where people get all secretive and jerky as soon as you get past the basic knowledge? Why share knowledge when you can be a jerkbutt and hoard it so people have to be as miserable as you were learning it?

"I see." He had told her what she wanted to know, though. How to form a domain. *In the most generic way possible. Yet given the depth of differences among paths, maybe that's not intentional vagueness, but actually because of differences in how people view their own powers. Is that the result of there not being a grand unifying system, where everyone walks an individual path even for the same powers?*

"Thanks, Eldarion. Had you heard there's going to be a hunt for Nidhogg in a year?" Now it was time to gossip.

"There is? I might have to stay here longer than I planned. Opportunities like that don't come along very often. The city levels are usually just a chance to recuperate, restock, blow off some steam, and deal with your trauma to face the rest of the tower. Nidhogg will be as strong a tower boss as you'd encounter on Floors Twenty-Five, Fifty, Seventy-Five, and One Hundred. Stronger, even, since it's not a single contest." The elf rubbed at his hairless chin in consideration of changing plans. "Have you told other Climbers about this yet?"

Aetheria grinned.

"I'll take that as a no. Well, thank you for the heads-up. I appreciate it. If you need any help with forming your domain properly and not relying on the Flames, I'm staying here."

"I'll keep that in mind. Have a nice day." With a casual wave of her hand, Aetheria wandered out of the Hanging Tree and hurried back to the villa. She scribbled a note to the queen of the Bane and sent it off with one of the clergy of Odin. She spent the rest of the afternoon trying to create a domain in the villa's garden.

Time after time, she almost created the field of energy around her, but it fell to pieces at the last moment. *Am I visualizing wrong? Do I not possess something necessary to project a domain? What's missing? I'm doing everything Eldarion said.* No matter what Aetheria tried, she couldn't form a domain from Aether or Nether. She didn't want to force Ethereal energy into being on Nidhogg's Bane unless she had to; it would draw attention. *Would switching to Ethereal energy even matter? I* am *on the Ethereal Path, but maybe I just don't meet some requirement?*

Displeased, she changed gears, withdrawing the scroll covered in runes that Odin had given her. She was relieved when she found it inscribed in the language of Ath.

Descend into the abyssal expanse of Erebos, source of Nether. Ascend into the celestial expanse of Aetherius, embodiment of Aether. Forthwith, erect a vessel within thyself, that thou mayest amass and encapsulate Ethereal energy. Thereafter, kindle a spark of Origin within thy vessel. Pray thee, mayhap that thou canst endure.

"Gee, thanks, Odin." Aetheria refrained from letting her teeth grind in annoyance. "Okay, I've got this. Erebos is Darkness, counter to Aetherius. So probably one embodiment of Nether, like Aetherius is Aether. Right? Right. Vessel within myself... means inside my repository? Seems about right. A Spark of Origin must refer to starting the reaction with Ethereal energy. The other books all refer to it as the Origin Energy or an Origin Point. Pray to survive... oh, this is just going to be awesome. Ark!"

The cat showed up shortly, not actually having heard her words but feeling Aetheria's call through their bond.

"What's going on, Red?" The winged cat was gnawing on a fish.

"How many of those have you eaten already? I'm going to blow myself up a few times with this cryptic-ass scroll from Odin. Monitor me and convince anyone who comes to investigate that everything is fine, yeah?"

The StarMane rolled his eyes. "Fine. But if you take too long, no promises I won't eat someone before you get back. I'm positively famished."

"Greediness is a sin, you know." Still, she pulled one of the large fish she'd bought at the market from her repository and tossed it to Arkaziel.

"This should hold me over for... oh, a day. Maybe. Don't take too long, and try not to explode on me. Actually, explode on me. You taste awesome, but your bits always disappear into energy before I can eat more than a few bites." He displayed his sharp fangs in a grin.

"And *you* are my companion." *Fuck my life.*

CHAPTER 41

Heart Engineering

The soul repository remained one of Aetheria's largest weak points of knowledge of her path and capabilities. According to Aoibhe, she could evolve her soul repository into an inner world between Tiers Four and Five. For now, though, her repository seemed to be an infinite void that could hold anything and everything she threw at it. An important facet of the void, however, was the omnipresent quantities of Aether and Nether. Inside her soul or not, there seemed to be a nearly infinite presence of the two energies, much like anywhere else in Creation.

The flavor of the Nether was more like Nyx than Erebus or Khaos, though. Not that it seemed to matter in the grand scheme of things. Nether was Nether, as far as combining it with Aether went. *I wonder if that's because Aetherius's Flame is the pure deal. Are there other Primordials who share his role in other cosmologies? There must be.*

Her awareness of the repository was nearly perfect. She always had total knowledge of everything inside of it. Withdrawing and stowing things had become second nature. This would be the first time that Aetheria tried to impose something on the place. Her first effort created a water fountain. It served no purpose but was easy to visualize, and that seemed to translate into not being a challenge to create.

The scroll Odin gave her supposedly would help with her path and energy conversion. Conversion of power reminded Aetheria of engines, and for humans, the heart had always felt analogous as the engine of the body. Four chambers seemed unnecessary, but she felt confident she could make it all work while retaining the idea and aesthetic of a human heart. Logic seemed to be weak in the face of a universe-altering power like that of the Ethereal.

The first chamber of her imaginary heart would be where the Aether flowed in. She directed Nether to flow into the other upper chamber. The third chamber would be where Aether and Nether mixed and pushed into the final chamber, where a spark of Ethereal power would ignite the two via a process similar to what her Aetherflame Nova did, resulting in Ethereal power or Ether, which could fill her repository and wait for use.

That was the idea, anyway.

Visualization seemed to go fine. *This feels like I'm building a cultivation core. Is that what I'm doing?* She molded together Aether and Nether and ignited the mix via the Aetherflame so it took on the form of Ethereal energy. Using will, Aetheria then crystallized it into the shape of her imagined Ethereal heart engine. The crystallization of power took time. How long Aetheria forged, smoothed, shaped, and reshaped, she wasn't sure. Arkaziel's bored annoyance in the back of her mind assured her it was taking her longer than the StarMane wanted.

In the end, a gleaming red structure dominated the soul repository. It towered over stacks of fruit, piles of chests, organized weaponry stacked like cordwood, the portable tent, and all the other things she had accumulated since her rebirth.

Aetheria placed a copy of the Flame of Aetherius into the Aether chamber, while a double of the Flame of Nyx went into the Nether chamber. These mimicked Flames would draw Aether and Nether to the associated chamber. Without them, the engine would need some kind of intake.

Alright. That looks good. Structure seems sound, no cracks, I'm doing good. Yay me.

Aetheria checked over the Heart again and again to make sure everything was as she imagined it. Only after her tenth review did she stop and acknowledge she had entered procrastination territory. She had not found so much as a spot to smooth since the second pass. Delay would not change the results.

What's the worst that can happen? I blow up my proto-inner world?

The last chamber would need a combustion element. She had initially visualized it as something like her Aetherflame, but the scroll from Odin said to use Ethereal energy. Remarking on her ice affinity, Aoibhe had said that Ethereal energy could take on the qualities of any energy. In the last chamber, she imagined a star-shaped orb. It would suck in Aether and Nether and then explode in a flash of Ethereal sparks that would fuse the woven Aether and Nether into Ethereal.

The third chamber broke the visual and aesthetic comparisons to a heart, since both Aether and Nether chambers connected to it, and it was more like a loom than a mixture chamber. The entire purpose of the third chamber was to weave the strands of power into a fuel to burn in the last chamber. The last chamber was also out of place slightly, being more of a combustion engine than a heart. *Still, incongruities aside, there's no reason it shouldn't work. Right?*

There was only one way to find out. Aetheria created a spark of Ethereal power to ignite the process. Anticipation and nervous excitement built within her. The first explosion of power from the last chamber kick-started the entire process. The Flames pulled in Aether and Nether, which were woven into fuel and pulled into the combustion chamber. It expunged Ethereal power from the heart as crystalline bricks.

Will that work?

Aetheria tried to draw power from the brick, and she could feel it flow from her soul aperture into her body. It was a sensation like no other—vivid, raw, and utterly alien. She felt her cells soak up the Ethereal power like dehydrated people in a desert at a newfound oasis. *It works!*

When she opened her eyes, a pale face was looking into her own. Darkness and night surrounded them. She didn't recognize the face: alabaster pale skin, black hair, mysterious eyes. A beauty that haunted the mind. A dark black gown covered the woman's pale frame and billowed around her in imitation of a dark cloud.

"I shielded you from prying eyes. Just in case you took out Nidhogg's Bane with a mistake." The voice was unmistakably her friend Callie's. The face and the primordial night around them were undeniably of Nyx. Which meant either Callie was a goddess, or the happenstance of a similar voice was a joke. If deities had been in her raid group, especially if they were her sort of adopted internet parents, her selection for this life after an untimely death made a lot more sense.

"Hi, Callie." A warm smile accompanied her lightly stated, half-questioning words.

"Hi, Aes." Simple words. Words that Callie had said to Aesca hundreds of times over the years when she logged into Discord. Nyx bundled familiarity and reassurance with those words, and an old friend returned after a long absence.

"Nyx, huh?" Aetheria tried to wrap her mind around the situation.

"Yep. How are you enjoying your new life, dear?" Nyx was unperturbed, her voice smooth as silk and her demeanor calmer than a still pond.

"Quite a lot. I found love, got a cat, am learning to kick ass. All the stuff I used to dream about when we'd play *EFWO*."

"I'm glad to hear it," Nyx said, her voice filled with pride. "I always knew you'd make a fantastic heroine, even if Pete put his hand on the scales more than he needed to. And be careful with that cat. StarManes are vicious menaces."

"Pete's Aetherius, then?"

"I just won the bet on when you'd remember. Good job." Nyx's voice suggested this was only natural. After all, she was Nyx. One of the oldest, most powerful, and craftiest Primordial beings in existence.

"How many people in our guild were actually gods?"

"Only Pete and me. Well, a few demigods here and there, but most didn't stick around long enough to make the raid team. Adam and Yziiie are both plane walkers, though."

"So did I just do something dumb, or awesome?"

"Something new-ish. Without the Flames, it wouldn't work. Like your repository itself is a proto-world, you've constructed a proto-core. It is stable, generates Ethereal power in a usable form, and isn't running out of control. Impressive."

"So this wasn't what Odin's note meant to do?"

"He would say that yes, that is what it meant for you to do. Odin has wisdom beyond most gods. He investigated your fate and plucked a thread of possibility. Yet his vague note could have taken thousands of forms, and your results could have destroyed the floor if you lost control. Apparently, it was a gamble Odin found agreeable, despite his fondness for the Nidhogg's Bane. We've all shaped city floors, and that is obviously his. He dotes on the Natives there and tempts Dwellers to it with great frequency."

"I could've wiped the floor out. Should I just assume that's a possibility any time I'm about to do something involving the Ethereal Path?"

"Yes, and yes. You walk a dangerous path, not just for yourself, but for everything around you. You still don't remember receiving my Flame, do you? Even with my deft touch, thanks to that clod Aetherius overdoing his Flame, you spent the equivalent of twenty years in a cycle of exploding and regenerating before your new body found equilibrium."

"I spent twenty years dead and exploding?" The words hung heavily in the air, each syllable a hammer blow against the anvil of her preconceived notion of how things had come to this point. Aetheria had known she was missing something, but that it had caught her in a twenty-year cycle of pain felt like a stab in the heart. *No wonder I blanked some things out. That's a long time to be maimed again and again while always healing. Maybe I've got something in common with Prometheus now.*

"Equivalent. We formed your body in a pocket dimension with a time differential. Oh, Odin's about to notice I stopped time and shielded you. Time to go. Good luck, Aes." Her old gaming partner waved, then vanished. With her went the total darkness around them, to be replaced by the villa, the garden, and a bored-looking Arkaziel who was mid-yawn.

"Took you long enough. No kaboom, though. Did I... Oh, wow."

Aetheria frowned at Arkaziel, but she could feel what had made him widen his eyes. Her Ethereal heart had starting beating. With each beat, flows of power became accessible to her, which her cells greedily lapped up, her Ethereal physiology truly awakened for the first time now that a constant power source was available to it. There was no pain this time. No red energies ripped her skin. No parts of her exploded. Aetheria imagined this was how a plant felt when put in the sun.

"You're ridiculous, you know that? You're not supposed to form a core until you're well into Tier Three and about to cross into becoming an Ethereal Scion. What else should I expect from a human with four Primordial Flames?" The StarMane stared at her intently, then laughed. "Don't look so concerned. I'm growing faster than I should, too, thanks to you. We'll just be two freaky powerful, young, good-looking, super-amazing, Ethereal Path walkers together." Arkaziel was in good spirits, at least.

"That's the attitude. Besides, I'm sure you'll get a similar boost when you eat part of Nidhogg."

"Oh, I will, alright." The light in the cat's eyes would have been terrible had she been his enemy. *Then again, he is basically a cat mixed with a dragon. It's kind of disturbing even for me.*

"The priests left a message from the queen on the coffee table in the parlor. You were only out for just under a day."

"Thanks, Arkaziel. I'll go see what she said to my suggestion." She ruffled the cat's fur and bounded inside to check on the missive.

CHAPTER 42

Nidhogg Strikes

In the year Aetheria spent on Nidhogg's Bane, she saw land only one time. The massive Magitech vessel anchored itself off a slightly larger island than itself. Not that there was much land to disembark on and wander across. Yggdrasil, the world tree, dominated the entire island. No other tree Aetheria had ever seen compared to the mighty ash tree that was Yggdrasil.

They launched the smaller vessels attached to the Bane's sides and the rest once fully anchored. Within two days, Drottning Brünnhilde's forces had erected a series of massive Magitech gun towers. The process seemed well planned out. Each of the Bane's regiments erected powerful weapons and defenses. Aetheria and Arkaziel spent the week leading up to Nidhogg's arrival solidifying the gains they had made over the last year.

The Climbers who had stayed were put in regiments with the locals and assigned to fight against Nidhogg. As a Dweller, Drottning Brünnhilde had seen the value of retaining some Climbers to deal with Nidhogg. However, she had been quite selective of those to whom she offered advanced pay to stay and fight.

The promised day arrived. Nidhogg, Dragon of the Apocalypse, approached from the south. The monster appeared as little more than a dark brown blob on the horizon at first. Minutes ticked by and the blob grew ever closer, ever larger. The colossal dragon was almost a quarter of the size of Nidhogg's Bane itself, with sickly looking scales and sharp protrusions covering his hide. The air darkened with his toxic aura, and even the sun seemed to want to warm other waters.

Massive magic cannons fired beams of coruscating blue and black energy at the dragon. The first beam to strike Nidhogg's hide elicited a terrible scream. Toxic black breath concentrated on the fortified gun tower. At the very last minute, a familiar bubble expanded to protect the tower, and his breath attack dispersed into the wind.

"We're up the moment he breaks past the perimeter. You ready for this, Ark?"

Aetheria and Arkaziel stood on a floating piece of ice near the boughs of Yggdrasil. Today, the red-haired form of Sarka was gone. Her standard accouterments—the red trench coat, her black fingerless gloves, leather pants, and a tank top with a scarf— were all she needed to fight a legendary dragon. Drottning Brünnhilde had offered her one of the flying Magitech vessels, but Aetheria had declined, suggesting they serve those who couldn't fly on their own.

Black veins of ice formed the exterior of the wings she had formed, with red ice filling in along the wings themselves. She could have shapeshifted wings, but she found that using etheric ice gave her far better control. Real wings required a lot more work, too.

More volleys of energy assaulted Nidhogg, and when a tower blocked his breath attack, he just swiped his tail and demolished the whole tower in one blow. However, this, too, led to a terrible roar from the dragon, as a strange form of fire had stuck to his tail and kept burning. *Let's see, that's Andry's Poison Eating Flame. Hopefully, Andry made it out of the tail strike. No shock that a toxic monster like Nidhogg isn't a fan of an Art that does damage the more poisonous the target is.*

Each tower delayed Nidhogg's advance, but nothing stopped it.

"Let's eat this jerk," Arkaziel snarled and leaped off her shoulder. Within moments, the small black cat had become his true draconic-feline self, with a length from snout to tail of about fifteen meters. The StarMane had feasted heavily to grow so much. Sunlight bathed him, showing off black scales under purple, glittering fur. The claws on his forelegs glowed with a malevolent intensity. And then, like a bullet, he was off.

Before Aetheria even got to a count of five, Nidhogg was raging and screaming again. The red glowing claws of the StarMane were the first thing of the day to truly pierce its thick, vile scales. *Knowing Arkaziel, he stopped to take a bite out of Nidhogg to add insult.*

"And now it's my turn."

Aetheria jumped off the floating ledge of ice and let her aura unravel around her. Today, that aura was Ethereal red and danced with wild abandon at the thrill of such a legendary encounter. Her flight was direct, and she maintained a speed just under the speed of sound. She had crossed that threshold once unintentionally and learned a painful lesson about creating sonic booms.

Aetheria's soul repository contained somewhere around twelve metric tons of items. Mass that she shifted into her right hand at the last possible moment. The arrogant dragon looked as if he were about to laugh her off. He took the strike to the face, instead, shaken by horrible pain. Cracks ran through scales on his face, his body flung backwards. Nidhogg landed on his back in the sea.

Oh, cripes, that hurt my hand. No getting distracted.

The aforementioned right hand looked fine, but internally her bones were already being realigned and straightened after fracturing from the strength of the blow. Nidhogg's armored hide was no joke.

Aetheria clenched her left hand in a raised fist. The sea around Nidhogg churned as the Flame of Thalassa formed in the water. Appendage-like bands of water thickened and bound the dragon. Arkaziel passed over the exposed underbelly of the dragon in a black flash, leaving deep wounds across Nidhogg's softest spots. Following the StarMane's attack came volleys of fire from the remaining Magitech towers, while the smaller flying vehicles launched large prepared spells or rockets at Nidhogg's belly.

Aetheria summoned Ymir's Flame, freezing the water and locking Nidhogg even more in place. Spears of red ice shot from the watery restraints to pierce the flesh of the dragon. Her construct of etheric ice darkened and pulsed as if it had a heartbeat of its own. She was mimicking the effects of her Death Ice, the freezing cold of Ymir leeching the life force of Nidhogg bit by bit.

Damage accumulated quickly, and Nidhogg went berserk. Rage gave strength to the legendary dragon, and the etheric ice shattered. Nidhogg was back in the air before anyone could stop him, and his next roar, fashioned from his anima, carried the wrath of a godly dragon. Not only did the sound shatter eardrums, but the monster's energy disrupted the mind and stunned others.

With fast healing and Flames bolstering her, naturally Aetheria was one of the first to recover. She'd barely regained control before forcing her wings to steer her to the left, the jaws of Nidhogg missing her by bare centimeters. The monster's teeth ripped half of her wings to shreds. She conjured new wings with a simple thought, just in time to dodge the follow-up swipes from Nidhogg's claws and tail.

Nidhogg opened his mouth and spewed toxins across the second perimeter. Nidhogg's breath had a potency that transcended simple descriptions like poisonous, corrupt, or miasmatic. It was as if the dragon had an affinity all on its own that blended all the terrible toxic powers of acid, industrial waste, poison, and radiation together into one terrible, gray-green-yellow breath attack. Boats in the water rusted; those without shielding jumped into the ocean. Barriers and defenses were immediately erected on most of the boats.

Nidhogg's breath attack ended just as Arkaziel's began. With his increase in size, the cat-dragon's black and white beam attack was now the width of a school bus, and it punched into the wounds along the side of the larger dragon. Scales cracked and shattered; flesh and contaminated blood created a terrible mist until the beam ended two seconds later. The agile StarMane deftly avoided Nidhogg's tail strike.

Flares went up above the Bane itself, which made the third barrier between Nidhogg and Yggdrasil. Yellow, yellow, red. The ritual attack magic was ready.

~Get clear, Ark! The Bane's ritual is coming.~

The only response through their bond was an arrogant snort ringing through Aetheria's mind. Just because the cat could talk telepathically to her didn't mean he always chose to.

Tentacles of water rose once more from the ocean to entangle Nidhogg's feet and tail. It took Aetheria's full concentration to hold the dragon in this fashion, and the drain on her Ethereal energies was immense. Block after crystallized block of energy in her repository was consumed by the second to keep Nidhogg contained.

Five seconds after the flare, a massive rune appeared in the sky and a spear shot forth from the rune. The spear pierced into Nidhogg's shoulder repeatedly. With each thrust, the rune grew dimmer, until the spear vanished after the ninth attack.

I kind of thought we'd at least see Odin's hand holding it. If that's how a Conjuration of Odin and Gungnir work, I'm glad I'm not a summoner. Talk about lame.

The damage inflicted by the spear was considerable. Impressive looking or not, the mass conjuration spell worked by the faithful of the Bane sent fountains of cursed toxic blood into the air and ocean. If the blow should have stopped Nidhogg, though, no one told him. The dragon's eyes were terrible and red with rage. Waves of destruction emanated from him. Everything within fifty meters of the dragon ceased to exist. Then Nidhogg was on the prowl once more.

Random cruel attacks took down multiple boats and vehicles of the second line, the dragon's anger driving him toward Nidhogg's Bane.

Aetheria got a little altitude and then flew down like a pile driver. Right and left, hands ahead of her like a flying superhero, energy spinning around her like a drill. Her Ethereal energy shot black lightning as she added the Primordial Flame of Nyx to it, and then aqua lightning when the Primordial Flame of Aetherius joined in. This time, the scales parted before her attack, and the energy-drill around her burrowed deep into the corrupted flesh of Nidhogg.

Nidhogg's back shook and roiled when the bright form of Aetheria shot inside of it. Then even more attacks rained upon the legendary dragon. The black and white breath attack of Arkaziel vaporized one of Nidhogg's eyes and left deep wounds across the dragon's face. Magitech cannons, rockets, and missiles launched from Nidhogg's Bane impacted the massive dragon across his colossal form.

Into one of the deep wounds created by a missile dove the StarMane. Arkaziel's breath attack melted flesh before him as he plunged into Nidhogg's torso. The StarMane had a unique attack in mind, other than what Aetheria intended.

On the command deck of Nidhogg's Bane, Drottning Brünnhilde laughed like a madwoman.

"Are they truly fighting it from inside?" The Viking queen's tone carried amusement and a touch of wonder.

"It appears so," the Priest of Odin, who was conjuring the scenes in the viewing pools arrayed on the command deck, agreed with their leader. "I cannot scry inside Nidhogg, however. There is no doubt that is not a flying *cat* but a *StarMane* fighting with the Lady Challenger."

"Both of whom have Odin's Blessing." The sternness of Drottning Brünnhilde's tone brooked no dissent. "If we defeat Nidhogg instead of just driving him away, you'll have to write heroic prose about a StarMane. The absolute horror." Her humor, however, was contagious. Even the priest smiled ruefully.

"Something's about to happen," one of Drottning Brünnhilde's aides exclaimed, pointing to the third viewing pool. Nidhogg had recovered from the two attackers burrowing into his flesh, and seemed to shrug off the continued volley of attacks. The dragon sucked in copious amounts of air in a way it had not done previously.

"All shields up! Anti-Corruption activate!" The order spread like wildfire. Bubbles, barriers, and cleansing auras activated everywhere.

The indrawn breath of Nidhogg held such power, a few smaller vessels were sucked into the air and shredded in his maw. A sickly yellow-green light glowed at his mouth's edge before the legend unleashed the apocalypse.

Sullied, toxic energy exploded forth from the maw of the dragon. The entire second perimeter vanished like an illusion. No barrier or shield had the strength to stop the full power of Nidhogg at point blank.

CHAPTER 43

Arkaziel Strikes Back

Deep within Nidhogg, Aetheria had no clue what was happening outside of the dragon. Nor did she realize Arkaziel had committed to an attack similar to her own. She did not know that the dragon was unleashing his ultimate attack upon the defenses and fleets arrayed against him.

Darkness pressed in on Aetheria, and vertigo struck like a viper. Her body felt vague, numb, and spectral. She was a glowing ball instead of herself. In this darkness, there was another glowing sphere. Sickly yellow, the other ball radiated corruption and poison. She needed no one to explain to her that this was undoubtedly Nidhogg himself. Somehow, the dragon had pulled them into purely mental combat.

"You are strong. Nourish me with your blessed blood and I shall not feed on Yggdrasil for another turn of the ages."

"Why would I do that? I'll just beat you into oblivion, and then someone else will beat you into oblivion the next time you incarnate. It's your lot in life, isn't it? Giant punching bag." Aetheria didn't entertain the offer even slightly. Her bonds with both Arkaziel and Aoibhe provided constant reminders of reasons to strive and struggle.

No answer came forth from Nidhogg. The dragon was not known for his diplomatic abilities, cleverness, or anything other than his brute strength. His toxic light tried to swallow her own aqua light. Tendrils of corruption shot forward to burrow into the light that was Aetheria. Those tendrils froze, cracked, and shattered into millions of pieces.

"You should have stuck with fighting me physically. I keep getting told how human flesh isn't up to snuff, and how the human soul is inviolable."

The darkness surrounding her became the Flame of Ymir. Darkness turned into a pale blue, almost verging on white, coldness that froze everything. Everything other than Aetheria, to whom the cold offered comfort and solace.

"No matter how many Flames you have, I am Nidhogg!" Power flared from the mind of Nidhogg to assault her own mind. She centered herself within the Primordial Flame of Nyx. A cloak of night shrouded her mind and deflected the initial attack, and then the dark flame went offensive. Aetheria conjured the Primordial Flame of Nyx within Nidhogg's yellow sphere and commanded it to *feast*.

The immense cold slowed the reactions of the dragon and froze the outer layer of his being. A perpetual cycle of a tiny patch of Nidhogg freezing, turning to dust, and blowing away repeated itself while darkness took root inside of him.

"I win!" Nidhogg roared as corrosive appendages shot at Aetheria and tried to pierce her glowing mental self. Only one succeeded, and the pain was excruciating. Yet no strength leeched from Aetheria to the dragon. In fact, the opposite happened now that a linkage was in place. Dark pulses of energy were visible inside Nidhogg's toxic core, and all too late did the dragon realize he had attacked when he should have defended.

The Primordial Flame of Nyx ripped the incarnation's soul and core to shreds from the inside while Aetheria mentally imagined her hands inside of Nidhogg, ripping and clawing the dragon's essence apart.

In the real world, hoarfrost formed at Nidhogg's giant maw. Ice crystallized in the heavily moist sea air. A thin coat of frost ran along the gigantic form of the dragon. Then the ice turned black, and the legendary figure of the dragon mottled and wasted away. Nidhogg's chest cavity exploded outward, and another dragon flew into the sky. Arkaziel carried the legendary dragon's heart, already two-thirds eaten. Corrosive fumes rose from the StarMane, his black fur and scales showing moderate damage.

Heart gone, the rest of Nidhogg turned to solid ice and shattered from the inside. None of the dragon hit the ocean, though, the corpse being shunted into Aetheria's repository. She herself hovered in the air, her red ice wings restored, surrounded by a wicked halo of Ethereal power—all the energies she had absorbed from Nidhogg. Aetheria pushed what felt like never-ending torrents of absorbed power into her Flames. Each Primordial Flame hit its cap at Tier Two and now possessed a deep inner light.

She could feel each Flame bursting with power. She was the only obstacle preventing the four Flames from progressing to the next level. The torrent of Nidhogg's power did not stop coming, so Aetheria pushed it into her repository and crystallized it for later use. Corrupted yellow Nether crystals formed inside of the repository.

"Nice job, Ria. Did you eat the whole body? I was kind of hoping for a few more bites." Arkaziel was still in his much larger form, although once he tossed the last bite of Nidhogg's heart into his mouth and finished chewing, the StarMane became a small flying cat and landed on her shoulders once more.

"Nah, I've got some of him in my repository. I don't think anyone, other than you, could eat that nasty meal. The scales might come in handy for something…" Her red eyes took in the desolation Nidhogg had caused before his defeat. The dragon's caustic breath had caused rust, corrosion, and damage to Nidhogg's Bane and had destroyed nearly the entire second perimeter and half of the first perimeter.

"We'd better help with cleanup."

Aetheria spent hours using the Flame of Thalassa to control the seas. She salvaged debris, pulled people to boats, sent predators of survivors fleeing, and created multiple boats of ice to ferry people back to Nidhogg's Bane. It was a productive use of her abilities, but it also offered her all too clear of a glimpse into the desolation Nidhogg had wrought upon the people. In the back of her mind, she wondered if anyone would have survived without her and Arkaziel to do the heavy lifting against the dragon.

Five days went by in a blur. Memorial services for those who died. Awards for those who had survived. A feast for both. Aetheria had shared a portion of Nidhogg's scales with the leadership of Nidhogg's Bane, plus allocated ten extra scales to be sold and profits split and given to the families of the dead.

A week after the battle, an old leatherworker by the name of Angulus brought her what she had commissioned from him.

"And you're sure I don't owe you anything more?" she asked the man, who shook his head and grinned.

"The extra materials you let me have are more than enough reward, Lady Challenger."

"Alright. Did you name these boots?"

"Nidhogg's Fury." The old man gestured to the boots. "See how they're almost black, but the red of the dragon's fury still shows through?"

"You've a good sense for naming things, Angulus." To the astonishment of the old man, the boots already on Aetheria's feet just vanished, and she started pulling on the new boots and working on the straps.

"The fit is perfect."

"Well, I measured quite a few times, although the stories around town are that the Lady Challenger has a touch of the weird about her. Folks like you have a magic of your own, and things just kind of fit you, I hear."

Aetheria couldn't contain the laugh. It was such a roundabout way to say she was a shapeshifter. Although maybe the old man didn't know that? It didn't matter. She wasn't about to explain to him that the amazing boots he'd just fashioned for her were now part of her because of a trick she'd figured out with her soul repository.

"Thank you again, Angulus." While patting his back, she slipped a small purse of coins into his rear pocket. If the leatherworker noticed it, he had the grace to at least pretend he hadn't, but Aetheria felt like she had succeeded in her reverse pickpocketing skills.

There was now only one task awaiting her before she left Nidhogg's Bane.

"Let's go." Ark purred and headbutted her neck. The StarMane was once again the size of a house cat, and in the form of a black cat with wings.

The path to the Temple of Odin was smooth and contained no obstacles. Most of the Climbers who had fought Nidhogg had already departed or were still recovering from their wounds. In the following months, many new Climbers would end up at the Bane, the queen had said. When wares made of their share of Nidhogg were available, the forces behind the towers would send the worthy to purchase them.

The interaction made Aetheria wonder just how the decision of who went to what city worked. If happenings like these occurred on the regular in the tower, then the mere chance of being nearby to capitalize on it might shoot a Cultivator far ahead of their peers who had missed the opportunity.

"Quit questioning it, Blue. Good things just happen to us. We're good-looking, powerful walkers of the Ethereal Path, and sponsored by Primordials! If you went places and all they had were rusty iron swords, it wouldn't help our crusade for righteousness." Arkaziel's eyes glimmered with loot-whoriness and delusions of his own grandeur.

When the duo crossed the temple threshold, they instead found themselves in Odin's study again. The single-eyed deity sat in the same high-backed chair near the fire as before, although this time he sipped at a mead with a familiar scent.

"You beat an incarnation of Nidhogg. Very good. I see the power coursing through both of you. Ate its whole heart, did you, StarMane?" Odin seemed impressed by the cat's greed.

"I have a last gift for you, Aetheria." Odin hefted a book and tossed it to her. The cover had the distinctive look of dragon leather. Each page was a thin slice of incredibly durable wood, with a painting mounted to the wood. Small annotations in Ath, carefully scripted, filled the margins. *Notations on biology and physiology?*

"You might be a human, but you are a true shapeshifter now. Learn some of your options of other races. It'll help you as you climb the tower. Now, off with you, before your dumb cat tries to eat my remaining eye."

"Aw," Arkaziel whined as reality shifted around them, and they appeared in front of the Rune Gate in the middle of Nidhogg's Bane.

"Stop thinking about eating people, you mangy cat," Aetheria scolded Ark.

"Did you buy all the food on that list I gave you?" Arkaziel sulked.

"Yes, I got it all. Why do we need to carry so much food? And you don't even drink alcohol!" Aetheria narrowed her eyes. "Do you?"

"Oh, no. The booze is for trades. People love good booze, and the mead here should sell like gangbusters on other floors, or at least open some closed doors. And it's not that much food. I'm a growing boy, remember?" Arkaziel gave her his most pathetic look, and Aetheria could have sworn he was on the verge of meowing at her.

"Oh, stop it. I hate that sad look. How big are you actually now?"

Arkaziel stared at her, not blinking.

"What? Am I not supposed to ask that?"

"It's a horrific cultural taboo to ask a StarMane how big they actually are."

"Seriously?"

The cat laughed at her. "Nope. Got you."

"You are the worst cat ever," Aetheria snarled. She stepped through the Rune Gate. Internally, she bid Nidhogg's Bane good luck before the world blinked black.

The duo appeared on a cloud.

Cripes! Clouds aren't things you can stand on!

Despite this, the cloud held the weight of Aetheria and Arkaziel easily. Near and far, all that filled their line of sight were clouds. Clouds, clouds, and more clouds as far as the eye could see.

Arkaziel took a bite out of the cloud they stood on.

"Tastes kind of sweet, real creamy. I could eat a couple of these. I haven't been able to shake that Nidhogg heart aftertaste yet."

CHAPTER 44

Fluffy Stuff

Against her better judgment, Aetheria grabbed a handful of cloud and took a bite. It had a strange consistency, between gaseous and sticky marshmallow. As she took in all the clouds around them, she prayed to Aetherius that the point of Floor 16 wasn't to eat all the marshmallow. No messages came back, though. No announcements from the Tower Administrator, either, not even taunting. *Maybe he got in trouble for calling Mommy.*

"So, what do you think, Ark?"

"Well. I'm going to eat a cloud or two because, seriously, I need to get the after-taste of Nidhogg out of my mouth. That was the vilest dragon my family has ever eaten. Maybe our trial will show itself after I remove some clouds for a better view?" Arkaziel leaped off her shoulder and, once he was away from her, grew to his larger form. Large sections of clouds disappeared to assuage the unending hunger of the StarMane. *I can't really blame him, though; damned dragon's corpse is smelly even in my repository. I should really do something with it sooner rather than later.*

Bite by bite, Arkaziel diminished the clouds. Every cloud the StarMane ate just revealed another cloud behind it. *This must be like heaven for him. A massive field of food he can go hog-wild on.*

At first, it seemed like a StarMane paradise. Yet as the minutes ticked on and nothing new showed up, Arkaziel grew bored. After two hours, by Aetheria's rough estimate, the cat flopped back onto her shoulder with a disgruntled *hmph*.

"It's all the same. No variety in flavor. I think I'm getting a tummy ache."

"You ate Nidhogg's heart with no complaints, but marshmallow does your stomach in? I don't understand your race at all."

"Our glory transcends human comprehension. That's true." The cat nodded sagely, then nuzzled against her neck and went to sleep. *How does he do that and not fall off my shoulder?*

From experience, Aetheria knew that if she poked Arkaziel, he'd just squirm or bat at her hand with his claws, but he wouldn't fall off. *Some kind of magic? Why wouldn't a race of genocidal gourmand cat-dragons have spells to sleep peacefully wherever they want? Makes as much sense as everything else about them.*

"Guess I'll just experiment, then."

Experiment the first: freeze a cloud. Projecting the Mark of Ymir into a cloud that looked like a car seemed to break whatever magic kept the marshmallow clouds aloft. It immediately plummeted downward and kept going, taking any other clouds beneath it along for the ride.

Experiment the second: burn a cloud. A ball of flame appeared in Aetheria's hand and she tossed it at a nearby cloud. The flames spread like the cloud was gasoline, and it turned brown and gave off a terrible smell. Then the cloud deflated, and rinds of burned marshmallow debris fell on the cloud below it. There was no chain reaction of burning clouds catching each other on fire, though, oddly.

Experiment the third: use the Flame of Thalassa to leech all the moisture out of a cloud. The leeched moisture was a strange white liquid that left nothing of the cloud behind.

This reaction intrigued Aetheria enough that she converted several clouds to liquid and stored the strange stuff inside her repository. *That's enough, that's enough,* she had to tell herself after the tenth cloud, as her desire to loot all the things pressed her to keep going.

Between Aetheria and Arkaziel, they had cleared almost a half-kilometer area of clouds. They revealed nothing.

"This is stupid."

Aetheria touched upon the Ethereal power slumbering in her repository and summoned a series of etheric ice nets. Just as Aether and Nether had properties natural elements didn't have, etheric force could take on multiple esoteric aspects. Here, she created nets of ice that could fly under their own power.

"Round them up." Verbal orders were unnecessary, but Aetheria found that speaking orders out loud helped solidify commands to construct. A defect of her control process, no doubt.

She could not deny the satisfaction of watching the ice nets gathering up clouds and drawing them to a concentrated spot. From there, she leeched the moisture out of them and added to the growing collection in her repository. *Note to self: buy a lot of glass containers in the next town.*

With another expanse cleared, something new was now visible. Floating on a cloud was a small castle. She nudged Arkaziel and bounded across the clouds to the front gates. The castle's gates and walls had been built out of a white stone that was almost indistinguishable from the fluffy clouds. No guard appeared to be present, so Aetheria wrapped a knuckle against the door.

A face appeared in the door. Elven.

"You aren't an elf. Go away." The face vanished.

~What elves would live in a place like this, Ark?~

+Mm. Sky elves? I think Mom saw this castle before, a few hundred years ago. Yeah, definitely sky elves.+

~I suppose that tells me what happened to the inhabitants. Stick to your flying cat form—no letting on you're a StarMane, okay? What's a sky elf name?~

With telepathy accorded by their bond, Arkaziel could now fill her brain with the derisive noise of sticking ones, tongue between the lips and blowing. Some called it a Bronx cheer, others called it blowing a raspberry; she called it the sound that means Arkaziel is an asshole. The StarMane did this for a solid thirty seconds before a hand moving for his head urged him to action.

+*Elvarr'ie. Claim no clan.*+

Aetheria concentrated. Her hair shifted from blue to silver; her skin tone lightened, her ears elongated. She now wore an armored dress, mimicking an outfit she'd seen an elf in Nidhogg's Bane wear. A few minor alterations of her eyes, nose, and chin, plus a couple more inches to her height, and she was content with what an ice mirror showed her. She rapped on the door again.

"I thought I told you to go aw—oh. A sky elf! Welcome, welcome, to the Keep of Mellow Mallow." The face in the door seemed pleased to see them. The gates opened. "Come on, come in. All the Mallow family are long dead, so I'm afraid it's up to me, faithful Archibald the steward, to entertain company."

Aetheria stepped into the inner courtyard and let out a small gasp. The castle was on the smaller end, but its diminutive size did not hold back its beauty. Graceful curves and arches and delicate works of crystalline lattice held weight just as much as blocks of white stone. *This is going to be my castle.* Decision made, she just needed to figure out how to claim it as her own.

"How long have the Mallows been dead, Archibald?"

The steward's face appeared on a nearby wall, answer ready at hand. "It has been seven hundred and thirty-nine years and two weeks since the Mellow Mallow sky keep encountered a draconic species known as a StarMane, and the residents subsequently became dragon food. I don't suppose you are of a noble family, Miss...?"

Aetheria smiled coyly, then shook her head. "I'm afraid I'm just a commoner who's struck out on her own, Archibald. I'm called Elvarr'ie by my friends."

Arkaziel's laughter in her head was a bad sign.

"Elvarr'ie?" Hope blossomed in the steward's eyes. "Pray tell, would you do me a small favor, Mistress Elvarr'ie?"

Aetheria suppressed the desire to spray Arkaziel with water. "I'll certainly try. What do you have in mind?"

"When the vicious draconic cats attacked, one heir to the family managed to teleport away, but we never had confirmation if she safely made it somewhere—or if the wretched beasts caught her, anyway. If by some chance you match her essence, you could take control of the keep and free me from this wretched servitude to an empty castle."

-*Your mom ate Elvarr'ie, too, didn't she?*-

+*You know it. Mom made it a point to never let a teleporter escape. Enough people want to hunt down StarManes as it is. Why give them more reasons?*+

Aetheria held in the sigh. "What happens to the keep if I free you, Archibald? I quite fancy it, and I'd love to take ownership if I could."

"Hmm. Well, once I'm freed, the keep would revert to a basic command core. You could always install a new servant in my place, if someone's foolish enough to make the same mistake I did in taking this job to begin with. The basic core is more than capable of maintaining cleanliness, flight, steering, and mallow generation."

"Mallow generation?"

"Oh, yes. The lord just loved the stuff. He implemented many varied alchemical recipes to create defensive mallow, obscuring mallow, and corrosive mallow. I've generated obscuring mallow since the incident."

"I see. Show me to the controls. I'll get you freed if I can."

They crossed through parlors, down a hidden doorway, and down sets of stairs. Eventually, the stairs ended in a room lit by arcane light. Crystals and runes covered every surface. Some even acted as gauges and indicators. It was a fairly sophisticated Magitech engine room.

"Address the core by identifying yourself as Elvarr'ie, and request administrative access."

"Hello, Core, I am Elvarr'ie and I would like administrative access."

Silence hung in the engine room.

::Granted.::

Aetheria grinned, and Archibald clapped.

"Now give the command to Terminate Contract 03-A, and release servant."

Should she? Archibald clearly knew the keep, its commands, how to fly it. *No. He's done his time. I'm not going to become a slave driver.*

"Terminate Contract 03-A, release servant."

::Acknowledged.::

Along the side of the room, a tubelike structure glowed with magical power. The cylindric tube hissed, and a door opened. A tall elven male stepped from the misting insides into the engineering room. Aetheria did not like his smile.

"Poor Archibald. All those years, slaving away to maintain my keep. I just couldn't let him walk off and stop maintaining everything." The elf looked nothing like Archibald, and his clothing was certainly not that of a servant.

"Body-swap spells work even in stasis, you know. Poor Archi's body has been dead for seven hundred years. Little matter, though, because now I shall have my revenge on *the wretched StarManes!*" A cloud of green glitter shot forth from the elf to envelope Aetheria and Arkaziel, who began to cough up blood.

I knew it! I knew StarManes were nothing but trouble. Wow, corrosive fumes are nasty. Aetheria didn't enjoy the feeling of her skin, lungs, and throat liquifying. All around her, the air turned blue-white as her domain activated. The green fog froze, dispersed into crystals on the ground, and then disintegrated as the cold went further and further. Arkaziel was the only one spared from the cold, creating a safe little bubble within the domain.

"You shouldn't have killed Archibald. He was loyal, sweet, and had a silly name. I liked him."

"Oh, please. He was planning to trap you in the core and become the new Lord Mallow. How naïve are you?"

Aetheria frowned. She hadn't gotten that impression from the servant at all.

The elf lord gestured and chunks of burning mallow shot toward her. Her domain had blocked the flames and prevented them from reaching further than four centimeters in. This displeased the elf lord.

"I've decided you can die the way your family did. Ark? He's all yours. I'm going to figure out how this system works."

"What? No, I forbid you fro—*Noooooo!*" The elf screamed as the StarMane crossed the distance in a flash and took the elf's head off in one large chomp. A chomp that confirmed to Aetheria that Arkaziel was also shapeshifting, because it was comical watching a house cat's head grow big enough to eat a humanoid head.

"Think we could retrieve Archi's spirit or anything?" she asked the cat.

Arkaziel didn't answer her verbally. He was busy eating. *~No way. This douchebag sent him to the great beyond. Maybe we'll see him again in his next incarnation. Maybe he'll be a superior race to these stupid elves. A snail, perhaps.~*

The StarMane's mental laughter filled her head while she fiddled with the controls and determined that Archibald had told her the truth. The basic core could do all the things he said.

"Alright. Time to see if I can dump this thing into my repository."

CHAPTER 45

Dwarfsketball

Transferral of the keep into her repository worked, surprisingly. It also left Arkaziel and Aetheria floating in air. They landed on mallow clouds. A door to the next floor opened. Neither wanted to belabor the point, so Aetheria took on her blue-haired form and they jumped through the door to Floor 17.

The pair found themselves in a large valley nestled between mountains. The slopes of the mountains that shaped the valley were marked with elaborate cave villages. From just a glance, it was apparent each of the mountains had different architectural styles, but all had their large size in common. Different clans of giants populated each mountain. One mountain was shorter than the others, but it had no peak; instead, it was clearly an active volcano belching smoke into the sky. The giants had transformed an area of flat land between the mountains into a makeshift sports field.

Before Aetheria and Arkaziel, five giants stood, frowning at the small human.

"You no giant," one declared observantly.

"She smells like Ymir," a blue-skinned giant noted.

"I crush her dead," declared another with reddish skin.

Not liking where this was heading, Aetheria borrowed mass, and her form rippled and grew. No longer was a small human woman before them, but a tall giantess who stood equal to the tallest of the giant men. Aetheria maintained her blue hair and pale skin. Ymir had not had the looks of any of these distinctive giant groups.

"You'll crush who?" she challenged the red-skinned fire giant, keeping her ruby Ethereal eyes on him. Arkaziel, yawning, cuddled against her now much bigger neck.

"Uh... Ignar crush you? You not so big or strong." The fire giant was large, but slow. He didn't stop the fist that halted inches from his face.

"I would turn you into a paste, puny Ignar. Why are all the clans down here?" Steam rose from her exposed skin as she erected the tiniest of domains a centimeter around her, then blended the Primordial Flame of Ymir into it since the frost giant seemed to sense it anyway. The sudden manifestation of primeval power and cold appeared to take the five giants aback slightly. They seemed to all agree to ignore it.

"We compete at the greatest tests of skill to see who controls valley and leads unified clans to greatness for next fifty years." The light-purple-skinned giant had a strange sense about him. She couldn't place it at first, but he was the most eloquent of the giants to speak so far.

"We crush dwarves outside valley and take more mountains." The yellow-skinned giant was the smallest of the five, but his eyes fully conveyed a love of violence—especially against smaller and weaker beings.

"Our conquest of Obsidian Throne will honor Surtur." The fire giant pointed at a distant peak, barely visible, that looked like another volcano.

"No, no. We go south, conquer the dwarf cities. They labor good, and make great stew." The frost giant spoke definitively. Aetheria thought he didn't mean that dwarves made a great stew, but could be made *into* a great stew.

Maybe there's a solution that doesn't come down to me rampaging and murdering five clans of giants.

+Awww. Giants have the tastiest livers. Just something to keep in mind if you maim them—leave the livers intact. +Arkaziel was, as ever, the most helpful companion in the history of companions.

"Can I compete?" *Worth a try, right?* She put the pressure on her Flame of Ymir.

The frost giant spoke first. "You take Thokk's spot. Ymir strong with you." The other four giants eyed Thokk warily, then her suspiciously.

"She no chieftain. She a she. Rules say no woman," the yellow giant objected immediately.

"You've failed my test." Aetheria's features shifted into those of a blue-skinned giant male, larger than the five before her. She copied the build of Ymir with the face of the scary giant from *Game of Thrones*. "Submit or suffer the consequences."

Bravado and threats seemed like the way to go with these giants, and they reacted much more strongly to her male form and the Flame of Ymir than they had to her female form. The casual cultural misogyny thrust in her face meant she didn't need to act to show anger. *I hope I get to punch people, because some giants are getting punched in the throat.*

"What is your name?" the rocky toned giant asked. As befit a rock giant, his skin looked like limestone, varying from light brown to a deep gray.

"Hyrromir," she answered. *Please don't be a swear word or one of their actual names.*

"Never heard of you," the mountain giant grumbled.

"Hyrromir carries strong blessings of Ymir. Watch your tone, rock. That one is Roknir. The hill giant is Thrumm. Fire giant called Ignatius. Cloud giant is Nimrod. I am Thokk. You represent frost giants, best giants. Crush them all." Thokk's smile was disturbing to look at, but Aetheria felt like she would indeed enjoy beating up most of these giants.

"All assembled, then. We pull sticks and finally start." Nimrod, the most eloquent of giants, held a container with a myriad of sticks. Aetheria ended up in the middle, with Nimrod and Roknir ahead of her, and Ignatius and Thrumm behind her.

"First event. Dwarf Toss. Whoever throws furthest wins five points. Second place, three points. Third, one point. Most points after all challenges wins Belt of Leadership for fifty years."

Nimrod stepped up to a two-meter-tall building and pulled the roof off it, revealing several cowering people inside. Despite the name Dwarf Toss, only a third of those inside the cages were dwarves. There were halflings, gnomes, elves, humans, and even one wolf-man. *I'm as tall as them, and they all distinctively aren't dwarves, so it's not a matter of perspective. Ignorance? Arrogance?*

Nimrod grabbed a human, took two steps, and hurled the being through the air like a fast-pitched baseball. Aetheria winced inside. *Okay, so this is far worse than I thought it was going to be. Let's see, I don't have telekinesis. I can't catch him, maybe... Nope. He's out of my range.*

The inevitable crash sounded like a melon hitting rock, which was close to what actually happened. Roknir was already stepping up with a dwarf in his grasp.

"Can't we just fight for leadership? These contests seem cowardly and unfit for prominent leaders," Aetheria growled in the most masculine and challenging voice she could imagine.

Thrumm hissed at her words. "This is valley tradition! He who win becomes leader and takes giants on glorious rampage across small races!"

"Of course, that's what a hill giant would say. As the weakest and dumbest giants, you wouldn't stand a chance in true contests of might." Nimrod the cloud giant's smirk made Thrumm shake with fury.

"I like this one's thoughts. Let us fight; the last one standing shall become king of the giants! Enough of war leaders, chieftains—all shall serve under my thumb! Bow before King Ignatius!" the fire giant shouted loudly. His hair burst into flames with the challenge, and he looked eager to begin the violence.

~Arkaziel, wake your butt up! Go release all the prisoners and get them out of here. Discretion is less important than evacuating them all. NO EATING ANYONE, if you want a single giant's liver.~

+Fine, but I really want the cloud giant liver. You better not ruin this for me.+

"Roknir shall win, and Ignatius will be his fool." The mountain giant wasn't one to pass up on the shit-talking, and his already rocky skin took on the properties of stone. He slammed his jagged fist into Ignatius's steaming face. Aetheria smiled inwardly until she felt a purple fist crash into her cheek. The pain was surprisingly less than she expected, coming from a cloud giant chieftain. She casually looked Nimrod in the eyes and smiled.

Nimrod's eyes widened, and she slammed her fist between the purple cloud giant's eyes, sending him tumbling end over end. Her year in Nidhogg's Bane had given her time to learn more than just her domain. She had gained an increased degree of volume, mass, and density control through her ability to shapeshift. The other giants gazed wide-eyed as the strongest of them was sent flying like a child.

Aetheria capitalized on their stunned reactions, stepping forward and blasting Ignatius with a punch to the face. The fire giant fared worse than the cloud giant, as vulnerable as he was to the immense cold of her still-constrained domain. A massive burst of steam clouded the air when her fist hit the fire giant's face, the flames of his hair extinguishing in the blast of cold. Ignatius stumbled, crashing into Nimrod on his way to the ground.

"Get them! No outsider will be king!"

"I prefer the title of queen." Aetheria's flesh rippled and flowed, returning her to her pale human visage, but she remained giant-sized. Her eyes shone with the Ethereal power that fueled every cell in her body. Roknir and Thrumm leaped at her simultaneously, but she let them take the initiative. Hill and mountain giant struck, one after the other. Roknir's boulder-like fists slammed into her stomach, pushed in, and then rebounded with more force than the attack had contained. He punched his own gut and doubled over.

Aetheria bent her head just slightly to the left and completely avoided Thrumm's attack. She brought up her left knee, grasping a handful of Roknir's stony mane, and slammed his face into her knee. Pieces of stone fractured from Roknir's form, and the mountain giant fell to the ground, unconscious.

Aetheria had forgotten about Thokk, who struck her from behind with a stout club. *I always forget how effective weapons are.* Light and stars filled her vision, and Thrumm took advantage of her distraction to land a powerful blow to her back when she hit the ground. *I wonder if hill giants have the equivalent of a small-man complex?* The surrounding air dropped below zero, and with a light flip, she returned to her feet—and her normal size.

"I'm done pretending to be a giant." In a flash, she was standing before Thrumm, covering his shin with hoarfrost. By the time her fist made contact, her domain had frozen the giant's left leg, and her punch shattered it.

If Aetheria had her way, all the giants would surrender now. Even expanding her domain to ten meters—completely denying even the frost giant the ability to combat with her—didn't make the giants yield. They were sentient creatures. They could talk, but they were also... evil? Cruel? Indifferent? *I could never torture a puppy, or make up games of throwing armadillos for fun. What kind of messed-up people play Dwarf Toss?*

"We will never yield to a human trickster's rule!" Nimrod tested the tried-and-true method giants had fallen back on forever. He threw a large boulder at Aetheria. When it crossed into her domain, a pillar of ice shot up and shattered it.

"She can't block all of us at once! Throw everything at her!" Ignatius threw a burning tree. The same fate awaited it: freezing, then shattered by a pillar of ice.

"I actually can. Last chance: yield or I feed you all to my cat."

The giants laughed, mocking her. *I just bitch-slapped them all like kids, and they're acting like they have the advantage. Even the idiot whose leg I obliterated.* Annoyed, Aetheria flashed across the distance between her and the fire giant. A pillar of ice propelled her up to his height, and she flicked him in the nose. Her domain had already frozen his face, and like a poorly made house of cards, Ignatius shattered into thousands of pieces and made a mess of the ground, while she stood on the pillar of ice.

"So, no surrender?"

"No surrender!" Nimrod screamed, and charged at her.

Aetheria sighed and dropped her domain. If nothing else, the four surviving giants would provide her with practice against larger enemies.

Ten minutes later, Arkaziel arrived. "Oh," he said. "You tenderized them for me!

CHAPTER 46

Conflict Resolution

Floor 17 ended with the deaths of the five chieftains and Aetheria giving the subsequent new leaders a firm warning to stop treating other races like sporting goods or snacks. In the back of her mind, she fought the nagging sensation that maybe she should just wipe the giants out, but they were also sentient (if seemingly innately evil) beings. So, they could have their chance until the next Climber got sent to this place—if it even continued to exist after their departure through the door to Floor 18.

Arkaziel, at least, was happy to feast upon giant livers. The gourmand cat-dragon muttered about still needing to wash away the aftertaste of Nidhogg.

The duo appeared in the middle of a small rustic village. The few people walking the streets were dressed like medieval farmers: not well and covered in dirt. The small town smelled of human waste, and the citizens were pale and gaunt. Many appeared to be suffering from the early stages of starvation, and there was a noticeable lack of men who weren't old-timers.

Cracks of thunder filled the sky, yet there were no clouds. On the horizon, brilliant displays of a magical battle took place. Blinding bolts of lightning countered vast explosions of fire. Aetheria could not make out all the goings-on from the great distance, but whoever was fighting had to be powerful to create disturbances this far away.

~ This smells like a scenario floor. I hate scenario floors. The Tower Administrator gets so pissy when you just eat everyone, or don't solve things the way they want you to. ~

Arkaziel's thoughts echoed Aetheria's own. It seemed this wouldn't be a simple trial by combat. Still, it had to be better than the puzzle level, or the time she had to make a sculpture of Arkaziel.

"You just be a good little kitty and take a nap. I'll wake you up if there's someone to eat." Arkaziel purred when she scratched his chin, then gave her a dirty look and shut his eyes. He kept purring, though.

The appearance of a clean, well-dressed, well-fed woman in the middle of the village square attracted attention. An older man in slightly nicer clothes than the rest of those in the square approached. His hair was gray, his hands only lightly calloused. His eyes bore a shrewd look. Thankfully, the man spoke one of the multiple human languages she'd picked up between Solace and Nidhogg's Bane.

"Haven't seen you around these parts before… ma'am." After careful consideration of the quality of her clothing, the man had opted for a middle ground of respect. Not lady, but not *hey you*, either. Aetheria's red eyes seemed to draw wariness from people, regardless of whether they were Dweller, Native, or Climber.

"Oh, I just arrived. I'm a wandering Cultivator—name's Ria. I seem to have wandered into some kind of conflict, though?" She gestured to the far horizon and the magical battle happening there.

"Ah, you must be from the far islands. Aye, that battle has been going on for nigh on ten years. Lord Lamberys, our liege, was forced to answer the cowardly Lord Conton in a duel. That rotten Conton was about to lose and erected some vile curse that trapped them in time, repeating the battle each day." The man gave a heavy sigh. "If I weren't the mayor and in charge of keeping order here without all our young men, I'd go over and give that rotten bastard what-for, I tell you, or my name isn't Brannigan." The old man barked a laugh. "It *is* Brannigan."

"I see. Nice to meet you, Brannigan. If the conflict has been repeating for ten years, why are there no young men to be seen? Are they also trapped in battle? What of those who came of age after the battle?"

Brannigan sighed and rubbed at the back of his head, where his hair was thinning.

"Well, Lord Lamberys's knights still come around every season and collect the levees and war taxes. Each season, things around here get more dire, and no amount of militia being thrown into that meat grinder is going to stop the vile magics of that wretch Conton."

"People can still enter the time loop?"

"Aye. People enter. No one leaves."

"Then how do the knights join their liege?"

"They don't. They force the conscripts in, then retreat to Castle Lamberys."

That's not at all suspicious.

"Do you know if the same thing is happening to the Conton lands?"

"Who knows? There are only a few ways to the Conton lands. Through the battlefield is the most direct. You could go through the Cursed Woods, but those woods aren't named for a laugh. The mountains are barely passable, and who would risk them just to get to the land of that swine?"

"I see. Well, since I'm here, I think I'll scout the area and see what I can learn to maybe end this for you fine folks." Aetheria tipped an imaginary hat to the man and brusquely walked away before the mayor could get another word in. A brisk pace took her out of the village toward the mountains, but she waited until she was away from prying eyes before she grew ice wings near her back and jumped into the air. She shot up into the sky.

"You need to work on your flying more. You fly like a human—badly." Arkaziel opened his eyes just long enough to insult her before going back to sleep.

Only one road went to the small village. Going east, the road led to a castle. *About six kilometers to the castle. Three kilometers to the west are the battlegrounds.*

The chaotic magics surrounding the battlefield prevented Aetheria from discovering the lay of the land on the opposite side. What became very apparent from her position in the sky was that a pass was being excavated in the mountains to allow an alternate route from the Conton lands toward Lamberys's lands and castle.

Since they had so politely made a path for her, she flew over the pass and followed the mountain road toward Conton. Outside of a small work crew at the end of the road, she saw no other people on the ground. As best as Aetheria could tell, no one saw her flying in the sky, but when the battleground had been circumvented, she landed in a copse of trees. There, she altered her clothing to better match what she'd seen in the village. Her trench coat flowed into a red cloak and light leather armor, and that was good enough, she figured. *Glowing red eyes and aqua hair stand out, but it's annoying to change my eye color. It always feels like I've got an eyelash stuck in my eye. I wonder what I'm doing wrong for that to happen?*

After a twenty-minute walk through light woods, she came across another village. This was not as bleak as those in Lord Lamberys's territory. Children played in the streets, men of all ages went about their business, and the farms were fully worked. Intrigued, Aetheria walked into the village and was promptly stopped at the west entrance by two guards. They wore only minimal armor—pauldrons, gauntlets, and a chain shirt—but it was still a far cry from the rags people had worn in Lamberys's lands.

"Halt. Name, origin, business?" the younger guard asked. His coworker eyed Aetheria, much more interested.

"Ria. Nova Azura. Mercenary." She infused her aura with Nether. Not enough to become visible to the naked eye, but enough to send goosebumps up the neck of anyone within a meter of her. Most humans instinctively found Nether repulsive, or at least registered it at as danger. Both guards stood a little straighter, the older man's hand drifting toward the cudgel on his hip. The younger shook his head at him.

"Purpose for visiting Lamley?"

"Passing through, unless there's work on offer."

The old guard laughed dismissively. Aetheria felt her fists clench, but calmed herself. *Casual misogyny is nothing new.*

"Entry is five coppers per day for outlanders."

Aetheria sighed. While she had gold and silver pieces, nowhere she'd been previously dealt with denominations as small as copper. If this were a tabletop game, she'd accuse the game master of putting roadblocks in front of her to discourage her entry into the village. Instead, she slipped a hand into a pocket, pulled a silver coin from her repository, then handed it over to the young man.

"This will cover you for a ten-day."

"Good. Is that all?" Her matter-of-fact tone made the younger man look a touch embarrassed as he got out of her way. She felt the older guard's eyes on her as she walked off.

It didn't take long to find the village tavern. There were few patrons, still being an hour or two before lunch. Aetheria sat at the bar and waited for the barkeep to come to her. The man glanced at her a few times and delayed serving her just long enough to make the point that she should know her place.

"What can I get for you, outsider? Name's Jayden, I own the Red Boar."

"Whatever your best lunch is, and a bottle of your best whiskey."

"You got the coin? Strange to see a mercenary without a weapon."

Aetheria slapped three thick gold coins on the bar top. "I don't need weapons." Again, she let her Nether aura flare up, to intimidate the man.

Jayden coughed a little into his hand and nodded. "Guess you don't. One of them Cultivators, like the lord? Should've said so. The call for Cultivators has been out for eleven years now. Lord Conton's son will pay hefty if you can help with the Lamberys problem."

"The Lamberys problem?"

"Yeah, old story in these parts." Jayden gestured for his daughter to get drink and food for Aetheria. "Former Lords Conton and Lamberys got into a duel over poaching. Lord Conton slew Lamberys, but it didn't end there. The new Lord Lamberys swore revenge, hired a bunch of wandering Cultivators, and started this fool battle. Old Lord Conton saw the writing on the wall, though, and had built up a force of his own. What he didn't foresee was that goat-shagger Lamberys using dark rituals to trap the battlefield in time like that."

"Who's in charge now?"

"Conton's son, Derran. There's plans to end it all, but you'd have to get hired on by Derran to hear the gist of it all."

"Right. How come the ritual hasn't ended? It's been a decade."

"Lamberys's men still make sacrifices that power the ritual."

Aetheria sighed. That checked out with the extent of people being conscripted. What good would a bunch of farmers be against a Cultivator? None; they were nothing in a battle against people who walked a path.

"Where do I find Derran at?" It made sense, this version of the tale, but she wasn't going to accept this blindly as truth, either. The best lies were forged with truths.

"Castle Lumley. Twenty-minute walk out the east gate."

"Thanks, Jayden." Aetheria had been about to say to keep the coins, but his daughter came out with a large platter of steak, bread, cheese, and a soup that smelled fantastic. The warm bread's intoxicating scent wafted toward her, and her stomach growled.

"I'll be having that lunch now. Can't show up at a castle with a growling stomach. Oh, and do you have any fish for my cat?"

The man looked startled by the question, then realized the black fur wrapped around her neck and shoulder was a sleeping cat, and not a fur lining.

"Sure, get some bass for the kitty, Emily."

CHAPTER 47

Castle Lumley

~ That bass was good, but not worth the indignity of letting the little girl pet me. She wasn't even a Cultivator! Only Cultivators get to pet me.~ The indignation of it all still lay heavy on Arkaziel.

+If it was such an indignity, why were you purring so much?+ The StarMane brooded quietly in response. *+You even thumped your hind leg when she scratched you under the chin.+*

The walk to the castle took Aetheria only five minutes. If she had stretched her legs and gone all out, it would've been less, and flying would've taken travel time out of the scenario entirely. But just flying into a Cultivator's castle seemed like a bad idea, and she still wasn't sure if the acting Lord Conton was an ally or enemy. If nothing else, his rule was certainly more prosperous for the common people under his thumb.

Castle Lumley was moderately impressive. Its highest towers were three stories tall. The outer walls were thick, and the facade was made of an interesting gray stone with lines of black and white through it. It made Aetheria think of marble, but as she approached the gate, she saw the stone bore no resemblance to marble. *More like a granite, really.*

"Hold. Name and purpose for visiting Castle Lumley?" a soldier called from the shadows of the open gate. Unlike the town guards, these soldiers were clad in scale armor and carried spears.

"Ria, wandering Cultivator. I was told by the tavern keep that acting Lord Conton is hiring Cultivators."

"You look the role, sure, but I've never heard of you. Can you show your power? The lord gets awful annoyed if we let a pretender through." The soldier grinned.

I'm not sure if he just wants a show, is doing his duty, or is trying to piss me off. Aetheria gestured behind her and ice coalesced into the form of a miniature Nidhogg, only thirty feet long. The dragon stretched out and snapped its jaws at the air in a menacing fashion. Cold radiated from it in waves that made Arkaziel squirm against her neck for more warmth.

"Adequate?" Aetheria asked with a raised eyebrow. "Or do you want to fight it, to ensure its lethality?" Her tone was exceptionally flat.

The guard who had asked swallowed but didn't answer. Instead, the gate officer answered from the shadows.

"I'll accompany you to Lord Conton, Miss Ria. No need to keep your dragon active. The demonstration is more than enough. It's been some time since we've had a master of the Frozen Path come through Lumley. The last one made a fortune at enchanting cold stores for the innkeepers and here at the castle."

Aetheria smiled and refrained from correcting the sergeant about her chosen path. She snapped her fingers and Nidhogg vanished in waves of steam.

The guard took her on an elaborate route, clearly trying to impress her with the wealth and grandeur of Castle Lumley. *If this had been my first floor, that might've worked. After the glory of Aoibhe's castle, the sky keep in my repository, and even Castle of Dread, this is just another place.* When she didn't *ooh* and *ahh*, the route became slightly more direct toward a private study, inside of which three men already waited.

The man sitting behind an elaborate wooden desk appeared to be in his early twenties, with sandy blond hair and elaborate clothing befitting an acting lord. His aura was in the second tier and felt aspected to wind. *I'm going to guess he's early, very early, in Tier Two. He's puffing his aura up as much as he can to impress me. A noble with self-esteem issues? Unheard of.*

The man standing next to Derran Conton appeared to be in his sixties and had no aura of cultivation at all. The man looked every bit the dutiful retainer, and Aetheria assumed he served as an aide, steward, castellan, or what have you.

The last man in the room looked to be in his early thirties, had brown hair, brown eyes, and wore an assortment of leather armor that veered into utilitarian more than visually impressive. He had a Cultivator's aura, mid-to-high Tier Two, filled with fire. He, too, was flaring his aura to impress her. Both Cultivators frowned at Aetheria, whose aura remained concealed. The sergeant announced her as "Ria of the Frozen Path" and departed. *No doubt a runner had already come while we took the long way to tell them about the ice dragon.*

"Ah, Miss Ria. In Lumley and the surrounding territories, it is customary to show your aura to those you are meeting for the first time, thus allowing for establishment of social hierarchy and relative strength," the fire Cultivator spoke.

"Oh, I was unaware." Her aura awoke like a sleeping dragon; as if a nuclear blast had gone off, the blue-green and black-purple of Aether and Nether swirled around her, visible to even the steward's eyes. Aetheria exposed the three men to the pressure of her aura, the older man almost collapsing before she retracted it from him. Derran's eyes widened in horror, and the fire mage seemed to have trouble breathing.

Her aura retracted, concealed once more.

"I trust that was adequate?"

"Gods, woman, you could have held back a little." The fire mage wheezed, but seemed able to gain breath now that her aura wasn't suffocating him.

I did. "My apologies. I sensed both of you pressing your aura, so I did the same." Her smile was as sweet as sugar, but her tone was flat and hopefully conveyed her lack of amusement at their posturing.

"How does a Cultivator on the cusp of Tier Three travel unknown? We should have heard of you before," Lordling Derran asked with frank curiosity.

"As you can see, I am adept at concealing my aura. I only get involved in things of my own choosing, as my whims and fortune dictate. Thus, the life of a wandering Cultivator and not a sitting ruler. Which brings me to why I am here. Tell me about the battlefield."

"Are you here to end the Curse?" Hope filled the lordling's voice. "By all means, have a seat. Geoff, go fetch some wine for us all. Wayne, pull it together and have a seat. If she crushes us, there's little you could do. Her aura alone nearly incapacitated you."

"I am here to end the Curse. I would like to see this entire territory enjoy the prosperity of your subjects. Things are quite stark in the lands of the Lamberys— worse than the common folk should suffer under any lord."

"Thank the many gods. The wretched knights of Lamberys swore allegiance to a dark god called Nergal. Lamberys turned to the vile god when his father was slain, and converted many of his inner court. The ritual originates from a tablet Nergal gave to Lamberys, and his men used to enact the sacrifices of his people to fuel. So long as the ritual continues, the battle will reset each day at midnight, until Lamberys is victorious or the ritual is interrupted."

"So I just need to go marauding through the Lamberys keep and wipe out the knights, and it's all done?"

"Unfortunately, no. We are currently clearing a safe pass through the mountains to effect a strike, but it is not the castle that requires a strike. There is a hidden ritual somewhere near the battlefield. We know not if it is a cave, a barn, an ancient hidden temple, or just a big hole in the ground they throw corpses into. We must purify the ritual site for the ritual to truly end. They have sacrificed hundreds of peasants over the years to fuel it. We do not know how long it would last if we stopped it now, and uncertainty breeds fear."

Aetheria rubbed her chin, then held up her hand to stop the lordling from continuing. "I'll find the ritual site, cleanse it, and end it. You have your men ready to assault the battlefield and end all of this when I do that."

Wayne laughed at her statement, then swallowed nervously when her red eyes focused on him.

"You want no aid at all, Miss Ria? Not even in cleansing the ritual site? I am unaware of any purification rituals available to the Frozen Path."

"You assumed my path wrongly." A globe of glistening golden water appeared in her hand, slowly twirling and sparkling.

"Holy water? How? What path do you walk, miss?" Derran and Wayne were both perplexed by this.

"A powerful one. Now, I'll be going to find this secret ritual chamber. I'll wait until just before midnight to destroy it, so be ready to save lives when the battlefield resets."

"How will you find it?"

"I'm very attuned to Nether. A ritual like this sounds like it subsists on Nether."

Both men just nodded. She had taken the planning and discussion out of their hands, but left the role of valiant heroes to end the battle.

"Good luck, Lady Ria," Derran offered with a grin, seeing the political realities available to him. Wayne looked like he had a mouth full of Atomic sour candy, but he didn't contradict his boss. *Good training. I should get minions. Then again, they'd just be like Arkaziel and ignore me and eat people.*

After a glass of wine in the awkward atmosphere, Aetheria left the castle and took to the air once she was a few minutes away. Derran had earned *most* of her trust, simply because he had revealed the reason for the mountain pass without her prompting. If things were as the lordling said, this seemed like a pretty clear-cut case of who was righteous and who was evil.

Her flight around the cursed battlefield took little in the way of time. She focused her attention on Nether. To trace lines of power required little in the way of effort, but much in the way of concentration. Aetheria opted to land in a tree so she didn't need to worry about witnesses to her flight. The tides of Nether were frequently associated with the ground and the depths of the earth more than the sky, anyway. Proximity to the earth allowed for an even easier time tracking flows of Nether. Within twenty minutes, her consciousness had followed multiple flows of the dark energy. She found a subterranean location in which multiple streams of Nether were being pulled out of their natural flow.

Her senses could not penetrate to the origin of the disturbance. *Warding? I suppose I am dealing with second-tier Cultivators. It'd make sense they have resources like that. Makes me wonder how many intricacies like this I'm blind to, with my patched-together Cultivator education.*

So many of the novels she had read on Earth had revolved around Cultivation Paths being difficult to the point of requiring mentors and help at all the steps. Her own path, outside of the mentors of Solace, had been about self-discovery. Of course, she had Primordial beings interfering, which she felt was one of those outlier factors like video game protagonists had. *Better to get the unique experience than the slow, boring one.*

"Ark, you awake?"

"Nope. I'm sleeping. What do you need?" The StarMane made an exaggerated yawn, exhaling fish breath in her face.

"Do you sense that disturbance in the Nether flows? I need to get down there. Can you find the entrance?"

Arkaziel laughed and hopped off her shoulder. The cat-dragon darted around, a black and purple blur, before suddenly he took on a fifty-foot-long form and slammed a taloned claw into the ground. Debris rained down, clouds of dust shot into the air, and then the house-cat-sized Arkaziel flopped back onto her shoulder.

"I found an entrance." His yellow eyes stared at her.

"Good job," she said flatly, rolling her eyes. "Did you forget about discretion?"

"What's discretion?" the cat deadpanned back.

"Are you actually asking or yanking my chain?"

"Actually asking?" Arkaziel purred and looked super cute.

Aetheria took a deep breath and explained it the way she would to a child. "Discretion means making good choices about what to say or do in different situations. It's like having a little voice in your head that tells you if something is a good idea or not. For example, if you see someone drop their fish, discretion might tell you to pick it up and give it back to them rather than eat it yourself. It's about being thoughtful and making choices that show you're a good person."

"Why would I not eat it myself if it's good? They dropped it on the ground. If they care so little about their food, the fish is better off being eaten by someone who respects it as a meal enough not to drop it. Also, I'm not a person. I'm a StarMane, Chronos's glorious gift to the universe, Supreme Sentient Being In All Existence, Best of Felines and Dragons, Handsomest in all the Land, and Ria's best boy." Arkaziel smirked, his fangs disturbingly prominent.

"Wait, are you proud of the whole 'drunk god dreaming your race into existence' thing?"

"Why wouldn't I be?"

Aetheria's head hurt.

CHAPTER 48

Evil Rituals of Evil

S o, do you have a fish for me, or was that just rhetorical?"

Aetheria could feel the veins in her forehead throbbing. A deep breath and a flood of warmth through her soul bond to Aoibhe were all that stabilized her emotions enough to let her pat Arkaziel on the head and pull another fish from their time in Nidhogg's Bane out of the repository for her cat.

Arkaziel munched on his prize. Following the "no eating Ria" rule, he levitated a few feet behind her while he made quick work of the fish. Not for the first time, Aetheria wondered what the real extent of the StarMane's powers were. Ark seemed to be capable of feats on par with her, even with her possession of four Primordial Flames. Were all StarManes this ridiculous, or was it the tower and trials pushing both of them to grow? She couldn't exactly ask him. Even if the StarMane wanted to be honest with her, his arrogance and supremacist views wouldn't result in genuine answers.

The dust from Arkaziel's excavation finally settled. At the bottom of a hole, dirt and stone lay an ancient stairway going into the depths. This route seemed to be a long-disused path to the ruins, seeing as it ended in rocks going to the surface. Lamberys's knights must have had another entry to wherever the steps led.

"Eat your fish. Then we're exploring ancient ruins." She failed to keep the grin off her face. Once again, Aetheria was partaking in the sort of adventures her books, games, and anime contained. The fact that she was jumping into a hole in the ground where knights of an evil god were sacrificing people to fuel a strange time warp felt like a total vindication of her progress as a... heroine? Adventurer? Cultivator? One of the above. A large burp from Arkaziel broke the moment of levity.

"Hey now, some respect. We're heading into a place where they sacrificed innocent people for evil."

"Oh, right. Sorry? I'll burp less." Arkaziel did not sound apologetic.

Annoyed, Aetheria jumped into the hole. There were no lights down the stairs. Two orbs of white-blue Aether manifested on her shoulders, and she continued downward. The orbs only generated a pale light out to about two meters, for now, but on command, they could provide light up to ten meters. Goosebumps rose on her skin the farther down the stairs she and Arkaziel went. The flows of Nether grew stronger.

Eventually, the staircase ended at a sealed stone door. Primitive and worn inscriptions marked the doorway, but they meant absolutely nothing to Aetheria.

"Ark?"

The StarMane peered at the pictographs.

"Praise for the great Nergal, who rules over war and death, blah blah blah. No magic." Arkaziel's genetic memory proved useful once again. "It's not trapped, that I can sense. It's locked."

"I brought my lock pick." Aetheria touched the door, and hoarfrost lined it. With her pointer finger, she tapped the stone. It quietly disintegrated into dust.

"That was a new one. Netheric ice?" Arkaziel's curiosity piqued at the display.

"Yeah. I can't make it work with pure Nether, but using ice, I've been able to sort of make it... rot? The things I freeze. Fighting Nidhogg made me realize I wasn't utilizing Nether fully."

"You aren't using any of your powers fully, Ria."

"Shh." Aetheria held up a hand to quiet him. With the dark of the hallway revealed beyond the door, sounds quietly echoed to them. Whining. Pleas. Begging for help.

"It's probably a trap," the sharp-eared cat-dragon noted.

"Doesn't matter. Gotta save people if we can. No need to hold back on people who commit ritual sacrifices." *Is telling Arkaziel that safe? He might just bite their heads off.*

Despite her misgivings, Aetheria darted down the dark hallway, which opened into the upper level of what had once been the chapel of a temple. The upper floor, seemingly just a viewing floor, seemed unused by the cultists. Below, the room featured a stone altar, a terrible-looking pit, and a cage containing four peasants.

Five very evil-looking people also occupied the shrine. Standing at the altar in oversized black and red robes was what Aetheria could only assume was a demon. His skin was black and red skinned, and he carried a crown of thorns around his bald head, a malevolent Nether aura, and a jagged blade in his hands. His black eyes gleamed. *Definitely a demon.*

The other four looked to be human knights, although their armor had blackened and become tarnished. Although none of the four had Cultivator auras, they held some weird power to them. *Maybe the demon strengthened them somehow?*

+Ohhh. I like demons. They taste like pepper. Dibs on his corpse. The knights I could take or leave—they're corrupted enough to taste spicy but aren't Cultivators, so eating them would be empty calories.+

~Alright. Like last time, you get the innocents out of here. Kill the knights if they get in your way. I'll take on the demon.~

+Fine, but I better get to take on a boss soon. It's not fair that you get to do all the murdering. At least you don't try to steal my meals, I guess, but I'm a growing boy. I need to stretch my wings and let loose sometimes.+

~You literally just got to eat the heart of an incarnation of Nidhogg!~ Aetheria's annoyed snort drew attention from below.

"Intruders! Slice the peasants' throats and throw them in the pit, and then kill the wretches!" the demon priest ordered without hesitation. Arkaziel, however, was faster than the knights. In a blur, the StarMane was at the cage. He casually shattered the prison door with a swipe of his claws. Once he was through the doorway, a wall of ice rose around the prison.

~Use your breath to drill a hole to the surface and get them out. When you're back, I'll drop the wall.~

The StarMane didn't back talk. Aetheria felt the surge of power that accompanied a blast of his breath weapon. She vaulted over the railing and delivered a hammer kick to the shoulder of one knight before landing. The blow slammed the man against the floor so hard, he bounced multiple times, then didn't move again.

"Four on one—not bad odds, I guess." A brilliant smile crossed Aetheria's lips as her mocking tone sank in for the three knights and demon priest. Her aura sparked to life, red energy with just the subtlest hue of gold to it, fueled by the Primordial Flame of Aetherius. The next closest knight charged at her, shield first.

Right before the knight reached her, a pillar of red-gold ice rose up from the floor, crushing him against the ceiling so hard, the whole temple rumbled.

"Holy... ice?! Kill her, you fools! If she's a holy Cultivator, she could bring this whole temple down. We mustn't let Lord Nergal's blessing diminish."

"You know I can hear you, right?" Annoyed by the casual dismissal of being talked around, Aetheria walked toward the demon priest. With their attention on her, no one realized the pit was filling with gold water.

The remaining two knights approached her slowly, wary of any manifestations of ice. None came, but the men wasted precious seconds in their slow approach. The demon priest seemed to realize they needed to apply pressure on her and chanted in a language that sounded even harder on the throat than Orcish. For the moment, Aetheria ignored him and kept her energy going into filling the pit with holy water. And a few holy ice badgers who were excavating under the shrine.

The knights seemed to at least understand the concept of basic teamwork. They separated to flank her and moved in to strike with their weapons simultaneously. The knight on her left had a thick-bladed longsword, while the knight on the right had a well-used mace.

Aetheria caught the mace with her hand, making her palm squishy like a marshmallow and elongating her fingers to trap the weapon. The knight grimaced and tried to overpower her, to use his brawny muscles to yank the mace free. Her Ethereal physiology, filled with power from her Ethereal heart, did not let that happen. She caught the sword nimbly between two fingers as the knight swung. He struggled to free it. A casual twist of her wrist shattered the blade.

"You shouldn't send normal people to fight a Cultivator." A tail slashed out from her coat and knocked the swordsman into the wall with extreme force. She pulled the mace free from the knight's control and bashed him across the room with it. Adding insult to injury, Aetheria threw the weapon after the man.

"What are you? There's no Tier Three Cultivators in the kingdom! It doesn't matter. Lord Nergal, feast upon my offering!"

The demon priest cut a gash across his arm, and blood spilled down the altar. From there, it ran down engravings in stone to drip into the pit. Nothing immediately happened. The demon priest frowned and smeared a streak of his blood across the altar.

A dark and misty form appeared in front of Aetheria and punched her in the gut. *Oof! That hurt!* Blood actually splattered out of her mouth.

"Aha, hahaha! Nergal will eat your soul himself! The rewards from Lord Nergal shall be immense!"

Aetheria's aura turned golden, and she sucked in huge breaths of Aether and Nether. The Aether converted into holy water that blasted out of her hand to strike at the shadowy avatar. The Nether she used to coat the shrine's outer walls in Nether ice. Ice that would leech power from anything inside of it except what she gave a free pass to, which certainly wasn't the avatar or the priest.

The avatar *poofed* out of existence, then appeared behind her and struck with tendrils of darkness. A sensation of death, chaos, and darkness flooded through her. She cleansed herself of Nergal's corruption with pulses of Aether, and blasted the avatar with holy water again.

Aetheria spoke, but not in the human language the priests or knights had been speaking in. She spoke in Ath, the divine language.

"Are you my enemy or just a facsimile?"

The avatar didn't respond, which she felt answered her question. She felt like this Nergal couldn't hold a grudge if she curb-stomped some non-sentient summoning of him. Her hand flashed forward, fingers becoming talons that plunged into the smoke, and then holy fire raged out of her hand in the form of the Aetherflame Nova. When the golden flames of the nova vanished from the room, the avatar was gone—burned out of existence.

"What? No! Rise, souls of the damned, rise and protect me!" The demon priest pointed to the pit, but nothing rose... until water filled the pit to the level of the floor and sloshed into the stone of the temple.

"Yeah, that's not going to work. Tell me how to undo the ritual, and I'll give you a quick death." *Weird how easy it is to say things like that now. Maybe the fact that he's a literal demon priest of a dark god makes it easier.*

"Never. The ritual has feasted upon so many souls, it will last for a century on its own! Lamberys is bound to kill Conton by accident at least once in that time! We've already won!"

"I don't like my food to talk." Arkaziel had returned, and Aetheria let him quietly through the walls of ice. Ark started as a house cat, and with each step toward the demon, he grew bigger. First the size of a dog. Then the size of a lion. Each step, a larger feline.

"Too bad. Enjoy the meal, Ark." Aetheria turned to the altar. She covered it in hoarfrost, steam rising from it. Then the altar shattered, obliterated by her frozen wrath. Holy water still rose from the pit and surged over every surface in the shrine.

"What... what are you two?!"

"Oh, I'm a StarMane," Arkaziel answered, his form rippling to reveal the black scales, the glorious ephemeral purple fur, and the large draconic wings. "She's my sidekick." He casually took the last step and chomped the priest, while Aetheria eroded the ritual and any lingering presence of evil. The shrine's Nether concentration was too strong for her to purify it into a holy place, but she hoped she could transfer it to another god of darkness.

"I consecrate this shrine in the name of Nyx, Primordial Goddess of the Night." The light managed by her and Arkaziel's auras dimmed and flickered, and a dark presence seemed to settle into the shrine. With a gesture of her hand, two permanent ice statues formed in the depiction of Nyx. Aetheria thought, for a moment, she heard a golf clap.

Then nothing.

CHAPTER 49

Ever Upward

It was well past midnight by the time the two made their way to the surface. The chaotic curse had dissipated, no longer powered by the ritual in the shrine of Nergal. When they made their way to the battlefield itself, things had already been settled.

A victorious elder Lord Conton had slain the weaker Lord Lamberys, and without the ritual to reverse time at midnight, Lord Lamberys's soul was off to meet his patron, the God of Death, Nergal. Aetheria briefly considered leaving and not dealing with the Lords Conton, but annoyingly, the trigger to the next floor had not activated in her mind yet.

She left her aura on display to keep the rank-and-file soldiers from disturbing her, and followed the sense of power to find the elder Lord Conton, whose power was solidly into the third tier. A full third-tier Cultivator would go far in explaining why the priest and Lamberys had gone to such lengths to make a trap. There was almost no possibility of victory in a fair contest.

"The ritual breaker, Father," Derran Conton stepped forward from the gaggle of Cultivators and soldiers. He made a sweeping gesture to the aetheric aura-clad Aetheria, a smile bright on his face as he attached her actions to his reputation.

Glory by proximity is no glory. "Ria."

The elder man looked to be in his late thirties, despite being twice that in years. Life expectancy for Cultivators could be exceptionally long, depending on the physiology one gained from their path, but also thanks to alchemy and treasures. Throw in access to the towers and they could get virtual immortality for the right price. One look at the man reminded Aetheria of a thunderstorm, and she knew he was the one who had been casting the lightning.

"The heroine of the hour. Lamberys explained his dreadful plot to me multiple times over the last decade. The little prick took a sick satisfaction in taunting me with my inevitable failure, even as he lay dying each day. What an odious man, tied to an odious god."

"Indeed. We killed the priest of Nergal, some kind of demon. The knights guarding the shrine all suffered the same fate. The shrine is no longer consecrated to Nergal, but is now a temple to Nyx, Goddess of Night." The assembled Cultivators frowned at that, but no one complained. "I wouldn't pick a fight with Nyx if you don't need to."

"No doubt. Come to the keep in the morning, Ria. I would give my heroine a reward." The old man grinned. "Unless you are the sort who can't wait even a day to see new lands now that the fight is done?"

Nope, I love loot. What kind of stupid idiot would wander off without a reward?

"Until the morrow, then, Lord Conton." Aetheria tossed a salute toward the lord and sauntered into the darkness. She'd throw down her tent in the mountains, away from these people.

The next morning, Aetheria and Arkaziel wandered into Castle Lumley an hour after sunrise. A large welcome awaited them. Expectantly, the guards all stood on display. It took nearly twenty minutes from the gates to being escorted into the presence of Lord Conton in his receiving hall. It was the sort of pompous cut scene she would mash the Escape button to skip if this were a game. Instead, she had to grin and bear it through the speeches, the platitudes, and Derran trying to associate himself with her actions, until he gave her a gift: a gaudy tiara that supposedly helped with mana recuperation. Which, of course, was complete trash for Aetheria, but once the ceremony was over, the door to the next floor became triggerable in her mind.

She waited until after a private audience with the elder Conton, where she pressed upon him her desire that he rule the Lamberys lands fairly. The lord seemed tired of bloodshed and was amenable to her request that he not punish the already starving peasants, so she and Arkaziel hit Floor 19 just before noon.

The next level turned out to feature a return of her annoyance.

"Well, if it isn't the Primordials' favorite human. Enjoy this floor. I know I will." The obnoxious laughter faded into the harsh winds of Floor 19.

"I don't like tundras," Arkaziel opined as he and Aetheria took stock of the unending plains of snow in every direction. A number appeared in the sky: 3,650.

"I kind of like it. The cold is refreshing. Pretty bland view, though." She counted the seconds in her mind. After a minute, the number did not change and Aetheria had a bad feeling in her stomach. The clouds in the sky darkened and took on an ominous wormhole shape.

"I think you got a boring draw this time, Ria," Arkaziel hissed at the sky.

"Remembering something?"

"My dad saw this level. It's a decade-long slog of demons coming through portals in random waves. At least, if there was a pattern, Azrael never noticed it. He really developed a taste for spicy things with all the demons he ate." The house cat hopped off her shoulder. When he landed on the tundra, it was as a twenty-meter-long draconic feline in all his glory.

"Bigger again, huh?"

"I've been digesting Nidhogg. Plus all those giants, the marshmallow clouds, the elf, and that demon. You haven't figured out StarManes cultivate by eating?" The slight scoff, the tilt of his head—Arkaziel seemed to be reassessing her intelligence.

"I figured, but you're all secretive about your abilities, how big you are, what kind of stuff you can do…" She narrowed her red eyes and met the StarMane's gold ones, and they both laughed.

"If you kill more demons than I do over the next ten years, I'll tell you how big I actually am."

"Oh, a contest? You are on."

"If I win, buy me all the food I want every time we go to a city."

"You can't buy out all the food. We'll buy the food within reason, but we're not going to create a famine because you want snacks."

Silence dragged out while Arkaziel mulled over the counter. "Fine. Deal. We've got incoming. Do you want to alternate waves or fight simultaneously?"

With a deep breath, Aetheria shrugged. "Let's alternate for a bit. We've got ten years for this."

"I'm up first, then," Arkaziel cackled, and he shot off into the sky.

The first wave of demons were imps. While Arkaziel darted between clumps, Aetheria practiced control of her eyes. Eagle vision in video games was as simple as the press of a button. She had to imagine the process of altering her eyes: increase the number of photoreceptors, play with lens shape and size, alter the retina—it was all trial and error. Arkaziel continued to dart between flocks of imps, his speed drastically outpacing the slow, levitation-like flight of the imps. Afterimages of red claws lingered where the StarMane sliced, and only periodically did the cat-dragon dash down to snatch a corpse into his maw before they touched the ground.

~Can I netherize the ground ones?~ Aetheria inquired, and the answer was prompt.

+Go for it. I'm eating the ones that smell palatable or have more nutritional value.+

A nearly twenty-meter Arkaziel could eat a lot of imps before getting full. *Actually, can Arkaziel get full?*

~Oh, can you pop one of Nidhogg's femurs out? I'll use the demons as a digestive aid to gnaw on one of those giant bones. So many nutrients…~

Aetheria groaned at the audible salivation in the StarMane's tone, but dropped a skyscraper-sized femur from the repository onto the tundra.

"Huh. I could go into butchery." The bone had transferred clean of connecting tissues and organic bits. Could she dismember bodies without a mess just by pulling only certain parts out of her storage? *I'm definitely going to have a lot of time on my hands to experiment with that.*

From there it became a matter of simply walking the rapidly filling tundra to netherize the demon corpses. The only eventful occurrence while Arkaziel rampaged waves of imps was the occasional corpse that almost fell on her. The plummeting forms gave her a chance to work on her Nether sense as she worked to avoid getting squashed.

Day 30

The imp waves broke for a twelve-hour window. Then they resumed, with the addition of a portal that opened on the ground. No imps from the sky.

Day 37

They added hellhounds in addition to the imps. Although physically weak, the imps brought firepower and ranged attacks into the mix, while the hellhounds only contributed physical attacks and flamebreath.

Day 90

Arkaziel and Aetheria slept and ate merrily during what turned out to be a twenty-four-hour break. Afterward, hate demons came out of the ground portal. This incarnation was a horrific flesh abomination in a barely humanoid shape, but the monsters had high levels of strength and durability. Aetheria experimented with the creation of more etheric ice constructs, predominantly ice turrets that fired spears of ice.

Day 100

Succubi and incubi showed up. Arkaziel did not feel the call of their siren songs of seduction, and the four Primordial Flames in her mind allowed Aetheria to ignore their attempts of influence. After the tenth one died, the type of demons changed.

The next day, a second ground portal opened up half a kilometer from the first. Half human, half demon soldiers replaced the succubi. The variety of enemies covered multiple archetypes: casters, warriors, and assassins, both melee and ranged. Aetheria and Arkaziel no longer could alternate.

Day 120

Aetheria's further experimentation with turrets now included making kill boxes and corridors with etheric ice walls. While the demons could scale the walls with difficulty, they were nearly impervious to damage and self-healed, just like the Ethereal turrets.

Day 150

The sky began spitting imps again, and hellhounds intermixed with the half-demon shock troops.

Day 200

Then, the gluttony demons appeared. These abominations against goodness vaguely resembled the xenomorph, only they were yellow, and when killed, they exploded into a corrosive cloud. Fast, agile, and physically strong, they were exceptionally annoying. For whatever reason, they never attacked Arkaziel, and zoned in on Aetheria.

Day 430

The Administrator gave the duo a day's break. Aetheria made herself a hot tub and pampered herself.

The next day, a new type of monster showed up—greater fiends. Three meters tall, with large bat wings, built like giants, they used flame whips and breathed fire. Each one had a shock troop of half-demons with it as support.

Day 999

The heart of the murder maze Aetheria had created had not been breached. Hundreds of walls made up a complicated tunnel system. Some tunnels had roofs, some did not. Hidden in walls, floors, and ceilings, Aetheria had made turrets that flung ice spears, and freezing turrets that pulsed an aetheric freeze pulse every thirty seconds. And since Arkaziel flew, all the floors were ice and leeched life force from anything that walked on them, excluding her.

A day's respite. That was all they got, after a solid year and a half of constant combat. Apparently, Aetheria's need for sleep was completely counter-acted by her regenerative capabilities and energy absorption. Arkaziel, likewise, did not need sleep. Both were cranky as hell.

Day 1,830

New enemies entered with each wave. Most never even saw Arkaziel or Aetheria. They died from traps, turrets, energy beams, auras, or the toxic power of Nidhogg. Aetheria deployed Nidhogg's toxicity via ice, while Arkaziel had gained a second breath type and now had the corrosive, toxic-ridden, awful breath of Nidhogg that melted demons just as easily as humans.

The StarMane also showed another new ability: duplication. The exact method of it eluded Aetheria, but there were three smaller Arkaziels running around committing a one-cat demonic purge while the real Arkaziel gnawed on Nidhogg's bones, greater fiend corpses, and anything that looked tasty.

Aetheria roamed the tunnels. She repaired walls, altered the maze, and added turrets, traps, and other nasty surprises. The power of her freezing domain killed everything but the greater fiends and the ice demons outright. At first, this confused her, but she slowly realized the test was not truly a combat trial—none of the demons stood a chance against Arkaziel or her. The test was about how long she could hold on to sanity in the face of constant violence, lack of sleep, no human companionship, and limited breaks to even eat or deal with bodily necessities.

Her solution? She started talking to Arkaziel more telepathically. She told him stories about Earth mythology, history, culture. She told him about One Piece, the *Iliad*, even the story of *Eldest Fantasy Wars Online*. That helped, significantly, as did the warmth that radiated in her soul from her connection to a certain blond nephilim who was out there on another floor. Her mental health rose from abyssal to getting by.

CHAPTER 50

Worst Tower Defense Game Ever

Day 3,640

A fourth portal opened on the ground, but Aetheria immediately boxed it in a sphere of yellow etheric ice. The ice radiated the power of Nyx, and anything that generated inside of it that didn't die to the Night's Hunger was killed by ice spear turrets. Ice spears were a comparatively merciful death, unlike the brutal, inescapable drain of life force provided by the Primordial Flame of Nyx. It was the same process she had taken with the third portal on the ground. The constant pressure from inside the first two ground portals prevented her from simplifying the tunnel design those portals were set up with. This worked relatively well, as it allowed her to supervise one tunnel and one of Arkaziel's clones to supervise the other. The StarMane's other two copies handled the two sky portals with prowess, aided by the rapid-fire ice spike turret that sat atop large pillars.

The wear and tear of almost a decade with less than a few weeks' breaks interspersed throughout had allowed both Aetheria and Arkaziel to develop brutal efficiency in the elimination of demonic forces. Greater fiends, fiend lords, wyrm fiends, pit demons... it didn't matter what they were. Arkaziel and Aetheria had mastered the fine art of slaying demons. That both walked the Ethereal Path, which apparently counted as holy power, did the demons no favors.

In fact, both of them had mastered the art of adding aspects to their Ethereal energy. Aetheria had reached the height of three simultaneous aspects, while Arkaziel did not seem to go beyond two. Whether this was the StarMane's limit or just choice, he refused to answer. He favored his mixing his Ethereal energy with the toxic aspect he had gained from his digestion of Nidhogg, although just as frequently, the StarMane mixed Ethereal energy with light or darkness. Arkaziel's light had the holy attribute on its own, and his darkness carried a form of unholy power that Aetheria thought matched what her books called dark divinity. It did not appear to make his attacks count twice for holy power, though.

Aetheria had found she favored mixing ice, what she thought of as Nyx's Hunger, or leech, with her Ethereal energy. This allowed her ice to be nearly indestructible against demons, and a portion of the life stolen from them helped strengthen and fortify the ice itself. She couldn't be sure even she could break through the walls that were over a year old now if they weren't under her control. She felt certain her oldest walls could withstand a nuclear blast.

Aetheria also had new suspicions about how Aoibhe had constructed her crystalline tower. Reinforced over years, even a delicate tower like Aoibhe's could become nearly indestructible. She suspected words like "indestructible" should have quantifiers. Her current destructive capabilities far outstripped those she had when first reincarnated, or when she had advanced to the second tier of the Ethereal Path.

Every day on this level had infused her with increasing energy. Aether swallowed from the dense air, Nether taken from the earth, and the uncountable legion of demons they slaughtered. Aetheria's soul repository, filled with Nether crystals, demonic cores, everything she had taken with her in her adventures so far, and a literal mountain of crude armor and weapons taken from the demons towered over every other stack in the repository.

Maybe it's time to start thinking of a better way to sort things than giant piles? Maybe I shouldn't take everything I find. No, that's silly.

Her summation of the trial, however, had felt incomplete. The challenge of constant battle, no contact beyond Arkaziel, and no real time to eat or sleep had taken a toll. A massive toll, in fact, but Aetheria's faith in their ability to endure had held steadfast in the face of depression, loneliness, and doubt. Arkaziel seemed to be free of any such issues. The StarMane's ego and supreme confidence translated into a mind free of self-doubt.

Aetheria's body had continued to adapt to her Ethereal physiology. With over a decade of experience built up, constant exposure to Ethereal power from her Ethereal heart, and perpetual battle and exertion, every aspect of her body had become adept at making use of Ethereal power to become more. She still couldn't teleport, though.

She was on the cusp of entry to Tier Three. To join the ranks of Ethereal Grasper, she needed to open a path to the Origin and pull the power into her location. No matter how good she got with merging Aether and Nether into Ethereal, she would never advance until she successfully grasped the Origin and made that infinite source of Ethereal power her own. *Just a little hole in reality. No big deal, right?*

How did one go about safely boring a hole in reality to draw power from the Origin? And then repeat the process every time one needed to access power? This was the problem Aetheria had reached. Nothing in her books mentioned a path forward, and Arkaziel's cultivation process seemed to be unique to StarManes and not applicable to her. The obvious answer she repeatedly came back to was to upgrade her proto-core heart into a full core, and pull power through her soul.

Day 3,644

A precious break. Aetheria locked downed the tunnels with more turrets, traps, and orbs that pulsed with freezing waves. She added more turrets to the roof as well. When the sadistic Administrator gave them a break, it meant whatever came next would be awful.

The last waves started at dawn the next day. A third sky gate and a fifth land gate opened.

+*I've got the sky gate. Our setup should hold. Why don't you just handle the new gate?*+ Arkaziel's suggestion came as the enormous form of the StarMane lofted into the air. The thirty-five-meter-long draconic cat shot into the air, ascending to become a blur of murderous destruction.

~*Sure, might as well see what a fresh portal looks like.*~

Flight was fast, but Aetheria just jumped onto the roof of her tunnel maze and ran toward the new gate. She leaped into the air at the end of her construction, her coat billowing to catch the air and slow her drop at the last moment. The soles of Nidhogg's Fury hit the crunchy tundra.

The portal was a red and black glob of energy that offered a partial glimpse into a dimension of hell.

"Goat-men? Really?" Aetheria shook her head a little as the humanoid figures of goat-demons came through the portal. They ranged in size from two to three meters tall. Their eyes were either red, orange, or black. Armor and armaments varied per individual, but only one in three had visible ranged weaponry—at least, Aetheria assumed the strange scepters with a fiery glow were range weapons.

The goat-men talked in a terrible-sounding language she did not understand. They launched balls of fire, crossbow bolts, and orbs of darkness toward Aetheria. The fire fizzled out before it could get close to her. Even against the lowest strength of her freeze domain, it would take a powerful fire to get to her. Crossbow bolts slammed into small walls of ice that rose to provide cover. Aetheria dodged the orbs of darkness and watched them explode against the ice structures behind her. The shadows inside struggled against her ice wall, but the darkness slowly faded.

If enough of those hit walls, it might actually bring them down.

Aetheria accelerated like a shot, then fell among the goat-men like the wrath of a furious god. Her fingers elongated into fierce talons that glowed with gathered Ethereal power. She slashed through the metal and leather armor of the demons like a butcher's knife through lamb. Red Ethereal energy filled her cells. Her Cultivator's physiology pushed her strength above even the normal levels she could reach with shapeshifting alone.

Those goat-men who were backhanded were subject to the enchantment of her gloves. The magic of Punch Drunk Punchers increased the disorientation of her blows, and if she struck the same being repeatedly, it created an effect similar to excessive alcohol consumption. Few were hit more than once, as a slash of her talons swiftly followed the backhanded blows to steal each demon's life.

Goat-men bellowed terrible screeches as she fell among them. She kicked one in the chest with Nidhogg's Fury while pushing her Ethereal power into it. The result was that noxious fumes erupted from the goat-man as he shot through the air and slammed into another batch of demons. The kicked goat-man screamed before he exploded and coated his fellows in a toxic cloud that ate their fur, armor, weapons, and skin until the ever-present wind dissipated it.

That's so nasty, but damn, if it isn't effective. I love magic items. I hope I get more soon.

Day 3,650

The goat-men came and died by the swarm in Aetheria's domain. The number in the sky flipped to 0 and then disappeared. The demonic gates closed. It took Arkaziel and her another hour after the gates closed to finish off the rest of the goat-men, and hours more to sort the corpses. Ark separated ones he thought would be super tasty, and the rest Aetheria netherized.

"Want to bet if I can throw some of my ice walls into my repository?" she inquired of her companion.

"Why wouldn't it work? Of course it would work. Take them with; drop them on people. Splat." The StarMane laughed at that, an unrestrained viciousness on display after the last decade.

Aetheria touched a wall and sent it into her repository. It worked. She wasn't sure why she'd assumed it wouldn't, while Ark had been confident it would. *Perhaps it's because I think that's poorly balanced to work that way, while Ark just thinks in terms of the cold rules of reality as he understands them, with no regard for fairness.*

A massively bright light filled the world, refracting off the snow and ice of the tundra and blinding them. Silence reigned for three long seconds.

"Shit, that was bright." Aetheria rubbed at her eyes, and the StarMane cackled.

"Let me guess: You're immune to bright lights?"

"You know it, Ria. It's like freezing you. I don't know why I should care about a seed."

"Seed?"

Arkaziel lifted a foreleg and pointed at the sky. An orb of bright light descended to touch the ground. The tundra cracked when the orb blessed the ground, and then soil opened to accept the seed held within the light. The earth shook, heaved, and shook again. From the seed, a massive tree grew higher and higher into the sky. The energy in the area changed.

"Thank you, Walkers of the Ethereal Path."

Aetheria blinked. The tree had no face, but it was talking somehow.

"Uh. Yeah, sure. No problem. It was the job, y'know? Who are you?" she inquired, shooting Ark a questioning look. The cat shook his head.

"I am the Tree of Harmony. The demonic energies built up here have allowed me to balance my divine energies and take root once more. For this, I will offer each of you a boon."

Arkaziel didn't even take a moment to think about it. "Got some fruit or nuts? I'm hungry." The expression in his eyes had nothing to do with physical hunger. He wanted cultivation food.

Aetheria wandered closer to the tree, and let its peaceful and serene aura wash over her.

"I could go for some esoteric knowledge. Namely, how to cross into the third tier of my path."

"Sit with me and meditate, child. I will reveal the secrets to you if you are ready."

Arkaziel snickered. "Leave me some Nidhogg meat while you meditate. It'll go super good with whatever Harmony has for me."

Aetheria rolled her eyes, dropped a haunch of Nidhogg on the cat, and went over to meditate under the tree.

CHAPTER 51

The Paw-sitively Hiss-terical Riddler

Meditation had not played a large part in Aetheria's progression as a Cultivator. She liked it that way. Advancement through violence felt like it had a higher rate of return than time spent in solitude. Surely, there was merit to the lives of those who dedicated it to ideas, dogmatic routine, and obsessive repetition. But that life was not for her. So, she took little joy in meditation beneath the tree. But an irresistible sense of peace radiated from beneath the Tree of Harmony.

Muscles she was unaware of relaxed. Doubt and fear washed away in the tide of serenity. Her mind and body joined in serene ease. In the newfound tranquility of mind, body, and soul, pathways of thought previously blocked off opened like a flower. Fragrant blooms of knowledge filled Aetheria.

That's it. I align my soul to Ethereal power. Draw it in as flowers pull in insects to pollinate them. Well, not quite like that. I'm not reproducing with it. Bad analogy, Tree. This will take some time, but a little each day should get me there.

When Aetheria opened her eyes, it was to the sight of Arkaziel's big yellow eyes. The StarMane was staring at her, and when her eyes opened, he bopped her on the face.

"About time. You were out for a month. Any longer and I would have eaten the tree."

"No eating trees."

"I didn't want to eat it, but if you didn't wake up soon, I would have made the valiant sacrifice for the good of all."

"Thank you for not eating me, Arkaziel," said the tree. "I see you have found your knowledge, human. Thank you again for returning balance to the area. Balance is important." The last words hung over the duo before the tree and floor faded from sight. The Tree of Harmony had triggered their transport to Floor 20.

Ark and Aetheria found themselves on top of a strange stone glyph in a desolate valley. Littered across the sandy valley were the ruins of pyramids, temples, and abandoned city structures.

"Undead floor?" Aetheria inquired of Arkaziel and his predecessors' memories.

Arkaziel sniffed the air. Then sniffed it again. He hissed.

"No. Worse. Sphinx."

"As in, answer my questions to pass?"

"As in, tries to eat you even after you win, because they're lying liars who smell bad."

"Not a fan of them?"

"My great-aunt was tricked by a sphinx. We declared a blood feud."

"On the entire race?"

"Obviously."

Aetheria forced herself to take a deep breath. The peace of the Tree of Harmony seemed so far away now. Instead, she smiled. Riddles and (most likely) violence appeared to be the order of the day, and those were orders she could handle.

"Well, let's get it over with. We talk first, murder second."

Arkaziel gave her a small hiss, but turned into his house cat form and jumped onto her shoulder. The little jerk flexed his claws a little before he settled down.

"You know I still feel pain, right? Just because I heal almost instantly doesn't mean it's okay to hurt me."

"My bad. Really. It's been a decade since I was in kitty form. I'm not used to the differences in paws anymore."

The explanation sounded like bullshit, but she let it go. About fifty meters away, on a pedestal in the middle of the path, sat a sphinx. Its eyes opened slowly, as if it were fresh out of a long slumber.

"Ahh. Travelers. Answer my riddles three, and you may pass me. Fail, and you shall be my lunch. I'm starving, so get them wrong." The malicious smile on the feline's face mirrored the hunger Aetheria often saw in Arkaziel's features. *No wonder they hate each other.*

"Fine, let's get this over with. Give me your riddle."

"What has a bottom at the top?" the Sphinx asked smugly.

Aetheria frowned, but before she could say anything, Ark filled her mind with the answer telepathically.

"A leg."

The sphinx hissed. "Beginner's luck. I am a word of letters three, add two, and fewer there will be. What am I?"

Again, Arkaziel filled her mind with the answer, even as Aetheria rolled her eyes at the awful riddle.

"Few."

The sphinx hissed again. "Third time's the charm. You'll never get this one right. What has keys but can't open locks?" Smugness radiated from the sphinx as it beat its tail against the pedestal it sat on, licking its lips in anticipation.

+It's a piano. Can we eat him now? I want to eat him.+

"A piano." Aetheria wouldn't admit she hadn't immediately gotten that one, but she felt confident she could have if given a few minutes.

The sphinx frowned in agitation at being beat. For a moment, she thought it was going to pounce off the pedestal to eat her.

"You may pass." The words came out like a curse, but Aetheria shrugged and walked past the sphinx and its spot in the middle of the road. She didn't make it far before Arkaziel became a black blur, and the sound of struggle came from the two felines. By the time Aetheria turned to take in the scene, Arkaziel had the sphinx gripped by the neck.

"A StarMane? A tho—" The sphinx got no more words out before Arkaziel bit its head off and swallowed. Rather than watch the gruesome scene, Aetheria took the time to scan the path forward and the horizon. No door, so there was more to this floor than just the sphinx.

Minutes passed. Arkaziel descended upon her shoulder once more.

"He was startlingly tasty. Let's see if we can find a female sphinx. They taste even better."

"Why would there be more?"

"I can smell them. This valley is lousy with sphinxes."

"Is it okay to just... eat them, like that? He was going to let us pass."

"No, he wasn't. He was already stretching to eat you in one bite. He said he would let you pass, not that he would let you pass *safely*. They're worse than lawyers. Not that eating you would have worked, but I enjoy showing inferior beings their inferiority to *me*. Him knowing he was inferior to you doesn't matter."

"Fine, but I want to try some more riddles before you eat them—and don't tell me the answers until I've had a moment." This time, the StarMane rolled his eyes at her.

Ten minutes later, they encountered the next sphinx. This one had the face of a human woman on the traditional winged feline body.

"Answer my riddle, and you may live. Fail, and you will die."

"Yep. I've been through this once already. What have you got for me?"

"What comes once in a minute, twice in a moment, but never in a thousand years?"

Arkaziel's tail beat against her back impatiently. Aetheria could feel him tense up as each second passed. A small smirk flickered across her lips and she held her tongue. She made a show of being thoughtful and unsure about an answer. Second by second, Arkaziel tensed more and more, and his murderous intent rose closer to the surface. Before the sphinx could sense it, Aetheria ended the game.

"The letter M."

The lady sphinx hissed.

"Fine, then answer this one! The more you take, the more you leave behind. What am I?"

"Now, now, you said *a riddle*, not multiple. Are you going back on the deal?"

"No, no, surely your fallible human ears failed to detect the plurality of riddles. Answer the question." The sphinx hungrily licked her lips.

~Okay, I'm seeing why you hate sphinx, Ark. So do they just always eat the person, anyway?~

+I think they let people go sometimes, just to perpetuate the idea that they are actually fair. It's not a bad con—you fell for it.+ Aetheria wanted to rebuff the StarMane, but

the truth was, she *had* fallen for it. In hindsight, her instinctive trust of mythology probably was a trait she needed to fix. Anyone, human or monster, can use propaganda as a weapon.

"Footsteps are what you leave behind you, the more you take."

The female sphinx let out a disappointed growl. "Final riddle, human. What gets wetter as it dries?"

The first thought that popped into Aetheria's mind didn't answer the riddle. Yet there would be satisfaction in killing the sphinx with the Primordial Flame of Thalassa. Death by magic dehydration seemed a proper fate for a sphinx.

+*Oh, do it, do it. I bet sphinx jerky tastes great.*+

Aetheria controlled her violent urges. She wouldn't attack the sphinx unless it made the first move.

"A towel. I win, lady." She focused her red eyes the feline.

The sphinx pounced, its hunger palpable in the air. Just as fast, Aetheria formed a pillar of ice that filled the stretched mouth of the sphinx. She then struck the sphinx in the face to sending it crashing hard into the ground.

"Seriously?" Aetheria asked, forming a ring of blue ice around the sphinx. The ice lit into a blaze of the Flame of Thalassa, and moisture melted the sphinx before their eyes.

"Get to it, Arkaziel." Aetheria's vexation was clear in her voice.

While the MurderCat ate the RiddleCat jerky, she took a few moments to focus her mind and visualize changes to her soul repository. Minor changes needed to be wrought to synergize with the Origin. *I wonder if Aoibhe had to do this? As a nephilim, she had instinctive connections. Did she start as a higher tier? Arkaziel didn't start life at Tier One. What other species have distinct advantages?*

"That was nice, but now I'm thirsty." Arkaziel let out a yawn. Aetheria summoned him a keg of beer from her repository.

"Thanks, Blue."

She sighed and started walking down the path once more. Arkaziel caught up with her a few minutes later.

A final pedestal stood between the duo and the door to Floor 21. Upon it sat a much larger sphinx. This one had the face and wings of a hawk and the body of a lion. It radiated palpable danger, unlike the other two sphinxes. This one actually seemed to be on their level.

"Answer my riddles three, and you may pass to the next level. For each wrong answer, I will eat one of you."

"There's only me and my cat."

"I'll eat the cat first, then. Best not get two wrong, human."

"Fine, let's get this going. What's your first riddle, oh great Sphinx?"

"I can be cracked, made, and told. I am not a joke. What am I?"

+*Dead is what he is. Let me eat him! He killed one of my family!*+ Arkaziel's tail hit her back with great agitation.

"A code. Easy. What else have you got?"

The hawk's face snorted in annoyance. "What is so fragile that saying its name breaks it?"

Arkaziel's agitation continued to grow in the back of her mind. Like a volcano, the StarMane would erupt soon. Aetheria had better put the sphinx off its game before it happened.

"Silence. Duh. Do you need a few minutes? These are basic-bitch riddles." She filled her voice with condescension and put on her best "Can I talk to your manager?" pose and voice.

The sphinx narrowed its eyes and crushed some of the stone pedestal with its claws in a burst of anger.

"You see a boat full of people. It has not sunk, but when you look again, you don't see a single person on the boat. Why?"

+*Can I eat it yet?*+

"That's the best you've got? They were all married, so there were no single people on the boat. Lame. Alternatively, they all jumped in the water."

The sphinx lunged its beaked maw forward to bite her head off. Aetheria shot her head back, neck stretched in an inhuman posture. Ark launched off her shoulder and left gashes across the neck of the sphinx, then turned to loop around for a breath attack.

Stopping her head's strange stretch backward, Aetheria then shot forward as though launched by a slingshot. A horn emerged from her forehead right before she spiked the surprised sphinx between the eyes. Blood fountained and the sphinx screeched, and then coruscating black and white energy from Arkaziel's breath attack shot the sphinx in its open maw, exploding its head in a fountain of gore.

"Ew. It's all over me. I'm going to make a shower and wash up while you... eat that thing." Disgusted, Aetheria picked off the largest chunks of sphinx and tossed them onto the corpse, then erected a shower in which to clean up.

CHAPTER 52

Chess Match

As the teleportation effect of passage to Floor 21 faded, Aetheria and Arkaziel found themselves in a small room. There was a singular occupant, sitting at a table. On the table was a chessboard.

"Ah, if it isn't Sparkle Princess and her cat," said the holographic projection of the Tower Administrator sitting at the table. "This floor is easy. We play chess until you win a game—just one game."

Aetheria arched a brow at the Tower Administrator in contempt, trying to recall the last time she had played chess.

"Isn't it a breach of the rules for you to play such a direct role in a challenge?"

"Nope. All who reach this floor get the same challenge, so it's perfectly fair. Unless you think I would dishonor my position by intentionally losing to a Challenger?" It was the demigodling's turn to be vexed and cross.

"Ugh. Let's get this over with." *~Do StarManes know how to play chess, Ark?~*
+Oh, yeah. I'll tell you what to do. We won't lose a single piece to this scrub.+

"You cheated! I don't know how you cheated, but you cheated!" the Administrator ranted like an insane man as the doorway to Floor 22 opened a half hour later.

"Sorry, pal. Tell your folks I said hi." Aetheria saluted the Administrator as she and Arkaziel cruised onward to Floor 22.

~He was terrible. I wonder if he ever won a game before?~
+Maybe you are just that good?+
~Well, of course I am that good, but he was exceptionally bad, too.~

When the darkness turned to daylight, Aetheria and Arkaziel were separated. Aetheria found herself on a patio. Nothing connected to the patio. They had constructed the structure of light wood. There was a table with an umbrella above it, a pitcher of lemonade, and two glasses. Aetheria immediately disliked the look of this level.

She dropped into one of the Adirondack chairs, poured herself some lemonade, and kicked her feet up on the table.

"I raised you better than that, young lady."

Really? You're pulling my mom out?

"Hi, Mom."

"Don't you 'Hi, Mom' me! You die of a brain aneurysm in your sleep, leave me and your poor father all alone, destroyed by the death of our daughter! And now here you are gallivanting in some fantasy dungeon, sleeping with elves and nephilim, killing monsters with your fists, and you don't even find a way to say, 'I'm actually alive, Mommy' to me? That is not the child I raised you to be, Aesca!"

Aetheria let a deep sigh escape. *This isn't my mother.*

Despite that knowledge, flickers of power escaped from her eyes and hands as a sign of agitation. She doubled down on control over her emotions. Sure, she could go off on this copy of her mother, but it would serve no purpose. This was not her mother.

"I died," Aetheria said softly. "I died, and I watched the EMTs come and try to resuscitate me. Then I got asked to go on a quest by a *god* with a chance to live again. Of course I took it."

"That was no 'god,' sweetheart. That was a demon. You've trapped yourself in a fantasy that's keeping you from moving on to be with the one true God. Stop letting the wiles of demons trap your soul and keep you from basking in *His* glory."

Aetheria blinked. That was not the path she had expected this to go down. Her expectation had been that this would be a guilt trip, an attempt to cause a trial of the past. *I guess I wasn't totally wrong.*

"So you want me to, what, accept death and move on to the afterworld?" She arched a fine aqua-blue brow at the facsimile of her mother.

"Precisely. This is a trap—one giant delusion, dear. You are not a chosen one. You don't have magical powers, a talking cat, and a body made by demons to lead you astray. This is all ephemeral, a distracting dream. Accept that and it will just fade away, and you can know the peace you should have when you died. I love you, Aesca, but this has gone too far. You were a librarian with a video game addiction, not some action heroine."

It would be easy to let doubt ease up with this argument. *Why did Aetherius and Nyx choose me? Why wouldn't they choose someone more impressive? Is that the line of questioning you're trying to get out of me, Administrator?*

"Yeah, no." Aetheria shot her domain outward. The air froze. Hoarfrost covered the patio. Her breath became steam. The patio shattered into nothing, and Aetheria found herself alone.

"You really should have tried that *before* I'd been in the tower for, what, fifteen years now?" She should have kept tabs on how long she had been in the tower.

"What? You can't just freeze a trial!" the Tower Administrator's voice boomed around her.

"Just did. It was stupid, and I wasn't going to fall for it. What, did you want me to play along? Fake-cry, wail about how I've been deceived? Where'd you go?" The last Aetheria asked after the Administrator failed to respond to her flatly delivered questions.

No response came from the Administrator.

Aetheria gestured and then sat on the ice throne she'd created. She might as well get comfortable until Arkaziel broke free. Something was blocking her telepathy with the StarMane, but the empathic aspect of their bond functioned now that she had freed herself. She pushed love and support at the cat. *He might be a murderhobo, but he's my murderhobo.*

Aetheria lost track of time, but it seemed on the shorter side before she felt the bond with Arkaziel come back fully. Her eyes opened just in time to witness him appear in a burst of darkness and light.

"Quite the entrance."

Arkaziel snorted, and she noticed shadows escape with his breath.

"Biggest waste of time ever. As if one of my descendants would ever act untoward with me. I have their memories, you stupid Tower Admin. I played along with it until I got bored and was certain that there wouldn't be anything good to eat."

"So you would've kept playing along if he gave you some fried chicken?"

"Well, fried cockatrice, maybe. I'm a growing boy, remember?"

"I've wondered, just how long are you going to be a 'growing boy' for?"

"Another million years, plus or minus a couple of centuries."

"Even with your accelerated growth?"

"Growing faster just means I have more time to keep growing. Prophecy speaks of a StarMane so large that he could eat a galaxy. We all strive to become the chosen one who can devour galaxies."

"*Galaxies?* Plural? I thought the biggest a StarMane could eat was a planet?"

"So far!" Arkaziel's conviction sent shivers down Aetheria's spine. The general distrust of StarManes made more sense the more she learned about them. *This must be what it feels like to have a demon for a companion, or a necromancer friend. If they're such a threat, why do all the gods I've met so far treat them like a nuisance at worst?*

The door to Floor 23 opened.

The two appeared on a flat, sandy training ground. They seemed to be alone. A sign before them read:

Arkaziel: Become proficient at manipulating Twilight.
Aetheria: Freeze the flame of the ever-burning torch.

As the sign suggested, not far to one side stood a post holding a burning torch. When Aetheria waved a hand to put the torch out, it relit a second later.

"Oh. Maybe we can keep the torch after we're done. You need anything from the repository to get this started?"

Arkaziel made a tremendous show of doing absolutely nothing, then yawned. "Oh, I'll take another real gigantic piece of Nidhogg. Do you still have one of his legs?

Plus some demons—any that used shadow or light powers. Maybe two or three giant trout from Thalassa's floor, too."

Aetheria laughed, but agreed to his wishes. A massive pile of fish, dragon, and demons appeared over a layer of ice to keep things fresh.

"Hey, Ark? What's Twilight, anyway?" Aetheria couldn't resist asking any longer.

"Twilight? Oh, it's the common name for the mixed element combination of light and darkness. Technically, it's sort of a hodgepodge between light, dark, and shadow. Fire and earth can give you magma, fire and air give explosion, and so on."

"Thanks." Arkaziel grinned, took on a thirty-meter-long draconic form, and began to gnaw on one of Nidhogg's haunches. The StarMane gave no sign he would spend any time on the assignment, not when he could focus on food and the realization of gains from digested prey.

With that, she walked back to the torch and considered the task at hand. *Freeze fire. No big deal. Just freeze an intangible, magical flame. How hard can that be?*

She started with her domain. That just extinguished the fire. She applied the Flame of Ymir. Also extinguished the fire. Aetheric ice extinguished the fire. Nether ice did the same. Aetheria tried each Flame she possessed, then tried combining them. That did not work.

So, none of that works. The answer is some kind of Ethereal freezing that breaks the rules of Aether, Nether, or ice itself. Actually, is freezing the same as ice? Time to revisit those books.

She popped her tent out of her repository, and she wandered inside to settle into a rocking chair to review the books.

"I have always been fascinated by the mysterious and otherworldly properties of conceptual ice. Unlike mundane ice, which can be understood and manipulated through scientific means, conceptual ice is governed by arcane laws and ancient magics that are beyond the understanding of mortals.

"To freeze a flame, one must first understand the essence of fire. Fire is not merely a chemical reaction or a physical process—it is a primal force of nature, a manifestation of the raw energy and passion that burns within all living things. To freeze a flame, one must first master the art of manipulating this primal energy."

"Oh, my gooses. I know how to use fire already. Kind of. I'll worry about that after a nap."

Aetheria stifled a yawn, wandered over to the cordoned-off bedroom of the tent, and took the most glorious of all things: a nap.

Troubled dreams haunted her. Dreams of red oceans of power, crystallized fire, a gateway into the unknown—even dreams of Arkaziel eating Earth. When she awoke, she decided it might be best to take a shower and get back on topic.

This happens when you don't sleep regularly for a decade. Maybe I should slow down a little, like Arkaziel.

The StarMane had not moved. His tail lazily flapped around, smashing the ground, while he happily pigged out on Nidhogg and demons.

Ugh. Am I really telling myself to be more like a cat?

Day 3

"Frostfire! Hahaha."

Blue-white flames danced in circles around Aetheria while she laughed like a madwoman. This was not the quest she had been given, but it felt like an appropriate step along the way and added another dangerous tool to her arsenal. The blue flames emitted a cold so intense that it burned. *Somehow. I don't think science can explain magic, and I think that's working against me. I want to know why that works, why I can make it, but not explain it. Hand wave and magic, blah blah blah. Why??*

Aetheria snapped her fingers and pulsed a changed version of her Aetherflame Nova Art. She named the new version Frostfire Ether-Nova. *All the advantages of fire and ice, twice as nice.*

It put the ever-burning torch out.

"Oh, for Pete's sake."

Day 7

Freeze. Freeze. Freeze. Freeze.

The word was a mantra repeated like a prayer in her mind. Aetheria's aura raged around her, a massive red tide of Ethereal energy. She had spent dozens of bricks of Ethereal power forged by her proto-core heart. Her aura was wild and barely contained.

Flickers of red Ether lashed out like tongues that licked the ever-burning flame. Dozens of tendrils of much thinner power separated from her aura and probed more minutely at the flame.

Aetheria repeated the mantra and imagined the Flames—and new flames generated by the torch—crystallizing into ice.

An odd crinkle sound filled the air as the fire *froze*.

"I did it! I froze fire!" Aetheria grabbed the now frozen-solid torch and examined her handiwork. "Ark! I did it!"

"Good job! Could I get another fish? This bit of Nidhogg has the worst aftertaste. I swear that jerk peed himself as he died just to spite me."

CHAPTER 53

Trials of a Shifter

Aetheria spent the next week in meditation. The process of altering her repository environment progressed at a snail's pace. Anytime she tried to make broad changes at once, it all reverted the moment she concentrated on something else. Small incremental change seemed to stay in place.

The repository now had a red sky that churned with clouds both dark and light. Aetheria had decided she wanted to make the gateway to the Origin be the sun that lit her proto-inner world. A constant high-output source of Ethereal energy would make the small output of her Proto-core heart seem insignificant. In fact, the four-chambered combustion heart would be utterly redundant once she established the gateway to the Origin. At least that is what her books suggested.

"It seems like the power gap between Tiers Two and Three is going to be enormous. If the tower's scale is relative to the Climber, everything is going to get a lot more dangerous soon."

In the background, she heard a sound like laughter. Since the only other being was Arkaziel, she left the tent to investigate the StarMane's activities. Around Ark, three of his clones were throwing balls of murky energy at one another.

"Ria, check it out. I've made Twilight duplicates. Who's the best? I'm the best. Also, I'm out of food. Meat? Please?" The StarMane made his yellow eyes enormous when he said the last word.

Aetheria tossed him one of the last of the fish from Thalassa's lake.

"Oh, there's the portal to Twenty-Four. Eat your fish. I'll pack the tent back up. Good job, Ark!" *I wish I could cultivate by eating. I suppose I could eat the rest of those ambrosial fruits, but better to let them be preserved until I can get someone who can tell me what they do.*

When the darkness of teleportation faded, the duo found themselves in the middle of a ring of white stones atop a flattened hill. The inner ring contained sand and a single stump. A white-haired, blue-skinned, wrinkle-faced man sat on a stump in the center of the ring. The old man ignored them until Aetheria walked closer to him.

"Hail, candidate. Pass my trials ten, and I shall impart upon you knowledge of a secret shapeshifting technique."

Arkaziel didn't pipe up with alternatives to cooperating with the old man's tests. Aetheria quickly realized the reason for that, though. The man was talking to her, not Ark. So the murder-cat had already shut his eyes and gone back to sleep on her shoulder.

"Okay. What's the first trial?"

"Transform into... this!" The blue man held up an empty bottle that looked like it had once held wine.

"A wine bottle?"

"A wine bottle."

Aetheria couldn't help but release a gigantic sigh. *I've never tried to turn into objects. I guess...*

Mass and volume were immaterial, since she could transfer them to energy temporarily. Glass, tinted slightly green. Classic wine bottle shape. Aetheria visualized the bottle, then shifted. The sudden loss of so much of her normal mass went beyond strange. Clunking onto the sand sent strange sensations through her tiny body. None of her normal senses were in place in this form. She held it briefly before turning back into a human.

"Uffda." Breathing, while a luxury in some forms, was comforting.

"Good. You have passed the Trial of the Bottle."

"If you tell me to turn into whiskey so you can drink me, we're going to have a big problem, old-timer."

"The last shapeshifter I ate gave me terrible indigestion. No, the next trial is to turn into... this!" With a grand gesture, an illusionary form appeared next to the blue man. The illusion depicted a scorpion the size of a large Ford F-350 Super Duty truck.

"Seems a step down in difficulty from the bottle..." Aetheria muttered under her breath and focused on the image. Pincers. Stinger. Exoskeleton. Creepy eyes. In less than a minute, a large scorpion clicked its claws at the old man until he nodded in acknowledgment.

Aetheria grumbled as she became human again.

"Speed test. Change into me, your cat, the scorpion, the bottle, and back to me."

Rather than waste words, she immediately shifted into the man. It took her a few tweaks before he grunted assent. Arkaziel proved to be easy. She saw the cat every day and knew his appearance almost as well as her own. The transition from tiny house cat to giant scorpion felt odd, just as going from the scorpion to a bottle felt strange. To shift that much energy into mass and then shift it back could only be described as mystifying. When the old man nodded at his own face again, Aetheria felt slightly unstable.

"You should practice fast shifting more. You're clearly not used to it, but you did well enough for a novice. Now, become this statue and don't move for an hour." An hourglass appeared out of nowhere. The illusion of a statue that appeared looked like an homage to Aetherius.

Aetheria stifled a groan before she became a statue. The experience provided a certain form of enlightenment. She had no muscles in this form, yet every part of her yearned to move. She didn't need to breathe, but she wanted to. Her vision could not swivel; her stone eyes were locked in place. Perhaps she had been too literal in her mimicry of the statue, but she would endure to pass this trial quickly. By the time the last sands of the hourglass fell, Aetheria found herself in a state of calm meditation.

"Not bad. You know, most shifters can't or won't do that—become the statue. Most just *look* like they're a statue. Extra credit for the super dedication."

"Oh." It had not even occurred to her to not literally become a statue.

"Stand next to this wall." The old-timer gestured to a wall that had not been there previously. "I will conjure environmental illusions. Camouflage yourself. We will start with the basic wall."

"Behold, I am the human chameleon." Aetheria stood against the wall, and let herself become "looser." She flattened against the wall and took on its colors. The old man watched, frowning.

"You can actually go flat?"

"Yep."

Illusions then appeared. Rain. Grass. Wood. Jungle. She blended herself the best she could.

"Fire."

"... Fire?"

"Fire."

"I can't become fire."

"Good." The old man grinned.

I can't become fire... can I? And why did he say 'good'?

"We're skipping to the last trial. This is a bat. It uses echolocation to find its way. Mimic it."

"Sure, want me to fly around you?"

"That's fine. Don't get in my hair, though."

In many of the books Aetheria had read about adventurers, changes like these often required an understanding of how and why things worked. Her experience had been more akin to the way druids shapeshifted in tabletop RPGs—slight familiarity with the concepts seemed to be all she actually needed. She didn't need to know that bats could reach up to 140 decibels or covered a range of 14,000 hertz to over 100,000 hertz.

Strong intuition guided her once she took on a new form. She didn't know exactly the best way to fly or echolocate, but she had a strong gut feeling on how to do it. Trial and error solved the rest. The experience of weak sight, chirping to echolocate and view the world, felt surreal. She had previously experimented with minor things in shapeshifting: talons, muscle changes, improved telescopic vision, but this took it to a whole new level of strange. The possibilities were so wild and mind-boggling that she suddenly felt a deep dissatisfaction in her soul. *I don't know if I'm creative enough to make use of this to the level it deserves.*

Bat-Aetheria chirped and flew circles around the old-timer until he passed her.

"Impressive." The old man grinned, his image rippling to that of a young man. He still had blue skin and white hair, but now his appearance matched hers. Somewhere between his late twenties and early thirties.

"Do people not take you as seriously if you don't look wizened?"

"It's been a problem in the past."

"So why did you skip me past a few steps of the trial?"

"They were unnecessary. You exhibited the traits on trial in the initial trials. Do you enjoy wasting time? Doing things only for the sake of doing them?"

"Not really. I've gotten stuck with enough time-sink floors."

"Good! Now, on to the secret technique. By mimicking races with magical anatomies, you can copy their powers. Seems obvious, right? Except what's not obvious is that it does not mimic these abilities with your own affinities, but with those of the Origin. Poison from the depths of the swamps, fire from the mouths of dragons, spears of darkness from the sad Oni. All possess the power of the creature and their strong affinities."

"Is that true for all shapeshifters?"

"No. Not even slightly. My trials were to determine the type of shapeshifter you are."

"And what type am I?"

"I don't have a label for you, Lady. What I can say is when you reach Tier Three, they will label you an Asura."

"What's an Asura?" *Somehow, I doubt it's the same answer I learned in comparative religion.*

"One of divine stature. A powerful force, a demigod, a demon, someone who is a force to be reckoned with beyond the standard ranks of Cultivators."

"Alright. So, back to the 'technique.' I've got a book of different races and their unique biology. Turning into them would let me copy their unique attributes?"

"Yes. The true secret to this kind of shapeshifting is mixing and matching your forms. Many small pieces can make for a powerful whole. The eyes of the Sages of Naada, that see through the tides of Aether. The bones of the Oliniin, who came from a heavy-gravity environment and have the strength of the next two races combined."

Aetheria could not stop her grin. She had, in a way, been doing part of this technique with her usage of talons, rubberized body, and eagle vision. She had barely scratched the surface of possibilities, it seemed.

"My thanks. Any other tips for a novice?"

"Only that the more time you spend as someone else, the more important it becomes to remember who you are."

The world turned dark around them as she and Ark were sent to the next floor.

Aw, man, I really wanted to take a bite out of that diva. He would've really hurried my cultivation up.

I'm glad you refrained, Arkaziel. It's important we don't eat people who help us.

I suppose so.

Floor 25. Darkness gave way to light. The duo appeared on a tower. The structure seemed to go up and down infinitely, with no glimpse of an end to the atmosphere above or land below. The tower was a skeletal construction of unfamiliar metal beams with no floors or ceiling, just braces and cross braces.

Arkaziel coughed and leaped off her shoulder to take on a five-meter draconic feline form.

"This might get messy, Ria. I smell something bad. This is the battleground for Typhera Echidra, the Chimera child of Typhon and Echidna."

With his words, a roar that deafened the world followed. The bare-bones tower vibrated with the frequency of the monster's cry. Aetheria's eardrums regenerated almost instantly, but she knew Arkaziel's ears would take a minute or more.

~Lion head?~

+Yeah. Oh, and Typhera Echidra flies. Who gave Chimera wings? Typhon. He's a total dick. He really hates StarManes, because Chronos made us and we don't give a shit about his whole "Father of the Monsters" thing.+

Aetheria formed wings of ice along her back. Her fingers elongated and became reddish, long talons that looked evil. Even Arkaziel, ever inquisitive, did not look too long at the menacing claws.

CHAPTER 54

Typhera Echidra

When Typhera Echidra came into view, Aetheria had to reassess if Nidhogg was still the scariest thing she had seen. Sure, Nidhogg had been the size of Manhattan and a dragon of the apocalypse, and Typhera was only the size of a house. Yet the Chimera radiated an unrestrained aura of power. *Floor Twenty-five, quarter-way boss. This thing probably isn't scaled down the way so many other monsters have been.*

A lion made up the largest part of the Chimera's form. A winged lion with large golden eyes that emitted harsh, Aetheric light. Behind the lion's head, there sat a second neck with a goat's head atop it. The goat's eyes were a shrouded mix of black and red. To be the target of the goat's gaze made Aetheria feel sullied. Its Nether energies were corrupt, dark, and offensive.

While the foul gaze of the goat momentarily distracted her, the viper-like head at the end of the tail gazed at her, and spit streams of poison. Aetheria froze the poison just before it touched her. The frozen liquid fell to the ground and shattered, which brought Aetheria out of a momentary lapse. *Are those glimmering green eyes hypnotic?*

Arkaziel's thirty-five-meter-long form appeared behind the Chimera, his mouth open. The StarMane unleashed his Twilight beam on the Chimera, but his aim was somehow off. He missed by a narrow margin, and the snake head bit his rear left ankle before the Chimera took to evasive maneuvers through the clouds.

+*The goat is using curses and dark magic.*+ Despite the pain that flared through their empathic bond, Arkaziel's telepathic voice was clear and steady.

Typhera reappeared when she ambushed Arkaziel from another cloud bank. The lion's claws ripped at the StarMane's scales but had an issue with the draconic hide. This bought Arkaziel a moment to roll and rake one of his own claws against the side of the lion's left flank. Blood fountained from the wound, but it was a graze, and the move exposed Arkaziel's softer belly. The snake head bit the StarMane on the other rear leg, while the lion exhaled fire-breath. A powerful darkness gathered at the goat's head.

Aetheria appeared out of the clouds and came down with a massive hammer kick with her right leg. A terrible sound of physical damage filled her ears. Then the enchantment from Nidhogg's Fury kicked in, and Typhera dropped from the sky in a cloud of toxic energy.

The sound of physical damage had been to Aetheria's own leg. Pain flared through her body in unbelievable waves. Nearly every bone in her right leg fractured, and her shin was bent at an impossible angle. Flesh reknit; bones reset. The process remained horrifying to watch. Flares of Ethereal power hastened her regeneration.

~Yeah, no. What the fuck was that bullshit?~

+Thanks for the assist. Dark magic. Reflect? Retaliation? Something like that. Goat head needs to die fast.+

They did not have long to mull over what had just happened. Typhera had once again entered the clouds.

~Can you track it in the clouds?~

+No. It's using some kind of enchantment, or it cultivated some kind of affinity with these clouds. Get rid of the clouds?+ Arkaziel's assumption matched her own. Her sense of the Aether and Nether that the Chimera represented faded to nothing the moment Typhera entered the clouds.

Aetheria held a taloned hand out and created an etheric ice wyvern, imbued with the power of the Flame of Thalassa. It had only one command: absorb the clouds. The construct immediately flew to obey. Its icy maw opened, and the ice wyvern sucked in whole clouds per breath.

From a nearby bank of clouds, Typhera emerged to ambush Aetheria. There was no sign of the toxic energies of Nidhogg still infecting the Chimera. *Can it cure its own ailments? Which head would do that? The lion with Aether? Or does the snake or goat have some way?*

The lion's claws and teeth should have missed her. Aetheria moved with more alacrity than the Chimera, yet her body did not respond the way it should have to her thoughts. Claws ripped her midsection to shreds, and quick alteration of her right shoulder was all that kept her from losing a limb to the lion's bite. Aetheria jabbed the talons of her left hand into the neck of the goat, and pulled as much Ethereal power from her repository that she could in one big pull. She released the energy as the coldest blast she could imagine and backed it up with the Primordial Flame of Ymir.

The lion hissed and scorched Aetheria in searing aetheric fire. The pain of the fire was bad enough. The snake bit her in the throat and actual pain stalked through her veins. The lion kicked her with its back legs and flung her hundreds of feet to impact hard against the tower.

Arkaziel—three Arkaziels—appeared and ambushed Typhera. Even the Twilight clones' claws glistened with red Ethereal energy. The kid gloves had come off, and a vicious melee erupted between the three cats and the Chimera. Wounds piled up on all four combatants.

+You okay, Ria?+ Arkaziel had caught her in one of his massive paws after she had rebounded from the seemingly indestructible pillars of the tower. Heedless of her situation, the ice wyvern continued its mission to fly around and remove as many clouds as possible.

Aetheria couldn't even think straight enough to form a response to Arkaziel. Instead, she focused on her body. Ethereal energy flooded her body from her soul aperture to increase her regeneration. Aspected with the Flame of Aetherius, the Ethereal power greedily burned any ailments, such as the poison, from her body. With the abatement of the poison, the usual pain of regeneration came and felt quite tolerable compared to the neurotoxin.

She generated a new set of ice wings behind her before she jumped into the air to fly under her own power once more. Arkaziel dropped his pawn once she was off it. Her impact with the tower had destroyed both of her old wings and shattered her spine, but that had barely slowed her down, unlike the poison.

~Better now, thanks, buddy. We definitely need to kill that goat.~

Two of the duplicates had already been destroyed in the brutal melee with Typhera. The last of the duplicates had its jaws around the lion's throat while it slashed again and again with its claws at the hoarfrost-covered head of the goat. The viper ended the last duplicate with repeated bites to the throat and underside. The concentrated Ethereal power that had made up the duplicate dissipated in a *poof.*

~Go scorched Earth on the goat. I'll distract it.~

Aetheria altered her entire form. Her skin turned red and took on a crystalline appearance. Her book from Odin spoke of a race from a strange place called the far realm. These crystal people were known as the Luxentians. They were made of an exceptionally powerful crystal that became stronger when infused with energy, and the race specialized in absorbing energy, predominantly light. Aetheria's crystal form glowed with the input of power she gave it, and then she launched herself toward the Chimera. The goat's head was still encrusted in hoarfrost and unable to get her into view as she flew around the creature. Her interest in meeting a Luxentian paled when she learned the far realm was the home of creatures of Lovecraftian horror, and terrors like Elder Abominations.

The first strike of her crystalline talons nearly decapitated the viper. She let the snake try to bite into the crystal, its fangs unable to find purchase, and her counterstroke left the viper almost bisected. Her follow-up attack finished the job—the viper's head and a meter of its length fell. The lion and goat heads both went berserk at this, and the hoarfrost around the goat shattered. Aetheria and the Chimera clashed in a dance of slashes and evasive moves—she trying to stay out of the goat's gaze, and the monster constantly trying to get her back into view.

Eventually, it succeeded, and Aetheria felt her strength and speed take a massive hit. Unexpectedly, a jade form shot around the lion's side and hit her in the neck and shoulder area. The viper had regenerated, only now its scales were crystalline like hers. Its fangs pierced into her crystal form, and again she knew the pain of poison.

~Here it comes.~

Out of the cloud that the wyvern hadn't touched yet came a glimmer of Twilight. Then the car-sized beam of coruscating light and dark energy edged in red lightning. The beam took Typhera solidly in the goat's head. Unprepared for such a powerful attack, the head vaporized in the continuous stream of light and dark. The beam burned and disintegrated a large piece of Typhera's back.

Aetheria's body was already working on the poison, but she endured and activated her domain. Hoarfrost immediately covered the Chimera. Typhera's blood froze in the air, took on the form of long ice needles, and then slammed back into the body of the Chimera. The jade viper's head came to strike Aetheria again, only to be sliced in half by one of her ice wings.

Typhera's life force flowed into Aetheria every second the creature remained inside her domain. Life force that helped regenerate her wounds. She felt the temptation to drain the Chimera dry, to eat its essence, but her partner cultivated that way, not her. Her talons slammed into the lion's mid-body, and she froze the blood inside its veins, which then expanded like thousands of miniature ice spikes inside of the creature.

While it roared in pain and denial, Aetheria threw the injured Chimera to Arkaziel. The StarMane was waiting, and his jaws went to work. He ate the lion's head first, then the stump that marked the regeneration of the goat's head. The rear end was third, to ensure no snake bites. Only then did Ark slow down and enjoy his meal.

"They aren't going to regenerate inside you, are they?"

+*No. When I eat something, it stays eaten.*+

"That poison was bullshit. How did it hurt me when I was made from crystal?"

+*Magic, I would assume. It hurt me considerably until I neutralized it with purification. Why were you so slow to use purification?*+

Aetheria, mid-shift back to her flesh and bloody normal form, blushed brightly.

"I kind of forgot I could do that? It seemed like my regeneration was taking care of it well enough."

Arkaziel's silence to that made her flip off the cat-dragon.

+*You're only going to have more power and versatility at your control, Ria. You haven't realized all of your gains yet. That's understandable. Not everyone can immediately understand their own potential and incorporate all aspects of it cohesively into their repertoire.*+

While Arkaziel lectured her, she found herself confronted with energy. Typhera Echidra must have died in the StarMane's stomach. Aetheria absorbed the energy, letting it flow into her repository to aid in the changes she continued to make there.

"It's a work in progress, boss."

Arkaziel failed to notice Aetheria's eye roll or the flat delivery. "Well, just remember, I'm the senior partner in our team, and it'll all be fine." The StarMane licked his lips after he spoke.

"So, where's the door to the next floor?"

"It looks to be over on the tower. Are you ready to go to the next floor, or do you need some time?"

"Let's go, you mangy cat."

"I am not mangy."

"When was the last time you got brushed?"

"Oh, my god, we don't have a brush. *We don't have a brush!*" Arkaziel sounded distressed.

After landing on the tower, Aetheria gestured, and a brush made of ice appeared in her hand. "Is it brushing time?"

"Yesss!" Arkaziel's tail batted back and forth in excitement as he shrank down and pranced in front of her in his black cat form. Even though Aetheria could do the same thing, it felt remarkably off to see such a powerful creature turn into a "simple" house cat. Ark's control of his aura was so fine that she could find no sign that he was a Tier Three scourge of worlds.

CHAPTER 55

Rick the Trapmaster

After a thorough brushing for Arkaziel, the duo stepped through the portal to Floor 26. When they materialized, it was under a warm afternoon sun. They stood in the ruins of a long-fallen castle courtyard. Before them lay a set of unearthed stairs that led down into the darkness. Behind them stood a young man with a torch in one hand, a sword in the other, and equipped in leather armor. His hair was bound up not unlike Aetheria's own, although the youth had dark brown hair, not blue.

"So, what do you think? They say the riches of Nabonidus are in these ruins." The young man had a deep voice. Eagerness made him talk just a little too fast, and he bounced back and forth between heels and toes. He emitted no energy that Aetheria could detect, but the way he held his sword seemed to show he knew that the pointy end stabbed people, at least.

"Remind me, are you proficient in detecting traps?" Aetheria asked with an arched brow. "It is not one of my strong suits." They were speaking a language she had picked up while on Nidhogg's Bane. Arkaziel, not willing to speak to a mere peasant or lower-tier Cultivator, slumbered on her shoulder.

"Oh, yes. I've got my poking stick, thieves' tools, and a bag of rocks. I can safely trigger anything I'm unable to disarm. They call me Rick the Trapmaster for a reason, after all. Aren't you going to light a torch?"

Aetheria flicked her fingers lazily. Aetherial light manifested into a blue-white orb of frostfire above her fingers and drifted up to form a halo over her head. Cold seeped from the flames, but the light it provided would be useful and prevent her from relying on infravision.

Rick eyed the halo warily.

"The whispers in town said you were a witch, but I thought that was just an exaggeration. Makes sense, I suppose, with your strange clothes and the black cat. Who, other than a witch, would walk into a legendary dungeon with no armor? Lord Felsir must have paid you handsomely for this expedition." Envy crept slightly into the Trapmaster's last words, but superstitious fear remained dominant in his tone.

Aetheria smiled and went with it. "Who indeed? Let's explore this dungeon. After you."

+ *This guy is totally going to betray us,* + Arkaziel opined telepathically.

~ *I'm expecting the same, honestly. Almost seems* too *obvious.* ~

Rick the Trapmaster took the lead and went down the stairs. The darkness of the ruins seemed reluctant to part for the torch. Aetheria followed a few steps behind the leather-clad man, her attention repeatedly drawn to the unnatural way the shadows cast in the dungeon moved on their own. The trio descended ninety steps. A single path lay ahead of them. The ceiling stood at approximately three meters, and the passage's width was the same. *Square tunnel? Weird.*

The pale light of her Frostfire halo and Rick's torch illuminated faded iconography recorded on the passage walls.

"What was the story of Nabonidus again?"

Rick seemed to pay no attention to the art on the walls. *Can he not see them, or is he totally focused on finding traps?*

The Trapmaster grunted. He stopped every few feet to poke and prod at suspicious tiles with his stick.

"Nabonidus was the last ruler of an ancient kingdom. His decision to replace the head god of their pantheon with the Moon God caused upheaval with the nobility, clergy, and commoners. Before it came to internal strife, another kingdom conquered them. Some kind of natural disaster wiped both countries out not long after." Rick shrugged and looked as if he might spit to the side for a moment. "Stories say he took all the valuables of the head god, Marduck, and had them hidden so they might not steal from the grandeur of the moon. For years, no one could find the entrance to the dungeon until Lord Felsir got the map."

Rick's story seemed to match the story that played out in pictures along the tunnel. A deity and church struck down by a king; new monuments of the moon risen to replace them. More strife; the moon iconography struck down and the old god risen once more. Finally, different-colored invaders slaughtered everyone, and the moon and other god looked on sadly.

Pulses of power lay ahead. Double doors sealed the end of the tunnel. The thick miasma of Nether lay heavily on the other side of the doors. No inscriptions covered these doors, save what looked like chicken scratches across the one on the left.

"Looks like someone tried to write or carve something here," Rick muttered. He tried to clean it enough to make something out of it.

+ *I smell ancient blood.* + Arkaziel told Aetheria. He opened one yellow eye to regard the door.

"Perhaps someone wrote something in blood?" she said aloud.

"That's a dark thought. I've disarmed about sixty traps in this hall so far. The door itself has no traps or lock. It *is* locked somehow, though. Magic?"

"Large concentrations of Nether lie on the far side of the door. That could mean multiple things. Monsters, darkness, items of the moon..." Aetheria shrugged.

"Felsir is offering too much to fail." Rick grimaced and pulled out a belt knife. He slashed a minor wound across his left arm and smeared the dripping blood onto the door where the scratches were.

The blood moved by magic, forming into the alphabet of another human language Aetheria recognized. She read the words to Rick.

"*You shall not have the treasures of Belshazzar. Instead, you will guard it for eternity.*" The door suddenly opened, each side moving into recesses into the wall.

"No wonder it didn't have a lock. It slides open. Tricky, that. I don't much like the words you said, though. Belshazzar was supposed to be Nabonidus's kid, who assassinated the previous king so his father could ascend. The historian Felsir hired said that Belshazzar was the power behind the throne, or some such. Doesn't much matter to me. We're here for the treas—"

Darkness reached out and snuffed Rick's torch. With a scream, Rick vanished into the farther reaches of the ruins, leaving Aetheria standing in the pale radiance of her Frostfire halo. Arkaziel opened his eyes fully and jumped to the ground. He grew to the size of a massive black tiger, walked up to the open door, and roared in challenge to the entire dungeon. Three shimmering white tigers made of light jumped from his aura to lead the way.

"Let's go treasure hunting."

"Sounds like a plan. Think Rick's already dead?"

"Oh, yeah. I heard his death gurgle as the undead dragged him away."

"That was pretty fast for undead. Vampires?"

"Vampires. I suppose there's the possibility of specters or shades, but I heard footsteps."

The halo above Aetheria brightened to shed more light, and a multitude of appendages of sanctified holy ice formed at her back. They almost looked like wings, but were in fact more like ribbons of ice that she felt confident she could attack with. Her hands shifted as well, taking on the usual Luxentian crystalline talons instead of fingers.

"Let's cleanse this place. We're getting close to another city, you know. Think of all the treats waiting for us." With the reminder of what awaited them, the three light cats lead the way into the dungeon, with Arkaziel and Aetheria right behind them. The ancient dungeon opened into a large, round room past the open doors. Pillars obscured their visibility and cast a multitude of shadows with the light from the cats and Aetheria. Smears of fresh blood covered the floor toward a door to the right. Another door went left.

+*He's already dead. Why don't we go left?*+

Aetheria considered. There was little point in immediately giving chase after Rick if he were dead. Arkaziel's hearing far outstripped her own. The Administrator would expect them to go right. The undead would expect the living to chase after the taken corpse. Unpredictability registered as a valid tactic in her mind, since they didn't know what undead they were dealing with. Level the field.

~*Alright. Lead the way, oh valiant cat.*~

The door opened easily. No obnoxious, loud creaks. No alarms. Yet the moment the three clones walked through the doorway, figures emerged from the shadows of pillars in the first room to swarm at Aetheria, who brought up the rear. The ribbonlike appendages on her back flexed and shot out to slash, pierce, and strike the shadowy visages.

"Shades," she said flatly. "Light them up, buddy."

Arkaziel yawned and lifted a paw. A ball of light coalesced, and the cat lazily flexed a single claw to send the ball to the middle of the room, where it exploded like a fireball. Light filled the room while holy power bathed and clung to everything. Dozens of shades screamed out in a mixture of anger and satisfaction as it burned them out of the world of the living.

"That was a pretty sweet move."

Arkaziel smirked and lapped up the praise.

The three cats of light had decimated the shades in the next room before the duo arrived. This room held dust-covered shelves that were barely intact. The few objects that had not disintegrated from age on the shelves held a touch of mana to them. Preservation magic, perhaps, or just enchanted items that resisted the all-devouring ravages of time. Aetheria pulled everything into her repository, shelves and all.

The room had only two doorways—the one they had entered through, and one to the right, which had no door in the archway. It lead to a tunnel with a door on the far side. When one of Arkaziel's duplicates went through the empty archway, dozens of horrific black blades shot out of the doorway to destroy it. Arkaziel grunted in annoyance and summoned a new one, while Aetheria walked up to the doorway and shifted almost fully to a Luxentian.

"Hit me with some light, if you'd be so kind. I haven't really figured out how to change Luxentian physiology to use Ether or Aether yet."

Arkaziel opened his mouth and breathed a beam of light right into her back. Her skin absorbed it, the light illuminating her crystal body from dark red to almost pink.

With a shrug, she stepped into the archway, and the metal blades stabbed out once more. Awful sounds filled the air, metal against denser crystal. Metal shattered, broke, and fragmented. Only a few superficial flaws showed in Aetheria's form, and those quickly regenerated. The twelve-meter hallway unsurprisingly held a plethora of traps, which she tanked and destroyed with stomps or punches.

"You're better than a trapmaster, Ria," Ark encouraged her.

"I still feel pain, you know. I'd rather have a trapmaster," she grumbled. The stone door before her appeared similar to the one in front of the dungeon. Aetheria kicked it until it shattered.

"Blood and stone aren't on my agenda today," she quipped, but Arkaziel just looked at her like she'd lost it. *Oh, right, I never told him about that game.*

Ark's clones rushed ahead of her into the room before them. Aetheria's vision filled with flames. The entire room became a giant mass of fire. *One... two... three... four...* she counted until, ten seconds later, the flames vanished.

"More tanking." The surrounding air shimmered as Aetheria's freezing domain activated. *Fire is my bitch. Freeze the flames.* She stepped into the room and it filled with fire once more. Fire that solidified and froze, then vanished into her repository.

"That was cool. You're getting close to entering Asura territory, Ria. How's the bottleneck to Tier Three going?"

"Not the place, Ark. It is going slow." Aetheria walked across the room and pulled the enchanted traps into her repository. They left holes in the floor, walls, pillars, and ceiling.

"Oh, are we taking *everything?*"

"Yes. It's what they get for killing your cute little Twilight duplicates."

CHAPTER 56

Loot!

Looting the fire room went quickly. To work each trap free by normal methods would have taken time, especially to ensure they remained in working order. Aetheria just had to walk near them and pull them into her repository. The smirk on her crystalline lips hinted at the deep satisfaction she found in this. *Who doesn't love taking their enemies' stuff?*

The room held no other secrets or enemies the duo could find. With an annoyed sigh, Aetheria opened the room's only other door. She suspected the layout of the dungeon was a looped box, with an offshoot going deeper in the next room. Traps attacked her with each step to the stone door at the end of the tunnel. Those that were reusable, she claimed into her repository; those that weren't, she destroyed with her domain.

+ *This would probably be a lot scarier if normal people came through here.* + Arkaziel's lazy telepathic voice echoed Aetheria's own thoughts. Adventure should be exciting, fun, or at least scary. So far, the dungeon had proved to be mostly just annoying.

When she reached the stone door, she froze and kicked it until it shattered. This room differed dramatically from the last two. Beautiful mosaics filled the walls. Magical lamps cast green-tinted light upon the circular room. This room had four doors, one at each of the cardinal directions. Pillars like those in the first circular room cast shadows everywhere, but these pillars were full of writing and iconography.

At the center of the room stood an altar. On it lay the body of their missing Trapmaster. At the head of the altar floated a specter, and opposite it stood a corpse that Aetheria could not decide if she would call a mummy or zombie. It had a powerful Nether presence, but it looked like a zombie in decrepit robes. The amount of embroidery on what remained of the robes made them look once royal. The purple faded dye also hinted at royalty.

The specter held some kind of ghostly energy in its hands, energy it continued to draw like threads from Rick's corpse. It hissed commands at the mummy, who turned to approach the duo. *Maybe I shouldn't have just kicked the door to dust...*

A ball of light shot over her shoulder, struck the altar, and exploded brightly. Temporarily blinded, she missed the sight of hundreds of lesser shades being burned from existence by Ark's sacred light. The mummy and the specter, however, only grimaced. The specter kept working the soul-threads of Rick, while the mummy lumbered slowly toward them.

"I'll take the mummy," Aetheria grumbled, and moved forward to meet the slow undead. Scraps of fabric from its robe elongated to attack her as she approached. The fabric met her ribbons of holy ice, and purple fabric fell to the ground and turned into a puff of smoke.

Arkaziel flew past her. His three light duplicates ran ahead of him to start their assault on the specter. Before they could close in on it, though, a river of gold flowed from around the altar to form a golden golem that interposed itself between the cats and the specter.

Aetheria's domain created a thin layer of hoarfrost over the mummy when it entered her domain. She approached the shambling horror confidently, darted in and went to cut the thing's head off with her talons. The superdense, pink-colored crystal hit the mummy but found no purchase.

"Oh, jeez. Seriously? What kind of bullshit is this?" she cursed. The slow-moving mummy slapped her. It hit her so hard, she hit the wall, denting a solid meter into the rock structure, cracks traveling up and down her crystal form. Pain, her second-best friend, had come for tea time.

Aetheria's fractures healed quickly. Almost all of her form had become whole by the time she extracted herself from the wall. The only solace in the embarrassment she'd just suffered came when she noticed a lingering sizzle of damage where her talons had touched the mummy's neck.

"Immune to physical? I always hated that cop-out, and here I am without a MacGuffin." Thoroughly annoyed, she made her Luxentian crystal form fade into her flesh and blood body. Her aura spilled out to encompass her in the red glow of Ethereal power. One of her red eyes filled with the burning blue Primordial Flame of Aetherius, and the other filled with the pale blue of the Primordial Flame of Ymir. Red Ethereal power, flecked with shades of blue and white from the Flames, billowed from Aetheria's hands and feet as she dashed back to the mummy and began a high-speed chain of attacks. Her entire body shifted and changed slightly, focusing on speed instead of physical strength.

Each punch or kick became a love tap, yet carried Ethereal power fueled by the aspects of two Primordial beings and caused a sizzle of undead flesh. With her seventh hit, the mummy combusted. Holy flames flared through every Nether-rich cell of the once-presumably great king Nabonidus, until all that fell to the ground in the chamber were ashes.

Arkaziel, meanwhile, had let his clones take on the golem while he engaged the specter in a duel of magic. The specter held the threads of Rick's soul in one hand and cast spells against the StarMane with the other. Ark countered the death-based attacks with contempt, using only a single finger of his right front claw, then countered with a similar gesture that sent a dozen bolts of light to race at the specter.

Did he alter his spell after I told him about magic missile? Aetheria watched, interested. The StarMane had the genetic memory of thousands of years of his ancestors' knowledge. Not just in what foods tasted great, but in magic, paths, and martial prowess, and presumably they all majored in the greatest of all feline skills: being assholes.

Aetheria also noticed Arkaziel was only half paying attention to the fight. Those yellow eyes of his kept drifting to the door to the left of the one they came in, a doorway that revealed a full treasury behind its barred gate.

She rolled her eyes and conjured a wave of holy ice spikes that shot toward the specter. *It's nice to be the one to do the ambush now and then.*

"Kill stealer! You told me kill stealing was bad!" Arkaziel whined as the spikes ripped the injured enemy to shreds.

"Oh, shush. It's not like you can eat specters... can you?"

"I can."

"How does that eve—you know what? Go ahead. It's not completely dead yet. Deader?"

"How... dare... you.... mock... the... great... Balshazzar? Curse... you... for... eternity..."

Arkaziel hopped over the altar and chomped the fading specter. Aetheria nodded when the feline let the soul threads of Rick go free, though.

"Your efforts have been valiant. Tithe unto me the treasure in the vault and I shall restore this brave soul of your companion to life."

"No, tithe unto *me* the treasure and *I* shall restore him to life."

Aetheria pinched the bridge of her nose as two illuminated figures appeared before the altar.

"And why would we do that? It's *our* treasure," Arkaziel hissed at the deities.

"I'm curious as to why I should choose either of you." Aetheria put on a face of bravado she hoped conveyed that she might choose neither and simply keep the treasure for herself.

"What would a vault of holy artifacts do for you, Asura?"

"What would a—quit saying what I'm saying as I say it." The two masculine gods glared at one another.

"Well, since it's supposedly a vault full of your relics from when Nabonidus wanted to replace you, and full of his because they had brief warning of Cyrus coming... why would I give either of you the treasure of the other?"

The gods glared at her in silence.

"See? Can I eat them?" Arkaziel begged.

"Not yet. What if you each get your due, resurrect Rick here, and give me something I want?"

"Sounds greedy."

"Impudent mortal!"

"You can't have it both ways, calling me a mortal and an Asura, can you?"

"You aren't Tier Three yet, human."

Aetheria met their ghostly glares. "Oh, and you have to give my cat something to eat. A good meal."

"That's asking too much!"

~ *Which gods are these?* ~ she inquired of Arkaziel.

+*Marduk and Sîn. Not worthy of our respect. They are fodder for my cultivation. Not Primordials.* +

Aetheria pushed the Primordial Flames of Ymir, Nyx, and Aetherius into her aura and let it bleed across the room. The light of her aura made the two gods seem more incorporeal.

"Fine," Marduk said. "You have my agreement."

"Your terms are acceptable," said Sîn.

"Then you may take your rightful treasures." Since the treasury did not immediately empty, she stalked over and kicked open the ornate gate. Cursed energies traveled up her leg, but Aetheria invoked the still-active Flame of Nyx to consume the curses, and absorbed the energy. The last of the cursed energies broke apart. The gate opened fully and she took stock of what lay beyond. None of it seemed particularly potent to her senses, although one or two minor items held enough power to be interesting to her. An amulet came close to the power of Nidhogg's Fury, but she had made a deal.

The treasures vanished in a *poof* of godly magic. Semi-transparent Marduk spoke words in a language that was not Ath. Aetheria couldn't decipher it, but Rick the Trapmaster's body glowed. Wounds healed, and the gods restored the soul to life. The same second Rick's eyes opened, Arkaziel's maw also opened, and he ate Sîn in a single gulp.

Marduk eyed the StarMane warily, like a hiker watching a viper.

"I guess that was part of the agreement. You could have waited for your companion's reward to be delivered first, Eater of Stars, but little else could be expected from a Child of the God Devourer." Marduk's displeasure caused sweat to bead on the newly revived head of Rick, but it didn't disturb Aetheria or Arkaziel in the least.

"Azrael is famous? Sing me the song of his full name, godling." Arkaziel's teeth bared in what the StarMane thought of as a smile.

"Quit tormenting Marduk, Ark. My reward now, please. I want something to help me redecorate my soul repository."

"Oh, yes, only small asks, I see."

Oh, he's totally rolling his eyes at me. What a jerk.

A few seconds passed with no sign of the god doing anything. Just as Arkaziel was about to advance on the spirit, its incorporeal hand rose. The air shimmered and glowed above his cupped hand. A strange metallic sphere flipped through the air and landed in Atheria's hand. Marduk vanished. The sphere squirmed, wriggled, and took on the form of a multitude of interlocked rings. After a quick glance, it vanished into her Vault.

"So, no treasure?" Rick asked nervously.

Arkaziel stretched his neck and gave a great yawn that showed his sharp fangs and teeth.

"Well, there's the golem here." Aetheria kicked the remains of the gold golem that Arkaziel's duplicates had destroyed. "And maybe something in the other couple of rooms we didn't clear yet. Let's do that and you can be on your way back to your lord."

Rick's nerves had frayed, but he still caught the implication that the cat and Aetheria would not be with him upon his return to Lord Felsir. Wisely, the man didn't anger those responsible for his resurrection.

"C'mon, Ark, send the kitties ahead of us and let's finish this up quick. I want to get on the road, and I bet you could use a nap while you digest that god. Did he taste good?"

"Like a dessert wine mixed with way too much sugar, with a dash of high-quality sheep. Weird combination for the essence of a god, but then, they're all weird. Dad said the more powerful, the better they taste, but alas, Marduk didn't give me a chance to do a live comparison."

CHAPTER 57

Ride the Dragon

Floor 27 began in a very different way from the previous floors. For starters, Arkaziel appeared full size, in his forty-meter draconic cat form. Second, Aetheria appeared sitting in a saddle atop him.

"I'm going to eat the Administrator. I'm blind, Ria," Arkaziel growled miserably. His dismay transferred through their bond and made her heart hurt a little. She stroked his hide.

"I can still see, buddy. Also, you've been saddled, and I have your reigns."

Anger, rage, and unbridled humiliation all flared through their bond. Arkaziel stood on a large fifty-by-fifty-meter platform high in the air. Clouds filled the sky as far as Aetheria could see.

The dreaded shock jock cadence of the Tower Administrator boomed across the vast clouds.

"Are you ready? In this amazing challenge of teamwork, the pestilent, plundering, perennial Primordial parasite must ride the noble StarMane through a series of rings. You only get one chance. Can the human stow her ego to work with the valiant, chonky cat-dragon to get the most points possible? My bet is no, she'll bring shame to such a majestic creature."

+Why is he sucking up to me?+

–You did just swear to eat him.–

+Right, right? Maybe he can live for a few more days...+

Silence reigned. The Administrator seemed annoyed that neither Aetheria nor Arkaziel showed any reaction to his antics. The duo just waited. And waited. Aetheria counted to 3,600 before the Admin finally broke the silence.

"Anyway. Arkaziel is blind, Aetheria silenced... now! Your telepathic bond has also been silenced. Aetheria may only use the reins to guide you, Arkaziel. Get the most points you can!"

Loss of bodily autonomy infuriated both Aetheria and Arkaziel.

"Three... two... one... go!" A deafening beep rang through Aetheria's ears.

She flicked the reins, and Arkaziel leaped off the platform. While their telepathic bond had been silenced, their empathic bond remained active. Both were bubbling cauldrons of annoyance, but Aetheria's indignation at this scenario paled in comparison to what boiled within the cat-dragon. She wondered if the Administrator realized he had committed to his own death sentence. Their prior interactions had been annoying, but this one... this one would be paid back a thousandfold.

Arkaziel's anger transformed into laser focus on the commands Aetheria gave through the reins. Despite both of them using the rage as fuel, they almost missed the first giant red ring for Arkaziel to fly through. *Go figure, a forty-meter-long dragon is harder to drive than a car.*

She imagined all the times she had seen Arkaziel fly in his larger form. The sharp turns, the instinctive shifts on currents of air, grace personified. She tried using sharper and more firm commands to translate pressure into navigation. The next ring they flew right through, and Aetheria laid on the speed more with another flick of the reins.

They finished the course without a single miss, although there was a near miss when they had to land on the finish platform.

The Administrator was nowhere in sight. Next to the platform appeared a massive leaderboard.

"CONGRATULATIONS!" text flashed, and then the leaderboard populated:
Odin, Sleipnir
Vishnu, Garuda
Aetheria, Arkaziel

"We only got third? I knew we should've gone faster," Arkaziel huffed. That he read the board meant he could see again. Which meant Aetheria could talk again, too.

"Hey, third isn't too bad. Those two and their mounts are notoriously connected. We beat out most of the other big names. That's pretty impressive, isn't it?"

Arkaziel puffed a mass of shadows in annoyance. "Dad lost a race against Sleipnir once. He always regretted it. He probably still has dreams about catching and eating Odin. I know I do."

StarManes. Aetheria held in her sigh and smiled at Ark, then patted his shoulder.

"We did good. I know you could've gone faster, but we've never done this before."

"Choose your reward: StarMane saddle, Reins of the Ice Queen, or Barding of the Ferocious Feline."

"Your call, Ark."

"Reins." The decision came nearly instantaneously, unsurprisingly. The first and last options spiked indignation in the StarMane.

A pair of slender, almost translucent reins appeared in Aetheria's hands. When she channeled Aether into them, nothing happened, so she tried Ether. It accepted the Ethereal power, and she dumped more into the reins and felt a probe of her mind. *Probably wants me to picture a mount?*

Aetheria imagined a pure ice form of Arkaziel, which quickly came into existence, attached to the reins. Arkaziel hopped onto her shoulder in cat form, seemingly uncaring about the ice facsimile being their ride. "You could've made it look like Azrael instead, you know." *Not so uncaring after all.*

As fun as it was to ride an ice version of Arkaziel through the sky, it had disadvantages. It didn't have breath weapons or magic; in fact, it wouldn't attack at all. But it freed up Arkaziel himself to operate as mobile artillery. The StarMane fell somewhere in the middle when it came to melee versus ranged, but compared to Aetheria, who had relatively small ranged attacks, he was a ranged specialist.

It felt like a disappointment of a reward when she or Arkaziel would have been much more potent mounts. *Ugh. I'm going to end up becoming a dragon and he's going to ride on me as a house cat, I just know it.*

On Floor 28, the duo appeared on a sparkling sand beach. Beautiful green-blue water stretched out infinitely before them, and behind them, a jungle. Before either had time to wonder what the trial would be on this floor, a pair of pincers rose from the sand to bisect Aetheria. The pinchers slammed shut, and only a small bit of her left thigh was caught and the flesh rent before she fell onto the sand. Arkaziel tumbled with her. The small black house cat hissed and jumped off her, and grew wings. In flight, Ark grew to twenty meters.

Aetheria rolled along the sand to the edge of the water. The liquid reached out and pulled her to her feet as she demanded its cooperation with the Primordial Flame of Thalassa. The crab that emerged from the sand had a brownish-red shell and beady evil eyes, and she estimated it to be the size of an Olympic swimming pool, somewhere around fifteen meters.

Unimpressed with the water helping her, the crab's baleful eye fired a beam of heat that struck her in the shoulder. The red trench coat took the brunt of the heat attack. It smoldered but did not actually burn before Aetheria's leg healed enough to become mobile. She brought her freezing domain to life around her; hoarfrost formed, melted, reformed, melted, and formed once again on the crab's shell.

"I don't like my seafood frozen, anyway," Arkaziel quipped before a ball of energy formed at his mouth and he fired a Twilight beam at the crab's shell. The shell didn't fracture, crack, or take any type of damage.

"How are things becoming immune to us so easily now?" Aetheria asked in annoyance. She blurred between the crab's legs and delivered a series of blows with her gloved hands to a single leg. Almost no damage at all showed on the crab's exoskeleton.

"Higher tier. This thing is mid-Tier Three. It also isn't being suppressed much. They're meant to train you to overcome enemies you're theoretically weak against, devise battle plans separate from your normal, and maintain diversity in your combat capabilities." Arkaziel sounded bored. "I could kill it if I go to my full size, but the challenge is for you, so I'll just watch."

Aetheria bit down her retort and just said, "No, yeah, I get it." Even though she did not, in fact, get it.

The crab, annoyed by her skittering under it, dropped its body down to crush her, but she made it out in time. If freezing didn't work on the monster, she suspected the Flames would. Red Ethereal energy flowed over her skin. The shadows in the area deepened, and she channeled the Primordial Flame of Nyx into her Ether-infused hands. Aetheria further adjusted her body for speed and darted in to deliver a flurry of blows against the crab's shell. Each strike was a touch of the Punch Drunk Punchers' enchantment, while the Flame of Nyx stole portions of the crab's vitality.

No visible damage showed. The crab, without the dragon attacking it, jumped high into the air and spun like an unidentified flying object. "Cripes, I've got a bad feeling about this."

With almost no sign of what was coming, the giant crab suddenly shot downward, and sand exploded into the air. For those brief moments of blindness, the crab burrowed beneath the sand and came up and ambushed Aetheria from below. One pincer almost took off her left arm; the other she avoided by shapeshifting her body just slightly out of the way of it bisecting her. To add insult to injury, the crab, apparently not stupid, shot its heat beams at her injured arm to finish the job.

Aetheria dropped a kick against the crab's shell and activated Nidhogg's Fury. Toxic energies shot into the crab, and she put some distance between her and the crab while her arm regrew.

Chomp-chomp +*He really got you there, Blue.*+

~*Did you just eat my arm?!*~

+*You're already growing a new one. Why, did you want it back?*+

~*...No.*~ Aetheria decided now was not the time to mull over the ethical or moral implications of Arkaziel's actions.

The crab had chittered after her and Aetheria had only seconds to decide on a new battle plan. *It's a real pain I haven't figured out how to teleport yet. Flames work on it, though.*

Eight orbs manifested around the giant crab. Four copies of the Flame of Aetherius, four of the Flame of Nyx. Essence, vitality—all the energy that drove the crab—flowed from it to the orbs, and its power became hers. Enraged, the crab charged in with the attempt to just bowl over her. A massive jump shot her into the air, and she altered her mass and gave a quick bat of temporary wings to shoot her back down to land atop the crab. She immediately began delivering more blows in the precious few seconds between her landing and the crab, getting its pincers up to remove her.

The last series of blows stacked her gloves' enchantment while the Flame orbs continuously worked to drain the crab. The crab's movements slowed. Aetheria easily dodged the pinchers and moved to deliver another set of blows. Each additional blow caused the crab to move in a wobbly manner. Once the thing just fell over, Aetheria focused on ripping its life force out with the Flames.

"I'd say that's a win for you. Now let's eat it!" Arkaziel cried excitedly from his position, levitating in the air.

"Go for it, kitty. I'm going to sweep the island for any worthwhile ingredients before we hop up a floor. Know this floor at all?"

"Yeah, Azrael liked to sneak into this one for some of the fish, and there's this crocigator that's just so amazing. Catch a few of those if you can. Oh, and there's an orange fruit the size of your head that makes a fantastic sauce. Just grab everything, maybe—this is a great floor for food."

Aetheria laughed. She hadn't expected the cat to actually put in a grocery order. "Alright, then you're on fish duty while I scour the island."

"Sure. Oh, there's these flying birds, like that one over there. They taste great marinaded in the orange fruit..."

"I get it. Birds, fruit, and crocigators."

"Oh, the crocigators have psychic blasts, so don't get surprised."

CHAPTER 58

Nivathar, the Silver City

Floor 29 proved to be one of the annoying sort, where Aetheria had to complete a series of 3D puzzles. Each puzzle became part of the next, in ever-increasing difficulty. Arkaziel was useless at the puzzles and asked why they didn't just destroy them. Still, she completed fifteen stages of increasing complexity without the StarMane's help, which brought them to another bastion of civilization.

The duo appeared inside a cable car. Outside, lines of people waited to get inside a similar cable car. There were five platforms for cable cars to load and unload, with bored-looking employees in silver uniforms directing people.

+Jackpot, Ria. This leads to Nivathar, the Silver City. Sometimes called the City of Song, sometimes the City of the Moon. We should be able to get some good food here.+

The cable car had four other occupants, who looked like Climbers. One of them blinked a few times, looking at Aetheria's blue hair and the cat on her shoulder, before he finally asked his friends, "Is she real, or am I still hallucinating things from the squadrik's toxins?"

A slender young lady with glasses gave Aetheria a judging look, followed by a frown. "I can't read her."

The largest of the group, a red-skinned woman with two horns on her head, grinned at Aetheria. "Don't mind these rude arseholes. Tower dumped you right into a cable car? Nice. We had to wait out in line for two days! Jerky buggers, the city levels are."

Aetheria immediately liked the large woman. "I'm Ria, and this is Ark. We're climbing the Tower of Aetherius. You?"

"Cindra, that's me. Glasses is Pyra, the dumb one is Jonol, and the wily one there is Asher. We're climbing the Tower of Svarog. Lots of fire, but we're all good with fire." The large woman slapped a hand against her breastplate to show toughness. "Aetherius? Isn't that the tower what poisons people with high energy concentrations?"

Aetheria grinned and shrugged slightly. "I haven't really run into any problems with it, but people keep saying that."

"Know anything about the city? Our primer didn't have no mentions of Nivathong."

"Nivathar," Pyra corrected Cindra.

"Oh, only a little. It's got a few nicknames. The City of Song, the Floating Citadel of the Moon, but mostly they just call it the Silver City. It's the creation of the moon goddess, Selene. Lots of crafters and entertainment, but there are strict rules about fighting in the city, even in the training areas. Don't pick fights with the locals or other Climbers, or they'll toss you off the side of the city without the benefit of a cable car to get down. It's one of the most peaceful of the cities." Aetheria relayed the information Arkaziel offered her to the other group.

"Huh. You must be pretty legit to be a solo Climber. Ain't many solo acts in our world. We're from Volcaria."

"Well, I'm hoping to round out my entourage more for my next tower climb. I've got two candidates in the back of my mind."

"Next? You planning to conquer a whole tower solo?" Asher entered the conversation. He was red-skinned with horns, like Cindra, although more slender, with the look of a rogue of some sort.

"That's the plan. You four aren't planning to conquer your tower?"

"Naw. We're hoping to get up to Floor Sixty this time. We made it to Forty-five to end up here. Floors are getting a lot more dangerous, though. If it isn't traps, monsters, curses, or mind tampering, it's strange puzzles or blacksmithing." Cindra's contempt for the mind puzzles seemed to embarrass Pyra and Asher.

"I hear you. I just had a three-dimensional puzzle with fifteen increasingly difficult stages."

"That sounds terrible. Just how high in the tower are you?"

"Uh. Not very. This is Floor Thirty for us."

"The Tower of Aetherius sounds awful." The other group all seemed to agree on that.

The cable car ascended through the clouds, and those inside finally saw the city. The platform the city rested on was flat on top and convex on bottom, constructed from a brilliant white stone. Worked into the foundation were silver runes, glyphs, and other magical constructs that kept the city skyborne. Nivathar itself climbed high above its base. Over two-thirds of its buildings were high spires, and skyways and elevated paths formed a complex series of intersections in the sky between buildings.

With only a hundred feet between the cable car and the city, Aetheria glanced at the other party.

"Get ready for bells and what have you."

Cindra picked up her meaning and laughed. "You're a Challenger? No wonder you can solo climb a tower." Pyra adjusted her glasses and reassessed Aetheria.

With a light jolt, the cable car came to a stop against the platform, and a silver-clad city worker opened the doors with a lever pull. The Native working the platform winked at Aetheria.

"One at a time, if you would. Welcome to Nivathar, the Silver City!" The city employee looked human at first glance. The lupine yellow eyes, slightly too large canine teeth, and fingernails that looked just a little too much like claws gave away that he was not. Cindra's party made their way out first, and Aetheria brought up the rear. As expected, the moment her boot touched the ground of Nivathar, bells rang, shafts of moonlight illuminated the city, and from out of nowhere, white sakura blossoms filled the air with a sweet scent.

As if that were not enough, a large silver moon eclipsed the sun, sending twilight across the city. Fireworks filled the sky, explosive blooms of a color cast from out of nowhere. Their noise resounded like thunder, and all around the cable car platform, people alternated their attention between the spectacle and Aetheria. A single intense moonbeam illuminated her for all to see.

Awkward. No hiding this time, I guess.

~No, not this time, Child of Aetherius. Let slip some of your aura. Capture the imagination of my people and my city's visitors.~ The mental voice was as soft as a feathered caress, smooth as silk, and deeply feminine. Aetheria immediately guessed it belonged to the designer of the city, Selene. Yet by the time she thought to answer back, the slight mental presence she had felt was gone. *Gods.* Aetheria rolled her eyes at the sky and let her aura leak out just enough to become visible to others. Red Ethereal mist roiled along her skin and looked like steam rising from water on a frosty morning. The usual soft glow of her eyes amped up as red energy swirled in her eyes before leaking out. Overall, it wasted very little energy while providing a view of something very few people saw even once: an Ethereal Cultivator.

"Damn, and I thought old Greyfox and his tales about seeing an Ethereal Path Cultivator were full of it." Cindra laughed, but Aetheria could no longer see the camaraderie they had shared in the cable car in her eyes. Now Aetheria was a Challenger, or a walker of a rare path, instead of a peer. For a moment, she felt exceptionally alone. She was who knew how many light years away from her home—if she was even in the same universe—and years had passed since her death on Earth. Loneliness and homesickness were on the verge of completely overwhelming her when Arkaziel pushed his nose against her neck and purred.

+You've got me, Ria, and your witch.+ Ark purred against her neck, and she scratched his chin. She replaced the reserved expression on her face with an amiable smile and waved to the people she had shared the cable car with.

"It was nice to meet your crew. It appears I've got a welcoming committee to deal with. Safe travels, Cindra, Jonol, Asher, Pyra. If we meet in a tavern, I'd love to hear some of your stories." With that, she offered a light salute, then walked toward the approaching group of official-looking people and consigned herself to being a spectacle for a while.

The rest of her day flashed before her eyes. Aetheria rode around the Silver City with the governess of the city, a former Climber, now Dweller, and her entourage. The governess pointed out useful places, while her entourage (who were Natives) mostly just pointed out things vapid courtiers of a theocracy would care about. Needless to say, Aetheria rapidly tuned them out.

The governess did not have the canine tells of the silver-clad dock worker, nor did any of her entourage show such signs. *I'm pretty sure the governess is a type of fae, actually.* Oriana Solaria had pale, slightly ashen skin. Her eyes glowed faintly with a silver light that matched their hue. Oriana's ears tapered just a touch, but were no longer than a human's. Her fingers, arms, and torso all looked just slightly too long to be normal. Her entourage appeared to have most of the same characteristics, minus the glow in her eyes. *Path-related, like my own eyes?*

Aetheria endured the tour and a welcome dinner in Oriana's mansion, where the governess insisted that she stay with them. With darkness truly in the city now instead of the fake night of the eclipse, Aetheria agreed and was led to a tastefully minimalist suite. Arkaziel seemed disappointed by the lack of overwhelming luxury, but she found it easier to sleep that way.

"Figure out what you need to accomplish in Nivathar, Ark. I don't think we'll stay too long."

"Why's that? Sick of people after one day of being fawned over?"

"A little. We're over a quarter of the way through the tower. I want to keep our momentum going. Unless we get a quest like on Floor Fifteen, we bail in a few days."

"Alright. Then we're going shopping tomorrow. You said I couldn't buy *all* the food, not that I couldn't buy *almost all* the food."

Before Aetheria could respond, the cat had claimed the whole bottom of the bed to lounge in, and he snored. She pulled out one of the two items Aoibhe had given her and channeled some Ethereal power into it. In the blink of an eye, her mind was pulled into a replica of Aoibhe's quarters in the crystal tower.

"I wondered how long it would be before my sweet brawler sought me out." The nephilim sat lazily at her desk, fingers interlocked and hands steepled before her. A full smile lit the room as she took Aetheria in.

"Hi. I've missed you. A lot. Got stuck on a ten-year demon-killer floor. That sucked. Can we touch here?"

The blond shook her head sadly. "We're both just projections, unfortunately, my dear. I've missed you, too—and I hated that floor. You've gained more Flames. Powerful ones. Only a human with your physiology could pull off such a ridiculous feat as having four Primordial Flames."

"Yeah, that's what Nyx said. Guess it took even Aetherius and Nyx quite a few years to get the physiology to match the good old human inviolability of the soul. I never thought about it, but does that make me a gene-engineered super soldier? That's going on my business cards. 'Primordial-Created Super Soldier, Tower Climber.'"

CHAPTER 59

Shopping in Nivathar

You've spoken with one of them while in the tower? Interesting. Usually they are very hands-off inside towers."

"Uh. Yeah, she appeared to shield a city floor in case I botched the creation of my proto-core."

Aoibhe laughed. The sound was like music to Aetheria's soul. Warm, vibrant, full of life, and a denial of pain and suffering. It really sucked that she couldn't at least hug her.

"Is this just a catch-up, or did you need help with something?"

"Well, I could use some advice. My current plan to break through to Tier Three is to create a 'sun' in my repository, to function as the Gate to the Origin. I am changing my repository to make it more like the Origin to facilitate the breakthrough, and I'm using these metal rings to empower the Gate. With a surplus of built-up Ethereal power in my repository, I figured I could use the like-calls-to-like rule to make the permanent Gate. Thoughts?"

Aoibhe listened with interest, her smile growing wider the more Aetheria talked. "That would annihilate most people—a direct link to the Origin in your soul. For you, I suspect, it might feel like indigestion for a few days. It should work the way you think it will, darling, but do be careful about the formation of the Gate. That is the most important part of forming a true link to the Origin."

"How did you build yours?"

"*You'll* have to tell *me* that next time we meet for real. I'm sure you'll figure it out."

Aetheria had an idea about that, actually. The crystal tower would be a perfect link. The tower's base could extract Nether from the ground and Aether from the sky, and then combine them to fuel a permanent link. With Aoibhe's power, she could move the tower at will, including into her inner world, where it should function the same way it did anywhere else.

"Ria? Make sure you look over those metal discs. Have a few crafters look them over and make any changes to them you want. Or just alter them yourself inside your repository. You don't want any surprises when you form your Gate. Have you passed the fiftieth floor yet?"

"No, we just got to Floor Thirty."

"'We?'" Aoibhe did not look jealous, but she was very curious.

"Ah, I am bonded to a StarMane companion. He's on the Ethereal Path just like us."

"A StarMane?" The blond looked shocked. "I didn't know they even bonded to other races, but Aetherius has set you up. Try to teach it basic manners, such as empathy and compassion for others, before we join." After a moment, the Soul Witch laughed. "On second thought, maybe getting it to acknowledge that other people have a right to exist would be a good start.

"Anyway, knowing your luck, you'll wander into a strong Ethereal location before the fiftieth floor. Break through at a location like that if you can. If you are diligent enough, you may leave Aetherius's tower as an Ethereal Scion. If you can't find one like that before the fiftieth floor, use the environment of the halfway boss. I have faith in you, Aetheria, and I love you."

"I love you, too. Our link and my bond with Arkaziel are all that have kept me going through some of these levels. I don't know how you solo-climbed the tower and kept it together so well."

Aoibhe started to answer her, but the room faded away, and Aetheria woke up on the bed in Nivathar.

The next morning, she and Arkaziel found a pair of guards outside their rooms, who were to act as their entourage while in Nivathar. The duo abused the two as navigators to get to where they needed, which perhaps had been Oriana's plan to begin with.

Three hours—*three hours*—spent buying food. Arkaziel insisted on food first, so they wandered the market and bought some of virtually everything. Aetheria gained more liquors and beers for the fun of it.

A sage by the name of Olgos helped her examine the metal discs she intended to use as part of her Origin Gate. Neither could find any traps or problems with the inscriptions on it, and Olgos even found a few places she could improve the enchantments. He chalked out the additions for her and suggested a blacksmith and Enchanters who could do the work.

She ended up paying a smith named Jonas, and then hired a lore master and Enchanter by the name of Houff to aid her in the light rework. Getting the two to commit to the work had been easy enough when she offered a few of Nidhogg's scales as payment. Both were more than happy to do any other work she wanted, but the only thing she wanted wasn't possible until she found a fifth-tier Enchanter, and Houff was only third-tier.

After that, the expedition through the markets of Nivathar proved a disappointment. Neither had much use for weapons. The armor was subpar and weaker than their own gear. But then they stumbled into the alchemy district. If not for bartering away cores, crystals, and remains of strong opponents or demons, Aetheria would've spent a significant amount of money in the Alchemist Quarter.

With healing potions, burn salves, mana potions, Ether potions, cures for all kinds of ailments, and resistance potions galore, the duo were better prepared to deal with issues they could encounter. Arkaziel seemed to view the healing potions as a waste since Aetheria regenerated and he could heal through light magic—something she had suspected but now had confirmed.

The sky had darkened by the time they left the Alchemist Quarter, so they had the guards guide them back to the mansion.

The duo had planned to spend the last day on Nivathar acquiring knowledge. But outside of a few texts on moonlight, Nivathar lacked any useful books, scrolls, journals, or other knowledge when they perused the shops. So it was barely past noon when Arkaziel and Aetheria hopped on the portal sigil to leave the Silver City behind.

They appeared on a similar teleport rune on Floor 31. White clouds made up the platform for the runegate they stood on. A black abyss filled with stars, comets, planets, and other universal elements seemed to go on forever in every direction. A pair of stairs rose from the clouds, ascending toward a series of other clouds and more stairs.

"Climbing the stairs seems pretty easy," Aetheria noted dryly.

"I hate levels like these. This stinks of fortitude and mental trials."

"So, let me guess, you're just going to ride my shoulder?"

"Obviously."

With no upside to an argument about a cat being lazy, Aetheria just nodded and approached the stairs. The risers appeared to be made of rainbows, while the treads had the look of volcanic obsidian. With the first step up, a weight settled on her. With each step she took, the sensation of pressure grew.

"What're the odds of reaching the top of this one?"

"Pretty solid. You're strong, a shapeshifter, and I bet you can get all the way to the final stair without activating your Ethereal physiology."

"Let's see how right you are." She didn't make a wager, just climbed. One foot in front of the other, with ever-strengthened pressure as her opponent. She made it up the first, second, and third series of stairs without her stride being slowed. On the fourth set of stairs, a new type of pressure set in—a sense of bone weariness, total exhaustion. Aetheria redoubled her focus and pushed through the exhaustion.

On the top step of the fourth staircase, there was her clone.

"No passing without giving something up," the copy said.

"Here, take this." Aetheria handed over the belt knife she no longer needed.

"You give up your first weapon, forged by the gods. You may pass."

The clone vanished. It took her knife with it.

The fifth staircase proceeded in the same pattern. She struggled to ignore the increasing pressure on her mind and body, and another doppelgänger appeared at the top.

"To enter a higher realm, you must transcend what you started as. What do you leave behind?"

Aetheria considered. It felt like the clone wanted something intangible—a concept, not a solid item. Her gut had frequently led her well in the past, so she trusted it.

"I leave Earth behind. Even if I ever see it again, it is where I *came* from, not where I'm *from*."

"You give up the past to secure a future. The past is not always willing to be forgotten." The doppelgänger vanished with the words.

Did I pass that one? Whatever.

The sixth set of stairs marked the start of struggle. If the stairs had been made of wood or metal, the pressure Aetheria struggled against would have shattered them in seconds. Every single step to climb the sixth staircase made her clench her fists, bite her lower lip, and push past the exhaustion and counterforce to reach the top... only to meet another clone.

"What will you leave me?"

Aetheria eyed the duplicate. This one gave no indication, no hints of what it wanted. Any answer would be enough, perhaps?

"I leave you with the fear that I am nothing more than the gifts the Primordials gave me. I am more than my powers, gifts, and blessings."

The clone smiled.

"So it will be."

Aetheria felt something in her disconnect at that moment. The fear, the self-doubt, the uncertainty seemed to fall away from her and vanish with the clone. Obviously, some small portion of self-doubt remained, but most of it was now gone. Her first step up to the final set of stairs felt lighter than when she had started the trial.

At the top of the seventh set of stairs stood the door to Floor 32, and no clone stood in her way. Yet every step seemed to double the pressure and weight. Halfway up the set of thirteen steps, Aetheria's aura broke free. Her cells scarfed the Ethereal power to give her the strength to push on. Two steps from the top, even sheer strength couldn't get her foot up to the next stair, and so limbs of ice stretched from her torso to pull and push her up the next step. When she tried that on the last step, the ice shattered.

Aetheria had never believed in the shounen rationale of just doing things harder. If you tried something and failed, you were better off with an alternative approach. Thus, she flared all four Primordial Flames inside herself. Ymir had told her that all four of her Flames shared a component of shapeshifting. She fortified her body to stand up against any pressure, until at last she took the last step.

She made it, but then the pressure seemed to retaliate and slammed her into the incredibly hard, yet fluffy, cloud floor. The force abated, and Aetheria stood to frown down at all the lower platforms and stairs she had crossed.

"Cripes! What the gosh-darn heck was that about?"

"The tester got annoyed you beat it so easily." Arkaziel murmured and lifted a paw toward the door. "Let's go, this level was super lame."

"How come only I had to take the test?"

"It tested me too. Mentally. It was dumb, and I didn't like it."

"Do you want to talk about it?"

"It made me decide between you and food. I chose you, by the way. Can we go?"

"Aww. I love you too, Ark." She gave the StarMane a scratch under the chin before they walked through the door to Floor 32.

CHAPTER 60

The Stagnant Swamp of Sogginess

Ew. I'm not stepping in that, and you can't make me," Aetheria scolded the uncaring heavens. She stood on a stone platform in a narrow gulley that opened up into a swamp as far as the eye could see. Which wasn't far, because gas bubbles, vine-choked trees, and swarms of insects limited her vision.

Arkaziel, usually fine with sleeping and trusting her to keep him dry/safe/cuddled, hopped into the air and levitated while his wings appeared.

"I think I'll be staying in the air. This smells worse than Nidhogg's asshole."

"Did you smell Nidhogg's asshole?" Aetheria choked with laughter.

"I thought about flying up it in my compact form and turning full size, but the smell made me change my mind."

"Huh. So even StarManes have limits." Aetheria's laughter drew movement across the surface of the swamp toward the stone platform. Disgusting black, slimy creatures the size of a loaf of bread crawled up the stone in search of prey.

"Oh, hell no." Aetheria's domain shot five meters out around her. The leeches froze, but before they fell into the swamp, Arkaziel snatched one to take a bite. He spit it out.

"That tastes like it looks. How disappointing."

The swamp froze in her vicinity.

"Scout the area and find what we want. I'll play bait and draw the locals out." With those words, Aetheria's aura expanded to the full ten-meter range. Swampy water, mud, and some of the water in the air froze just the same. *I don't need to fly. I'll make this wretched swamp into a frozen work of art.*

With an exaggerated gesture, Aetheria sent three large frozen orbs of Ethereal power ahead of her and out of the gulley. The orbs froze everything around them. Hundreds of tiny spikes of ice were volleyed at leeches, frogs, mosquitoes, alligators, snakes, and any other terrible thing to be found in the swamp. The crack and sizzle of things freezing was soon the only sound around her. Nothing she encountered survived first contact with her domain, and the more she progressed into the swamp, the more she spread her frozen glory across the creepy crawlies.

One-woman ecological disaster! Wait, am I the bad guy on this level? Ugly things deserve to live too.

Aetheria stopped her forward momentum and stood, considering. The ethics behind "it's disgusting, so I killed and destroyed all of it" were villainous for sure. Since she had already frozen where she stood, she just waited for Arkaziel to return from his scout mission. The minutes dragged on as she felt increasing guilt for annihilating generations of swamp denizens in minutes. After an eternity, or five minutes, Arkaziel returned.

"Big swamp. Huge swamp. There's a series of temples throughout the area. I found a Temple of Aetherius, a Temple of Nyx, a Temple of Khaos, and one of Gaia."

"And do any of them actually have substructures under the swamp?"

Arkaziel grimaced at her.

"I sent my duplicates down them. Thought I'd trick you into exploring them, too, but sure, just ask me straight if I found the right one." Disappointment and annoyance dominated the StarMane's tone. "Aetherius and Nyx both were dead ends. Gaia's is a trap. Khaos seems to be the right path. How come you stopped freezing the swamp?"

"Felt wrong."

"That's the silliest thing you've ever said. Is this some kind of crisis of faith? I hear you humans get those. Weird to feel bad about killing a bunch of mindless leeches and never bat an eye over the total genocide of entire tribes of demons."

"Not helping here, Ark. Lead the way to the temple." Large draconic wings rose from Aetheria's back, and she shot up into the air. Her dedication to not destroying the ecology of the swamp lasted until she saw mosquitoes as large as her arm. That assuaged the guilt of destruction, and by the time she and Ark landed in front of a temple half sunk in the swamp, she no longer felt any guilt for her massacre.

"I'm really not a fan of swamps. Like the famous Dr. Jones once said, 'I hate snakes.' Oops!" Aetheria's voice was not at all sorry, despite her exclamation, when one of her draconic wings brushed against a terrifying snake statue, causing it to fall and crash into the water outside the temple.

"Were the insides dry, or are we going to be swimming?" They were halfway up the pyramidal temple—the higher portions apparently had been destroyed at some prior point. The center of the pyramid had a set of stairs going down into the darkness.

"There's water in there."

Aetheria changed forms. The book on races she'd read described a race called Dragonids. This species of half-frog, half-dragon, all-bastard, came from the swamps of a world called Drakonia. They possessed the ability to breathe water or air, could swim as easily as walk, and had a highly potent venomous tongue lash in addition to the ability to release a poison cloud. Best of all, they could see in exceptionally low light.

"Non-feline dragons are just sad. No fur, no wings. I mean, what good are they?" Arkaziel mumbled under his breath. Aetheria just smiled. Or tried to smile. Having a snout made facial expressions take on a whole different feel.

"Maybe, let's find out." She jumped down the shaft into the mucky water below. The water went down some thirty meters before the shaft came to an abrupt end. Thanks to the low-light vision, Aetheria actually spotted the horizontal tunnel with no issue, and explored down it. After fifteen meters, the tunnel sloped up and opened into an air-filled chamber. Runes and sigils marked the area and created a small field that prevented water from coming into the room.

~Alright, come down all the way and then hang a left. There's a room with air, and it looks like the rest of the dungeon is dry.~

Twenty seconds later, Arkaziel popped up out of the water and shook himself. When no water came off, he noticed the water-field and nodded sagely.

"Alright. That wasn't so bad for involving water." Dry or not, the StarMane still looked annoyed.

"You want front or rear?"

"I'll have my duplicates bring up the front," Ark answered. "You can take the rear until we find traps."

Aetheria became human again and fell in behind Arkaziel.

The chamber had only one other exit. Walls, floors, and ceiling all looked much better-made at these depths. For being constructed ages ago, the temple still seemed structurally sound. Along the walls were pictures detailing the story of fates. If there was a deeper message hidden within the iconography, Aetheria wasn't seeing it.

The tunnel they were in suddenly forked into three short hallways, each ending in a door. All the doors remained intact and closed. Arkaziel watched intently as his clone cats went up to each door and pawed at the latches. The left and center opened fine; the right door exploded when opened, and rubble filled the tunnel.

Arkaziel chose the left door to explore first. The room appeared to be a barracks. Rotted wooden bed frames lay arrayed in neat rows. A small side room functioned as a washroom. Although Aetheria and Ark looked through each bed, dresser, and chest, all they found were tattered old clothes and a single pendant with a holy icon. The symbol showed a circle of darker metal molded into a circle of air, and swirling inside the air were all the other elements mixing. *Maybe it's supposed to represent the Primordial mud of Chaos?*

Aetheria stashed it in her repository, and the two went back to the other door. This room appeared to be a single priest's office. The books along the shelves had all rotted, and the desk fell to rubble when Arkaziel brushed it with a claw. Yet they found some things of value: golden candelabras, a tattered bag full of metal coins, and a chest all in one piece. Rather than deal with traps, Aetheria tossed it into her repository and checked its contents that way.

"Couple of grimoires. We'll sort those out later. There's also a map." An ice version of the map appeared in Aetheria's hands. "I don't know how flimsy it is. So, we're here. It looks like there's a hidden door to the next level behind that bookshelf."

A touch, and the rotten shelf vanished and revealed steps that spiraled down into the darkness. Small crystals mounted against the wall every two meters created dim light to see by. They descended the stairs quietly, spiral after spiral, into the depths. A half hour later, Aetheria looked back at Ark. "How far down do you think this goes?"

"Another fifty meters."

"How'd you guess that?"

"I sent one of my kitties ahead while you weren't looking, just now. Got to be more observant, Ria."

She rolled her eyes at the cat and stalked down the last few spirals before the steps ended at an archway. The archway itself flickered and flashed with different elemental powers. Even Aether and Nether were present. Aetheria stuck her finger into it and could feel a spatial enchantment about to take effect. She stepped through, and after a dizzying few moments, she entered a large chamber. Alcoves dotted the side of the chamber, each full of different hobbies that all looked long forgotten.

Upon a divan lounged a woman. Almost a woman. She had no skin or flesh, only the feminine form crafted from dark mists, like the snake that lazed upon her shoulder. The snake had red eyes and a dark red misty tongue.

"Oh, hey, Oro. That you? Long time no see." Arkaziel waved at the snake. "Oh, yeah, er, I'm Azrael's kid. We haven't met yet." A faint sound of laughter, feminine, filled the room.

"It's rare that I am ignored and someone addresses Oro here before me. StarManes." The misty form shook its head, yet she sounded amused.

"I take it you're Khaos?"

"Hmmm, and you're the Challenger that Aetherius and Nyx are cashing all their favors in for. A human with the power of Primordials, walking unbound and untethered by my daughters, the Fates. You could be very entertaining, Aetheria."

"While you two sort that stuff out, we're playing dice."

Aetheria blinked as Arkaziel and the shadow serpent slithered off to a side area, and the clatter of dice followed shortly thereafter. Khaos seemed like an amused mother as her snake went off to play with another kid. *Maybe Arkaziel will mellow a little, having a playmate for a bit.*

"I could be entertaining?"

"Well, you already are. But when you aren't limited to the goals of Aetherius and Nyx, or that little world called Grief, that's when you'll be truly interesting. Your dream to walk the planes interests me. Nyx and Aetherius tried to buy my aid, but I am not for sale. So you must make me a promise, little human."

"What promise do I need to make? You're not about to stuff a Flame in me, are you? Ymir said I wouldn't be able to handle another one until I ranked up."

"Oh, you're close enough you could handle it now, if I'm gentle. The others were all 'now-now-now,' but I am in no hurry. Delayed manifestation is easy enough. I want you to promise you'll climb the Tower of Moros next, and the Tower of Khaos after that."

"Moros... that's Doom? You want me to climb the Tower of Doom?"

"Yes, yes. And my tower afterward."

"What do you get out of me climbing the Tower of Moros?"

"Entertainment. You, who are freed from the Fates, from the Samsara itself, clashing with the essence of inevitable doom? I want to see it. Just as I want to see you clash against my nature, beautiful chaos, and what manner of experience will be born out of that."

"I didn't really plan on any particular tower next, so this works well enough. I promise to climb the Tower of Moros next, and the Tower of Khaos afterward."

"Excellent. Now take my hand, child. I shall impart the smallest of sparks of my Flame within you, and it shall grow to blaze brightest of all those you possess."

When the misty shadow hand met Aetheria's pale one, goosebumps rose across her skin. For once, she was thankful for the fingerless gloves, for the limitation they placed on sharing physical contact between her and the Primordial.

For all Khaos's talk of gentleness, the torrent of power that flowed into Aetheria felt raw, uncontained, uncontrolled, and like it would run roughshod over her. She rode that power into unconsciousness, and the dark mist swallowed her.

CHAPTER 61

A Touch of Khaos

The world was not darkness, but formless energy that cascaded in all directions—colliding, exploding, and redirecting other energy. This was a place where order did not exist. Yet before this, Aetheria somehow knew there had been another place. A familiar place... That sensation faded as the calamitous power raged in every facet of this reality and overwhelmed Aetheria's senses. She fell deeper into vortexes, deeper into chaos.

Among the surreal energies, she occasionally caught glimpses of things that tickled the back of her mind. Concepts that had names. Darkness. Light. Water. Night. Fire. The nebulous forms of Primordials lumbered through these storms. Aetheria continued to fall, and glimpses of the building blocks of reality glimmered in the storms.

The power she fell through could not be described. It encapsulated everything all at once. It represented the power to form galaxies—or crush them. The surface of the vortex seemed random, but within chaos, probability held strong, if haphazard, power. Every power Aetheria had ever encountered could be found somewhere in this vortex of energy.

She suddenly appeared on a floating platform of rock. A small villa rested among a stand of trees. It was complete with a small garden, a well, and a cave off to the side filled with massive mushrooms. *Whoever owns this place has interesting tastes.*

"That is unnecessarily obnoxious, don't you think?" A man stood behind her. His pupils were golden hourglasses. Aetheria thought she could see sand flowing inside of them, but her eyes fell into the black sclera the hourglasses stood out against. This man represented a power every bit as great as the vortex.

"Cripes, don't sneak up on a lady! No, yeah, it's a lot to take in at once."

"Indeed. Khaos slipped through the Gate when I did. Well, slightly after, really. Imitation is the greatest form of flattery, they say, but I feel she just wants to take over my minor project."

"And what project is that?"

"Day drinking for eternity." The man nodded toward his cave. "My still."

"So you came to day drink. What did she come to do?"

"Oh, the same thing I came for. To make a new universe. We traversed through the Origin and came out here. We expected a higher realm, possibly even a lower realm. Instead, we found a blank realm."

"What kind of realm were you from before this?"

"A very violent one. We thought we could do better."

"And the Primordials lurking in the shadows?"

"They are unrealized. Only I and Khaos seem capable of existing without Time, or so I thought. Apparently, you can as well. I sense Khaos's essence upon you, which solves that riddle. As for the Primordials, we have surmised they are something like a do-it-yourself kit for creating a universe. Prepare the field, plant the seeds, and watch what grows seems to be the idea."

"You don't know for sure?"

"No. I am not omniscient. I once was mortal, like you. I walked the Path of Time, climbed to the peak, and became a sovereign. Just as dear Khaos did upon the Path of Chaos. There could be others who traversed the Origin here. Not everyone is so attention-starved and thus as easy to spot as Khaos. The Primordials *could* be like Khaos and me, but I do not think so. They would wait for eternity, never enacting creation, without someone like us pushing them."

"So why haven't you done so? Khaos has clearly manifested herself. All that's stopping a new universe from being born is Time. I assume you are Chronos?"

"Indeed. And who are you, that bears the touch of four unrealized Primordials, and Khaos?"

"I'm Aetheria. I'm a human Tower Climber on a quest to fire a goddess, and then explore the wonderful universe you and Khaos are creating."

"It's wonderful, is it?"

"I've only seen two planets, and a tower. I might not be the one to ask, but as far as realities go, it seems pretty okay."

"Hmm."

"What's keeping you from manifesting Time?"

"The Primordials. We don't know how they'll react when they become realized. Will they be more powerful than us? As unlikely as that is, there are beings who dwarf even a sovereign of Chaos or Time."

"Not to belabor it, but I think you're probably more than that now. Look at Khaos. Her power seems to have expanded when she manifested herself."

"We both have already transcended apotheosis in our ascent to sovereignty. I sense things our equal or superior in the void. But you come from a time when I have already manifested myself, so further discussion is redundant."

Chronos lifted a hand, but Aetheria held up her own to have him hold a moment.

"What is the Origin?"

"Who knows?"

"What?" Aetheria felt stunned. Chronos was about to make a universe, had transcended to the highest points of cultivation in his old universe, and he didn't know? *What a bunch of crap.*

"Anyone who claims to know with certitude is likely wrong. It is as far as we can tell a nexus that connects all realms in some fashion. It is the culmination of all elements and none, and its power can create or destroy universes. Some think it is some kind of god beyond gods. Some think it the essence of Creation used to make the first worlds. I ascribe to the idea that it relates to some form of higher being. It *fights* you sometimes, and *assists* you other times."

"Thank you." Aetheria thought he'd only just reiterated his first answer of "who knows," but at least he explained himself.

"You shouldn't worry about it too much. What it is matters very little. Focus on what you are—that is the heart of the path you walk. Now, I can feel your tether has strengthened, so back to your body with you. I have work to do."

"Wait! Can I have a bottle of your booze?"

Chronos burst into laughter, and a bottle flew from the cave to her. The bottle was not glass but a strange crystal, and its contents looked like liquid rainbows.

"You might not survive drinking that." Chronos's warning marked a gentle tug that pulled Aetheria from the vision back to her body in the tower. Only now she had a beautiful bottle of rainbow in her hand.

"You got the miser to part with a bottle of his precious old-world alcohol? Impressive. When you decide to drink it, offer a cup to me in prayer."

The Temple of Khaos seemed brighter now than it had before Aetheria had passed out. Why would that be? The goddess still took the form of mists.

"Sure, I can do that." The bottle vanished into her repository before Arkaziel could see she had something he'd want.

"So why the vision?"

"A side effect of my impartment. I do not impart myself to others, but you represent a promise to make this universe worth watching again."

If she was human once, or mortal anyway, how bored must she be? Can she and Chronos even improve still? "Was what I saw true?"

"It happened. It is how I knew to nudge little Nyx and Aetherius into playing with you. I didn't speak, but I heard your whole encounter with Chronos back then. I would never have agreed to impart my essence without a reason beyond Aetherius and Nyx begging."

"So you sent me to convince Chronos to do what he would do anyway, to reveal to you that you should impart yourself to me in the future. That's convoluted."

"My entire requirement was that you entertain me, dear. Convoluted and absurd are the perfect ways to entertain me."

"I don't suppose you'll tell me any more about the Origin, or forming the universe?"

"I could, but again, you digging it up yourself will be more entertaining."

"Your Flame isn't lit within me yet?"

"As with Nyx's Flame, you'll need to feed it before it fully ignites." Khaos sounded bored.

"Any hints on what your Flame will let me do?"

Laughter. "I think we're done for now, darling. You'll find the door to the next floor in the alcove with your cat." The dark mists that made up the form of Khaos dispersed. Aetheria looked around.

"Absurd, huh?" she walked through the alcoves, dumping everything into her repository. *Stealing from Khaos seems nice and absurd to me.* She gave herself a mental pat on the back and swiped everything until she found Arkaziel at a table playing with dice by himself.

"You get abandoned too?"

"Yeah, couple minutes ago. I saw you looting, but that damned snake used enchanted dice. I can't stop playing." The StarMane hissed. "Stupid snake."

The dice froze and shattered into stray atoms.

"Thanks, Ria. I'm going to eat that bastard again next time we see him."

"Again?"

"Uh. Yeah. I sort of ate him this time. I rolled snake eyes. He made a joke. I ate him. It's just how things go between friends."

"You know, this reminds me of you eating my arm last time I got hurt. I'm not sure how I feel about you eating my severed appendages. It is really weird, and kind of creepy."

"What, you want me to let all that power go to waste? That's dumb. It's not like I'm taking a bite out of you, but if you get a leg or arm hacked off, what's the problem with me having a little snack?"

"Um, I could just reabsorb it?" Aetheria said flatly.

"Wait, you can do that and never mentioned it? Damn it, Ria. We're bond-mates, and I've been slowing down your cultivation to the benefit of my own. That's a big no-no! If I knew you could reabsorb your dismembered limbs, I'd have let you reclaim the lost power instead of eating it. No matter how good your limbs taste." The StarMane's 180 impressed her. His race's strange rules regarding things never ceased to amaze her. *Is he making it up to give me an out, or is he trying to guilt me with how good I taste? What the hell kind of guilt trip would that even be? Goddamn cat.*

"Thanks, Ark. Now, I've looted all the hobby holes, you ate a cloud snake and got tricked into playing dice. Good job. What did the cloud snake taste like?"

"Awesome, actually. Like a stew with many flavor hints—jam-packed with power but airy at the same time. I would put it in the top five meals I've had, taste-wise. Cultivation-wise, I'd say top ten."

"Don't gods and immortals ever get mad at you for eating them?"

"Oh, all the time! But it's not like they actually *die* when I eat them. If it was permanent, I wouldn't have eaten Oro. He's a good pal. I would eat the real Nidhogg, though. That guy's a major asshole, and there's only room for one apocalypse dragon around here."

"Apocalypse dragon?"

"Small apocalypse dragon?"

"No. I will spray you with water. No apocalypse. We're the good guys, remember? We help people, then you eat the bad guy."

"I do like the part where I eat the bad guy. They are always either powerful or tasty, or both."

"See? Altruism has plenty of rewards for StarManes."

"Maybe. I'm not fully convinced, but no apocalypse. For now."

"Oh, keep an eye out for strongly aligned Ethereal spots. I'm just about ready to break through to Tier Three."

"You could try here, but I wouldn't. Temples always result in interference from their owners. Even if Khaos likes you, you don't want to be at her mercy. Especially after I just ate Oro."

"Duly noted. About temples. Do we need to worry about the gods we've upset in the tower outside?"

"Nah. It's why I eat most of them. Other than Thalassa, Ymir, and Khaos, the others have all been fakes. Fraction of the power, but still tasty. Only absolute badasses enter another god's tower; it weakens them. Those jerks in the tomb were fake. No need to worry about reprisal. It's why the towers are so awesome for my race. Administrators spawn fake gods all the time. They're great food."

CHAPTER 62

Not-So-Secret Garden

The duo stepped into a veritable forest on Floor 33. At first glance, anyway, it looked like a forest. A small cottage lay immediately before them. Slate roof, stone walls, an adorable little winding path curved up to the wooden door. A small bell hung next to the door.

Like everywhere in the Tower of Aetherius, the air was exceptionally rich with Aether, and within the ground below them were powerful tides of Nether. The plant life here pulsed with long-absorbed power, and Aetheria had a feeling in her gut that there would be alchemy equipment inside the cottage.

"I'm going to look for something to eat." Arkaziel's yellow eyes lit up with anticipation.

Probably smells a squirrel. "Didn't you just eat Oro?" Aetheria chided.

"I'm a growing boy! Besides, he was *really* light. I need something more filling!" The StarMane resorted to the dreaded begging, eyes wide and his tail twitched.

"Fine. Don't go too far. I'll check out the cottage."

The cat vanished into the woods before she made it to the cottage door. She rang the bell once, and then another time when no one answered after she counted to two hundred. Aetheria knocked on the door instead. Still no answer. When she tried the door, it wasn't locked, so she slipped the latch and opened it.

Her intuition proved correct. The main room was an alchemy workshop. The herbs that hung from the wall and ceiling were still all fresh. A quick inspection of the structure revealed glyphs of preservation had been carved into the stone. Each fed off Aether and thus would never run out of power. Not all the herbs were magical, though. Next to the cauldron, a smaller cooking cauldron hung on the wall, surrounded by wreathes of garlic. Preserved onions, potatoes, and other roots filled some baskets neatly arranged.

Besides the alchemy workroom/kitchen, the cottage had a small bedroom, a bathroom with magical plumbing, and a study with books all written in the same hand. No signature covered any of the books, and they all appeared to be recipes. The only problem was they had been written in a language Aetheria couldn't read. *Maybe Arkaziel can read it.*

Finished with the cottage, she wandered back outside to observe the woods. If she ignored the undergrowth, the forest almost looked like an old garden left to go wild. After a circle of the house, she felt even more confident in the idea. Behind the cottage, small fields of three different crops ran wild and unharvested for who knows how long. The mystery of how the patches had not been overrun troubled Aetheria, until she found more glyphs in the fence around each plot.

"Preservation wards in the house, weeds-be-gone glyphs here, magical plumbing. Someone went to a lot of effort to just abandon this place."

The crops interested her. The first field held an orange plant that rose in climbing spires. The stalks were thick, tough, and covered in overly large thorns. *Those look painful.* In fact, the thorns triggered a memory. She had seen them before, in the kobold alchemist's workshop back in Solace. *Let's see: Regro said these are called Sunspires, the key component of which is the thorn. Correctly used, they make vitality and stamina elixirs. Incorrectly used, and you go on a bad trip.*

The second patch held a light blue crop with leaves that looked remarkably like snowflakes. No name came to Aetheria, but the plant's association with cold could not be more obvious. Without a real name for it, she dubbed it Frosty the Plant.

A dark-leafed plant that reminded Aetheria of kale filled the last patch. Large leaves held only the faintest hint of green hidden within the dark coloration. *"You can always tell Shadowleaf by the way it grows toward the nearest shade. Don't eat it raw. It will poison you, make you sluggish and slow. Properly prepared, it makes shadow camouflage potions. Excellent for avoiding detection, or gathering plants in peace."* Regro's words came back to her easily.

"Knowing two out of three isn't bad, since Regro was pretty much the worst teacher in Solace. Secretive little shits, kobolds." Aetheria tossed a few samples of each of the plants into her repository. The theme of this floor seemed clearly related to alchemy. Her time with Regro had taught her only the basics of alchemical science and herbology, so hopefully this trial would not require her to make any master-level potions.

Arkaziel lay sprawled in the sun in front of the cottage when she returned. The house cat-sized StarMane lazily opened one eye to regard her. *+Ate too much. Nap time.+*

Slightly annoyed, Aetheria headed into the cottage and back to the study. She summoned a small journal into her hand and read over the notes Aoibhe had given her. Her control of Aether had advanced enough that she shouldn't be at risk of making a Chaos surge. *Unless maybe I should? Nyx's Flame feasted on Nether. What will Khaos's Flame eat?*

"Let's see. I need a candle with a magic flame." A wave of her hand and a candle appeared from her repository. She narrowed her red eyes, and flames burst upon the wick—blue Frostfire flames. *Regular fire is so uncool. Hahaha. It's okay to laugh at your own puns when no one else is around to appreciate them.*

"Candle, magic fire. Visualize my desire, tie it to an idea, dump Ethereal power into it until the magic either explodes or works."

Aetheria picked one journal from the wall at random, then placed it next to the candle. She chose the word "understanding," the ideal behind her need for a translation spell, and visualized the books containing the language of Ath instead of whatever they contained. *Is that enough?* She pushed Ethereal power into her concept, and a spell-form flared to life before her eyes and then vanished.

A thin layer of hoarfrost covered the desk, but the journal now contained words she understood in the language of the divine. *Victory! I didn't even destroy the cottage. This means I'm ready to learn magic!*

Luckily, Arkaziel dozed outside, so no one witnessed Aetheria perform her victory dance.

Arkaziel was roosting on the cottage's slate roof. Periodically, a shadow swooped across the front yard, another high magic-infused creature caught by the voracious StarMane. If their quest lasted too long, the forest might truly become depopulated. After three days, they had yet to encounter any form of monster, wildlife, or plant that was a deterrent to the StarMane.

Aetheria had been in the middle of processing Shadowleaf into powder when a small ring came from the bell in front of the cottage, followed by a rap of knuckles on the front door. Unsure of what to expect, she approached the door and slid it open. A young human boy and girl stood in the stone entryway. Their eyes flicked this way and that, and both appeared stunned that an attractive young woman had opened the door. They both stood still, a perfect mimicry of deer in headlights.

"Can I help you, children?" Aetheria tried first one human language, then another, until a look of understanding finally lit the kids' eyes, and their fear eased. A little. After all, the strange woman had been talking in strange tongues at them while a black cat had slowly walked along the roof giving them baleful, hungry looks. Arkaziel currently sat on the slate roof above the door, a house cat the size of a panther, until he felt Aetheria's disapproval and shrank to the size of a normal cat.

"Um, hi. There's stories that an ancient witch used to live out here. Everyone says it's malarky, but Grandma said in her time they still bought medicines from her that could fix most that ails you. Even the plague!" The boy had quickly jumped into imagining Aetheria as a witch who could help with whatever his "quest" was. The girl, however, seemed distrustful of her.

"Well, I can say for sure that the witch wasn't me. I've only recently arrived, and I'm going over the journals and recipes she left to learn from her skill. Is there a specific problem you need help with? I might be able to help." Internally, Aetheria hoped they didn't say a plague. Plagues sounded awful.

"Dad caught the Black Cough from the Spore Creepers during his last turn on guard duty. The stockpile of old medicine in town ran out four months ago. Everyone who gets the Black Cough dies." The girl frowned at the ground. "The last time a healer of any sort came through town was over three years ago. With the raiders coming by sea, no one in the kingdom cares about the frontier anymore."

"That's rough." Aetheria dropped to a crouch to be on the two children's levels. She estimated the girl to be about thirteen, and the boy to be eleven or twelve. "My name is Ria, and I'll do my best to help you. Have you had lunch? I've still got some stew left. Let me see if I can find mention of this Black Cough or Spore Creepers in the books, and you two eat as much as you want, alright?"

The boy's stomach growled when she mentioned food. While neither looked like an orphan, they visibly had not been receiving the nourishment their growing bodies required.

"I'm Cody!" The boy showed no reticence in going right for the stew pot once Aetheria had set out bowls and spoons. "She's Mabel, don't mind her. She doesn't trust people much since Dad got sick and Mom started working at the inn."

Mabel just grimaced, but once Cody had eaten half a bowl of stew to no ill effect, her hunger overcame her distrust.

"Arkaziel, why don't you keep these two company? See what you can find out about the Black Cough, Spore Creepers, and anything else."

The lazy cat walked in through a window and meowed at her. It was his "I don't want to" meow.

~Are you seriously going back to your being too good to talk to people? Fine. Just watch them. Make sure they don't get into anything while I look the books over.~

Twenty minutes later, Aetheria came out to find the children both fast asleep.

+Too much food on empty stomachs. They both passed out pretty quickly. Did you find the recipe?+

~Yes. It's straightforward enough. We do need some reagents from these Spore Creepers, though. Once they wake up, we'll visit the village, get some samples. There's always a possibility my Aether purification will cure them outright, but I'd like to make them a stock pile of medicine if we can, and maybe look at some other long-term solutions.~

Arkaziel hopped onto her shoulder and settled into his standard spot. *+I could cure them with my Light abilities, but I think your trial is to do it with alchemy. Save the magic for combat—these sorts of boring trials always offer a better reward if you complete them in the way you're meant to. If we just heal everyone with our normal magic, kill all the mushrooms, and dash off, we'll get a mediocre reward.+*

~You have a point. Since when do you care about rewards, though?~

+The general rule of thumb is that tower gains are distributed in thirds. The first third is mediocre, the middle third is good, and the upper third is usually quite good. Rules of thumb aren't always true, but it's close enough I'm willing to play along with the trials a bit more now that we're in the middle. Just think, it could be golden cat bed shoulder pads for you! Wouldn't that just be the most amazing reward?+

Water spurted from Aetheria's hand to spray Arkaziel with a light mist in the face.

~No.~

CHAPTER 63

Raven's Hollow

It was midafternoon by the time Cody and Mabel woke up and guided them through the forest toward their village. The children seemed slightly impressed that she could walk through the woods with a cat asleep on her shoulder, and that she also towered over the teenager and preteen. The two were roughly the same height, barely up to her chest. Occasionally, they whispered to each other, but she did her best not to listen in. She still caught the occasional comment about how weird it seemed that no animals attacked them on the half-hour walk back to their town.

The woods became sparser as they approached the town and the meager path became an actual maintained road. It took a mere ten minutes to reach the village from there. At first glimpse, Aetheria summed the town up in one word: "depressing." A wooden palisade ran around the entire town. A small moat complemented the palisade, and a drop bridge provided the only entrance to Raven's Hollow from the direction they came.

"Ya actually found someone out in the woods, Mabel? Guess I owe ya five bits." The boy who stood guard at the gate seemed too young to be a professional guard by Aetheria's reckoning, but in a low-tech, man-versus-monster world, Earth norms were not applicable.

"That's right, Tad! We found a witch who can make a cure for the Black Cough!" Cody cried out. "You owe Mabel five bits, and you have to put in a good word for me with your sister! That was the deal if we succeeded!" He strutted like a prize rooster.

Tad gave Aetheria an appraisal. She let just a little power leak into her eyes, red energy misting from them intimidatingly. Tad swallowed.

"Entrance to the Hollow is a gold piece for outsiders, ma'am." He seemed uncertain about whether he should be respectful, timid, or forceful with her. The youth grimaced a little, and Aetheria proffered a thick gold coin before the teen's distress at looking weak before Mabel became a problem.

"I'd like to see your father, Mabel, and then whoever is in charge of the town. Thank you, Tad. Good day." Aetheria gave Cody and Mabel each a gentle nudge to get moving. Reminded that their father lay ill, their pace picked up.

The scene in Raven's Hollow was disturbing. She'd expected poor sanitation, but all the people she saw looked malnourished, with hollow eyes; there was no sign of healthy, well-fed individuals anywhere. The construction of the town seemed solid, if basic, but weeks of neglect showed. The people of the Hollow had lost their battle and waited only for the loss to fully materialize and end their suffering. Despair hung heavy in the air. As the town's name suggested, dark, ominous birds cawed from rooftops. *I've never seen a place so hopeless.*

The house the kids led Aetheria to was no exception. It was small. Inside revealed only four rooms: an open communal area and kitchen, two bedrooms, and what Aetheria presumed was a cellar or pantry. *No magical bathrooms here.*

A woman with streaks of gray in her brown hair stood over a pot that contained what looked like water. The few herbs in it did not make it a stew.

"Mom! We found an alchemist! She's here to look at Daddy!" Cody cried out.

"An alchemist, you say? Come in, come in. Handrick is in our bed. Children, you stay out here." The deep worry in the woman's voice felt like a hand tightening around Aetheria's heart for a moment. *I'm going to make things better here.*

"I'm Ria. You've got two very brave young kids to venture out into the woods on their own like that."

"Hildy. Brave? Stones for brains, those two. They could just as likely have been eaten by a bear or wandered into a Spore Creeper or one of the Steel Webbers that lurk in the forest." Hildy gave a snort of annoyance but then opened the door to the small master bedroom, and silence fell between the two women. A middle-aged man lay naked and covered in sweat on the bed. He held a cloth in his hand and it was mottled with black bodily fluids. The man's lips had also blackened some. He was pallid and malnourished, and looked barely alive.

"This looks severe. According to Gladia's notes, he's in the final stage of the Black Cough, where her treatment is no longer effective." Aetheria walked next to the bed to give the man a quick survey of his condition. Results: bad.

"Is there anything you can do? We don't have much, but... well, Handrick is a good father and husband." Desperation filled Hildy's voice. *Two kids, a dying town, no hope. Poor lady.*

"I've got this." A golden orb of water appeared in her hand. Aetheria pumped Aether into the water, then manifested the Primordial Flame of Thalassa and the Primordial Flame of Aetherius. The previous golden glow became a dull comparison to the luminescent glory that the Flames imbued into the water. The orb flowed from her hand to hover over Handrick's dying body, where it seeped into the man's skin. For a few brief seconds, the inner glow gave the bedridden man's skin a holy radiance.

"Oh my," Hildy muttered under her breath and made a religious or superstitious gesture Aetheria did not recognize.

Black spots on Handrick's lips returned to normal color. His gaunt face and sallow eyes filled in, nourished by divine power. Handrick traversed from death's door to a picture of moderate health in seconds. It put a significant strain on the man, however, and he slipped into unconsciousness. Aetheria had expected that, though. *"Most races can't deal with speedy fast healing. Pass out. Great time to collect bill while loved ones are happy."* Regro's lectures remained with her.

"He'll wake up in a day or so. Now, can you arrange for me to meet whoever is in charge here? I'll heal anyone in as bad a state as Handrick was in before I make medication for everyone else."

Hildy was still gazing in wonder at the healed man lying on the bed, and Aetheria had to repeat herself to get the mother's attention.

"Oh, of course. My apologies, Lady Ria. I'll go talk to Eldred." Hildy nearly sprinted out the door. Aetheria shrugged and returned to the main room of the home, where she fiddled with the stew pot. She evaporated some of the water via magic, then added more vegetables, meat, and herbs. By the time Hildy came back, she had turned a watery cauldron of a few herbs into a fragrant stew.

"Eldred will see you at the town hall, Lady Ria. What's that fantastic smell? We didn't have any meat or vegetables left..." Hildy frowned in confusion, but Aetheria just patted her shoulder and smiled as she walked out the door.

It was easy to find the town hall, as there were few large buildings in Raven's Hollow. The structure stood as a testament to a previous era, when Raven's Hollow existed as a thriving frontier town with regular trade convoys back to the established areas of the kingdom. Its imposing weathered stone facade loomed over the desolate town square, a stark reminder of better days. Two stone ravens perched atop the entrance; their beady eyes seemed to survey the suffering below. Ivy and moss crept up the walls, finding refuge in the cracks and crevices of the aging structure.

The heavy oak door squealed when Aetheria opened it. No one had oiled the hinges in some time. The cavernous main assembly hall dominated the first floor of the structure, yet dust bunnies ran rampant on floors and spiderwebs obscured corners. It was empty and desolate, a cruel contrast to the tapestries of harvest festivals and happier times that covered the walls.

A massive oak desk sat at the end of the assembly room, and two men stood before the desk. They spoke in hushed tones to the older man who sat behind the desk. The screech of the door had given Aetheria an attention-grabbing entrance, yet only the older man looked at her. The other two were in a heated argument. Not with the old man, but with each other.

"Gentlemen, enough. We have an honored guest." Eldred stood behind the desk. He frowned faintly. Even with the slight dais for his desk, the older man stood a head shorter than Aetheria. Or perhaps he was frowning at the black cat sound asleep on her shoulder.

The other two men muttered at one another before they turned to regard Aetheria. One wore a set of chain and leather armor that had been reworked many times. He stood like a stone, ready to defy the Path of Water should it commit to wearing him down to naught over the years. The other man wore clothes of a finer cut. His well-fed features and the lack of callouses on his hands led her to the conclusion he was a merchant of some sort.

Eldred, on the other hand, was much older. He had the look of a man who had worked a long life and wanted to be fishing, not managing a town. *But maybe that's just me.*

"Hi. Hildy's kids ventured into the forest to find old Gladia. She's long gone, but they found me. I believe I can help you with some of your problems." Bold declarative statements seemed like the best way to go.

Eldred did not waste time with speculation, distrust, or bargaining. "Hildy said you cured her husband, even though he had reached the fifth night of the deep cough. She said you'd heal more who were that bad off, and make a medicine for the rest. What can we do to help you?"

"I did, and I will. I'd like the worst to be gathered together if possible, but if not, I'll need a guide to take me to each. Do you have any of the Spore Creepers' corpses? I need to dissect them to make the elixir that cures the Black Cough."

"Ol' Dolgin is gathering them together now. He used to gather herbs for Gladia when he was a kid. Learned a thing or two, but not enough," said the military man. "As for corpses, we don't have any. They go on the pyre immediately to prevent spread of the Cough. Next attack, we can set a corpse aside, but you'll need to claim it quick. No one wants to risk being near those things."

"And just what will all of this help cost us?" the merchant chimed in. "Our coffers are nearly depleted, and even those of us with money have little to no food left." *Shocking. Capitalism never changes.*

"I'm not after money." With a gesture of her hand, a few large sacks of food staples appeared from her repository. For a village of this size, it would be enough to get people on their feet, but it was a short-term solution. *I haven't seen evidence of a lack of prey, just a lack of hunters. The fields outside of town were sad, but they had crops. They just need to get strong enough to work again, without being killed by a plague or whatever these Spore Creepers are.* "Share these with the villagers."

Eldred and the soldier bowed their heads in thanks, but the merchant still frowned.

"I'd like a briefing on the Spore Creepers and other local problems after I've healed the worst."

The soldier grunted. "I'll brief her, Eldred, and show her around. Name's Brynmor Blackthorn, head of the town guard and militia. What's left of them, anyway."

The screech of the door marked the return of Ol' Dolgin, and the start of Aetheria's stint as emergency medic.

CHAPTER 64

Goblins, Redcaps, and Little More Besides

Healing the six people on the verge of death proved simple. The Flame of Aetherius and the Flame of Thalassa combined to eradicate the monster-spawned plague the locals called the Black Cough. Witness to the effects of the worst cases, Aetheria came away thoroughly horrified by the black sludge the villagers were coughing up. Unnecessary or not, she sanitized the black goo, clothing, bedding, and other tainted things in a large pool of holy water she created for the job. Leaving instructions for all tainted clothing to be washed in the water, she moved on to the next item on her list.

Brynmor Blackthorn, leader of the city guard and militia, led her on a tour of the settlement of Raven's Hollow, ignoring the mundane and starting with the palisades. Aetheria had entered the Hollow through the Forest Gate. Midway between the Forest Gate with its thick palisade walls and the extremely fortified Frontier Gate was the much less defended Traders' Gate.

"A week's travel on horse will get you to Minnarin. They've got real royal roads in Minnarin, and you can get to the capital in less than a month." Brynmor's pride in the kingdom had ebbed, but with a change of situation, perhaps it would rekindle. Aetheria made no comment on the times or travel distances; she was sure her or Arkaziel's flight could get them to Minnarin in an hour or two.

"And no one has gone to Minnarin for aid?"

"We sent reports and tax-exemption requests. No one we've sent has come back, and no one from the capital helps." Brynmor sounded bleak.

"Arkaziel, go scout the road. If there's monsters, bandits, or any kind of problem, take care of it." Ark's yellow eyes lazily opened to regard her before he meowed and jumped off her shoulder. Mid-leap, he grew wings, and flashed off into the distance.

"Your familiar is mighty impressive, Lady Ria. We hear rumors of powerful witches with equally powerful bondmates, of mighty wizards in glimmering towers, and of warriors with weapons that could slay gods. No one like that ever comes out to the frontier, where we've got goblins, redcaps, and little more besides."

"Novice adventurers do not come to learn their craft on weak enemies?"

"Nay, you can find goblins and whatnot anywhere, and no one's traveling for a month or two from the capital to hope they encounter a more powerful monster that might not even exist here. No dungeons, no ruins, no interest." Brynmor heaved an enormous sigh as they reached the walkway above the aptly named Enemy's Gate.

"The frontier lies out there. The Hollow got a lot more traffic when the king still wanted to expand into it. Costs too high, they say these days. Infested with low-level monsters and no resources worth eradicating the monsters for. Some say there's some big old evil things sleeping out there, but folks who go there don't always come back."

The forest looked the same as the one in which the alchemist's cottage was located, except the Aether to Nether ratios were wrong. *Something's lowering the Aether and amplifying the Nether. No wonder the town has such a gloomy feel and name.*

"The Spore Creepers attack the town itself or haunt the area?"

"Attack. In fact... look at those bushes there, under that elm."

Aetheria looked where directed. The only movement she saw belonged to a single bush, until a small mass broke through the brush. She had expected some kind of monster, but not literal anthropomorphic mushrooms. Beneath their dark black domed caps were glowing red eyes, woody limbs, and horrific, vicious teeth.

Aetheria watched until one of the mushrooms made it to within ten meters of the gate, then she vaulted over the side. The mushroom never saw what killed it—she froze it solid with a quick burst of her domain before it could detect her. She sent it to her repository as a block of ice.

Brynmor had not followed her. He still stood upon the palisade, open-mouthed. Aetheria jumped back atop the gate, so she could ask further questions.

"Do they come solo often?"

"Aye, aye. Usually, one or two get ahead of their groups and stumble into the defenses alone before their friends show up. How did you do that? It just froze solid, then disappeared. You never touched it, just glared at it."

Aetheria offered a small smile. "Witchery, of course."

"Captain! There's more coming." One of the other men on duty ran up to point back toward the forest.

"Why don't you boys take a rest? I'll handle this batch. That should give me all the reagents I need to make the elixir to cure the Black Cough." She smiled sweetly with the words, but no one argued. The men were all hungry and malnourished, and they didn't want to risk further injury or infection if they didn't have to.

Aetheria simply waited until the group of Spore Creepers were bunched together, then vaulted over the side to land on a pillar of ice that shot up to meet her. A terrible chitter arose from the Creepers, but they had no chance to do more than release a few spores before her domain struck them like the wrath of an angry goddess. The anticlimactic way in which she defeated and collected twenty-three Spore Creepers left the militia quiet and sullen. She knew that help from those with the power she'd just displayed usually came expensively, and with many strings attached.

"Okay, I think I've got everything I need now. I'll have to make a jaunt back to Gladia's cottage to finish the elixirs—unless anyone has some alchemical equipment here in town? No?" Aetheria nodded, expecting that answer. It suited her fine to not have people look too closely at her work, anyway.

~I'm headed back to the cottage to do some alchemy. How's scouting going? ~

+I've found some snacks. I'll explain when I get to the cottage. Traffic to town should resume. I'll leave some signs to get Minnarin to see the roads as safe now.+

~ That's remarkably decent of you, Arkaziel. I'm proud of you. ~

+Well, there's some big mammal that way, too, and it smells tasty.+

Why Aetheria expected altruism when hunger could explain all things, she didn't know. *Hope?*

That evening, Aetheria and Arkaziel descended into the frontier outside Raven's Hollow. The elixir for the Black Cough had been easy to manufacture, and she had dropped off more than enough for three times the residents of Raven's Hollow for now. If using Aether instead of mana in alchemy took the tier quality up a notch, using Ethereal power as the catalyst instead of Aether resulted in a tier up from that. The delivery of the elixir to town allowed for Aetheria to open the portal to the next floor, but she wanted to do one last service for the town first.

Arkaziel and Aetheria landed outside a cave.

+ They marked this on the map. I don't smell any orcs. Just those mushrooms and some type of goblin-y, fae-like things.+

~Alright, I'll take the lead. Have your kitties flank me. Let's wipe this threat out at the source if we can, then we'll move to the next floor. ~

As the vanguard, Aetheria lead the way into the cave. They made it less than five meters in before Spore Creepers dropped from the ceiling, emerged from alcoves, and otherwise became a nuisance. Unlike Arkaziel and the duplicate kitties, though, she did not exempt them from her domain.

+ This is boring, it's just small non-threats. Not even worth collecting the corpses or eating.+

~ There's something stronger ahead. ~

They cleansed the cave of Spore Creepers. Very few survived even the first contact with Aetheria's freezing domain, but Ark's Twilight duplicates quickly dispatched those that did. The telltale remnants of Ethereal magic she had used in Raven's Hollow were now directly above them, which meant the cave's pathways had descended, twisted, and meandered so much they ended up over two kilometers from the entrance, and deeper, as well.

The cave ended in a large wooden wall with a single door in it. To the side of the door, casually thrown against the rock wall and left to rot, lay a skeleton. No items, clothing or otherwise, had survived the damp rot of the environment. When Arkaziel had one of his clones brush at the white bones, a mess of black liquid underneath shot out at it. Quickly, the Twilight cat flared in a burst of power and killed the black ooze.

With a sigh, Aetheria kicked in the door. The entire wall shattered and crumbled, and Arkaziel laughed insanely.

"Only you would go to kick a wooden wall, find out it's a stone illusioned to look like wood, and still destroy the whole thing."

She didn't respond, instead focusing her domain to freeze the dust in the air. Before that took effect, a small blur of red shot out of nowhere, and brutal cuts formed across her throat and stomach. Aetheria's aura formed as she drew stored Ethereal power from her repository. Her cells filled with extra power and her Ethereal physiology kicked in enough that she could actually see what had attacked her.

The creature stood at just under a meter. It had pale gray skin, beady dark eyes, and sharp teeth shown in a snarl of hate. Its murderous intent elevated the simple iron knives in its hands into weapons that could harm the most stalwart of champions. It also seemed to allow the monster to bypass her domain completely. *Maybe an innate characteristic of its race?*

"Redcaps," Arkaziel snorted, and spears of shadow formed from the redcap's own shadow to ambush it. The fae creature avoided the shadow spears and darted toward Arkaziel, killing all three duplicates before it got to the StarMane. Arkaziel promptly bit its head off.

"How'd you just... chomp?" Aetheria asked, fingers pressed to her throat to make sure the wound healed properly.

"I'm Tier Three already, remember? You really need to tier up already."

"I'm trying, Ark, I just need a suitable place."

Her domain had cleared the dust, and the two preceded into the hidden base. The first room held cages full of humans with varying levels of the Black Cough. Arkaziel healed them in one spell. Holy Light filled the room. Divine Radiance sanctified the captives, purified them, and then healed them. The captives recovered lucidity after a few minutes. Most were couriers, merchants, or entourages to caravans headed toward Raven's Hollow from Minnarin. Once she calmed them down, Aetheria explained their situation and sent them back to the surface with two of Arkaziel's duplicates.

The noise and commotion did not go unnoticed. While they organized the civilians and sent them off, a trio of redcaps came through hidden doors. Arkaziel let two come to him and brutally engaged, claw versus knife, while Aetheria struggled to keep her speed up against just one redcap.

Since she couldn't rely on her domain to take care of the redcap, she instead waited for it to get within melee range and stab her. Aetheria took the wound to her throat—as tiny, goblin-like monsters, they were exceptionally acrobatic—and conjured the Flame of Thalassa. With a minor delay, she flared the Flame of Ymir to freeze the air. Bodily fluids were pulled out of the redcap, and then all froze solid.

"Asshole." She dropped the dead redcap into her repository, then turned to see that Arkaziel had already disemboweled his redcaps and was midway through eating them.

+*They taste better than they look. Fae always do.*+

"There's going to be a lot more of them, aren't there?" Aetheria gestured and an ice wall rose to block the tunnel exit. "Hopefully they don't try to flee, anyway."

CHAPTER 65

An End to Sorrow

Before descending farther into the redcap base, Aetheria left two ice turrets in the room they'd just cleared. That the ice constructs would be of any use felt questionable, but it wasn't in her nature to do nothing. The next room turned out to be a barracks. Its lack of occupants felt ominous. The redcaps did not sleep in beds. Instead, they created a bedding out of whatever they scavenged. Even Arkaziel, who had called them tasty, grimaced at the foul smell in the redcap warren.

The next room proved they had taken on cunning opponents. Right after Aetheria and Ark crossed from the awful warren into what looked like a ritual chamber, hidden doors slipped open and almost a dozen redcaps swarmed them. Insulted, Arkaziel unleashed a wide-beam breath attack that destroyed five redcaps outright, plus ten meters of solid bedrock.

Aetheria stuck with her Flames, and shards of aetheric ice circled her in a cyclone. The first redcap to rush to stab her became red mist.

"Oh, you could make me purees," Arkaziel commented, delighted. The sole clone he had kept with them ambushed a redcap violently, reducing the number to four. Those didn't seem intimidated by the sudden death of their friends. They split: three to Arkaziel and one to Aetheria.

The redcap to approach her twirled its knives and then, much to her shock, diced her aetheric ice out of the air until nothing remained. It charged at her with its seemingly plain knives. The redcap's intent dulled her reactions, but not so much that she couldn't catch each knife.

Can't stab me now! Her fists suddenly glowed with the Flame of Nyx, and she overpowered the redcap, ripped out its life force, took it for herself. Surprisingly, it worked. The sound of the knives falling out of her hands to the floor pulled her out of her shock.

"Regeneration really is the best power."

Arkaziel had already killed two of the redcaps. Even though he had gone up against three opponents, the StarMane had wings, claws, teeth, and a tail with which to attack or defend, on top of his magical abilities. StarManes, Aetheria realized, were truly terrifying. *I really am nowhere near his level, even with all I've been through. I need to break through.*

+Don't feel bad, Blue. If we were playing your video game, I'd be an S++ tier DPS. You're a brawler, or tank, I guess you called them? Your ability to one-hit kill things will fall behind the farther we go, but you can cheat it with the Flames. Most can't. Your domain is great for small fries for now, but you'll want to alter your intent with it the farther we go, to make it less offensive and more defensive.+

Shadows boiled underneath the last redcap, and hundreds of grasping hands pulled it down into the darkness. Arkaziel burped.

"Consuming darkness. A favorite move of all StarManes with the affinities to use it. Ranged eating at its finest."

With the redcaps dead, Aetheria and Ark finally could take stock of the room. Grates covered the floors, vats warmed over magical fire. Stone troughs and tubing lead down into the room below.

"Creeping Spore breeding program." Arkaziel seemed surprised. "Redcaps aren't that smart. You saw how they fight—all murder, no thoughts."

Aetheria gestured, and the Flame of Ymir, powered by Ethereal energy, filled the Creeping Spore breeding ground below with hoarfrost and ice.

Ark opened the next door to the sight of five balls of dark energy that slammed into his furry scaled hide. The blasts pushed the panther-sized StarMane back a few meters. He snarled and hissed at the doorway. Whatever had cast the magic now hid. The room held tables, pillars, bookshelves, and other equipment. The only visible figure was that of a desiccated skeleton working at an alchemy table at the far end of the room, oblivious to the chaos Arkaziel created behind it. Arkaziel growled and became a charging blur that dashed into the room, jumped over a table, and lifted his head to break the neck of a tall pale humanoid that had previously been concealed with invisibility.

With a sigh, Aetheria shifted to her Luxentian crystal form and followed the StarMane, hopping over the adjacent table and skewering the first thing she found with the thirty-centimeter-long talons her fingers became. The orc stood roughly at her own normal height, had pallid green skin, large canines, a face caught utterly in shock at having long talons lunged into her chest. For the hell of it, she tried out the Orcish that Werylin had taught her. "Surrender or die!"

The orc understood, and its answer was to punch her. Aetheria's sharp talons pierced into the orc's chest deeper before it could land the punch. The ease with which she pierced the hide confused her slightly, and she had to refocus her attention. *There are only four Tier Three beings in the room, counting Arkaziel.*

"Kill her! She desecrates our language!" another orc hissed from farther in the room, but hidden from her view.

~ There's three Tier Three enemies in here, Arkaziel. ~

+I can smell them.+

~ Really? ~

+No, but I can sense them.+

Telepathy had advantages. The speed of thought exceeded the speed of speech and allowed Arkaziel and Aetheria to coordinate at speeds others couldn't match without their own telepathic bond. Aetheria expanded her domain to five meters around her and chose a tank approach to the room. Desks or other furniture that got in her way went into her repository—a shock to the orcs who hid behind them, and a nice opening for her to launch a surprise attack.

Arkaziel prowled along the side of the room, a flash of his claws or a blast of Twilight energy eviscerating any attacker foolish enough to approach the StarMane. Suddenly, from the darkness, another redcap jumped. This one had blades that dripped black ichor, pitch-black eyes, and the aura of a high Tier Three enemy. A second redcap tried to flank Arkaziel, this one with knives that gleamed a sickly green. This redcap's eyes also were green, and its aura showed its strength at mid-Tier Three. Every time the enchanted weapons made contact with Arkaziel's claws or scales, showers of sparks erupted.

Since the StarMane was holding his ground well, Aetheria took the opportunity to flash between pillars and across the room, quickly putting an end to the orcs. None of the orcs could stand up to her speed or strength. *I guess not all orcs are strong, muscle-bound fighters, after all.*

Aetheria's gut suddenly squirmed, and a spellform activated at the last alcove of the room. Strange glyphs and sigils blasted her mind, and uneasiness and confusion settled over her, but she burned the confusion away with the Flame of Aetherius. A flare of Aetherflame Nova burned the rest of the curse off her. In a flash, she appeared around the pillar, and with her talons, attempted to pierce the final orc's throat. A staff met her talons, and the strength and speed behind the parry shocked her.

The pale orc with a skull painted over his face had the aura of a powerful Tier Three Cultivator. His leather-and-hide armor was not that of a warrior but of a caster, which the staff only reinforced. In a split second, the orc stabbed the staff into her throat, pulled back, stabbed into her stomach, and then pulled back a last time to smash the weapon into her sternum. Her Luxentian crystal body absorbed the blows, although hundreds of fine fractures spiraled out from the assaults.

Ethereal power flared through her soul aperture and flooded her body. The power pushed her regeneration to the maximum and ran through her cells as she shape-shifted back to her human form with adaptions for maximum speed.

"Asshole," she grunted in Orcish as she fixed her stance.

"You are ruining the reclamation of our great empire! You and your pet shall be the offering to restore our might, and the humans will know our rule!" the orc snarled, anger fueling its rant and a spell Lightning flared from the orc's hand, and Aetheria lifted her own hand and a blue Aetherflame flared to life, empowered by the Flame of Aetherius. Two-thirds of the lightning went into the blue flames, their strength becoming hers. The rest hit her, scorched her, and sent tingles through her body.

She fought through the pain, called forth the Flame of Ymir, and closed the distance while lightning still scorched her. She slammed her fist into the warlock's face, then the other fist into a kidney, and then struck again at the orc's throat, since he liked that trick so much. Bolstered by Ethereal power and using Flames, each one of her strikes had delivered such cold that the orc suffered frostbite from Ymir's frozen wrath.

The warlock's frozen throat seemed to impede his spells. Aetheria delivered a strong kick to his middle. The roiling toxic power of Nidhogg infused the orc as she delivered a much more powerful follow-up to knock him across the room. Yellow caustic power around the warlock quickly built up, but just as it should have exploded, the warlock laughed and took in a deep breath. Somehow, the orc cleansed himself *and* absorbed the toxic power of the attack.

From the corner of her eye, Aetheria could see Arkaziel still battling the two redcaps. All three combatants showed wounds, but none of Ark's seemed dire. His thick dragon hide and Ethereal fur were potent defenses, while the redcaps had no inherent defense against Ark's claws; thus, their clothes were as bloody as their caps.

Aetheria switched tacks and charged the orc. Just before she got to him, she summoned a two-meter-tall wall section of red ice. It fell and killed the orc instantly. She tossed the ice wall back into her repository and sent the smeared orc along with it, then bounded over to help Arkaziel. Her friend could fly or levitate, regardless of form. Redcaps could not. She turned the floor to ice and slid by to suck the life force from the first redcap she encountered, the green-eyed one.

With the redcap distracted, Arkaziel's tail slammed a barbed end she didn't remember it having into the redcap's throat. At the same time, the grasping shadows of Consuming Darkness pulled the green-eyed redcap into Ark's belly.

The black-eyed redcap went all out on offense in response, but Arkaziel fended off its attacks and blasted it with a breath full of darkness. Aetheria didn't know how Ark did it, but the breath seemed to push the redcap's soul out of its body for just a split second—long enough for the StarMane to physically bite the redcap's body in half and finish it as it regained control of its body inside the dragon's mouth.

Aetheria watched it closely, aware she needed to diversify and expand her own fighting style.

Silence reigned across the room.

"Kill me, please." The skeleton doing alchemy drew their attention.

"You look pretty dead to me." Arkaziel and Aetheria said simultaneously and then glared at each other. Aetheria said, "Jinx!" and the cat-dragon sighed.

"They'll send more shamans and more redcaps. The orc and goblin tribes have wanted Raven's Hollow back for years. If you kill me, it will deny them my help with the Spores and their own cultivation. Redcaps can become powerful by consumption of certain potions."

"They're dead now. So you want out, fine. There any treasure down here before I send you back to the cycle?"

"There's a hidden door there, with all the goods the bandit party raided, as well as relics of the old orc empire. There's also a small chest hidden under the flagstones in my old cottage, if it still stands."

"Are you Gladia?"

"Yes."

"How'd you end up here?"

"After I made elixirs to stop their plan forty years ago, the redcaps came and killed me in the night. One of the orc warlocks bound my soul to my skeleton, and they forced me to work for them."

"I'm sorry you had to endure that. Know peace." Aetheria gestured and Frostfire, powered by the Primordial Flame of Aetherius, fell upon the skeleton and burned it out of the world.

"You should use your Flames more," Arkaziel noted.

"Won't that weaken them or slow their growth?"

"Not much. They won't regress when you've got them maxed out at a tier unless you try to share them with someone."

CHAPTER 66

The Master

The time it took for them to loot everything in the cave and cottage was minimal. Neither Arkaziel nor Aetheria were big on examinations of new loot. Now that she had successfully cast translation spells, identification and knowledge spells might be within her grasp. Nothing they found provided an immediate use, so it all went tumbling into the growing piles inside Aetheria's repository. *This is getting as bad as my* Skyrim *playthrough, where I cheated with infinite carry weight.* Within her repository were still the assorted spears she had found outside the Tower of Aetherius. Give a gamer infinite storage and they'll hoard.

High on the satisfaction of making a difference for the town of Raven's Hollow, they opened the gate to Floor 34. They appeared in what looked like an endless expanse of stars, standing on a city-sized rock. The rock floated through the space, although they had no way to tell if its movement was fast or slow. Atmosphere bound itself tightly to the rock, but there were much bigger concerns. The flow of Aether and Nether was minuscule. Mana, although of no use to Aetheria, was similarly vacant. She could not summon cold or create ice here. She might be able to make a thin layer of frost.

"I can only fly by flapping my wings here. What kind of primitive bullshit floor is this?" The StarMane did not take limitations on his power well. "I don't think I can use any magic here, beyond innate capabilities."

Aetheria considered and shifted her form a few times. Elf, cat-girl, and her Luxentian form all worked. Shapeshifting, at the least, remained in her abilities. A rake of her nail across her arm showed her regeneration worked as well. The unending fonts of Aether and Nether that flowed within her repository remained, as did the built-up Ethereal power her proto-core continually made. She didn't mention it, though. Arkaziel did not respond well to people doing things he could not. *I'll just go along with my abilities being "sealed," like magic is supposed to be here, unless I really need it.*

The rock on which they hurtled through space, while mostly barren, also included a few small cliffs, a pond, and light forest ahead.

"Let's go meet our challenge."

"Good idea. I want out of here as soon as possible."

Arkaziel shifted his form to the size of a panther and prowled along next to her. Aetheria noticed the tense muscles, the twitch of his tail, and the murderous gleam in his eyes. Ark would feel like meting out retribution for being forced to walk or flap his wings like a pedestrian creature.

There were only three buildings near the pond. A simple house, a shed, and a greenhouse. Fish jumped and splashed in the pond. The sound of crashing water filled the air but came from beyond the house. *Sounds like a waterfall.*

Closing her eyes for just a moment, Aetheria could see Gooseberry Falls in her mind, her father taking photos while she posed and strutted.

"It's been too long since my last guest. Did you make mortal enemies of the Tower Administrator, or are you here by virtue of being a Challenger? Or both?"

Aetheria and Arkaziel had walked right past the man who was sitting on the little dock in front of the house, fishing rod in hand. *Where did he get a straw hat in a place like this?*

"Uh. Bit of both, I suppose."

She studied him. A piece of straw between his lips. He appeared very nondescript, or average. He wore simple white-gray trousers and a loose shirt of the same material. No shoes. If she tried to focus on him more, her head swam.

"Don't think too hard about it. You can call me Master, for now, or Sun Wukong if you absolutely must use a name. Usually, when one of Aetherius's gits makes it this far, they have put all their work into their 'vast cosmic power' and neglected their bodies, relatively." The Master gestured at the rock and sky. "For a better training ground, we have suppressed magic here."

Oh, my god. I get to fight the Monkey King!

"So, is this where you beat the crap out of me until I put up a decent fight?"

"After dinner and a rest. No excuses about being tired that way. I hope both of you like fish."

"I love fish," Arkaziel chimed in.

"Let's make sure you stick to eating only what is supposed to be eaten, son of Azrael." The man waggled a finger at Ark, who looked displeased.

"You may take your leisure in the house for now or join me fishing." With that, the man lapsed into silence and left the duo to make their own choices.

Sleeping in a bed had become a treat for Aetheria. Her reluctance to leave the warm covers proved to be her first enemy of the next morning. Arkaziel snored at the foot of her bed, and she left him to sleep. The upcoming challenge seemed only for her.

The Master was already sitting outside by the dock, and he offered her a nod before standing.

"Use your shapeshifting as you see fit. Attack me with everything you have—strength, speed, cunning, training, secret moves taught to you by a mushroom—whatever cards you have, use them. Your enchantments won't work on me, nor will any magic you've hidden in your repository."

Aetheria frowned at the absolute confidence the man displayed, then made minor alterations to her form to increase both speed and strength. In the back of her mind, she assumed this would be like training sessions with Ascyn back in Solace, where she'd attack, he'd thwart her, and then explain better options for what to do.

With a deep breath, she bum-rushed the Master, intent on delivering a blow to his midsection. Her hand never even got close. The Master's left hand moved so fast she couldn't follow it. He gripped her wrist, and his other hand casually slapped her in the midsection. Aetheria had planned to do something clever like shapeshift another limb, or use plasticity with her leg to deliver a hammer kick. Instead, she blasted through the air and landed dozens of meters away on hard rock.

No lecture came. The Master just gestured for her to approach again.

It happened again and again. After the tenth time, when she could stand and speak again while her body knit together, she frowned at the Master.

"How am I supposed to even touch you? You're faster, stronger, and a better fighter than me."

He laughed. "You aren't as obstinate as most of the children who come here. They repeat the process for days, sometimes weeks, before exploding in a rant about how impossible this is."

"That's not an answer."

"No, it is not. How do you beat a superior opponent?"

"Trickery, cheating, or gang up on them."

"Will any of those work on me?"

"I doubt it. I might hurt you by using one of my Primordial Flames, but even that's questionable, I think." She examined the man. It had become no easier to study him. Her eyes wanted to slide off him and study the pond instead.

"It is possible that might work. Why have you not tried it?"

"Because you're fighting me without magic. Resorting to magic seems counterintuitive."

"I'm not using magic?"

"Are you?"

"Am I?"

Aetheria groaned and conjured four Flames of Aetherius around the Master to drain any energies away. His form rippled, and she found half monkey, half man before her, instead of a perfectly average man.

"You broke my illusion. Does it change your chances against me?"

"Not even slightly."

"So, what is your actual strategy to fight me?"

"Flee and fight another day?"

"Aetherius should have had more mortal children and fewer godspawn. That is all you needed to learn to earn my leave to continue to the next floor."

"That I might have to flee a fight sometimes?"

"Yes. Most of the lessons in this tower are non-lethal, or beatable with time. A few are insurmountable, such as me."

"I don't suppose you'd be willing to teach me some moves after all?" In her hand appeared some of the fruit she had taken from the ambrosial garden. Their sudden appearance carried the sweet smell of fruit, scents that promised seductive flavors and power.

Sun Wukong laughed. "Sure. You seem like a good kid."

Strangely, Arkaziel slept the whole two weeks, while Aetheria trained with the monkey man. In fact, the StarMane didn't wake until she carried him through the door to Floor 35.

The world around them shifted, and the duo appeared in a darkened room. At first, the only light was given by the glow of Aetheria's blue hair, although after a hiss and a flicker of movement, a gas lamp built into a wall of gears came to life and provided a minor amount of visibility.

"That jerk put me to sleep! I had the most wonderful dreams, but that's beside the point. You can't just go around putting people to sleep for weeks! I've had to pee for the last three days!"

The air was heavy with the scent of oil and hiss of steam. More lamps lit, revealing walls and ceilings covered in clockwork gears, all going *tic-tock, tic-tock*. The brass steam pipes that ran throughout the complex machinery rattled now and then. The lanterns disengaged from the wall and swung on chains. *Tic-tock, tic-tock*. The sound of groaning metal filled the pair's ears as sections of the vast chamber moved. The ceiling fell lower. The floor rose. Walls closed in.

"That way," Arkaziel grumbled and flew toward the only visible exit. Without the limitations of the previous floor in play, the cat could fly via magic without effort once more. Aetheria fell into a jog to keep up with the flying cat.

"I hate machinery like this. It is so inefficient and loud, and steam leaves hot splotches of water everywhere. Yes, it looks cool, but it's dumb! Dumb, I tell you!" Arkaziel ranted as they entered the tunnel. The prior room continued to shrink as they went farther, until a loud gong sounded at the same time as the floor, ceiling, and walls met to close off the starting room. Farther on, other large movements continued unseen.

"Steampunk is cool, you take that back!" Aetheria scolded Arkaziel lightly. Ahead of them, the path ended in a series of staggered bars and five hand cranks. "Do you think we need to do this the right way, or just get it done?"

"Doing things the right way on Thirty-Three didn't really pay off, did they? I say we do things our way. Improvisation, trickery, cunning, and clever use of your abilities are far more impressive than spending an hour in tedious trial and error to figure out the right sequence to get past this roadblock. If they wanted us to do it the old-fashioned way, it would've been back on the first couple of floors, before you came into your powers." Arkaziel's reasoning resonated with her. If they wanted mundane solutions, they should have said so somewhere.

She pulled a few levers to see how the mechanism worked. One bar rose into the ceiling, showing the other side of the tunnel. Arkaziel glowed white, and a moment later, the StarMane appeared on the far side and casually hit a button on that end. The bars separated and Aetheria joined him.

"I wish I could teleport."

"You need a medium. I teleport through light or shadow. You could probably do it through ice?"

"Your method seems a lot better than having to create ice to use to teleport."

"Obviously. Energy has a lot of advantages, but you've seen some weaknesses, too. All the Ethereal Cultivators I've ever met learned a pure Ethereal teleport in the fourth tier, as a Scion," Arkaziel said comfortingly.

You haven't met any others, you dumb cat! Genetic memories are weird.

"Alright. Let's cheese this place good." Aetheria grinned.

CHAPTER 67

The Mechanical Labyrinth

The tunnel continued on for another dozen meters, where it ended with a door. Each step toward the door carried more strange sounds to their ears. Aetheria would not be upset when the constant background noise of steam, gears, and the rattle of pipes faded from her awareness. It felt incongruous to deal with steam and clockwork technology after floor after floor of fantasy settings. *Are there going to be science fiction-level technology floors? Or even tech like on Earth?*

The door at the end of the tunnel had three embedded interlocking circles made of brass. Each circle had elaborately detailed engravings on it. Inside of each circle was a dial.

The two studied the symbols. The first circle had shapes: squares, triangles, hexagons. Each shape connected to several gears. The second circle showed a series of moons, stars, and planets with elaborate lines and dots representative of their orbital paths. The last circle showed the elements and iconography of the interaction between the elements. Across all three circles, there were some elements that looked connected.

"The fire symbol over here matches the triangle here," Aetheria noted. Arkaziel traced one of his claws through the air to denote other connections. Where he wove a claw, a line of light lingered to mark his thoughts.

Through rapid trial and error, they found the shapes matched to the number of elements interacting in the third circle. Meanwhile, the orbital bodies corresponded to the orbital paths for each shape-element pair. In no time at all, they had the outer, inner, and middle circles aligned. The door groaned, rumbled, and opened to reveal a workshop. The pair high-fived.

The workshop was smaller than the first room, more intimate, but no less intriguing. Shelves stocked with glass vials, brass instruments, gears, and cogs climbed high above Aetheria's head. A massive automaton dominated the middle of the room. Elaborate controls littered the automaton's back, and work benches around the colossal figure were full of tools, control panels, and strange contraptions.

Aetheria grinned at Arkaziel and walked across the room, dumping everything into her repository, the inactive automaton included. When the room had been picked clean, Arkaziel walked to the gate embedded in the wall, gained mass and size, and ripped the gate open and tossed it back to Aetheria, who sank it into her repository as well. *Never know when I'm going to need a ten-ton gate.*

The whole maze shook, machinery worked overtime, steam pipes burst, gears shattered. Shattered gears, broken transfer rods, any debris that came near, Aetheria froze and sent to her repository, while Arkaziel just destroyed it with a swipe of a clawed paw.

The next room went on for what looked like a kilometer. Massive conveyor belts took component pieces, presumably parts of the robot, to an assembly location where a veritable colossus of a machine absorbed ever more pieces into itself. A head the size of a school bus swiveled to look at the intruders. Flood lights in its eyes activated, illuminating each in a circular pool of light.

::To steal from Mechanus is to be deleted from existence. Face extinction.::

Although a mechanical voice issued the words, they were full of the fury and rage of a sentient being. Immediately, Aetheria discarded the possibility of vaulting the behemoth. Its presence felt like a change of pace, a response to their thefts from the last room. *I'd rather fight than do puzzles, anyway.*

The sounds of machinery filled the air and shutters opened in the middle of the robot's hand to reveal an aperture. A red light filled the robot's eyes in brief warning before the aperture powered up, and then a beam of destructive energy shot at Arkaziel and Aetheria. Aetheria froze it just before it contacted them. Then she stashed the conceptually frozen extinction beam in her repository, only to pull it back out, reoriented and thawed—which meant she could now shoot it back at the behemoth. The destructive blast struck the brass armor. The hiss of steam, and steam itself, filled the air as one of the internal steam pipes shattered.

Arkaziel inhaled a breath of air, and a coruscating beam of light and darkness flickering with red lightning tendrils slammed into the already damaged armor. Chain reaction explosions began inside the automaton, and pieces flew everywhere. Aetheria calmly went about gathering and storing them into her repository. It all might have trade value, or at the very least she could just drop it on people or build some modern art out of it.

The hiss of the steam labyrinth quieted. Lanterns dimmed. A humanoid man appeared. Aetheria pegged his aura at rank 4, and the man had flecks of gold in his eyes and a self-important posture. He was a few centimeters taller than she was. Although she'd never seen him in this form, his voice gave away his identity immediately.

"Sparkle Princess! You can't just go treating my challenges like they're a joke! Take it seriously."

Aetheria rolled her eyes at the Tower Administrator. Arkaziel's form shimmered oddly.

"Pretty sure I can. In fact, I'm pretty sure it's *your* job to make floors that not only are a challenge to the children of Aetherius but also teach them meaningful lessons and how to use their vast and varied powers."

The Tower Administrator frowned at her, considering a retort. Aetheria decided it was time to nip this in the bud.

"Dad? Daddy! I need a witness, if you could come out."

To everyone's shock, another man appeared, in the form Aetherius had taken when they had talked previously. The Administrator paled.

"It's only fair that a doting father sees his daughter after her mother gets to visit. Leave it to Nyx to supersede me in my own tower." Aetherius laid it on thick, amusement dancing in his eyes. The Administrator seemed about to swallow his tongue, missing all the humor between their exchange.

The poor Administrator had no way to know that Aetherius (aka Pete) had been Aetheria's friend for over a decade while playing *EFWO* together, and had taken their relationship further into the realms of adopted father/daughter by reincarnating her as his own daughter. There were scores of useless demigods laying around Creation, according to Arkaziel, and the Administrator no doubt had assumed Aetheria was just another one of those, not someone actually important to Aetherius.

"I want to challenge this guy to a fair fight, and if I win, I want him to never take part in any of my tower climbs ever again."

"You can't challenge Tower Administra—" The demigod's mouth was suddenly sealed shut by a glance from Aetherius.

"That sounds delightful," the god said. A massive screen and two controllers appeared. Aetheria grinned at seeing the title screen for a certain kart-racing game populated with plumbers, princesses, and lizards.

"Best out of four is the winner," the Primordial declared, with no room for argument.

"This is preposterous!" The Administrator's mouth had opened briefly, only to be sealed once more with an annoyed glance from Aetherius.

"You've already broken a lot of rules, Superbia, which I've let slip because I didn't want to embarrass you to the point of sending you back to your mother, but here we are. Play the game. If you win, I'll halve your contract time. If you lose, you'll be *bound* to the terms."

"She cheated! The Blue shell is bullshit!" Superbia raged twenty minutes later. His mouth was promptly melded together again.

"That's three out of four for Aetheria." Aetherius waved a hand and golden-green light sheathed Superbia. The demigod raged against the binding. The air shimmered and Arkaziel, in full forty-five-meter-long draconic glory, ate the demigod while he was bound and helpless.

"Pity. He wasn't a poor Administrator for regular Climbers. Couldn't hack it with more prestigious sorts, it seems." Aetherius laughed and shrugged. "Maybe his next incarnation will be an improvement."

The Primordial's lack of care about the former Administrator being eaten struck Aetheria as strange. *Even if they come back, why do all these beings seem so unconcerned about it? It sure seems like gods die a lot more frequently than should be possible for divine beings...*

Aetherius noticed her discomfort. "No longer are you shackled by the unyielding chains of Samsara, my 'daughter.' You've transcended a cycle that even the mightiest of us remain captive to. It is a rare and extraordinary privilege you have been gifted, for your spirit now roams free, unburdened by the ceaseless ebb and flow of life and death. You see, even the gods themselves are not immune to the relentless turning of the Wheel of Life. They may be felled like the golden stalks of wheat, yet, in time, they too shall rise anew, reborn and destined to be reaped once more."

"You didn't make it sound like any big deal when you offered me this chance."

The Primordial laughed. "We pinned a lot of hopes on you, well beyond Grief, Aetheria. So far, you're outpacing our wildest expectations."

"Expectations are no fun. Isn't saving a world from Nyx's daughter enough?"

"Nothing like that. We just have high hopes for the path you are going to build for yourself."

"You make it sound like the whole 'save Grief from the tyranny of Oizys' quest isn't even the main reason you gave me this chance." Aetheria squeezed the bridge of her nose lightly.

An ungodly, loud sound broke the air like thunder. Arkaziel's massive belch drew stunned laughter from Aetheria and Aetherius.

"Thanks, Pete." Sincerity with a smile was all she offered Aetherius.

"It is what it is, Aes. Ignore the Administrator, climb the tower your way. I think your approach is the best way to take these things on. This is no mere game, despite the warped perceptions of some Administrators. This tower is supposed to teach you to live and grow. It is to be a journey of evolution. The manner of your climb is yours to decide." In a flare of light, Aetherius vanished. In the space he had occupied now stood the door to Floor 36.

"What'd he taste like?" Aetheria eyed the StarMane.

"Sadness, with a bitter aftertaste, like radicchio." Arkaziel rolled his large, scaled shoulders before he shrank down to his house cat form.

"Sounds awful. Need some time to digest him before we go through the doorway?"

"Yes, and some better-tasting food. Do we have any ambrosial fruit left? Oh, and a hunk of Nidhogg. I'll make Ambrosia-Basted Nidhogg with Ambrosia Sauce, paired with those starwhisp petals I picked outside Raven's Hollow. We should still have some elven wine from your flying castle, and I could whip up a dessert using the mallow." Arkaziel laughed a little crazily.

"You really took those stories about Gordon and Anthony to heart, didn't you?" Aetheria shook her head but sorted her repository to get the cat what he wanted.

"I'm going to be the first Michelin Star StarMane. If you didn't want me to look up to them, you shouldn't have made them sound so cool when you told me their stories while we fought demons."

"That would require us going to Earth. Also, I may have totally exaggerated some stuff about those stories. I doubt Gordon ever wrestled a fifty-foot snake, or that Anthony ever fought a group of assassins. I got pretty bored for a while on the nineteenth floor."

"We'll get there, eventually. Unless one of my relatives eats it before then."

Aetheria ruffled Arkaziel's head. "I think it'll be okay. Make your fancy-pants second lunch."

While Arkaziel busied himself with meal preparation, Aetheria settled into a meditative pose and considered her latest Flame. The Flame of Khaos had barely gained any energy yet. It took in minute amounts of Aether, Nether, and Ethereal power, but it did not seem to be truly hungry for any of the three energies. Until it reached the first stage, she could not use the Flame of Khaos. She was uncertain about the actual name of this Flame, too. Based on the vision, were Khaos and Chronos even actually Primordials?

Ugh. I feel like I've been handed a never-ending puzzle. The moment I get a glimpse of an answer to a previous conundrum, I am told of a new conflicting account of the forces and players behind Creation. Maybe none of these cooks had anything to do with Creation, and they're just blathering for all time about something they didn't even have anything to do with. Wouldn't that be fitting? They won't talk about this so-called Overgod, after all.

Is this all just a divine prank? Or maybe reality really is just too complicated for me to actually understand at this point? Grand complexity that will be revealed and peeled away as I ascend the ever-higher paths of the Winding Way. Or maybe that's the point of the Winding Way to begin with. To take you on a course past the myriad illusions and conflicting accounts of Creation? A journey to find the cosmic enigma. The needle in the haystack?

Or maybe, just maybe, there is no unifying truth in any of this bullshit and it's Khaos's world and we just live in it.

CHAPTER 68

Chamber of Stone

So, what happens now? Is the tower on autopilot?" Aetheria and Arkaziel stood before the door. Arkaziel's meal had been a culinary celebration worthy of epic poetry, or so the StarMane had proclaimed. Fed, napped, brushed, and eager for murder, Arkaziel stood ready, his eyes bright.

"There's more than one Administrator, otherwise we would've been annoyed by that want-to-be Wisconsinite much more often. Did I use that right?"

"Yeah, perfectly. So, you think we'll have a problem with other Admins?"

"Nah. Aetherius laid down the law, and it is his tower. Even if he isn't actively watching, which he probably is, overriding the will of the tower's owner is poor job security for Administrators. Although, I look forward to eating anyone who didn't learn from the last guy."

"Onward and upward, then." They stepped through the doorway to Floor 36.

They appeared in a magnificent chamber that stretched out far beyond the reach of Aetheria's gaze. She and Ark were struck by the sheer scale and grandeur of the space, with its towering, vaulted ceilings adorned with intricate frescoes depicting epic tales of heroes and gods. The hall was bathed in a soft, ethereal glow, an other-worldly light that cast dramatic shadows on the cold stone floor.

Row upon row of lifelike statues stood sentinel along the length of the hall, each meticulously crafted to represent a unique figure. These statues, fashioned from marble, granite, and other precious materials, showcased various warriors, scholars, mythical creatures, and even gods, all frozen in time. Each figure had been rendered with astonishing attention to detail, from the folds of their clothing to the subtle expressions on their faces, as if the sculptor had captured a living being in the moment of their greatest triumph or deepest despair.

"These things are so going to come alive and attack us, aren't they?" Aetheria quipped, but she still walked down the red carpet that seemed to go on forever.

"No doubt about it," Arkaziel agreed from her shoulder, lazily blinking sleepy eyes at the statues.

Their voices echoed down the chamber. When they faded, a heavy pressure fell thick upon the room. The oppressive silence attacked their senses, ready to smother and suffocate them. Thankfully, the click of Aetheria's boots against the floor warded off the silence, at least temporarily.

The first statue they approached did not come to life and attack them. Someone had masterfully carved the stone into the likeness of a female elf. The stone told no tales regarding what color her hair might have been, or the hue of her eyes, but it captured a fierce expression that refused to go unacknowledged. The woman had the look of a warrior-mage, and the weapon she held was a strange pole-arm crossed with a sword. *Maybe they called it a sword staff?*

The base of the statue had a name. The words swam and rearranged themselves into the divine language, Ath.

"Looks like the names are important enough to have a translation field in effect," Aetheria noted to Arkaziel, who yawned at her, bored.

"Karieth Sylveria. What was your story?" Aetheria murmured lightly, about to move to the next statue. Surprisingly, the statue answered.

"I stood against the Sixth Great Green Tide alongside the Imperator. We cut down orcs like wheat, yet like the real tides, the waves seemed unending. I held the flank of the Farwalking Paladin and the Imperator on the day of the war chief's defeat. When the charges came against the Imperator, I escorted his family to the tower. After establishing the contract with the tower, I climbed higher. Perhaps if I reached the top, I could release the Imperator from the punishment of the Elders and the machinations of Oizys.

"Although I mastered the Art of Aether, I still fell. I fell on the fiftieth floor of the tower. The bosses of the tower are difficult for a solo Climber, and my ego convinced me to stay on my own."

"That's unfortunate. I met the shackled ghost of your former Imperator and intend to free him from confinement and restore him to life. Can you provide me with any advice?"

"If the gods answer your prayers, one of the many bosses of the fiftieth floor is a phoenix. I prayed mightily to Aetherius on the forty-fifth floor and earned a chance to fight the phoenix. To win against a creature that rebirths itself proved to be difficult for me. Yet if you can beat the phoenix, they say its power may undo death."

"Thank you, Karieth Sylveria. Are there any words you would have me carry to Werylin for you?"

"No. Would you like me to join your side for this challenge?"

"What is the nature of this challenge?"

"You must choose your allies. When you have chosen five, we will fight the tower's choice of enemies, and this will continue until the team you choose wins without your intervention."

"I see. It would be my pleasure to have you join my side, Karieth Sylveria. My name is Aetheria."

The elven woman morphed from stone to flesh, saluted Aetheria, and fell in behind her.

"Are there any elite warriors here who you would recommend I recruit?"

"I may not speak of others, Lady Aetheria. I am sorry."

Aetheria gazed across the rows and her eyes rested on a sight she liked—angelic wings that made her think of Aoibhe. She approached the statue.

"Who are you... Sarielle?"

"I was called Sarielle the Just, angelic sorceress. I was a messenger of the gods until corruption came for my world. I could not defeat the corruption, so I fled within the tower to earn the power to defeat it, or to use my wish to cleanse the corruption. I fell on the one hundredth level, minutes from victory. My niece later succeeded where I failed, but it was too late for our world."

"Was your niece's name Aoibhe?"

"Yes, it was. I sense your ties to her, Flamebearer. Would you have me as an ally?"

Aetheria grinned and nodded.

Thus, Aetheria assembled her team: Karieth Sylveria the battlemage, Sarielle the angelic sorceress, Kael the runesmith, Thalia the centaur paladin, and Zanar the half-demon warlock.

"Now what happens?" Aetheria inquired of them, as row upon row of statues slid backward. In the now-opened space, the floor descended to make an arena. On the far side stood a gate, which opened, and five figures emerged. A voice she did not recognize announced the identities of their opponents.

"First up, we have Sarenna the Witch Queen. Who's the one who made a pact with a devil lord, then tried to flee into a tower to break it *and* keep her power? That's right. It's Sarenna." The woman was a race Aetheria didn't recognize, with red skin and black markings.

"Next up, we have Priestess Xaphina, the dark elf who sought power to bring about the end of her world! Between you and me, I don't blame her. I'd want to end the world too if I worshipped a god as awful as hers."

"Who's this? Behold, Cowzane the Gladiator. Doesn't seem that evil, right? Outside of his habit of killing everyone put in a ring with him, he also poops in public. There are few greater evils than public defecation. There he goes now."

"About to strike Cowzane is Thorgar, orc warlord. One of many orc warriors who have entered the tower to try to kill the descendants of the Amaryllis clan over the years. Behold the intense disdain between Karieth and Thorgar. It's delightful!"

"Finally, we have... ugh, really? Baron Vrynn, the Dreaded Vampire. He's a rich dandy whose only power is his familiars. This happens when you just throw a dart at the board for the last choice."

"You guys got this." Aetheria patted each of her allies on the shoulder as they jumped down into the pit to square off against the other team. When they did so, the scenery changed. Instead of a vast chamber, they now stood in a dark, cursed forest. Aetheria and Arkaziel watched from above, still standing on a stone outcropping not part of the new battleground.

"Three... two... one... fight!"

The first to charge forward was Karieth Sylveria. Bolts of powerful magic flew from her sword staff. Behind her, Sarielle took to the air, hands raised in divine pleading, and in response, holy fire and radiant bolts of power flew from her outstretched hands. Behind Karieth came Kael, Thalia, and Zanar. Kael unleashed a barrage of enchanted runes, each able to explode with amazing force. Thalia's centaur legs closed the distance swiftly, her holy spear and shield awash in the radiant glory of holy energy. A large contrast to Zanar, who conjured demons from the abyss to charge into the line of villains who stood ready to meet them.

Not to be outdone by a mere warlock, the witch queen conjured a horde of devils to take on those summoned by the warlock. Xaphina chanted dark incantations and prayers. The sky darkened, the ground trembled. Cowzane charged to meet Thalia in direct combat—cow versus horse. The orc and the foppish vampire flanked them.

Karieth's speed and magical power were impressive, and she had no intention of letting Thorgar flank anyone. She slammed into the orc and began a flashy duel of axe versus sword staff. Vrynn, however, was not a capable second, unlike Sarielle. A hole in the darkening clouds opened, and a pillar of radiant light shot down to vaporize the vampiric lord in a single hit. Kael and Thalia pushed toward Sarenna and Xaphina, but even with Zanar's demons, the witch queen's devils were too many to break through with just the two of them. Zanar remained in the back line, where he summoned more demons and cast a curse upon Xaphina.

The dark elf's apocalyptic prayers were interrupted, her words now a random mish-mash of nothing that made any sense. This pushed Sarenna into a rage, and a massive bone devil rose from the ground in an explosion of ash.

Devils fought against demons, and the demons were not winning. Thalia and Kael pushed back against the horde of devils, but the mighty bone devil prevented them from reaching Sarenna. A crack of blinding lightning crashed from the heavens into Thorgar, then chained into the devil hordes. While stunned by such a shocking attack, Karieth struck Thorgar down. Not to be outdone, a blasting ring of holy power radiated outward from Thalia and Kael, cast by Sarielle. Devils in the vicinity were ripped to shreds by the joint holy and lightning spells.

A second devil rose from the darkened ground. This one looked humanoid, and its mere presence sucked in the life forces of the heroes. With each second it existed, it ensured victory for the witch queen. But it did not exist for long. Thalia seemed the natural opponent for the devil, but she was locked in combat with Cowzane, and Kael still was engaged with her first devil. It was instead the warlock who spoke a single word that no one could quite hear, but it annihilated the devil entirely.

Sarenna truly became enraged. She screamed like a madwoman about true names and unleashed waves of pure destructive power at the heroes. None fell, but all were weakened, until a burst of holy life flowed across the team from Sarielle. "Be healed!" she exclaimed.

When the dust settled, four of the heroes remained. Cowzane had dispatched Kael. The room shifted. Before Aetheria could congratulate the remaining members of her team, they were once more unspeaking statues.

"Could've let me say thank you first, you know?" Aetheria chided the unseen Tower Administrator, before she offered a bow to her team of statues. "Thank you," she said.

The door to Floor 37 opened before her.

CHAPTER 69

Temptation

Floor 37, at the very least, had a magnificent view. Aetheria whistled as she gazed down the mountain to take in what she could from the incredible height. Once upon a time, her stomach would have quailed and protested at such a view. Knowledge that you could fly via magical wings, or simply shapeshift wings to fly manually, had all but eradicated her reaction to high spaces.

Arkaziel heaved a great sigh when he looked behind them. "Monks. I hate monks. They taste bad, they are boring, and they have no good loot or food. These guys aren't even going to have any good honey or wine on the top of a frozen mountain like this."

Aetheria turned and studied the temple before them. It reminded her of images she'd seen in university, or on the social media accounts of old friends who had decided to see the world. The largest resonance she had with the temple, though, was the call back to the cultivation novels she'd read. She fully expected the place to be populated by warrior monks cultivating an ancient fighting style. But when she approached the temple, she noticed very few signs of life.

No tracks in the snow lead to or from the entrance. The only sign of anyone having been here in recent time were her own footprints in the snow. The wooden outer door of the temple was covered from top to bottom in carved reliefs. Initially, she could not make heads or tails of the elaborate work, but the more she looked at the strange fractal design, the odd geometric figures, the more it seemed to make sense to her. *This temple is dedicated to the Ethereal in some fashion.*

A thin layer of ice over the bottom of the door was the only obstacle to its opening. Once the ice was shattered, the door swung open easily to reveal not an inner courtyard, as Aetheria had expected, but a spherical tunnel that led into the monastery. The tunnel was filled with elaborate fractal designs, much as the door had been, and opened into the temple proper to reveal that the building contained only a solitary chamber.

Abstract patterns filled the floor and ceiling, which had no true walls, as the chamber was half a sphere, and there was no delineation of where the walls ended and the ceiling began. A large, rectangular altar filled the center of the chamber. It was half white, half black, and made from crystallized Aether and Nether. The altar sat upon a square dais, each quarter of which was a different color: red, blue, brown, and yellow. From each of these segments, Aetheria could feel a resonance with one of the four basic elements.

"Those patterns are hard to look at, aren't they?" She shook her head a little and squeezed the bridge of her nose.

"All I see are stars and constellations. What's so bad about that?" Arkaziel gave her a quizzical look before his eyes slipped shut again.

"I see fractal patterns, weird shapes, abstract art. It's really loud."

"So cast your little language spell and change it." Arkaziel's words sounded almost like a dare.

"I wouldn't recommend that. No doubt you would survive, but even with the gifts you have been given, the time lost to heal the damage to your mind would be significant." The voice came from nowhere and everywhere. It sounded serene and ancient, and reminded Aetheria of the tone grandparents took with young children.

"Hello? Who are we talking with?"

+*I didn't hear anything, Ria. You going mad from the abstract patterns?*+

~*Old man voice, suggested I not translate the room, or I risk madness.*~

+*Oh, fun.*+

"You may call me Vihara Ananta. Once, I held on to mortality and flesh, like you. Our sect sought to become one with the infinite void, but instead I became one with this temple."

"Cripes, that is an enormous gap between intent and result! How'd that happen?"

"Our understanding of reality was flawed. We knew nothing of the Origin, only rumors of the Ethereal, and thought Aether and Nether to be the pinnacle of Creation and destruction. One by one, we sought Oneness and failed. I was the last to make the attempt, and cowardice left me unable to give up the material world. My ascendance failed, and I became bound to the temple. These designs are what I have learned in the long years since, from my own observations and knowledge gained from travelers such as yourself."

"Ouch, that's rough, Vihara. Why does my companion see a different inscription than I do?"

"He understands the meaning filtered through the knowledge of his ancestors. You see as I see; he sees as his kind sees."

"Your symbology is pretty good, but your acknowledgment of the Ethereal, Aether, and Nether seems flawed. You can't just push the two together like that and expect it to become Ethereal power. You must use an external spark to meld them together, like this." Aetheria held a hand out and twined strands of Aether and Nether together. Once she had a decent-sized mixed wick, she applied a spark of Aetherflame to ignite the process, which produced a small amount of Ethereal power at the cost of larger amounts of Aether and Nether.

"I see. Other visitors have alluded to this process, but none have ever freely showed me such a method. The efficiency seems low."

"It is. To make Ethereal energy in this way is the hallmark of those who are only at the second tier of the Ethereal Path. I've been told that Ethereal energy has been separated into Aether and Nether as a safeguard for reality—if that's true or not, I don't really know. I know that tiering up carries risks of destructive power capable of destroying whole worlds."

The block of crystallized Aether and Nether altered into a more liquid-like state, in which they flowed into one another in precariously controlled chaos, orchestrated by a meticulous will. Aetheria watched with great interest as Vihara controlled the forces with a level of skill she lacked. *I guess he's been at this for a very long time, though. Trying to walk the Ethereal Path without even knowing the name of your path is probably pretty time-consuming. How many people run out of time before even making it to the second tier of the path? No wonder many would opt for more well-known paths.*

Aetheria watched the process, intrigued as Vihara split the block into two sections, no longer vertically split, but horizontally at two-thirds up. A spark of energy she couldn't identify before it was gone caused the top third to flare into crystallized Ethereal power.

"That registers a lot closer."

"It worked. Something so simple and easy to overlook. Millenia spent trying to join powers through harmonization, synchronicity, rhythms, and frequencies. All wasted."

"It wasn't wasted, Vihara. Your control of energy is amazing. Your progress should be remarkable now. You're very attuned to the Ethereal already, more so than I am."

"In my sect we believed creations such as this have a lingering effect. A brush with one of these creations can aide in a breakthrough. Meditate upon my new Ethereal center, and we shall share more knowledge."

"Don't mind if I do." Aetheria grinned. She was so close to the construction of her Gate and the breakthrough into Tier Three. This seemed like the exact thing that would help her during her final stages of attunement. Once her repository and soul became attuned to the Origin, there were few steps left beyond finding a place of power to do it in. This temple wasn't that place, though. She feared if she created her Gate here, it would destroy Vihara and potentially the entire floor.

+You could just break through here. Let this temple be the fodder for your cultivation, Ria. That is what most people would do, especially after you just helped it break through.+

~What are you, the devil? That isn't the way we roll, Arkaziel. We're the good guys, opposing an evil goddess, saving a world, and looking fabulous as we do it. Not sacrificing people just to get ahead week or two ahead. The easy road is for the weak. We stick to principles and take a harder path.~

Arkaziel went silent for a few moments. Draconic arrogance at war with feline laziness. Aetheria scratched under his chin and gave him a kiss on the top of his furry head.

~If you're going to be the biggest StarMane to wander the universe, you've got to rise to that occasion, buddy. We punch up, not down.~

+I don't punch at all. What does, punch up, mean?+

~ We don't pick fights with people weaker than us without reason. We keep that for people as powerful or more powerful than ourselves. ~

+I'm still eating gods, even if some of them might be weaker than me.+

~Fine, I guess. But let's stick to punching up as much as we can with living people. ~

Arkaziel snorted, which Aetheria took as agreement when he didn't want to admit to constraints placed on his activities. There was always a small part of her that wondered how much of these discussions and lessons actually stuck with the StarMane, but he seemed content to remain her partner despite her altruism in the face of his laziness and greed.

"Alright, Vihara. Let's do a little meditation. Show me your interpretations of all these fractals and patterns, please."

Aetheria hopped onto the platform, where she crossed her legs as she dropped into a comfortable position. She opened her mind to the universe, to her surroundings, and tried to let the strange abstract designs make sense. The longer she considered the patterns, the more she gained minor insights into the nature of Aether and Nether. Vihara Ananta's comprehension of the two components of the Ethereal was comprehensive. She had not spent long pondering on things like divinity or dark divinity, yet lacking access to higher information, the monks of the temple had spent lifetimes on the subject.

The seemingly unlimited amounts of Aether and Nether within her repository suddenly made more sense to Aetheria. As a proto-inner world, it had the same energy presences existing space would have, even if it wasn't realized into a true inner world yet. It also occurred to her that there would be some form of divinity/dark divinity equivalent in the Ethereal ranks. *Is that what separates the Primordials from gods? Then mortals live in the world of mana? What does that mean for Aoibhe and me? Are we destined to be "more" than normal people?* Aetheria burst into laughter. *Who am I kidding? I can't even pretend to be normal anymore.*

The break in her meditation made her aware that small tendrils of presence were trying to slip into her mind, but were rebuffed at every touch by the sheer power of the four Primordial Flames that burned inside her. A quick scan revealed that all the tendrils traced back to the temple, to Vihara.

Aetheria sighed and stood up. Thin chains of Ethereal power attempted to hold her in place, but she broke them with a lazy gesture of her hand infused with Ethereal power.

"They wasted your powers on you, soft-hearted woman. Give me your body, so that it might live up to the potential the gods have unfairly given you. You do not deserve so much power!"

"Thank you for the insights, Vihara Ananta. Unfortunately for you, I gave you gifts freely, and you repay kindness by attempting to steal my body." On her shoulder, Arkaziel gave a light hiss at the temple, but otherwise left retribution to his companion.

"Freeze." Aetheria pushed her domain to its maximum range of fifteen meters. With a flood of power from her soul aperture into her body, her aura flared to life. Red snowflakes crystallized around her in a flurry. In moments, a blizzard spun around her and kept expanding outward in all directions. The only part of the temple that didn't immediately drop into sub-zero temperatures was the few feet around Arkaziel.

"You can't freeze a temple on top of a frozen mountain, you nitwit." Vihara attacked her psyche in earnest, yet even so, he kept being stopped effortlessly by the protective power of the Flames.

"'Some say the world will end in fire', / Some say in ice,'" Aetheria said quietly, quoting one of her favorite poems by Robert Frost. The blizzard around her continued to build up. Everything in the room dropped closer and closer to absolute zero.

"'From what I've tasted of desire / I hold with those who favor fire.'" Trickles of aetheric power fled outward into the Ethereal blizzard, followed by the dark threads of Nether. "'But if it had to perish twice, / I think I know enough of hate / To say that for destruction ice / Is also great / And would suffice.'"

The tendrils of Aether and Nether flared up with a spark of Aetherflame, and the entire blizzard became turbo-charged. The storm orbited Aetheria and wreaked total destruction on the temple. When the red snowflakes faded and the sunshine shone down on her and Arkaziel again, the whole temple was gone, down to the last atom.

"Oh, that was great. Except the poetry. Well. Maybe it was okay, but I still think a quip or one-liner would've been far more appropriate. Regardless, good job. Very Asura of you."

"I'm glad you approve of my annihilation of a sentient temple that tried to take me over. I'm in the mood to punch something now. Let's hope Floor Thirty-Eight obliges me."

The doorway appeared next to the duo.

CHAPTER 70

Tethorian Terror

Arkaziel and Aetheria appeared on a wagon. They were seated in the driver's seat, Aetheria holding the reins of large oxen. Behind them, underneath the cooler and shaded wagon bed, sat a small humanoid. Aetheria presumed him to be a gnome. With his reddish hair and beady, inquisitive eyes, it was a stretch to call the gnome handsome. Yet there was a ruggedness there that seemed out of place for a gnome. He wore a set of clothes well suited to traveling, rough and patched with many pockets, and several tool belts full of small contraptions and hand tools.

Prairie grasses swayed in the wind around them. Most of the grass exceeded the height of the wagon, and Aetheria thought anything could be hiding in it. The path the wagon was on had been made long ago and not maintained in decades. The oxen were slow, but the pace made the ride smoother. *Any faster and I'd be regenerating my spine every few meters.*

Silence reigned for a few kilometers until the gnome finally chirped up.

"We're almost there! I can feel the magic of the Maze of Argaulis. When we make it to the center and I activate my device, I shall go down in history as the greatest gnome Wizgineer in all of history! Me, Tethoril the Terrible! Aha hahaha!"

"That's a pretty evil laugh there, Mr. Tethoril the Terrible," Aetheria quipped quietly.

The gnome looked shocked that the hired help dare talk back to him. Who in their right mind would talk back to Tethoril the Terrible, the mightiest Wizgineer in all the land?! Apparently, the stupid, ugly blue-haired human, that is who.

The gnome coughed when Aetheria didn't back down or supplicate herself to his majesty.

"Right, well. Prepare yourself, mercenary. We shall navigate the maze as soon as we arrive. With my Magitech Mappinator we shall breeze through the dangers of the maze, set up my device, and make history! Why, if you're properly dedicated to maintaining my safety, I'll even see that you make it into the history books. At least as a footnote."

"How benevolent of you. So tell me about the Maze of Argaulis. What are we going to be facing? Enemies, or just traps and puzzles?"

"Ugh. Mercenaries. So dumb." Tethoril the Terrible's contempt was great. "This is what I get for not working with the Expedition Guild for this job, but their ten percent finder's fee is beyond ridiculous! So here I am, the greatest Wizgineer of all time, slumming with illiterate mercenaries." After another two minutes of inane ranting under his breath, the gnome finally returned to answering the question posed to him.

"Argaulis, the greatest wizard of the mighty empire of Caldoun, made the Maze. Because you are an illiterate idiot and uneducated in the ways of history, know that the Caldoun Empire was the most ancient and powerful of all civilizations to exist on our continent. A continent is a large body of land. The Caldoun are said to have ascended to godhood through a great magic ritual that destroyed the single Great Continent and created the modern world as we know it."

"Hm," Aetheria grunted, not that interested in listening to the gnome's monologue.

"We've long theorized the maze is actually the trigger to transport yourself to their last stronghold, the Skycity of Atlanta."

"... Did you say Atlanta?"

"Yes, Atlanta! Did I stutter?! While many have made it to the center of the maze over the years, none have activated the device at its center. That is where I, the bestest, most fantastic, greatest person to live, come in. I, Tethoril the Terrible, shall become Tethoril the *Truly* Terrible as I begin my reign from the Skycity of Atlanta, with all the powerful technology and magics of the lost city of Atlanta! Haha!"

Aetheria just looked ahead and rolled her eyes. Maybe she'd let Arkaziel eat the gnome after they secured the doorway to the next level. Whatever the political climate looked like here, surely they didn't deserve to be ruled over by a megalomaniac magic engineer with a narcissistic personality disorder.

"We are here, boss," she noted with a sigh and flicked the reins to get the oxen to park in one of the delineated squares with a hitching post outside a stable. Aetheria had expected a wild place with a barely seen entrance to a strange maze. Instead, there were five inns with large stables, street vendors, and many people meandering around. She narrowed her red eyes at the gnome.

"I thought you said there would be danger?"

"Only when we get to the lost city of Atlanta. Shhh."

Arkaziel cracked one eye to look up at Aetheria, then she felt the laughter through their bond. She fell in with the gnome, who made her carry all the heavy packs into the maze after he argued with a stable boy about the cost of parking the wagon. The maze itself required them to pay a gold piece each to enter, and the paths were well manicured, and signposts marked every intersection with sights to see and the proper path. There were no traps, no dangers, beyond the threat of death by boredom while being stuck behind slow packs of guided tours full of the elderly and the very young.

Hours later, it was their turn to enter the center of the maze, a ten-meter-square area with only one thing filling the space. A massive metal sphere sat on a dais, perfectly balanced. When Aetheria put her hand against it and pushed a little, it completely ignored the force and stayed in place.

"Alright, mercenary, guard the entrance so no one disturbs us! We only have five minutes, and I take ten to set everything up."

Aetheria resisted the urge to sigh.

~Can you throw an illusion up over the entrance to keep people away?~

+I can. They won't even know where the proper entrance was. It'll be hours before anyone figures out my amazing trick.+

Rather than doubt the genius of Arkaziel, she ruffled his head and waited for the spell to take effect. After that, she made a show of pretending to be busy so the gnome would leave her alone. If the insane Wizgineer wanted to blow himself up, she would let him. He could do it himself and not let him blame her for his own incompetence in setting up.

The contraptions that the gnome organized looked overall like a still to Aetheria, but Tethoril kept muttering, changing dials, and adjusting tubing before he started adding liquids to it. Then he chanted incantations, and the strange still and liquids glowed. The sphere vibrated in resonance with the magic. Lines of eldritch inscription lit up on the sphere, and the still sprayed magical liquid all over it. The hissing and stench were brutal to hear and smell, and then the sphere opened and emitted a flare of bright white light that seared the retinas.

When Aetheria's eyes had healed, she discovered they were no longer in the maze. The air was thin, clouds surrounded them, and they stood on a platform in the middle of a park. Massive spires and skyscrapers filled the cityscape of the lost Atlanta. Tethoril the Terrible started laughing like he'd lost his mind, and began jumping up and down and excitedly talking to himself in a language Aetheria could not understand. Without so much as a word to his mercenaries, Tethoril took off toward the tallest spire.

Aetheria could have dashed in front of him, but she just walked after him. With little to no warning, the air split with the force of an object breaking the sound barrier. A long metal spike, larger than the gnome, suddenly pierced his torso and pinned him to the ground. The gnome died before she could even react.

+There's a red dot on your forehead.+ "Oh, hell no." Instinctively, Aetheria tried to shove the entire floating city into her repository. Unexpectedly, it worked, and she fell. With a lazy sigh, Arkaziel grew and caught her, even as she formed wings.

"Thanks, Ark."

"No problem. I'm shocked that actually worked. Actually, did it work? Or did we get ejected?"

"It worked. Wow, that's just a massive death trap. Railguns, lasers, explosives... damn. What was a hi-tech flying city doing in a magical world?"

"Weird. How do we get out of here?" Arkaziel had just been levitating them, since he wasn't certain of what, precisely, had happened.

"Oh, well..." Aetheria gestured and created a platform of ice that floated on its own. The doorway to Floor 39 opened. "That counted as a completion for the floor. I'm going to have to spend a couple of days cataloguing all the crap in that lost city until I find what was supposed to be so interesting about it."

For a few brief moments, Aetheria thought she heard laughter fill the floor. Surely, it was her imagination and not an observer such as Aetherius or one of the other Administrators openly expressing their amusement at their solution to the problem. *I suppose after Aetherius approved of my cheesing things, they can't exactly force me to do things the way they mean it to be done. Thanks again, Pete.*

"At this rate, you're going to have an inner world full of flying cities. The people of Nivathar are lucky you didn't steal their city, too," Arkaziel joked, yet through their bond she could sense the cat was actually annoyed. Apparently, vanishing an entire city qualified as too much, even in his book. *Or is he just mad that there was nothing to eat?*

"Why don't we push through to Floor Forty-Five, and you can catalogue Atlanta there while I eat all of their food?"

"That should work, I guess. I doubt there was anything in the city we needed immediately, anyway." The moment she said the words, Aetheria regretted it. Not because anything happened. It just felt as though she had set herself up for failure by saying flag phrases. She'd spent so long in the tower now that things like flags, tropes, and Earth felt very long ago.

On Floor 39, she appeared on a cloud. Everything felt off. She couldn't see. The bond with Arkaziel had been dulled—only their empathic bond worked. Her body had been forced to take on a different form, and she quickly realized she was a dragon. A very large dragon, yet she felt agile and faster than almost any other form she had ever been in. The soft clouds had an abrasive quality against her new scales they previously had not on her last visit. More importantly, the clouds felt familiar to her.

"Oh, no."

The announcer's voice had changed, since Arkaziel had eaten the last Administrator. The new Administrator spoke in a voice more akin to a sports announcer, possibly trolled from Aetheria's memories since he sounded like Bob Uecker.

"That's right, sports fans, we're back on the racetrack for another run. How will Arkaziel, son of Azrael, stack up against the leaderboard? Will he triumph over his bondmate? Can he surpass the speed of his father's 'one that got away,' Odin? Will his trusty mount cooperate?"

"Mmhmhmhm." Arkaziel tried to talk, but couldn't. Instead, he gave the reins a light flick, and Aetheria felt deeply conflicted and more than a little annoyed. She had been a dragon a few times as a trial, but not nearly enough to feel confident. Still, she had years of watching Arkaziel under her belt, and she prided herself on being a team player. The competitive streak within the former raid leader awoke for the first time in ages.

"On your mark. Ready, set, go!" Aetheria responded to the precise control of the reins, the pressure of the saddled Arkaziel, and went all out. She filtered out the extraneous world, let the currents of air become part of her, and pushed a literal mountain of Ethereal crystals into her massive dragon body to enter the realms of speedsters. Her favorite comic speedster had always been a certain arrogant jerk with a witch twin sister and an evil dad. The closest comparison she could make to her new burst of speed was the vaunted bullet time of some first-person shooters. Based on the serenity she felt through their bond, Arkaziel had no problem with equivalent reactions to her new speed.

A massive draconic bullet, she shot through the sky and left a red Ethereal energy trail behind her. Others would have been aghast at the amount of power Aetheria wasted on this race; a god could have built a new planet with the amount of power, and she'd used it just to compete in a one-off level of the tower that probably only gods cared about.

"And they made it! Let's check the leaderboard. I think we've got an upset!"

LEADERBOARD:
Arkaziel, Aetheria
Odin, Sleipnir
Vishnu, Garuda

With their respective senses returned to them, Arkaziel could be heard wheezing with laughter. Clearly, the StarMane just didn't have familiarity with human form. He stood a few inches taller than Aetheria, his black hair in tight braided rows, his skin chocolate. The StarMane's gaze was disquieting. Ark still had the yellow and black feline eyes. He wore a stylish suit with a tailcoat, and the lapels were glittery and perfect.

"Looking good, Ark." Aetheria grinned, and realized she was showing a lot of massive teeth.

"Etheric ice dragon. I didn't know you'd ever seen one of those yet. The icy scales are a perfect touch, but they were pretty cold even through the saddle. You should be warmer next time."

"What do you mean next time?"

"We just took first place. That means I'm the best rider and you're the best mount. Know your role!" The cat laughed and laughed, even when the door to Floor 40 appeared.

"Worst floor yet," Aetheria growled before she returned to her own human form.

A screen popped up with a long list before each of the companions. The reward selection options were vast.

CHAPTER 71

Canoroth

Salty sea smells overwhelmed the senses of the duo when they appeared on the deck of a large galleon. Arkaziel had resumed his cat form, and Aetheria had once again become human. None of the sailors who ran about the deck paid any attention to them, as if they had always been there. *Another floor with a scenario. I can't decide if I like these or not.*

On all sides of the ship, Aetheria saw only unending water. Two paces in front of them, an older cat-man in ornate robes spoke to a man Aetheria could only assume was the captain of the vessel.

"You're certain then, Polyto? If the ne'er-do-wells have taken Alyssa to Abyss Island, the chances of getting her back approach zero, no matter how strong your mercenaries are."

The captain appeared to be a human man in his forties, with just a touch of gray in his brown hair. He was well built and radiated the aura of a second-tier Cultivator, one who had only recently broken through. He gave the impression of swords and water to Aetheria.

"This is no ordinary mercenary, Stormblade. Unveil your aura for Lysander, lass." Polyto grinned at her, and with a shrug, she obliged him. Her unsealed aura spilled out as a visible red blizzard around her, unlike the one that had destroyed the temple. This one only made people shiver and feel immense pressure. After just a few moments, she sealed it again.

"Do you require further demonstration?" Aetheria lifted a hand, and with a command backed by the Primordial Flame of Thalassa, the ocean heaved and water formed into a replica of the ship they sailed on.

"My apologies, ma'am." Lysander bowed his head and tipped his hat to her. "You conceal your power well, and that's a mighty fine rendition of the *Stormstrike*, if I may say."

Aetheria gave the man a smile and looked at the older man.

"Tell me about Abyss Island."

Lysander spoke first. "'Tis an island shrouded in perpetual night. Out of the dark, ghostly voices of the damned whisper curses and temptations to lead you to your doom. The vines and trees themselves try to trap you. There is a pit at the island's center that goes into the depths of the underworld itself, and at its heart lies an ancient evil that would overtake all the seas if it ever emerges."

"As the captain says, but the island has accepted some who consort with evil and use it as safe harbor," added the priest. "If they took Alyssa there, it can only be for the vilest of purposes. We must rescue her—as the Vessel of Freyja, much ill could come from her being on Abyss Island."

"Which direction is the island?"

The two men looked at her askance, but wings of red, blue, and black ice formed behind her back even as they watched. Arkaziel murmured and nuzzled her neck in annoyance at the burst of cold that radiated from her back.

"Let me show you the maps." The captain gestured to the wheelhouse.

Ten minutes later, Aetheria and Arkaziel were flying just outside the massive cloud of darkness that hung over the island.

"So what do you think, Ark? Do we play this like we're supposed to, wandering through tunnels in barely lit areas, or do we just go to the pit and kill whatever is there, then save the girl? Or better yet, we do that while you send one or two of your kitties to save her?"

Arkaziel let out a mighty yawn, and his gold eyes took in the darkness and the island.

"I'll destroy the darkness and save the girl. You kill the thing in the pit. I don't want to eat *that*. Just make sure you kill it."

"What is it?"

"A demon." Arkaziel had never shown a reluctance to eat anything before. Yet even he had limits, it seemed.

"Alright, buddy, do your thing, and I'll go fight whatever is in the deep, dark pit."

Arkaziel smirked and hopped off her shoulder into the air. His form shimmered and a fifty-meter-long dragon with cat features appeared.

"Oh, you've gotten bigger again. Finished digesting that god and the admin?"

Arkaziel laughed. In his massive form, the sound was like thunder. His dark black scales and purple Ethereal fur glowed. In seconds, the cat-dragon became as bright as a sun, and then holy light blanketed the island. Light fought darkness, and light won. Barely. It pushed back the darkness and ate it, but it took minutes to destroy the cloud around Abyss Island. Coincidentally, about the same time that it took Aetheria's eyes to heal from the constant exposure to such radiance.

"Have fun," Arkaziel muttered before his form shot toward the now-revealed edge of the island and a boat docked in a sheltered cove.

Aetheria darted to the center of the island and looked down into the depths of the pit. Darkness crawled and squirmed in the pit before her eyes. Already, tendrils were sneaking back out of the pit to rebuild the protective blanket that had previously covered the island.

Aetheria pushed a little power into her hair. Her aqua locks emitted an aetheric glow that repelled the darkness. Her eyes gave off a bright red Ethereal light that seemed even more effective. With a sigh, she dropped into the dark pit. She fell, and fell, and fell... until finally she saw a hint of crimson aura around a figure. She slowed her descent, and the light from her body revealed the heart of the island.

A demon hung in the air. Dismembered pieces of it each had a large root or vine embedded into it. The roots held the pieces of the demon in a caricature of one piece. The large snout opened, and it howled at her. Not-quite-dead eyes glared death at her.

"Seriously? A dog demon is all it takes for Ark to wimp out?"

Aetheria flexed her domain. Hoarfrost covered the demon, and the vines and roots, yet her domain could not seem to truly freeze the roots or the demon itself. The grotesque, corpse-like demon laughed at her.

"Stupid human. I am the island, and the island is me! No little freezing trick will work. My little cultists were supposed to bring me the Vessel of Freyja, but you'll do even better."

Roots and vines shot from the sides of the pit to entangle her. Aetheria dodged them nimbly. Magic flight felt like cheating for aerial battles. Yet the number of appendages that attempted to grab her continued to grow.

Snowflakes made of Ethereal power and the Primordial Flame of Ymir popped into existence and circled around her. Unlike her domain, these cut and destroyed the roots. With her snowflake shield deployed around her, Aetheria focused to create a thick layer of ice around the demon—she didn't want any of him falling farther into the abyss before she made a move.

"Poor, dumb human, haven't you realized yet that you can't freeze me? I am Canoroth, mightiest of my line! No pathetic human will best me, even in this wretched state!"

For all the demon's bravado, Aetheria could tell the wretch did not have its full power. It had some, but it was stolen from the island, not the demon's own.

"You talk too much." She made no gesture, but hundreds of new snowflakes appeared in the air around her. They whipped through the darkness to destroy the roots that connected the demon to the island. Finally, a look of comprehension crossed the demon's face when the first of the roots were cut.

"Stolen power isn't your own. Maybe you were powerful once, but you're just a pathetic sack of meat held together by plants now. Maybe the next turn of reincarnation will do you better. Do demons reincarnate?"

Only one root remained, and dozens of snowflakes stilled in the air, ready to destroy it. Aetheria expected pleas, or a bargain, or several other things. Instead, the demon looked like it was about to win. She refrained from cutting that last root while observing the demon again. Most of its broken pieces had somehow healed together when the roots were cut.

"Finish it, human."

"Hmm. No, no. I think I have a better idea, really." Aetheria gestured, and a seal of ice made a floor across the pit. Then she breathed deeply of Aether and summoned storm clouds. Rain fell in a deluge.

The demon looked confused as water filled up the pit. By the time it was a meter deep and the first bit of gathered water touched the demon, it realized what she had done. The rain was rain, but the ice floor was holy and imbued itself into the water that gathered above it.

"Just to be sure, though..." A single purple orb of energy appeared above Canoroth, a manifestation of the Primordial Flame of Nyx. Immediately, the Flame leeched the life and power from Canoroth, and gave it to Aetheria instead.

The dog demon howled in pure rage. Its lower extremities were now submerged in the holy water, which ate them. As if he were in a bath of lye, the demon dissolved where submerged. Simultaneously, the Flame of Nyx robbed it of power and life. Only then did Aetheria cut the final root, a small smirk on her lips. In seconds, Canoroth died a true death.

"Tricksy. I would've set him free, then had a much harder fight on my hands. He wasn't the one holding himself together like that. Someone trapped him that way. Who builds a trap like this, then doesn't warn future generations?" Aetheria snorted, then sighed. "There's probably a bunch of warnings carved into stones covered in vines all over the island."

The rain ceased, but she left the holy ice seal over the pit. *I don't know what's down there, but no reason to leave a hole to the underworld open. For all I know, the dog kept the path closed somehow.*

Aetheria shot up out of the pit and used her bond to track Ark. She landed near the cove where they had anchored the ship. Arkaziel was sitting next to a gorgeous cat-lady. The StarMane had taken on the human form he had previously used, adopting the same cat-hybrid race as the woman, whom Aetheria guessed was Alyssa.

"I killed the dog. Everything go okay over here?"

From the rosy cheeks of the Vessel of Freyja, Aetheria wasn't sure if she'd arrived too early or too late.

"Oh yes, everything is great over here. I shredded the pirates and freed dear Alyssa. Why don't you drop that ship into your repository? Never know when a pirate ship will come in handy." Arkaziel's tone and facial expressions were pleasant, but through their empathic bond, Aetheria could tell he was annoyed she had arrived so soon.

"Sure, I'll grab it soon. I'm going to take a quick look around the island. I thought I saw some useful reagents for alchemy, ore for blacksmithing, and some other ruins to loot. Why don't you two finish raiding the pirates' hideout and wait for me here?" Aetheria did not wink, but she did the equivalent through their empathic bond, and Arkaziel grinned in return.

She scoured the island. While it had just been a cover for Arkaziel to have some time with the lovely maiden, it actually turned out to be an excellent idea. The plant life had spent long years exposed to high-intensity Nether and attuned to Canoroth. Alchemical reagents would be worth a fortune to an alchemist with the skill to handle such dangerous materials. Best of all, near the pit, Aetheria found a strange petrified tree. Its stone roots pulled Nether from the ground to the surface, and where the petrified tree had once used it to grow, now it just broadcasted the power into the air.

It even transferred into her repository properly. *Another piece for the Gate.*

CHAPTER 72

Cryostrialis

Aetheria and Arkaziel delayed their departure from Floor 40 for a few days to accommodate Arkaziel's tryst with the presumably still holy maiden, Alyssa. When it came time to go, the transference to Floor 41 came with the usual few seconds of nothingness before they appeared in... nothingness. A vast black void at every angle—except for a small cottage with a few trees in its yard.

A holographic projection of an indistinct humanoid appeared before them.

"Study the Nether Tree you got on the last floor and construct an Ethereal Tree."

"Oh, sure, no mission for me?" Arkaziel piped up. "I just get to sleep in the corner while she gets treated like the hero, when she is *my* sidekick?" The StarMane shook his head. "What am I saying? Yes, give her the tasks. I'm taking a nap!"

As a black house cat, Ark stormed into the cottage, presumably to claim the bed for a nap. When Aetheria looked back at where the projection had been, it had already vanished. With an annoyed sigh, Aetheria summoned the petrified tree from her repository. It kept the same dead look it had on the previous floor.

"Make an Ethereal tree. To make Nether into Aether, I have to fuse the energies, and there's a loss. I don't think that strategy will work with the state of this tree, anyway." She ran her fingers along the petrified bark and pushed her senses into the tree. It was primarily composed of crystallized Nether, but there were hollow channels throughout it. Presumably, before the death of Canoroth, those channels had been used to pull power from the surface down to the demon, and such channels likely existed in many other plants on that island. The more Aetheria looked at the design, the more she studied the tree, the more she realized she had missed something important.

"It gathers Aether and converts it into Nether, on top of gathering Nether naturally. That makes sense, I suppose, since Ethereal energy should theoretically be out of the reach of a demon. Aether should too, but it circumvented those rules over who knows how long of a period?"

Her senses focused even more on the tree and its interior. Within it she found the hows and whys. The glyphs were not in a language she understood, but she knew how to fix that. Concentrating, she covered sections of the tree's bark in a layer of hoarfrost. When she examined the tree again, the glyphs were in a human language.

The Aether to Nether conversion seemed a relatively simple process and would work anywhere with abundant Aether, which was everywhere in existence she had seen so far. The process did have a downside, however, with its low efficiency. The lost energy became mana, a useless byproduct for her. Aetheria wondered if using a more suitable language, such as Primeval Sylvan, might increase the efficiency.

Aetheria created a swirling spire of ice with many glyphs in the divine language, Ath, inscribed on it. In no time, she had an ice tree that could pull Aether from the air and Nether from the ground. No Ether came out of the tree, though; instead, it just exploded into icicles that left wounds gaping across her body. Those healed in moments.

"Hmm. I can't use an internal combustion concept with a tree, and the quest is to make a tree. Photosynthesis makes oxygen and glucose. How do I adopt that concept to rearrange Aether and Nether into giving me Ethereal energy?"

As she pondered the enigma of divine forces, her mind strayed to the remnants of fruit she had collected from Aetherius's ambrosial orchard. A splendid plum materialized within her grasp, its aroma and flavor transporting her back to the memory of that hallowed terrain. The luscious fruit harbored an oversized pit, which she cast upon the earth, imparting the merest brush of Aetherius's Primordial Flame. Infused with the potency of the god, the pit burgeoned into a plum tree of three meters' height in under an hour.

The verdant being inhaled Aether through its foliage, imbibed Nether from its roots, and bore fruit of an Ethereal nature. Though its energy intake paled beside the quantities Aetheria had endeavored to funnel into her ice tree, the living tree's focus on creating fruit held great promise. The energy currents appeared amenable to manipulation.

Within a crystalline dome of ice, Aetheria conjured another frozen tree, its essence channeled through glyphs of shaping and creation to yield apples wrought from etheric ice. Or, at least, that was the intent. Instead, it detonated. So did the subsequent ten attempts. But the twelfth specimen remained intact, bearing divine ice apples filled with the vibrant red Ethereal quintessence she sought. Satisfied by twenty minutes of stability, Aetheria dismantled the dome and scrutinized an ice apple.

The Ethereal energy contained within would suffice for a single large attack, but that was not the crux of the matter. Success had been achieved with ice, and there was no longer a need to unravel the mysteries of applying alchemy or directing growth with the Flame to a living tree. She could proceed to the creation of these arboreal marvels within her repository. A copse, or better still, a gargantuan tree, could accomplish more than what months of unhurried meditation on nature, aspect, and attunement had wrought.

"Guess you get to stay here and reproduce on your own." Aetheria left the rapidly grown plum tree to its own business while she created dozens of ice apple trees and sent them into her repository. This felt like an unnecessary additional step for something she should be able to do inside the repository alone. *What's there to be afraid of?*

I'm just making living ice trees inside my soul. What could go wrong? If I pull a Sleeping Beauty, Ark, you better not kiss me.

With exaggerated care, Aetheria constructed a tree within her repository. It did not explode, and it was actually easier to control minute details inside her soul. When she had constructed an orchard of apple trees, she felt she had laid the groundwork. She now felt confident she could, in fact, create a Yggdrasil-sized tree within the repository. The scale of such an endeavor would be time-consuming, but the product should easily produce far more Ethereal power than her proto-core did, while simultaneously enhancing the Ethereal nature of her soul.

Thus, Aetheria dedicated day after day to fashioning an impossibly large tree that dwarfed everything else inside her repository. The small Mellow Mallow sky castle, the lost city of Atlanta, the piles of treasure—they were but ants next to the impossibly large ice tree that climbed into nonexistent skies. The construction exhausted but also invigorated her. The feeling reminded her of the high she got when she absorbed large amounts of Aether.

When she opened her red eyes to take in the physical world again, she smiled with satisfaction.

A bored Arkaziel gave her a lazy look. "Done yet?"

"Yes, I just finished Cryostrialis."

"What is a Cryostrialis?"

"That's what I named the ice world tree in my repository."

"Have we completed everything on this floor?"

"Yes. I didn't know you ever tired of napping."

"You've sat there with a stupid smile on your face for two months! Of course I got bored. Plus, there's nothing to hunt here. Nothing! Who makes space and doesn't even toss in any space whales for a poor StarMane to eat? A jerk, that is who."

Arkaziel's dissatisfaction pushed Aetheria to trigger the door to the next floor.

"Floor Forty-Two, here we come. The gourmand inside of me feels the promise from the other side already," the StarMane declared passionately, or perhaps desperately.

Aetheria tsked. "You have a gourmand inside of you? I thought we talked about you killing your prey before you eat it."

"I don't think you get to talk about chewing your food fully before making it a meal, Ms. 'I dropped a trap-filled ancient lost city full of who knows what right inside my soul without a second thought.'"

"Atlanta looks tiny compared to Cryostrialis."

"I win. Changing the subject is an acknowledgment of the defeated."

"Sure, you betcha. Get through the door, Ark."

Floor 42 was a circular platform of white granite. Past the five-meter span of stone hung thick red mists. Ethereal energy lay heavily over the entire floor, with traces of

Aether and Nether much weaker than they had been in previous locations. Aetheria smiled as if the first flowers of spring had blossomed.

"Ark, you are on guard duty. I do not know what this floor is supposed to be, but it's perfect for me to break through to the third tier."

"It is a mimicry of what primitive peoples mistakenly identified as the Ethereal Realm. Some worlds cast multiple shadows into slightly off dimensions. The Astral, the Ethereal, the Shadow, and so forth and so on. This is a replica of what the uneducated call the Ethereal Realm. Its Ethereal energy didn't even earn it the name. That's a lucky coincidence. It's usually associated with cheap invisibility alternatives and phasing."

"Phasing? Like going through matter? You can do that?"

"Of course I can. What kind of shadow cat would I be if I couldn't phase?"

Aetheria rolled her eyes at her cat. "Either way, you got my back?"

"Oh yeah, you know it, Blue. Short of a tower boss, nothing will bug you." The cat stretched out into a full fifty-meter form. He curled around the platform protectively. "Do your thing, Ria. Time you become an Asura."

Aetheria dropped into a cross-legged pose to get comfortable and then positioned things in her repository. Cryostrialis was the landmark she used. She placed the metal rings from Marduk, which she had reworked with Jonas and Houff in Nivathar, vertically relative to the crown of Cryostrialis. Horizontally, the distance between the rings and the crown exceeded thousands of kilometers.

From there, she began to weave layers of Ethereal energy through and around the rings that would be the foundation of the Gate. She empowered glyphs and phrases in the divine language, Ath, with every pass of the threaded energy. Time lost meaning as she worked. Eventually, the Gate became a large circular tube of Ethereal energy. When Aetheria finished, she was shocked to find that she had consumed every brick of crystallized Ethereal energy her proto-core had produced, and a third of the fruit of Cryostrialis.

And I'm still not done.

Next, she needed to create a flow of Ethereal power that would set the stage for the Gate, then activate the Gate before the energy that she imbued into the rings was exhausted. Creating the Ethereal flow was simple; she formed a mental image of energy flowing from the circular tube out toward Cryostrialis. From there, it would flow out of her soul aperture into her right hand, and then create a pillar of etheric ice.

Once the energy was flowing, she immediately sent pulses of power through the glyphs of the Gate. The Principles of Oneness, Rules of Three, Convergence, Law of Association, whatever it was called here, Aetheria used the unifying sameness of Ethereal power to tear open a Gate inside the ring foundation. The shape of the tube changed immediately as a massive influx of Ethereal power shot out, became bound by the Gate's enchantments, and filled and filled until an Ethereal sun filled her soul.

Outside herself, Aetheria could feel arcs of red lightning that emerged from inside of her. The Ethereal power fought her once more, refusing to be tamed and chained inside her soul, or even limited to the inside of her body. It sought freedom.

The results were unpleasantly painful, but she refused to let it be free. Any wisps of energy that leaked from her skin froze. Small, crystallized teardrops of Ethereal energy struck her as they fell, but she blocked out all sensations. They didn't matter right now. Instead, she imposed her will on the tides of energy.

"I see you're making good progress, Etherfrost."

Within her soul, a single eye looked outward from the sun.

"Hi, Themis. Give me a moment. I don't have everything stabilized just yet."

The Gatekeeper said nothing more while Aetheria continued her work. She provided the Gate's energy needs through Cryostrialis, besides siphoning a small amount from the Ethereal flow. The stabilization of the Gate lead to the addition of Ethereal Frostfire blazes across the new sun. Aetheria didn't think that was necessary, but it added a very pleasant visual aspect to her inner world's sun, which she dubbed Frostfire.

The immense tides of Ethereal energy now slowed, no longer overwhelming her physical form. The red lightning and crystallized energy creation ended. Aetheria directed some of the extra energy to bolster her regeneration, and her tattered body reformed itself quickly.

"Very few people open a Gate to the Origin inside their souls."

CHAPTER 73

Point of Origin

Despite the fact that the physical damage had already been repaired, Aetheria's mind, soul, and body were flush with power that she could barely contain. Pain, her ever-present friend, was like the third wheel on a date. Had she made a terrible mistake in creating a permanent Gate inside of her soul?

"Very few people create their Gate to the Origin inside their souls," Themis, Gatekeeper of the Origin, repeated. "Do you know why?"

"Why?"

"It would instantly kill anyone who wasn't a human, or who does not possess an inviolable soul. That unpleasant feeling you are experiencing would be soul-rending instant death for an elf." Themis did not seem worried, but Aetheria could not guess if that was because the Gatekeeper wasn't concerned about her well-being, or if things would be okay.

"A human would survive the soul-rending but then succumb to the physical manifestations. You have the regenerative capability to withstand the latter. Of course, such profound power often breeds hubris. You seem to have lost sight of the danger of the powers you are dealing with, child. While you will survive this, and nearly anything else, consider the ramifications before you act. After all, being locked in a vicious cycle of implosions is hardly a desirable lifestyle. Surviving is not the same as thriving. Many are the Cultivators who have crippled their progress along the Winding Way."

With the words bringing focus, Aetheria could feel the tides of Ethereal power within her soul withering her soul aperture, which immediately regenerated itself by consuming the attacking energy. *This doesn't seem sustainable.*

"So, did I do this wrong?"

"Do you know how minuscule the channel most Ethereal Cultivators create is?"

"Nope."

"Obviously. Tiny. You have created a Gate that will allow for power exceeding what most Ethereal lords can produce using their core. You, a coreless Tier Three, have created a full conduit to the Origin. Inside your soul! The idea of a core, as most Cultivators know it, will be pointless to you should you manage this situation and continue on the Ethereal Path. In fact, you may end up having to create an exceptionally unique core after this."

"So, did I do the wrong thing?"

"I wouldn't say wrong. Most Cultivators create temporary channels to the Origin from which to draw their power when they need it, or bind one to an item to draw power from. Your transition into the third tier is just beginning. When finished, your Ethereal physiology should be capable of adapting. You may earn yourself a spot in the records, though, for the most painful tier transition ever."

Memories of the pain she had undergone during the tier-up to second rank flashed through Aetheria's mind. The pain she had already endured, and continued to endure, paled in comparison to the pain of her body being totally reforged on subatomic and spiritual levels. *Shit.*

"Got any advice before it starts?" she asked hopefully.

"Endure. Reshape. Rule."

Before Aetheria could even think or comment on the less-than-clear answer she was given, the eyeball in her Ethereal sun blinked out, and Themis was gone. Aetheria's pain redoubled in earnest. Red and blue Ethereal power poured out of the sun and into her soul, and from her soul into her body. The tides of the Ethereal scoured every atom, every subatomic particle, every ounce of Aether and Nether and any other lesser energy.

It all happened so quickly, Aetheria could only partially conceptualize the damage wrought on her body. She was only dimly aware of sensory input as she watched her hand be consumed by fire, split apart into thousands of pieces, pulled back together, and then exploded again.

I am Aetheria. I am Aetheria, Empress of Ice. I am a sexy badass. I am stronger than this. She embraced the mantra of identification and purpose. She used the words and mental image of herself to buoy her sanity, too. With her will focused, she completed the first step. *Endure.*

Once she had disassociated from the pain, she could see what occurred with the tides of power. The simplest way she could rationalize the changes she witnessed was to compare them to evolution. Every time the power destroyed her body and reformed it, minor changes were wrought. Most were on a metaphysical level. Stronger cells that could hold more Ethereal power. Meridians that had their power capacity increased. Prior adaptations that let her more fully use Aether and Nether were improved on to prioritize Ethereal power.

As a shapeshifter, she could be whatever she wanted. Aetherius and Nyx had placed many a contingency within her body, which gaining a tier had triggered. Aetheria trusted the two Primordials and added nothing of her own to the process. *It would be nice if I could shapeshift just a little faster, though.*

A single, fleeting thought was all that was required, and with it came subtle transformations interwoven with monumental ones. *Reshape.*

As the relentless surge of power from the Origin threatened to engulf her, Aetheria diverted the excess energy toward the dormant Flame of Khaos. To her astonishment, the Flame readily absorbed the surplus force yet showed no discernible progress. Equipped with this newfound capacity to dampen the harshest of energy tides, she found herself able to command the flow of power emanating from her Ethereal sun, Frostfire.

With her newfound mastery, the process became more fluid. In a span that seemed an eternity, Aetheria's body finally ceased its violent detonations and fractures. She savored the tranquility of remaining whole.

"Cripes." Aetheria spoke the word in what felt like a new throat, her voice unexpectedly raspy. She was parched. A bottle of water appeared in her hand to ease the worst of it.

"That was quite the show," Arkaziel noted, his massive yellow feline eyes fixed on her. The StarMane maintained his full draconic splendor—which left Aetheria to experience his words like a tempest, each word a mighty boom of thunder that struck her down. Her body convulsed a little before her inner eardrums healed.

"Mercy, Ark. Use your inside voice, please." Her cat-dragon companion had transformed, too—or, more accurately, her perception of the world had shifted. Previously, her senses for energy required focus and deliberate effort. Now she could physically perceive the tides of energy. It was a disorienting experience, especially when looking at a fellow Tier Three Cultivator on the Ethereal Path. Arkaziel was magnificent in his aura, light and dark interplaying all around and within him, with the blush of Ethereal energy powering it all.

"Wow, you're a strikingly majestic kitty, buddy."

"Gained Ethereal Sight, huh? I *am* a majestic kitty, though."

"So do I just see all types of energy now, or what's actually happening here?"

"You can see most types. Ethereal, Aether, Nether, mana, the basic elements, maybe some of the affinities you know about, like Light and Dark. Usually only Temporal Cultivators can see Time, but outside of that, it's affinity related."

"Sweet. How come you don't use your Light and Dark abilities more often?"

"Haven't needed to." Arkaziel's answer seemed genuine, but through their bond Aetheria could sense his evasiveness. *He can keep his secrets for now.*

Even in the brief time they spoke, Aetheria marveled at the newfound clarity she had gained from possessing Ethereal Sight. The world around her seemed to pulse with life and energy, and she was more aware of her surroundings than ever before. Even with her bond to Arkaziel, she could now place the interplay of energies around him with the emotional resonance she felt in their empathic bond. *I bet Aoibhe is even more gorgeous this way.*

"This is a little like a cheat, isn't it?"

Arkaziel turned into his house cat form and hopped onto her shoulder. "Ethereal Sight is great. You get a much deeper understanding of the energies you manipulate; you can even see problems with flows before they become real problems. But you need to pay attention to it for it to be of any benefit. If you don't think about or understand what you are looking at, it's just pretty lights."

Aetheria grinned. She was eager to try out her new ability in combat.

The door to Floor 43 opened next to them.

"Did anything ever actually happen while I ranked up?" she asked as she contemplated the glowing dimensional door.

"Nope. Not a thing. I sat here for two months while you exploded, shredded, bled, and oozed."

"Two months! I thought it was a few hours. And I most certainly do not 'ooze'. Take that back." Aetheria felt like she'd been punched in the gut. The time didn't really matter, but her perceptions of tiering up had felt so dilated. How could that have taken two entire months?

"I saw what I saw, Ria. You oozed. And jiggled. It was creepy. Would you like me to play it back for you as an illusion?" Arkaziel grinned, flashing his sharp teeth.

"No, that will not be necessary. Seriously though, two months?"

"Time flies when you're being rearranged by the atom?"

"Whatever. Hey, do you have any idea what I need to feed my Flame of Khaos? It ate, like, an ocean of Ethereal power and didn't progress at all."

"Chaos, obviously. Shall we make some Chaos surges?"

"I'll think about it. That sounds like a bad idea."

"It would be a bad idea. For the people you do it against."

"Isn't that pretty much everything we do?"

"Yeah, we're great. Let's go through the door and ruin some people's days."

"Uh, Ark, we're the good guys, remember? We're going to go through the door and make someone's day better... probably by ruining someone else's day. With pain."

"This is why you are the sidekick and I'm the hero, Ria."

"Oh, shut it, cat. You are addressing the Etherfrost Asura. Show me the respect I am due!" Aetheria winked and laughed. Then she smiled and said softly, "Am I actually an Asura now?"

Arkaziel laughed. The sound of a house cat laughing never failed to feel wrong. She had gotten used to him talking, but laughter just seemed too weird.

"I do like the name, for sure. You qualify as an Asura now, Ria. You were borderline there in Tier Two, which is ridiculous, but now? You're far and away in Asura territory. Which is a hilarious thing, since you're such a goody two-shoes. Asuras usually destroy things. A lot. And slap people, saying things like 'You dare!' I guess you'll be a new type of Asura."

"You could have told me that before!"

"It's not my fault you're an uneducated hillbilly from the middle of nowhere."

"Hey now, I'm no hillbilly. Duluth may not be that big a city, but it is a city. Also, who taught you the word 'hillbilly'?"

"You did, when you talked about your first boyfriend. Did I pay more attention to those conversations on the demon floor than you did?" Arkaziel gave her an exceptionally judgmental look. Which, upon reflection, Aetheria decided was the normal expression of StarManes.

"Oh, right... Adam. He was a redneck, but he was a nice enough guy other than that. Anyway, let's move to the next floor. I want to see what I'm capable of now."

They stepped through the door, where they vanished in flashes of light.

CHAPTER 74

Happily Ever After

Aetheria awoke. A small hand continued to shake her foot under the blanket. An adorable little boy with shining red-gold hair and golden eyes that gleamed was the culprit. He shook her foot again, insistently.

"Wake up, Mommy." He shook her foot again until she sighed and sat up.

"I'm awake, Aurion, you can quit shaking my foot. Why are you up so early?"

The young boy grinned, and an ache filled Aetheria's heart. She grabbed him and gave him a firm hug.

"Jeez, Mom, why are you so huggy? It's past dawn and Momma said you need to get out of bed and come down for breakfast, or you are going to miss everyone for the rest of the day."

Aetheria desperately clung to her son for a few moments before releasing him. She ruffled his hair.

"Alright, go on. I'll be down in a few moments."

"Better hurry, or I'll eat all of Momma's doughnut before you even get downstairs." Aurion bolted. Aetheria laughed and shook her head, and got out of bed. A single step was all it took for her nightshirt to become jeans and a tank top. A quick look in the mirror still showed her youth, in spite of the thirty years that had passed since she'd conquered her tenth tower. Unsurprising, given that she was the Etherfrost Asura—immortal and immune to the ravages of time.

The bedroom had a hint of chaos to it but was otherwise the image of something from Earth—a large bed, immaculate nightstands and dressers crafted by the best carpenters, and crystalline ornamentation all over the place. Aetheria chuckled at the latest scene Aoibhe had created on the shelf near the door. Werylin and Arkaziel stared down a horde of Hoop-Snakes. *Why on Earth do all the gods seem to love Hoop-Snakes, anyway? They're just a dumb snake biting its own tail and trying to ram you like a wheel.*

The laughter of children lured her down the halls and stairs to the kitchen, where Seraphielle sat before a plate of waffles and an enormous glass of orange juice. She did not look pleased, but she did look ridiculously cute. The four-year-old's platinum blond hair had been braided into pigtails. Her daughter's pale blue eyes held all the sorrow in the world that only a four-year-old could call out and display so readily.

"Mommy! Momma says I can't have a doughnut unless I eat all my waffle." The desperate cry for help went up, but this was one battle Aetheria would not champion. Instead, she smiled and gestured. A thin sheen of ambrosial glaze covered the waffles. For a few brief seconds, her daughter looked displeased, then she breathed in the tantalizing scent and dug into her waffles.

The throat-clearing cough of her eternal partner brought Aetheria's gaze to the nephilim. Her hair was a slight mess, with a touch of flour and sugar left from running her fingers through it. Aoibhe's witch hat lay on the corner of her usual spot at the table. Even while baking, she wore her usual armored dress, minus the gauntlets but with the addition of an apron. The half-angel was gorgeous, and the bond between their souls resonated so strongly this close, it was like feeling her heartbeat next to her own.

"It's just a little. Besides, it'll help her affinities. If she wants to be a Temporal Cultivator, she needs all the help she can get with her Time affinity." Aetheria grinned and stole a kiss from her wife, and then a doughnut from the plate she guarded from the children. "What's on the agenda today, anyway? Aurion said I'd miss everyone if I didn't hurry."

"Their ride to school will be along in ten minutes. I've got to deal with the Purple Rose Sect today. They assure me they have an offer that will sway me to take on a new apprentice. You'd think by now people would realize that there's nothing we want for. You don't conquer ten towers and found your own Nexus City and still want things." The witch's eyes rolled in annoyance.

"Oh, come on, now, I can think of plenty of things I want. Well. At least one," Aetheria retorted, only to get bopped on the nose by Aoibhe.

"Not in front of the children, my dear."

"Yeah, Mommy!" Aurion agreed with Aoibhe. "Ew. Listen to Momma, she's always right." Seraphielle ignored the goings on in favor of her ambrosia waffles, which she had already almost finished, a gleam in her eye with each bite.

Aetheria held up her hands. "Sorry, sorry. Guess I'll make the rounds of the Etherium and see what new annoyances the council has come up with. Maybe I'll let Arkaziel eat them after all, if they can't learn manners." She laughed to herself, while her children and wife shook their heads at her.

"Don't encourage the children to feed people to StarManes, my sweet. That's a fate worse than death."

"Fine, fine."

By the time she finished her doughnut, the children were on their way to school, and Aoibhe was off to suffer the ever-reoccurring begging from the sects that she taught. Aetheria herself used to get those requests until her response became freezing anyone who asked her. *Teach them to bug me. Figure out how to break out of frozen Time, and maybe I'll teach you something.*

Alone now, she felt *off.* She was the Etherfrost Asura, Scourge of Gods, Heroine of Grief, Slayer of Misery. Why did she feel so weak? Beyond that, now that her family had gone off to their own day's activities, the world felt hollow. That was new. Where was Arkaziel, anyway?

~Ark? Where you at, buddy?~

No response came. That wasn't supposed to happen. With narrowed red eyes alight with the power of a sun, she tried again.

~Arkaziel? Where are you?~

+It's... a... trap...+

The response was faint, but distinct. Nothing short of being in a tower could interfere with the bond between her and Arkaziel. In a tower... The back garden swam around her, and when she opened her eyes, she stood in the council chambers of Etherium. Self-important fools in elaborate robes and suits argued with one another around a large table at which she sat, at the head. *What kind of idiot founds a Nexus and then puts up with this? Worst decision ever. Councils are the worst. A Magic 8 Ball would be more useful.*

"You have that look again, Aetheria," a familiar voice said from behind her chair, and upon turning her head she saw that Werylin had returned. The purple-haired elf wore light armor and elaborately embroidered clothes, a single sword on his hip, and a crystal flute that hung opposite it.

"What look is that, oh emissary of mine?"

"The one that says you want to replace the council with a Magic 8 Ball, or even a yes/no coin. You've mumbled about it ever since that visit to Fortuna."

"Because it's a good idea. On the surface, a council seems like a great idea, but the reality is so depressing that I am forced to rethink the founding of Etherium at all."

The minstrel laughed and patted her shoulder in a consoling way. Unfortunately, that was when his neck split open from a guard's blade sliding across his throat. The elf died a second time and fell limply to the floor. The councilors muttered and stood up from their heavy chairs. Aetheria blinked, and the armed guard froze into solid ice and shattered into stray atoms. Her dangerous red eyes fell on the council, who were all enveloped in their own auras.

"So it's treason, then?"

"You are no longer necessary, Etherfrost Asura. The Etherium is established, and since you have relinquished the soul-bind to the council, it's time to get rid of you, your party, your line. The gods have granted us great powers to bring you low. Even an Asura cannot stand against the gods, you pathetic wretch."

The leader of the council was a tall man by the name of Edwin. One of Aoibhe's former apprentices who had gotten bigger than his britches. He had never given Aetheria a good feeling, but murder and treason for the sake of power were beyond what she had considered his envy and jealousy to be capable of. Her misjudgment had seen Werylin killed again, but she still had one phoenix feather left that should be up to the task after she dealt with the council.

Edwin's words registered again in her mind. They went after her family.

She did not return words to the councilor. Instead, she let Frostfire shine out through her eyes. The power of an Ethereal sun scoured the chamber, and the building, from the face of Etherium. Arkaziel had warned her it was a trap. *No, that's not what he was talking about. No...*

Rage and indignation at someone daring to threaten her family expanded in her chest, yet her mind kept turning back to the warning. Only being in a tower could interfere with their bond, and someone was interfering with it. *Because... I'm still in a tower. I'm still in my first tower. This... is just an illusion.*

"Freeze."

To an outsider, it might have looked like Aetheria had frozen time itself. Nothing moved but her. She breathed shallowly and fought the instinct to run after her wife and children. Finally, her efforts to freeze paid off when the illusion shattered under the weight of an impossible cold. The limitations of what real cold or ice could do were not limitations to the Etherfrost Asura.

Aetheria found herself on a patio, where Arkaziel was feasting on a buffet of fried chicken.

"It's the Administrator's 'we're sorry for putting you through that. Please don't hunt us down and kill us' apology for this floor." The StarMane flashed her that scary fanged grin that cats should not be able to make.

"How wise of them. I'm not sure I'm in a forgiving mood. It felt very real."

"Yeah, it did. They couldn't replicate our bond very well, though, so it became obvious to me real quick that it wasn't real. Besides, a planet should've tasted way better than the illusionary one they made me. If that is how planets taste, I'm going to eat them all out of spite." Ark hissed a little.

"I hear that. But just so they know, whoever created that scenario is getting punched in the face. *One way or another, I will find you, and I will punch you.*" No one answered her threat, but Aetheria felt like someone, somewhere must feel threatened. She hoped.

She dropped into a seat at the table and let out a few deep breaths. It had been an illusion. It was not real. She had lost nothing. Aoibhe still waited for her. They had all the time in the world to have children. *How would we even have children? Magic? Shapeshifting? Do nephilim have children the normal way or do they, like, have eggs? Probably not eggs. They are angels, not birds.*

"I intend to eat whoever made mine, but they could always buy me off. *Just saying, you can buy me off if you're listening, but it's going to be expensive.*"

Aetheria nearly fell out of her seat, laughing. "Ark, if you're going to solicit bribes, don't do it in a tone that clearly says, 'I'm actually going to eat your face off, and then the rest of you, regardless of whether you bribe me.'"

Arkaziel hissed at her. "Don't give away the twist ending."

"Buddy, if you do it all the time, it's not a twist."

"I don't eat *everything*. I haven't eaten you."

"You ate my arm, and other bits of me that have been chopped off."

"Your blood tastes like the best syrup ever. It's not my fault you're delicious. Besides, I said I'd stop now that I know you can reincorporate your parts. Hindering the cultivation of our bond-partner is a huge cultural taboo. I'd never get a mate if I did it knowingly."

"StarManes..."

CHAPTER 75

Floor 44

Floor 44 was a tropical paradise of small islands. In fact, when Aetheria and Arkaziel appeared, standing on a cloud, the view took Aetheria's breath away, and she was not in the mood to have her breath taken away. As far into each horizon as she could see, chains of sun-kissed islands filled the equatorial seas. In the ocean, vast schools of aquatic life went about their own business. No attention was afforded to the levitating duo.

"Oh, yeah, this is going to be a tasty floor. Oh, look! Orcas! They're like the StarManes of the sea."

"That's the sort of warning you should give people before you bond with them." Aetheria stepped off the cloud and gravity asserted itself. She plummeted down toward a tropical island, red and blue ice wings forming from her back to control her descent before her stylish Nidhogg-scale boots lightly touched upon the soil. Ark followed.

"Your control of Ethereal energy improved with your tier up. What else improved?"

"Everything, I think. I'm looking for something to test that out on, especially after the last floor."

Arkaziel lazily lifted a paw to point toward an ominous cloud to the south. "Looks like something is going to accommodate your violent desires. Want me to hang back so you can test out your new capabilities?" Arkaziel's offer seemed incredibly out of character until she noticed the cat's eyes kept going back to the orcas.

"Go eat. I'll call if I need you."

Arkaziel vanished in a flash of light. Excitement overruled his usual reluctance to show off his abilities. *Or has he been holding back until I tiered up? Is there truly that significant of a difference between power levels in Tiers Two and Three?*

Aetheria waited for the dark cloud to approach. She studied the flow of Ethereal power through her body, the saturation of her repository, and the amount she could pull through her soul aperture with and without strain. Schools of fish and even the orcas had fled in the face of whatever approached with the dark clouds.

The first dark shadow she saw in the water made her a little queasy, because it definitely should not exist. The first ten meters of the thirty-meter-long fiend looked like a great white shark, only its hide was a dark crimson. The back two-thirds made Aetheria's stomach ache. Eight tentacles propelled the creature through the water at a rapid clip. Occasionally, one tentacle slipped out and caught a stray fish that had not evacuated before the terror's arrival.

"Not quite the type of test I was looking for, but whatever." Aetheria's pale skin flowed into the crimson crystalline form of a Luxentian. Her fingers elongated into glistening, razor-sharp talons. Similarly, her hair came free of its ponytail, the blue now the same crimson red as her body and talons, and it too elongated. The strange red-crystal hair glowed just the same as her blue hair had, even as prehensile razor-wire appendages. Aetheria stepped into the sea and walked across the water toward the oncoming predator.

The shark-faced creature came right for her, an apex predator that knew no fear. Its speed would have intimidated her if she were still a regular human, or even back in Tier One. Now, though, it felt slow compared to her own potential. Aetheria waited somewhat impatiently for the shark to open its mouth as it charged to eat her. She slashed lazily with her left arm while, simultaneously, hundreds of threads of her hair elongated and grasped the shark, preventing it from actually making contact with her.

Blood and gore spilled from the disastrous gashes her talons left across its nose. The scent of blood filled the air paled in comparison to the terrible smells that came from the shark's mouth. Tentacles shot from the creature's rear to attack her. Rather than engage them in a contest of strength, she tangled locks of hair around each tentacle and tightened them. One after another, a tentacle hit the water before she slammed her open right palm against the creature's nose. A massive shockwave of Ethereal power flowed from her palm into the creature, and gore exploded in every direction.

"Well, I'm stronger, faster, and I can channel more power. I need some bigger fish if I'm going to figure out what my limits are now." Aetheria could feel there were more predators on approach. Murderous intent and ravenous hunger swiftly approached with the dark clouds. The next shadow she noticed gave almost no warning before it broke the surface of the water.

She erected a wall of blue ice just in time for the shark's snout to slam into it. The shark's momentum broke, and the wall dissipated into mist. Pillars of ice rose to lift the creature into the sky before it could react, tentacles wrapped around the columns of ice to break free. Aetheria solidified the water under her and she jumped up. The talons on her right hand extended to a meter as she sliced upward. The slash attack continued as a red blur through the creature, which fell into the ocean, bisected vertically into six sections.

Again and again, Aetheria slaughtered the apparently stupid sharks, but the activity allowed her to get a grasp on the new baseline of her speed, strength, and energy manipulation range. After an hour, the dark storm finally hit where she stood from the water emerged a creature that bore no resemblance to a shark or an octopus.

Aetheria could only describe what rose from the water as a merman. A very large one at that, at least ten meters tall. With a roll of her eyes, she grew in a flash of red light to match the gigantic size of the fish-faced humanoid. It bellowed a challenge at her in a language she could not comprehend. Its words left a tingle in the back of her head, a gnawing of unpleasantness. The fish's eyes were alit with madness, and she turned off her sense of hearing. She did not want to find out if her regenerative capabilities could repair insanity.

The titan of a merman roared again and moved with deceptive speed to attack her. Aetheria let the series of blows land. She made only slight moves to lessen the impact of the blows, otherwise the giants, fists connected directly with her crystalline body. Blows that would have shattered her previously did not even leave fractures now. Terrible wounds appeared on the sea creature's hands, wounds that healed slowly when they contacted water.

Great waves smashed into Aetheria from behind and on the sides. The ocean attack carried the force of titanic punches, but they landed no more damage against her Luxentian form than the previous ones had. They did not even distract her as the enraged merman released another volley of attacks at her. When the combination of waves and punches did nothing, the creature became enraged and its flesh rippled. Chaotic power seeped from the giant, and a hunger awoke within Aetheria.

Mine!

She immediately siphoned the chaos from the creature, slowly at first. Then she stepped forward and shoved her talons into its torso. Flares of discordant power filled the air, ripped from the merman via the talons that impaled him. Aetheria consumed the cacophony of power like a woman lost in the desert for a month, except all the proverbial water went to the Flame of Khaos. The second the stolen Chaos came within the vicinity of the Flame, it was devoured. The more the merman struggled, the more Aetheria pulled, and the more that insanity lit the vicious merman's eyes. She could see his sanity fade as chaotic power surged in the merman's heart.

The Flame of Khaos was on the brink of bursting into life. Just a little more would unlock the power of a being beyond even Nyx and Aetherius. Aetheria could take her first step on a truly unique path, provided Khaos had been honest about never giving out her power in the past. About to crow about her achievement, Aetheria instead frowned as the merman withered away into dust in the ocean breeze.

Her opponents had not met her urge to fight, no challenges had arisen; she had found all them lacking. *Is this the essence of being an Asura? Disappointment? He couldn't even light my Flame. I was so close.*

The sky returned to normal, and Aetheria reclaimed her usual size and form with a sour look. The floor was done. She could now trigger the doorway to Floor 45. Another city floor. Maybe there would be someone worthwhile to test herself against in the city, or at least facilities to benchmark herself. If not, Floor 50 would come soon with the halfway boss.

~I've annihilated everything. I'm going to look at the islands myself. After I've filled my repository, we can meet up and see what city we got.~

+That was quick. Let me know when I need to be ready by.+ Arkaziel's response showed even the cat had picked up on her sour mood. *Perhaps the empathic bond isn't one-way, after all.*

"What the hell is Chaos, anyway? Is Chaos a type of energy? Is it a force?" Aetheria pinched the bridge of her nose. She cast her mind back to review classes in college, memories of subjects she hadn't thought about for a long time now. Some of it was quite fuzzy, but perhaps because of the superiority of her newly ranked-up synapses, she could recall some of what she needed to know. Or thought she needed to know.

"The vision I had... makes me think it is a state, maybe? Time is a dimension, Gravity is a force, Chaos is a state? Does that mean Khaos is just Chaos, or is she order, too, and a continuum? I hate talking in circles like this."

For a moment, Aetheria considered using her last communication crystal to chat with Aoibhe. The Soul Witch had knowledge on a wide variety of subjects, and had mentioned frequent employment of Chaos surges during her own tower climb.

"I need to figure this out on my own. Maybe I can find some resources in the next town." She heaved a great, tired sigh and pondered at her weariness. The more she probed at the source of her emotions, the more she realized *she* was not the one who felt tired or obsessed with chaos. The sensation emanated from the Ethereal sun within her. Frostfire had leaked such strong emotional projections into her soul that it had colored her own.

"Maybe another reason people don't normally do this." She kicked a wall of sand into the air in annoyance. *Is the Origin alive?*

Aetheria had swum through the red currents of the Origin, floated in its unending tides of Ethereal power. She had observed no people, no land, no anything. *So, it is another dimension. It can bleed emotions into my soul. Not only do I have to deal with the rush of constantly being full of power, horny, and ready to brawl, but now I'm also getting some other being's desires projected inside of me. If it is sentient... what is it? Is the Origin the Overgod? Maybe it is some kind of sentient energy field?*

With the pace of her breath under full control and her emotions on a tight rein, Aetheria pursed her lips. "I don't need to rush it. Especially if someone or something is trying to compel me to rush it without even so much as an 'Ope, let me sneak by ya there.' So yeah, no. I'll learn what I can in the next city and go from there. Maybe I'll meet my white-bearded wizard guide."

CHAPTER 76

Dragon's Roar

Floor 45 was like Nivathar in that Aetheria and Arkaziel appeared inside a small compartment that had been built and fastened to an immense creature. At first, she thought maybe a wyvern, but the scale dwarfed any wyvern she had seen so far. Aetheria flashed back to a brief time when she and Callie had experimented with a dinosaur survival game.

"Oh, sweet! This is Dragon's Roar. These arctic quetzalcoatluses are the only way to the mountain city. Goes awesome with your whole 'I'm a Challenger, bow before me' entrance. We might make a killing here." Arkaziel's voice rarely showed such glee and optimism.

There were three other people in the cabin, and they all had the look of Natives, not Climbers, with their merchant's clothing and weak Tier One aura. They minded their own business, remaining engaged in a lively discussion about prices and demand.

The only other person in sight sat outside the compartment, and they flew the massive dinosaur.

"Look, there it is," Arkaziel murmured and pointed a paw ahead of them. The dinosaur broke through a bank of clouds to reveal a massive mountain that climbed far higher into the sky than they flew. Circular rings encased the entire mountain, with steps leading between levels of the city. "Dragon's Roar, the City of Arenas. They compressed the entire inside of the mountain into a controlled dimension where they put on gladiator matches, monster fights, and just about anything else you can wager on.

"There's a lot of Climbers who stay here for decades at a time, thinking to make a name for themselves. Anything we need should be here, although we may have to fight for some of it instead of bargaining. Perfect for you to punch some people." Arkaziel purred with happiness, as if he had chosen the city floor himself instead of it having been assigned by the Tower Administrators, or random chance, or whatever it was that decided.

Aetheria's imagination ran away with the idea of a city full of brutish peoples fighting and gambling over everything. It didn't align with the beauty of the mountain-covering city, or the glimpse she saw of a Magitech train entering tunnels. A city with elaborate infrastructure, public transportation, and rigid order did not seem to be one built on primitive ideology. *Of course, I'm just hoping I can't forget how amazing ancient Rome was, and they had slavery, gladiator pits, and other cultural beliefs that don't align with modern sensibilities.*

While she was lost in thought, the quetzalcoatlus landed on the lowest ring of the mountain city, on a large platform custom-made for the job. Aetheria smiled at the merchants and gestured for them to go ahead first, while a two-man ground crew pushed platform stairs up to the cabin.

Arkaziel practically vibrated into another dimension from his place on her shoulder. He was so excited to get off the dinosaur and experience Dragon's Roar. But Aetheria did not start down until the merchants had passed the customs officer at the end of the platform's single gate that led to the lowest ring level. The soles of Nidhogg's Fury pressed against the platform, but no massive reaction occurred. *When I touch the platform, I bet.*

Someone had carved the highest point of the mountain into the face of a dragon. The carving suddenly moved, lifted its head straight into the air, and let loose a deafening roar. Pillars of pyrotechnics filled the sky, and a halo of fire appeared over a different platform when Aetheria was halfway down the stairs.

"Another Challenger! Oh yes, if we get a match between the two of you in the Arena, we'll be able to get almost anything we want! Yes!" If the StarMane had been excited before, he now registered at a thousand out of ten.

Aetheria gave the chaos of the other Challenger's arrival a few minutes to die down before she stepped foot onto the platform. The peak of the mountain once again moved, raised its head, and emitted an astounding roar. Pyrotechnics filled the sky again, and the city seemed to come alive even more than before, with crowds torn between which platform to rush toward to see. She expected most would go to the closer platform, or to the one who stepped off first; instead, the bulk of Natives came toward her platform and keen-minded Climbers followed the always-more-informed Natives.

"So much for being discreet."

"Discretion is dumb. You're the Etherfrost Asura, remember? Tier Three on the Winding Way, Walker of the Ethereal Path, and Crazy Human with Four Primordial Flames."

"What about my other Flame?" Aetheria asked, but Arkaziel's tail filled her mouth as she formed the word "other."

+*Don't talk about that, not on this floor. Not even telepathically.*+

The absolute belief in Arkaziel's warning silenced her and made her frown. A frown that only deepened as the whispers and chatter of the crowd beyond the customs agent grew louder and louder. *Suck it up, buttercup. Time to pretend you aren't an introvert.*

Delicate pale snowflakes formed in the air around her as she unsealed a minute portion of her aura to wow the crowd. With Frostfire at her disposal, concerns about energy expenditures were a thing of the past. The flush of red Ethereal light surrounded her form, and whatever force controlled the welcome to Challengers in this place even generated a column of light from the heavens to further enhance the effect she had created.

Already, hundreds of people had gathered past the slightly nervous customs officer, who looked at the growing crowd and then to the woman who walked right up to him. Aetheria let her frown go and put a softer smile on display. It was the red light of the Origin reflected in her eyes that made people nervous, on top of the usual associations of red being evil.

"Welcome to Dragon's Roar, Lady Challenger! You are welcome to enter our city, but please be aware that even for a guest of your prominence, you must earn accolades in the arena to gain access to the higher tiers of the city." Sweat beaded on the man's forehead, and Aetheria felt guilty. She gently set a hand on his shoulder and gave it a light squeeze.

"No worries, friend. You're only doing your job. I'll abide by all the rules of the city while here, just like everyone else. Could you direct me to the nicest inn on this level?"

The crowd behaved itself, so far, held back by the chill and flickers of Aetheria's aura.

"Certainly, m'lady. The best inn on this ring is the Gilded Drake. Some might say it's the Sapphire Wyrm Tavern, but they're booked full, the last I heard. You just tell Pello over at the Drake that Danby sent you. That'd be me, m'lady."

Aetheria smiled, and a few coins materialized into her hand. She slipped them to the man, who looked confused by the tip before he laughed a little and stepped aside from the gate to the street, and crowd, beyond.

Aetheria cleared her throat, but just when she opened her mouth, an arrogant voice called out over the crowd.

"Where's this other Challenger? I'll show you for ruining my limelight, coming in right after me! Shoo! Out of my way, you filthy peasants!" The figure who pushed through the crowd stood almost a meter above most of the humans and elves in attendance. He had red skin and bull-like horns on each temple. The man's eyes were also red, but a very different sort from Aetheria's—his were clearly demonic. He tossed any person in the crowd who didn't part before him with a careless shove. A dangerous move, since his aura registered as Tier Three and most of the civilians were first, or second at most.

Aetheria, in contrast, whispered. Her voice carried to everyone in the vicinity. "I am right here if you wish to speak to me, although I find it hard to think of any business I have with someone like you. What is it you desire?" Her calm demeanor immediately infuriated the man, who continued to stomp through the crowd until he stopped and looked down at her. Behind him trailed three men and one woman. All four were of the same race. All looked uncomfortable.

"I'm amazed this demon-monkey has the gall to talk to the Etherfrost Asura that way!"

"Oh, wow, he's talking smack to the Etherfrost Asura!"

Aetheria recognized the voices. Arkaziel had left her shoulder at some point and had gone among the crowd sowing rumors, although she felt he probably meant to stoke the fires of competition in the idiot even more. The next bit he said confirmed for her that the cat just wanted to cause problems.

"The testicles on this guy! He's talking down to a child of Aetherius!"

It took an inordinate amount of willpower to not roll her eyes. Somehow, she maintained a calm expression, even though all she wanted to do was laugh.

The other Challenger turned a brighter red, but she could not be certain if he had heard the whispers or if it just annoyed him that she had not backed down. Maybe, with his towering stature, he was not used to being treated like anything other than royalty, or the massive bully he seemed to be.

"You are full of yourself for a woman all on her own. Who are you even a Challenger for? The goddess of basket-weaving? Pathetic. I am Malforge Tormentis, Challenger for Ahriman!"

Spouts of laughter emerged from the crowd—no doubt Arkaziel again—but Aetheria kept her eyes on Malforge. She let his words ring out, then waited for silence to descend. Even Malforge showed signs of disquiet at meeting the aspects of Origin locked in her eyes, although the demon probably did not know why her eyes affected him.

"Impressive," she said dryly, her sarcasm cutting the demon better than any blade. The crowd seemed uncertain.

"I am Aetheria, the Etherfrost Asura, daughter and Challenger of Aetherius." Aetheria unveiled her full aura. Snowflakes filled the air as blue and red Ethereal light twined around her in a radiance that was almost blinding. No pressure descended upon the crowd; instead, the divine blessing of the Etherfrost Asura's benevolence filled them. Only five people experienced the unbearable pressure of her aura. Malforge's entourage faltered; their eyes rolled and each of them passed out. The statuesque demon visibly struggled to avoid being crushed into the floor.

"Ah, my apologies. I thought someone who spoke so brashly could at least withstand the mere presence of my aura." Aetheria's voice remained dry as she gazed at the hunched demon like he was a bug on her shoe.

"Since we are in the City of Arenas, what say you and I have a little match? We have to compete to raise to higher rings up the mountain, so we may as well get started as soon as possible. Say, tomorrow? Unless you have prior commitments? I'd understand if you'd rather just apologize and start over."

Malforge spluttered. The mere hint that he must apologize to her sent everything else out of his mind. His body shook with barely contained rage.

"You're on, pretender! Only an idiot would claim to be both an Asura and a daughter of a Primordial! I will crush you and expose your lies in our battle!" Malforge spit at her feet before he turned and threw all four of his entourage over one shoulder, then stalked through the crowd. Aetheria missed whatever rumbled through the crowd, but spots of laughter spurned Malforge to get out of it even faster.

~I almost feel bad about that. Won't revealing my ties to Aetherius and that I'm an Asura make it hard to get good odds?~

Arkaziel wandered from the crowd and hopped onto her shoulder, where he settled down to nap.

+*No way, this is perfect. It's just hearsay now. Some will doubt your power, especially the people who weren't here. That you only applied your aura to the demon will really help keep things questionable. Good job, you did better than I expected; I was certain you'd broker some peace with him.*+

~*Screw that. Being a heroine means putting people like that in their place. Let's go find the inn. I'm hungry.*~

CHAPTER 77

Aetheria versus the Train

Aetheria wondered whether she had made a mistake. She had eaten three meals for dinner, crashed out in the best room the inn had, and now stood in the holding room of the arena, where she waited for the signal to enter. She had no doubts about any of that; the food had tasted amazing. Still, she wondered whether she had handled the obnoxious Challenger properly.

Should she have lured him into this combat? Was she being malicious? Did he deserve it? Heroines were supposed to beat up the bad guy, but they weren't supposed to do it for fun and profit. *Well,* Arkaziel *is the one who will benefit from this. I didn't even make a wager.*

The symbol above the door lit up, and a stagehand gestured for her to step through the now-shimmering door. Smiling, Aetheria shrugged and walked through the door. She appeared in a truly massive arena—the ground granite, the sky endless. *How unoriginal.* Apparently, there were four arena dimensions within Dragon's Roar. The spectators were safely in real space while the combatants fought within the manufactured environments of the arenas. No doubt Arkaziel sat on a cushion in a VIP booth, where he could watch the action as if he were there, all while being pampered by an attendant.

A voice filled the air. "On this side, we have Aetheria, the Etherfrost Asura and daughter of Aetherius. Not only is she beautiful, but she also played a major role in the defeat of Nidhogg's incarnation on the floating city of Nidhogg's Bane. Note her boots made of dragon scale."

Aetheria half expected to hear a crowd cheer, but that expectation went unmet. Light flared, and Malforge and his entourage appeared. *Why does he have his entourage with him? I guess I never specified one-on-one?*

"And here we have Malforge Tormentis, Challenger of Ahriman. Renowned for his extreme power, violence, and ingenuity in punishing his enemies. Let's see what happens when someone on the Path of Transformation clashes with one on the Path of the Ethereal."

Immediately, Malforge flipped Aetheria a gesture she assumed was an insult in his home culture. Nonplussed, she smiled sweetly and allowed the first move to be made by the demon and his four henchpeople. Surprisingly, all five demons glowed with an infernal light and amalgamated into a single... train.

"Jeez, Louise!" Aetheria exclaimed. She laughed in disbelief.

The four demons had become a literal train, made of five cars. Sure, it looked badass. The dark red metal gleamed in the sun, evil spikes and blades jutted everywhere, and the steam whistle sounded like the souls of the damned who all screamed for release.

Arkaziel remained unimpressed. +*That's the stupidest transformation ever.*+

~*Screw that. This is the most metal thing ever.*~

Offended by her laughter, the train charged straight for Aetheria. A multitude of reactions lay open to her. She nearly dropped one of her indestructible ice walls right in front of the train, but how often do you get to fight *a train*? Instead, she pulled deeply from Frostfire. Ethereal energy filled every cell of her body in an exhilarating tide of power. She strengthened her speed, strength, and density and waited until just before the train would strike her to jump up and kick.

The demonic steel of the train's engine car crumpled with the force of her kick, and Nidhogg's Fury activated. The toxic glow of the eater of world trees surrounded the engine, even as the force of her kick sent it flying horizontally for dozens of meters. The other four cars, all connected, dragged behind it. Metal screeched and ground against the granite as the train cars rolled three times before they finally stopped.

"That just looks painful, folks. With a name like the Etherfrost Asura, you'd expect the Lady Challenger to be an ice mage, but that is clearly not the case."

Aetheria waited patiently for her opponent to right itself. Eventually, the train blew its whistle again. The sound of wretched souls was a perfect mix for the hellfire that suddenly billowed forth from the front of the train in waves and engulfed her. The train built up speed in another charge.

Shockingly, the flames hurt. They bore no true heat but burned the sins and wickedness inside of a person to generate torment and suffering. If Aetheria required a lesson that she was human and imperfect, this proved an unfriendly reminder. Unfortunately for the demonic quintet, if there was one thing she could handle, it was pain. She denied it long enough to pull one of the massive ice walls from her repository and drop it into the air above the train.

The front of the train, with its sharp implements, still slammed into her. Blades rent at Aetheria's skin, and crimson demonic steel sent her into the air like a rag doll. The ice wall crashed down on the train. The third car took superficial damage, while the fourth and fifth cars of the train were utterly demolished. They vanished from the arena moments later. The now three-car train once again went rolling across the rocky ground with the massive disruption in momentum.

Aetheria did not hit the ground. Wings of ice formed behind her and freed her from the tyranny of gravity. The assorted piercing and blunt trauma wounds had already healed, and Ethereal mists wafted off her from the excess energy she had thrown at recuperating so quickly. She did not stay aloft, though, and dropped back to the ground.

With both competitors righted once more, the murder train sounded its terrible whistle of torment before it launched at Aetheria. Cannons emerged from its roof, and volley after volley of fireballs exploded around her. The engine car once more sent waves of soul-burning hellfire her way. She gestured and a single blue flame appeared before her, and the fire faded just before any of it could touch her. Aetheria remained stationary while the train made increasingly desperate attacks. She finally made her move when it couldn't be countered.

Ice tracks rose from the granite under the train, lifting it high. A pillar of ice shot Aetheria up into the air. The train sailed off the tracks. Her hands and arms grew denser, thicker, more muscular, and her wings pushed her down. *Duck, duck, gray duck!* She looked over the three-car train and picked the middle car to be the gray duck. Her bare fingers ripped into the crimson metal. Hoarfrost flared outward from the contact. Instantly, every surface of the middle train had layers of ice on it, and a few layers appeared at the front of the third car and the back of the first. Dozens of ice pillars rose to brace her weight momentarily before she hefted the whole train. She held it above her head for a fraction of a second and then slammed it down to the ground, like a god casting meteors at the rocks below.

The middle car exploded in fragments of frozen metal on impact with the ground, while the other two cars rolled. Aetheria dropped to her feet in the crater she had just made.

"I always thought Sabin was the coolest. When he body-slammed the Phantom Train, it sealed the deal for me. Thanks for letting me fulfill a dream I didn't know I had." Her voice betrayed none of the pain and stress she had just subjected her body to.

The forms of the engine car and the third car wavered, flowed, and became Magitech motorcycles. These were clearly not meant to ride; they had no handlebars, were lower, and they had blades all over the front and sides, as well as flamethrowers and other weaponry. The engines of each revved, and a beam of hellfire connected the two demonic bikes.

I really don't get their fighting techniques. It seems to boil down to fire and running people over. Seems really poorly thought out. Maybe I should take pity on them?

"Ha, you'll never get us this way, you dumb bimbo!"

Aetheria heaved a sigh. *So much for showing them pity.* "Let's just end this. I'll take you both out in one attack." She let her exasperation at the ridiculousness of their Cultivation Path show through and beckoned them to approach.

"Burn in hell, human!" Malforge's temper flared bright—the bike revved its engine and shot toward Aetheria. The henchman bike followed. The two drifted apart slightly to put her between them, and the beam of hellfire hit her. The weight of sins tickled and burned at her, but she let it continue until the pair had made half a circuit around her. Then, with both hands, she gripped the beam of hellfire that connected the bikes together. The hellfire froze instantly, and she gave each side of the frozen flame hard pulls.

Both bikes were ripped from their trajectories toward her. Icy walls shot up to take the impact on either side of her. Another pair of ice walls appeared from her repository above the bikes—the walls from the demon decade that were hundreds of tons each. Their impact on the ground left two more craters, in which the last two demons were flattened like pancakes.

"Aetheria wins! Hail the Etherfrost Asura! Five on one and she still wins! With this fight, she gains the right to advance up a ring. Let's give her a good round of applause." The smug amusement in the announcer's voice left Aetheria under the impression he had bet on her.

The hours after that became a blur. Introductions with a whole sea of people, Arkaziel bragging about how much he had made, a stunted apology from a significantly wounded Malforge, a more eloquent apology from one demon in his entourage, and introductions to all the best merchants in the city. Unfortunately, she would have to fight in the arena more if she wished to do business with the best of them, as their stores were on the upper levels.

Days passed in a blur of easy victories. That part still had educational moments, like the demons of hellfire being able to hurt her, or a giant eagle's ability to use its feathers as remote missiles. The worst part came down to all the people who wanted to ingratiate themselves to her. Still, she endured it, and after a week they gained access to the highest ring of the city, and the best merchants—and the temples. She had several things to do.

She visited the Temple of Aetherius to pray for her mid-tower boss to be the phoenix, just as Karieth Sylvaria had instructed. She bought an elven heirloom from the private collection of the city governor. Aetheria even made vast trades of commodities she had gained over the climb for things she thought might help her, like every single scroll on Chaos, resurrection, and a lot of magic items.

The tide of emotion from the Origin continued to ebb and flow. While occasionally the emotion had secondary notes like sorrow and longing, the dominant emotion remained the same: loneliness. More than a few times, Aetheria woke up crying, unable to stop for over an hour. She once again wondered if the Origin was alive. If it was alive in some fashion, why did it seem to have been listening to "Boulevard of Broken Dreams" for the last five millennia on repeat?

Aoibhe had never mentioned a sense of sorrow in relation to the Origin. Aetheria had a mystery to solve. Two mysteries. *I need to figure out how to dull these emotions and where they come from.*

CHAPTER 78

The Great Depression

The inescapable funk of the Origin left most of Dragon's Roar a blur in the back of her mind. Aetheria went through the motions, acquired what she had planned to gain, added literal tons of items to her repository for Arkaziel, and crushed a few more opponents in the arena. Ark did not press about her state of mind, but hastened his enterprises. Unaware of just how long they'd spent in Dragon's Roar, the duo left the city quietly one night when Arkaziel said it was time to go. It didn't occur to Aetheria that she hadn't learned the reason for the systems behind the structure of Dragon's Roar until after the gateway activated and sent them to Floor 46.

They appeared on hilly terrain in front of a massive cave. The cave appeared normal, yet radiated an ominous aura. Something dangerous, extremely dangerous, existed within the cave. But the threat of danger did not really register for Aetheria, who was still overwhelmed by the Origin's loneliness and in the depths of depression. She gave the hillside a cursory look before she walked into the cave.

"So, we're just walking into the dangerous cave of danger without a plan? Great idea." Arkaziel's sarcasm didn't even get a smile from his companion. Instead, she maintained a leisurely stroll into the cave, even after it trembled and a rockslide sealed the entrance behind them. When tendrils of darkness arose from shadows cast by her luminous hair, Aetheria activated her domain. The tendrils of darkness froze solid before they disintegrated into stray atoms.

Arkaziel watched keenly, interested by her freezing domain. She had not shown such potent damage potential with the skill for multiple floors now, and Arkaziel recognized the difference in intent that powered the domain. The usual restraint she showed was nowhere to be found.

They trekked through the cave for roughly twenty minutes before it ended in a massive chamber. Stalagmites and stalactites decorated the large chamber, except for in the center, where a large, dark form slumbered. Baleful red eyes blinked open to view the intruders, and a head slowly lifted from a long sleep. A ten-meter-long bear glared at them before it shambled to its feet and roared.

The sound hurt Aetheria's ears, but the psychic attack behind it failed to penetrate the mental defenses granted by her Flames. Arkaziel's wince showed he could not shake off the full effect of the assault.

+*You can't beat that thing the way you are right now, Ria. It's a demon bear. Dark emotions empower it. The way you're acting, it will be practically invulnerable.*+

~*I'm not that bad.*~

Aetheria darted forward to deliver a punch to the demonic bear's snout. Hoarfrost covered its fur when her fist landed, and the bear rocketed through the room. The bear hit the cavern wall and the whole chamber shook, stalagmites and stalactites crashing to the ground. Yet the bear just stood back up. The ice had already melted from its fur and no sign of any damage remained.

~*Okay, so let's say I am depressed and I can't shake it because the Origin is dumping all these emotions directly into me. What do I do?*~

The demonic creature approached slowly; with each step, it grew another meter in size. The previously messy fur became spikes. Aetheria darted forward again, this time to deliver a kick with Nidhogg's Fury. The blow had even more power than the punch, and the toxic power of Nidhogg ate at the bear. Yet in seconds, the effect of the boots vanished, and the bear grew another meter before it stood.

"Yeah, no. This isn't great." Increased attack power did not seem like it would help. In fact, it might destroy the cave long before it would destroy the bear. Its regeneration currently exceeded her own. A ball of fire appeared in her hand, and she threw it at the bear. Frostfire consumed a third of the cavern, with no end to the blaze in sight.

But the flames died, the cold ebbed. An even larger demon bear lumbered forward and batted at Aetheria with a paw larger than her body. Massive claws and brute force sent her crashing into the cavern wall. Tendrils of light pulled a lost arm and leg from across the chamber to her ruined form, where she reached down and absorbed them back into herself.

"Thanks, Ark." The StarMane was apparently earnest about not eating her parts now that he knew she could reattach them. Flickers of purple and blue flames appeared around the demon bear. Aetheria flexed the Primordial Flames of Aetherius and Nyx. Yet her attempts to pull the power and life force from the demon did absolutely nothing.

+*Well, it is full-out invulnerable now.*+ Arkaziel sighed and emitted a bright light, but it did not seem to do anything that she could tell.

I need to snap out of this funk. Whether the Origin is alive or sentient or just a sad piece of cheese doesn't matter right now.

Gigantic walls of red ice dropped from her repository to block the cavern as she retreated. Once, she would have said those walls were indestructible, but based on the fight so far, she assumed they'd only buy a limited amount of time. Arkaziel let out a whoop as she zoomed down the cave without concern for the craters. Her feet smashed into the ground with each step. In a minute, they were back at the sealed entrance.

"Running isn't going to work, you know," Ark, helpful as ever, informed her.

"I get that. I need a few minutes to get my head straight, though."

"When I'm sad, I eat things. That makes me feel better. Try one of those white plums. We should still have a few from the ambrosial garden."

"What do they do?" Aetheria inquired as one appeared in her hand. The scent pulled the strings of her desire, and she couldn't stop herself. She took bite after bite.

"No clue! They made me happy when I ate them, though."

The ambrosial fruit seemed to perk up her spirits some. In moments, all that remained of the fruit was a pit she sent back to the repository. Warmth filled her stomach and slowly spread outward, seeming to give her permission to overcome the Origin, at least for a few seconds, and she embraced a new mantra. *The sadness of others is not my own. Empathy is a double-bladed sword that I shall not cut myself with. I am not lonely; I am with a good friend and connected to my love.* Aetheria gave the bright strand that connected her soul to Aoibhe's a gentle caress.

In her repository, an afterimage appeared before Frostfire. Briefly, she considered whether she should extinguish the Ethereal sun. Her investigation of the Gate to the Origin shocked her. She couldn't close it even if she wanted to. Even if she took the power away from this side, something in the Origin now sustained the Gate. *Guess that explains why Cryostrialis still has all its fruits.*

"Look, I don't know why you are so lonely or sad. What I know is I can't help you if you overwhelm me with your own emotions. I didn't know what I was doing when I connected us like this, but it is what it is now. We need to coexist, or I'm going to spend a few decades stuck in a cave getting curb-stomped by a bear. Please?"

Aetheria didn't know if her words or the emotions she directed at Frostfire were the reason, but the deep loneliness ebbed. It did not go away entirely, but the decrease in strength was like an EF5 tornado downgraded to an EF1. The difference allowed her to rally her own emotions, especially with the warm concern that flooded Arkaziel's bond, and the depth of love that lit her soul from Aoibhe's. She opened her red eyes to regard the cave and offered Ark a small smile.

"Sorry, Ark."

"It's not your fault. Well, it is, but you've been like this for two weeks. I should have intervened sooner. I just thought you were missing your half-angel or something. I didn't realize you were under some kind of influence."

"You need to work on your comforting."

In the darkness of the cave, sounds warned of their opponent. The massive bear approached.

"My head is on right, now. You got another one of those positive energy attacks in you? I'll take care of it if you can wipe the slate for me."

"Ugh. I hate using those attacks," Arkaziel bitched, but the cat's eyes filled with a radiant power that quickly filled the cavern. The positive power of the light burned away any negative energy. Aetheria felt her own mood skyrocket in the brilliant glory of Arkaziel's light. The demon bear, meanwhile, roared in protest when light ate away at its power, halved its size, and stole its invulnerability. Yet the roar couldn't compare to the rage of the demon when it realized its food source had dried up and it could not replenish the power.

Aetheria darted forward and punched the bear in the face. The sealed cavern exploded open in the aftershock. The blow obliterated her own arm all the way to the elbow, and the bear lost most of its front half. Its body, which did not immediately disintegrate, froze solid while it traveled through the air, hit a cavern wall, and shattered.

Arkaziel concentrated his light on the area to ensure the complete destruction of the bear. It wouldn't do to have to fight the thing again out of carelessness. The job seemed to be confirmed as complete, though: Aetheria felt the ability to summon the door to the next floor in her mind. They had completed the bare minimum, at least.

"That felt good," Aetheria said with a grin.

"Disintegrating your own arm in a punch felt good?"

"Yeah, no. That part sucks—a lot, holy *cow*, a lot." She scrunched up her face in pain as her arm reformed, and she channeled more power into her body to speed up the process. In seconds, she flexed a new right hand.

"What do you know about the Origin, Mr. Genetic Memories?"

"Honestly? Not much. Very few StarManes walk the Ethereal Path. It's the source of all power, so it's tied up with Chronos somehow, I presume. Beyond that, who knows? My ability to pull power from it is innate. I didn't have to make a connection like you did. Our Cultivation Paths are exceptionally different." Arkaziel had the decency to look disappointed because he didn't know anything useful to her.

Then he went and ruined it. "Did you have to kill the demon that way? I could've eaten it."

"Oh, bite me," Aetheria growled at the house cat.

He bit her on the neck with all his force. It hurt.

"It's an expression! You aren't supposed to literally bite me."

"Sorry. I am just *so hungry*. No bear, no Ria-amputated limbs, and you ate that white plum in front of me without even offering me one. What am I supposed to do? I'm wasting away!"

A few ambrosial fruits appeared, and Aetheria handed two to the cat while she ate another one herself. It proved a great distraction from the problem that lurked in her soul. Whatever the source of the emotions in the Origin was, it had toned things down to controllable levels for now. But how long would that last? A week? A year?

CHAPTER 79

Chaos Fragments

The door to Floor 47 opened onto an oasis settlement in a vast desert. A myriad of traders had set up shop at the oasis because of the plentiful water and continuous sandstorms to the east, which was the direction in which the nearest trade city lay. Stuck at the oasis, the traders had set up stalls and tried to peddle their wares to the other waylaid travelers. Little in the way of a goal or trials stuck out to Aetheria, so she and Arkaziel browsed each merchants' goods to eke out a clue.

At the table of one merchant, she discovered a small golden ball the size of her thumbnail on offer. It resonated with the unlit Flame of Khaos within her.

"Excuse me... Nazeem, was it? What can you tell me about this gold ball?"

"It's cursed. I bought it from a man in the Cloud District of Alium. Since then, nothing has gone right for me. I'll part with it for its weight in non-cursed gold."

"It's cursed and you want to sell it to me? Why not just give it to me and I'll dispose of it?"

The dark-skinned man shook his head. "No can do. It is part of the curse. It can only change hands when a price is paid."

That's not at all ominous. Is there a correlation between how much you pay and how bad the curse is? Whatever. I can just have Arkaziel break any curses.

Aetheria handed over the gold without further complaint, and with a nod from Nazeem, picked up the orb and examined it more closely. The ball emitted a faint red glow as it resonated with the Flame of Khaos, building tension until the tiny orb became a second red sun and shot up into the air.

Uh-oh.

The sky immediately darkened in all directions. Rain fell from newly formed clouds; winds whipped up and tore down tents and awnings.

Aetheria raised walls of ice around the encampment. Wind and rain assaulted the walls and roof, but the people of the encampment were glad of the shelter.

"You should all stay in here, I'll deal with..." She gestured to the only door she had made in the ice dome.

~Ark, stay and protect these people in case anything comes up in here.~

The cat jumped from her shoulder and prowled around briefly before curling up on the sand.

+On it.+

~No sleeping on guard duty.~

Aetheria emerged from the large ice dome to be greeted by powerful winds that drove the raindrops at a sharp angle. Peels of thunder assaulted her ears in the aftermath of brilliant lightning. The golden ball exploded in the sky. It had split into four pieces that fell to the ground like meteorites. She sped in a blur to the cusp of the nearest crater in the sand to see a horrible creature grow from the golden fragment. A fifteen-meter-long scorpion immediately began its approach. It disappeared into the sandy walls of the crater, only to reappear almost instantly behind her.

Even though Aetheria moved faster, somehow the scorpion caught her with a pincer, and its awful tail darted into her. Whatever agent it stung her with, her regeneration struggled to cope. She screamed with pain. Even throwing obscene amounts of power into her regeneration barely improved the rate at which her body fought the attack.

Thump. Thump. The Flame of Khaos flickered in time with her heartbeat and pulled in the power behind the attack to devour it. The scorpion stung her again, and the process repeated, but the Flame of Khaos activated slightly faster this time around.

Before the scorpion could sting her again, Aetheria forced its claws apart, slid on aetheric ice under its carapace, and slammed a fist into its abdomen. Hoarfrost covered its underside, and she slammed her other fist into it. Cracks formed through the exoskeleton, and she shoved a taloned hand into the scorpion's innards. The Flame of Khaos activated on its own, and she watched as the creature withered into nothing. A small fragment of the golden ball dropped into her palm, before it too fell before the all-consuming hunger of Khaos.

"Holy moly." Aetheria took a deep breath through a very hoarse throat. If there were three more fragments...

The sand all around her rippled as an immense maw emerged from underneath her. Until the ghastly worm broke the surface, she had not even sensed it, even with her new Ethereal Sight. Ring after ring of menacing teeth gleamed as far into its body as she could see, and she fell right into them. Each tooth was razor-sharp, and five of the blades impaled her near the top of the creature's mouth. The worm seemed okay with this, however, and feasted upon its prey. Each tooth inside her exploded in a growth of tendrils that expanded into her body, greedy to feed off her blood, flesh, and essence.

"Nope, nope, nope! You don't eat me! I use you to catch fish!" Aetheria landed a firm kick against the worm's mucus-covered mouth. She created just enough momentum to push herself off the teeth, nasty black tendrils ripping from her body as she fell. But the kick had activated Nidhogg's Fury and begun the toxic assault on the worm, sending tremors of pain through its interior. Aetheria hung in the air, ice wings formed on her back to allow her defiance of gravity.

Thump. She felt another irregular heartbeat in her chest as the Flame of Khaos vaporized the black tendrils that were still inside her and consumed the detritus. The multicolored flame had brightened and solidified. It bordered on the realization of Tier One, and it *hungered.* Recklessly, Aetheria flew into the wall of mucus and teeth, heedless of the pain of fresh impalement.

More black tendrils began their feast as they spread inside of her. She stabbed her own hand into disgusting mucus, and tendrils of her own spread out across the worm. If it had been displeased by Nidhogg's toxic attack, then dozens of flesh tendrils sinking across its body truly enraged it. The worm thrashed and rolled, bashing itself into sand and rock.

An indescribable pain ripped throughout Atheria's body as the black tendrils were again annihilated and converted into nourishment for the Flame of Khaos. The rainbow flame solidified. A new sense of power filled her, as well as a desperate thirst for *more.* She employed the now-accessible Flame of Khaos, and the spiderweb of herself she had dug throughout the worm lit with strange iridescence. Explosions of fire and air rocked the world, and Aetheria crashed into the sand.

The Flame of Khaos, however, had gained a quarter of the energy it needed for Tier Two in the consumption of the worm. Yet it still hungered.

A strange scythe-like appendage stabbed through her chest as an insectoid she had no name for rose from the sand. Again, she had failed to detect anything in the sand. *Is it a property of the sand that it conceals whatever is inside it? That'd be great if you wanted to bury treasure. Focus, girl; you're impaled again.*

Aetheria's flesh could not regenerate with the scythe-like part of the insect inside her, so she slammed a fist down to freeze it, and then followed up with another fist to shatter the appendage. But it did not shatter, and the momentum she imparted caused excessive pain as the sharp arm of the insect cut her open even more. The second scythe-like arm moved to behead her, but her hair entangled the appendage and dragged that arm backwards.

Thump.

The Flame of Khaos lit up her mind with all the colors of the world, and she reached through a third arm at her hip to punch talons into the insectoid. The Flame flared again and consumed the nasty war-insect and the third fragment. No trace of its existence remained. The Flame of Khaos had reached two-thirds of the way to Tier Two.

Where had the final fragment gone? Aetheria found the answer to that when the ground beneath her opened and pulled her down into a hole full of thick, viscous webbing. The webbing clung to her, and halfway down the hole, she could no longer even move, she had become so enmeshed in the white webs. Neither her domain nor any form of ice she tried to manifest affected the webbing, beyond a few chunks of ice also being stuck in the trapped hole.

Vibrations spread across the webs as something larger down the hole started its climb toward its prey. Primal fear awakened in Aetheria at the mental image of a horrible spider on its way to get her. In desperation, she employed the Flame of

Thalassa to rip the moisture from the webbing. Beads of water gathered into an orb before her, while the webbing hardened and finally succumbed to her domain. Void of moisture, the webs shattered under the weight of her and the ice. She plummeted toward the large black spider.

"Not sticking my hand in you! Ugh." Aetheria wielded the Flame of Khaos, and the water orb before her turned into an iridescent strobe light of color that she threw at the spider. It struck and covered the creature in a gooey, multicolored mix. Her eyes widened as the chaotic liquid ate the spider before she had even manifested wings to stop her fall.

"Holy cow. I've never seen something get eaten in the air like that," she babbled to herself before the strange-colored orb of water reformed and flew up to her hand, and she absorbed it and the power it represented. Even with Flames to see by, Aetheria found no remains of the spider or the final golden fragment, so she had to assume the prismatic liquid had eaten it already.

What the fuck is Chaos? I wasn't afraid of Aether, and Nether is creepy, but they made sense to me. I don't even understand what the heck I just did.

By the time she returned to the dome, she still did not know what had actually happened there. Inside, Arkaziel lay with three of his Twilight clones around him.

"Lots of tiny scorpions, spiders, scythers, and worms. I handled it, though."

Aetheria gave him a few good pets and let him climb back onto her shoulder. The storm had died with the spider's death, so she dropped the dome.

"Alright, everyone, problem solved, cursed enemies slain. If anyone knows anything about those things, please come talk to me!"

Reluctantly, a few hours later, she opened the door to Floor 48, and she and Arkaziel left the encampment to its own fate. She found herself alone in a small, square room. The walls were bland sandstone, and there was a torch on one wall and a small table with an hourglass on it. The wall held an inscription that began, *Welcome to the shifting maze.*

"I don't like the sound of that. Since when have any of the timed events had an hourglass? Where's Arkaziel?" Aetheria felt bummed, but she identified it as the seepage of emotions from the Origin amplified by her own, and clamped down on it with an iron will.

CHAPTER 80

Time Loops Bad, Library Good

Aetheria read the rest of the inscription aloud. "The rules are simple. Make it to the center of the maze before the hourglass runs out. When time runs out, the maze will reset, and you will start again from the beginning."

That was all the sign said. A previously solid section of wall became a door. The sands of the hourglass did not flow until she stepped through the doorway, and then the first grains fell. A long hallway spread before her for about ten meters before it split into two curved tunnels. Her third step triggered a pressure plate, and flames bathed her from the walls. The burns healed almost instantly, but Aetheria found her speed had been halved.

Five steps later, another volley of flames accompanied a loud clunk when she activated another pressure plate. Again, the trap barely injured her, but her speed was halved again. By the end of the tunnel, Aetheria could barely move at her regular pace. She opted for the right split of the tunnel, and the moment she walked around the curve, a series of darts struck her. Too late, her wall of ice appeared before her.

"Bullshit. It even slows down my powers. What a cheat." Her pace had become a crawl, and when she stepped onto another pressure plate to be slowed yet more, she heaved a sigh and waited. Eventually, her patience paid off, and time reset.

She stood in the start room again; no sand flowed yet. "Alright. Can't get hit, and I've got about ten minutes."

Aetheria lowered her density and generated small ice wings to allow her to stay off the ground. While it made no sense that the traps would slow her magic-based flight, she assumed it would work, anyway. Logic be damned. She flew out the door and immediately fell. She pulled herself into a ball and tried to roll through the tunnel with the momentum. Why had she fallen? The flight granted by her ice wings had failed the second she had crossed the doorway.

Still, maybe she could make it as a ball? While the maze was the same shape, the traps had all changed. This time they were laser-activated, but her speed was so much greater that the first five traps missed her, and she bounced to the right and sped around the curve, only to fall into a pit.

This sucks.

A pillar of ice took her to the top of the pit, and she made it through an S-shaped bend and came to a rope bridge. Rather than risk the bridge, she decided to run and jump. About five meters short of the top of her jump, her head struck an invisible barrier with great pain, and she crashed down onto the bridge. Moments later, she reappeared in the start room.

"Okay, okay. I get it. You're not going to let me cheat. I can't tank it, only dodge. Still, invisible ceilings are such bullshit! I don't think that's fair."

When she stepped out the door this time, Aetheria took the time to watch for traps. Ethereal Sight active, she could see where energy lay, such as laser beams, but in no way did it help her with pressure plates and spider-wire. Her answer to this problem came in the form of simply dropping much of her mass and volume into energy, and reliance upon enhanced agility. In her head, she looked like Catherine Zeta-Jones doing some crazy acrobatics through traps.

Aetheria made it down the hall without a single blow. She went right again, where she was met with a wide river and a rope walk above it. *Every instinct I have says to freeze the river and walk over it. But this is a training level still, right? It should let me use some of my powers. No, better not risk it.*

She jumped on the rope and began to glide across it. Halfway across, the wind picked up out of nowhere and her lack of mass meant she went flying like a piece of paper when confronted with the gust. Apparently, this counted as a failure, and she appeared in the start room. Again.

They should have called this the Maze of Suck.

Again and again, Aetheria met difficulties that arose based on whatever form she took. With a disgusted look, on her tenth try, she decided to just be "standard" Aetheria. No mass variance, no volume adjustments—just a high suffusion of Ethereal energy to enhance her reflexes.

"Speed!"

This method worked, almost. After ten tries, she had learned to spot pressure plates, and with heightened reflexes and the large jump in her baseline physicality with the jump to Tier Three, she dodged or otherwise evaded the tripwires she still had issues seeing. She made it past the first tunnel, through a spinning tunnel full of spikes, up a jump obstacle with timed wind gusts, and across a set of vine swings.

"Are you shitting me?" Past the last obstacle lay a pond with a series of alligators floating on the surface.

"You can't jump on alligators! That's stupid!" Still, she thought about what she had to do, so with a run and jump, she landed on the first gator, ran along it, and jumped to the second. The second did what she assumed a gator would do and snapped its jaws at her. She cleared the head, landed on the body, skidded, and jumped to the third, who did the same damn thing and sent her into the water.

Aetheria appeared back at the start. "Seriously?" Again and again, she encountered ridiculous obstacles that reminded her of retro video games. Jump across logs to get past a river, dodge cars to cross a road, swing from vines. The crocodiles kept showing up randomly, too, which kept Aetheria from bitching about other obstacles. *Someone is enjoying torturing me.*

On the fifty-third attempt, she ran out of time a half-meter from the finish line. Frustration at such proximity to victory hampered her next twenty attempts, and for a while, she just sat in the start chamber to clear her head. It took her a few more tries before she finally crossed the finish line and stood at the center of the maze. The chamber rippled, and Arkaziel also appeared.

"Took you a while, Ria."

"How long have you been waiting?"

"No clue. Time loops, ya know? A few seconds." Arkaziel laughed.

"Let's go."

The door to Floor 49 deposited them in a library.

"Books are terrible food," Arkaziel noted with disdain.

"Shut it. Let's look around. Maybe this is going to be helpful."

"It's the Climber library. It's a staple, and almost always Floor Forty-Nine. It's the last training level, really. Once you hit Floor Fifty, you've gone past the Aetherial Veil, and the tower starts for real. The only training or lessons from here on out are what you find for yourself. As for the tomes, it depends. There's some from gods before their ascendance, some from regular Climbers, and some from Challengers. The understanding of the Winding Way has improved significantly in modern times compared to, say, when Odin climbed this tower."

"Why'd gods climb Primordials' towers? Weren't they gods to begin with? Were they tenacious mortals who ascended?"

Arkaziel shook his head. "No clue. Maybe there's a book from Odin or Zeus here you could read. Give me some food to eat while you do. Food is the best source of power."

"If I turned into a StarMane, could I cultivate by eating too?"

Yellow feline eyes narrowed at her. "Yes and no. It would improve your StarMane form—or, I suppose any bestial cultivation shape you take might share a universal power—but I don't think it would help you on the Winding Way. I guess you won't know unless you try it."

Aetheria pursed her lips and put that on the list of things she might try someday, but Arkaziel's emotions in the bond and his tone made clear that the cat had been a little offended by idea.

The dubious nature of the library quickly revealed itself. Many of the Climbers had catalogued their lives with themselves as the hero, and the unreliable nature and exaggeration of their exploits made it obvious that most were not factual. And there was no organizational system in place; books, scrolls, and paper were shelved wherever the last person in the library had left things. This vexed her greatly, especially when skimming books on three levels of the library had not led her to any form of educational gain.

On top of the lack of quality control, there was no translation field in effect on this floor. Any language she hadn't encountered previously was gibberish. This seemed like a downside at first, until she realized she could skim books to see if any were written in Ath, the divine language. After another few hours, she had found four books.

The first was penned by Zeus and titled *My Erotic Journey So Far*. After two pages, Aetheria put the book down. The title was not misleading, and the book proved to be poorly written erotica. *Well, if any god was going to write smut, of course it would be Zeus.*

The second book had no title or author, and was a treatise on speed. While a very interesting subject, Aetheria had already learned most of its contents through experimenting with shapeshifting. It had some references to optimized energy acceleration, which she was eager to test. If it worked the way the unnamed author suggested, she might unlock real super speed, but the author did not know if it was a universal technique and seemed to have unknown requirements.

The third book covered a myriad of subjects; war, poetry, morality, a treatise on the Path to Power. All mildly interested Aetheria, but only a small passage that referenced Order and Chaos as the same, not opposites, really intrigued her. Unfortunately, the author had not expounded upon the idea, and neither Order nor Chaos came up again in the book. *At least I'm not the only one who thinks Order and Chaos might be a state?*

The fourth book held some interesting tidbits about the rules of reincarnation, life, and death. It outlined several methods of reincarnation, like spells to call a soul (including one already in bondage), items that could be used to circumvent resurrection options, and a treatise that suggested love was the strongest power in the universe. Prior to that, Aetheria had assumed the book had been written by a god of life or death, but as the book continued to talk about relationships and bonds, she revised her guess and thought maybe a love god or goddess. Indeed, at the end of the book, a single name was scribbled: Eros.

"Hey, Ark, do you have a locator skill or spell?"

"That would find you a book you want? Nah. But you could always ask the librarian."

"What librarian?"

"That one, over there." Arkaziel pointed at a potted plant.

"That's..." Aetheria blinked a few times when two previously closed eyes on the potted oak opened to regard her.

"Hi. Can you tell me if there are any books here about Chaos?"

"Follow the glowing arrows," the oak answered, and arrows of light appeared out of thin air to lead her through the shelves.

The oak librarian made things much easier, and Aetheria felt a deep appreciation for the tree. Even if he didn't organize his library by any system she could discern, at least he knew where everything was and could send her to the right spot.

A week later, Arkaziel and Aetheria left the library to challenge the halfway boss.

CHAPTER 81

The Halfway Boss, Pyreheart Emberwing

The duo had taken many a copy from the library and read what they needed. Rather, Aetheria had, while Arkaziel slept or complained about how useless written words were. The StarManes did not have a written language of their own, and instead relied on genetic memories to impart wisdom to their descendants.

When they appeared on the other side of the door to Floor 50, all of their senses were assaulted immediately. The powerful scent of burned matches and eggs—aka hydrogen sulfide—attacked the duo's sense of smell. Sight had to contend with ashes that rained from the sky or occasionally swirled up from the ground on chaotic winds. The heat parched Aetheria's throat immediately and contributed to the immediate dryness of her eyes. Beyond the wind, the most significant source of heat originated from magma that churned under the heavy stone, and surfaced as lava through a few fissures of rock.

The reality of their location came together like basic math. 1 + 1 = 2. Lava + Magma + Caldera = Volcano. Aetheria immediately deployed her domain to drop the surrounding temperature and get her bearings. The sudden appearance of cold within the caldera caught the attention of its master, and a powerful caw filled the air.

+*Pyreheart Emberwing, Phoenix Overlord. Good thing your daddy is a Primordial who can answer your prayers.*+

~*Awesome. Remember, I need a few tail feathers and a piece of the heart.*~

+*You got it.*+

Arkaziel wasted no time. He jumped off her shoulder and morphed into the full fifty-meter-long draconic feline he truly was. He lifted his head and released a dragon's roar of challenge up at the ash-filled sky. The heavens and volcano itself stilled, then trembled in answer to his roar.

Gouts of fire and lava broke through fissures in the rock, and a flame burned large patches of the sky clear to reveal Pyreheart Emberwing, Phoenix Overlord. Despite his feathers of flame, the crimson and orange colorations, and being slightly larger than Arkaziel, the phoenix looked remarkably similar to a golden eagle.

Not to be outdone by the dragon, the phoenix cawed again. This time, massive gouts of flame and splashes of lava shot out of the broken ground of the caldera. They took form, morphing into fire elementals, lava golems, and, jumping out of the fissures, flame imps.

"Play with our big friend. I'll clean up the trash and then join you." Arkaziel jumped aloft before Aetheria had even finished her words. The dragon and phoenix began their aerial battle, claws versus talons, teeth versus beak. Aetheria darted forward, but the volcano weakened her domain. The best she got from it was stabilization of her immediate area, so she was forced to deal with the trash in a more direct way.

Punching and kicking with etheric ice-empowered blows, she could destroy a fire elemental or lava golem in a single hit, between the mighty cold around her appendages and her domain. The resulting explosion of fire or magma proved annoying, so she opted to channel the Primordial Flame of Nyx into place to eat it. Night was ever cold and hungry. With flickers of purple power around her fists, Aetheria delivered blows that froze and stole all that gave life to the fiery beings.

The imps she just crushed underfoot. Despite her mobility and high damage output, the diminutive monsters still outnumbered her. Fireballs shot at her, orbs of magma exploded around her, and walls of flame repeatedly tried to block her progress. *Single target mode isn't going to work.*

Aetheria focused on the surrounding air, dumping significant amounts of Ethereal energy to create snowflakes immune to heat. Dozens of delicately beautiful creations appeared around her, then began spinning. She made more and more snowflakes and threw them into the blizzard she had started. After a few minutes, she had scoured the caldera for enemies. To be safe, she imbued them with enough power to maintain them for another ten minutes, then formed wings and flew into the air.

Arkaziel and the phoenix were still trading blows. Neither of the massive creatures seemed injured, despite the constant flash of claws and talons. Light manifestations that deflected flames and energy countered explosions of fire, or were just solid enough to take on magma. Arkaziel's light shapes that got hit by magma became encrusted and fell to the ground to explode.

Briefly, Aetheria considered if she should just watch. *How often do you get to see kaiju movies in real life?*

The question was not just a joke. Arkaziel had often proved to be as strong, or superior, to her. Could the StarMane take care of the phoenix on his own? Should she let him? Her hesitation ended when she saw the next exchange of blows. Pyreheart allowed the cat-dragon to get a good attack in on himself before raking his talons across Arkaziel's underside.

Immediately, Aetheria morphed into a monster herself. At fifty meters long, she matched Arkaziel's length but was broader and bulkier, and unlike the cat-dragon, she did not cover her scales with purple fur but displayed her icy blue hide. Arkaziel had called her an Ethereal ice dragon when he rode her to first place on the leaderboard.

She bellowed just as the other two had, before she swept into the fray. As the phoenix and Arkaziel broke apart after another exchange of blows, Aetheria lunged and bit her frozen teeth down into Pyreheart's neck. Steam exploded from their contact, and with her front claws, she raked devastation across the front of the phoenix. With a shake of her neck, she cast the phoenix toward the ground, her back legs clawing at him even as she gained altitude.

Before the phoenix fell even a quarter of the way to the ground, a mixed beam of light and darkness struck and slammed him down into the rocky caldera. But he had directed his fall just enough to splash into a pool of lava. Within seconds, an uninjured Pyreheart shot up through the still-spinning snowflakes to resume their fight. The snowflake blizzard dealt many wounds to the bird, but it was the equivalent of a storm of paper cuts.

Aetheria opened her mouth and blew. Frost, snowflakes, and terrible icy gusts emerged from her draconic maw to assault Pyreheart. The cold Ethereal winds were enough to extinguish a few of his flame feathers. Hoarfrost grew over the phoenix's body, and Arkaziel shimmered into existence behind his back. Before Pyreheart could retaliate, Arkaziel plunged the claws of both his forearms into Pyreheart's exposed back. Two Twilight clones appeared and attacked the giant bird's sides. Arkaziel vanished again, leaving his duplicates to take the counterattack of the phoenix. Pyreheart's talons destroyed the copies in a single blow each, but this provided time for Aetheria to swoop down, snap her mighty jaw around the bird's neck, shake, and then throw the dying beast into the heart of her blizzard in the caldera.

A shriek of pain came emerged from Pyreheart before his fires extinguished. Then his corpse exploded in a nova of plasma. All of her Ethereal snowflakes melted, and from the ashes of Pyreheart's corpse emerged... Pyreheart. Bigger, angrier, and more badass. The phoenix had increased his size by about thirty percent. The red and orange coloration had an extra element: silver flames.

+*His attacks will change now but will still be primarily physical,* + Arkaziel reminded her. They had gone over the fight in the library. The information Arkaziel knew about the bird and the hearsay in the library had included nothing about a silver form. Pyreheart let loose a series of silver streaks to hit the StarMane, while red-orange attacks hit Aetheria's draconic form.

Arkaziel took the blows directly, unable to dodge them, and hit the ground to form a crater.

+*Astral attacks. Watch out for the silver stuff.* +

The red-orange blaze that struck Aetheria's icy scales passed right through the ridiculous defensive power of her body. The phoenix's Flames of Life burned her from the inside. She, too, crashed into the caldera, although she resumed human form at the last second to avoid the creation of a crater as Arkaziel had made.

~*Ouch. Flames of Life, not proper fire. I thought that was supposed to be Tier Three?*~

Arkaziel didn't answer. Instead, the StarMane focused on returning to the fight. Aetheria purified the Flames of Life from inside herself. She ate them with the Flame of Nyx.

Both had recovered their bearings just in time to see a massive silver shape. A literal moon descended from the heavens to crash into the caldera. Aetheria threw up layers of ice, but it was no good. The impact fountained lava into the sky, and billows of flame and gases were released. Pieces of the caldera flew in all directions.

Aetheria and Arkaziel reappeared in a shimmer of light in the sky, the StarMane covered in a mess of wounds, his breath labored.

"Almost didn't get you before it hit." Ark grimaced.

Aetheria ruffled his fur and dropped dozens of Ethereal fruit from Cryostrialis onto the ice platform underneath them.

"Eat up, buddy. I'll keep his attention while you recharge."

With those words, she jumped from the illusion-obscured platform and fell out of the clouds like a blue and red bullet, forming ice wings to accelerate her dive into Pyreheart. The phoenix's eyes locked on to her just seconds before she impacted him from above, and she immediately put everything she had into a flurry of blows. The physical damage from her strikes was marginal, but each blow stole life force from Pyreheart, thanks to the Flame of Nyx, and left dead, icy patches with every strike, thanks to the Flame of Ymir.

For the nine millionth time, Aetheria wished for health bars—the ability to see the effects of her attacks would be a comfort. Based on the visible results of her rapid assault, she could only estimate she had caused no serious injury to the phoenix yet. Like her, it regenerated. Like her, it seemed to have unlimited energy. A potent reminder of how annoying fighting her must be for others. Yet the blows she landed with the Flame of Ymir seemed to reduce Emberwing's healing ability.

A flurry of snowflakes emerged out of nowhere. Made of Ethereal energy, imbued with the Flame of Ymir, they formed a circle and spun into an impromptu hole saw. The snowflakes hit the phoenix and provoked terrible roars, but the cries did not compare to the rage of Pyreheart when a circular hole punched entirely through the bird's torso.

That was not the end of Atheria's plan. The comparatively tiny human jumped into the wound, flying out the other side and holding one of the bird's organs in hand. The heart of the phoenix continued to beat in her hands while she fell through the air. Ice wings allowed her to swoop over the shattered caldera. The heart finally stopped beating, and she stashed it in her repository.

The cries of Pyreheart did not stop, and when she looked upon the phoenix, the hole in his chest was gone. While not completely unexpected, Aetheria still spit to the side, "Bullshit."

+*Ria, it's not like stealing* your *heart would kill* you. *I bet your heart would taste great with garlic, salt, and light frying.*+

-*Bad cat, bad!*-

The momentary distraction from Arkaziel delayed Aetheria's notice of six small moons orbiting Pyreheart. One after another, they flew toward her. On swift wings, she dodged the first rock and the second. The third moon struck her straight on. The first turned and smashed into her from behind. She lost all abilities to evade, and the miniature moons crashed into her until only a massive pile of rocky debris remained on the volcano's slope.

An angry roar shook the mountain, followed by a beam of alternating light and darkness. A corona of red lightning hit the phoenix in the head, decapitating him. Ark's beam showed no signs of lessening as it covered the upper form of the monstrous bird. Then, the shaft of annihilation slowed, and three Twilight clones of Arkaziel jumped onto the headless phoenix. Ethereal claws and teeth ripped the phoenix to pieces, and then Arkaziel himself joined his duplicates. He took massive bites from the bird until only feathers and entrails fell into the volcano.

"Now that's a spicy meal," Arkaziel hissed, and light bloomed around him and healed the internal damage caused by eating the phoenix.

Inside the demolished caldera, whirlwinds of flame and pillars of lava surged in the rebirth of Pyreheart. An alternative form took shape. At the same time, hoarfrost covered the debris of all the small moons, and then the rocks vanished into Aetheria's repository.

"Jeez, that hurt. Is that any way to treat a lady after she steals your heart?" Aetheria stood as herself, whole and hale. Ethereal power billowed from her in thick streams of mist. Hundreds of snowflakes flickered in and out of existence until, with a surge of energy, they solidified and became real. The destruction of the caldera had revealed the magma chambers beneath, and vast quantities of lava fountained into the air unpredictably. The combination of heat, fire, and strange life-aspected energies of the former caldera made the manifestation of ice, even etheric ice, difficult.

While she rebuilt her snowflakes and established her aura, the iridescent form of Pyreheart emerged from ash and flame. He bore a roughly humanoid form about Aetheria's size, with wings instead of arms. His aura had increased again, and Aetheria estimated it to be at the upper end of Tier Three now. Heat, light, and life clogged the air around Pyreheart, just as cold and ice did around her.

Aetheria's red eyes filled with Ethereal power and met Pyreheart's white eyes suffused by fire and life. In a flash, the two met in a melee. Pyreheart's talons were met with a storm of snowflakes to deflect his blow, and Aetheria thrust a fist into the phoenix with enough force to mangle her own hand. Momentum carried the phoenix across the ruined caldera until he crashed into a pile of rubble left by his previous destruction. But his counterattack came before Aetheria could react; silver and orange feathers imbued with fire, life, and strange astral energy snuck past her snowflakes and ripped her flesh with vicious intent, infecting her with a negative energy that tried to attack her from inside her own body. Pulses of the Flame of Aetherius burned away the hostile energy.

+*I've got the moons!*+ Arkaziel alerted her. She had missed the threat somehow. Once again, six small moons had appeared in the sky. This time, the energy beam of intertwined light and darkness destroyed one after another before they could come into play.

~Are you sure we only have to defeat it three times? What's stopping it from rebirthing again?~

Aetheria flashed across the shattered caldera. Behind her, ice sheets spread, and the sky darkened in response to the call of the Flames of Ymir and Thalassa.

+No, I'm not sure. We need to go all out. Oh no, rain? I hate getting wet.+

~Just deal with it,~ she chided before she and Pyreheart met in physical combat again.

Her fingers had become long, dark talons infused with the Flames of Ymir and Nyx this time. Although her talons could not cut through the phoenix's talons, she was able to steal life and weaken Pyreheart with each contact. On their fifth trade of blows, she shattered the deadened and frost-burned phoenix talons, and her own taloned hands became human once more to deliver another calamitous punch.

The momentum of the blow sent Pyreheart Emberwing crashing to the ground. He rolled and bounced, and then kicked up into the air—talons restored.

"Catch." Aetheria flung a small yellow ball crackling with a strange power the phoenix did not immediately recognize. The Flame of Khaos detonated the Thunderball and created a massive Chaos surge about a meter in front of the giant bird. Tendrils of chaotic lightning reached out to caress the phoenix while unstable mana entered him and assaulted him from the inside. A misty snake reached out of the broken Thunderball. It bit the phoenix on the leg before it faded away.

"Damn." Aetheria observed the results of her first creation of a Chaos surge. For such an unpredictable power, it had turned out shockingly well, and all it had cost her was a one-time-use item. Did it have anything to do with her employment of the Flame of Khaos?

A massive ball of blackness descended from above to strike the phoenix as the snake faded. The air filled with unpleasant sounds when the phoenix became enmeshed in the darkness. The night eviscerated and ate at Pyreheart and his life. Is that the whole attack of Devouring Darkness?

A flash of flame cleared the summit of the volcano again. Pyreheart's powerfully aspected Flame Nova destroyed the sphere of darkness, the lingering lightning tendrils, and a large portion of Aetheria's snowflakes, despite their reinforcement with the Flame of Ymir.

The magma chamber beneath the fight heaved, and barely cooled lava and ice sheets cracked. A forty-meter superior flame elemental emerged from the volcano to protect Emberwing.

Ark was right; we can't keep trading blows like this. This fight will never end. Aetheria darted to the flame elemental and leaped into it. Its fires burned at her, but once she made contact, streaks of blue power flared out from her in every direction. The elemental found its flames changed.

Pyreheart raged at what she had just done. A forty-meter-tall Frostfire elemental now stood on the battlefield, and it did not answer the phoenix's commands. Through their bond, Aetheria could feel Arkaziel's deep amusement at the elemental turning its powerful attacks upon the phoenix. Hundreds of snowflakes manifested around her, aided by the cold effect of the elemental, and joined the assault on the phoenix.

~Bust out your ultimate attack, Ark!~

No sooner had she asked than the sky turned dark, as if by an eclipse. Aetheria raised her eyes to observe the black scales of Arkaziel, the purple glow of his ephemeral fur, the only light in the sky and the only way to differentiate him from the black void the sky had become.

The phoenix had continued to emit fire and light. The enormous amounts of Frostfire and snowflakes that assaulted him glowed. But with each second, those lights dimmed, and a tiny speck of light appeared in Arkaziel's mouth. Every light source, every flame, all energy became dulled by the second, while the orb in Arkaziel's mouth grew more brilliant. As everywhere else became consumed by darkness, the most blinding and terrifying light Aetheria had ever witnessed emerged from Arkaziel's mouth to scour the phoenix.

Pyreheart tried to escape the beam of absolute destruction, but the Frostfire elemental grasped the bird in hand and held him in place. Aetheria thought it fitting that the elemental would join his former master in defeat and saluted the creatures as they shrank to nothingness. The world returned to normal in moments, and no sign of the elemental or the phoenix remained. No buildup of energies came again. They had destroyed Pyreheart Emberwing, Phoenix Overlord.

"Damn, Ark! What do you call that move?"

The cat landed on her shoulder and cuddled against her neck. "That? Oh, that's just my Apocalyptic Eclipse. It's not bad. I didn't think I'd need to resort to Twilight Apocalypse."

Aetheria eyed the cat. *Is he being arrogant, or does he actually have something up his sleeve worse than that? It looked like he took all localized energy sources the darkness consumed and turned them into a pure Ethereal light attack.*

"Well, either way, good job, buddy. Did you get those tail feathers for me?"

Two feathers appeared and floated next to her in the air.

CHAPTER 82

From the Ashes

Enjoying the spatial rings that you got in Dragon's Roar?" Aetheria made a lovely ice floor and altar, phoenix feathers in hand.

"They're nice. Not relying on you to store my snack hoard is a grand step for my dietary independence. So, you are going to do this now? Not wait until we hit a different floor?"

"Nope. I've got everything I need, so we'll do it now. Besides, we're past the Aetherial Veil now. No more training floors. No more lessons. Now they try to kill us for real, so why not have another person with us who can handle themselves in a fight?"

The cat seemed indifferent, yellow eyes closed.

Aetheria prepared the altar. First to go on the altar was the old energy bow she had gotten back on Grief. Next went the sword she had bartered for in Dragon's Roar. Then went the vials of blood. Not just from the elves on the second floor, but also from Werylin's direct children she had encountered on the way. Finally, she placed clothing she had gained from the former Imperator's son.

With the Flame of Nyx employed, Aetheria spoke a spell she had already memorized.

"I, Aetheria, the Etherfrost Asura, call the soul of Werylin Amaryllis to appear before me. No chains shall shackle you; no one and nothing shall bar thy path to this, your blood. Your blood calls, and you are compelled to answer. Now appear before me!"

Aetheria's aura turned into a thing of pure darkness. Despite that, she manipulated Ethereal energy instead of Nether; the ritual was touched with those dark powers. With each moment, she channeled tides of power into the spell, and the blood on the altar boiled. Finally, a specter appeared over the altar. The ghost did not hide its shock, but it did not speak. Instead, the undead spirit took in the altar and the items on it, and then Aetheria, conducting the ritual. The heart of the phoenix appeared on the altar, as well as the tail feathers.

"Do you want to live again, Once-Imperator? Do you want your revenge on Oizys?"

"I do," the undead rasped, and Aetheria smiled.

"By the power of the Etherfrost Asura, live again!" Power cascaded through the altar and all the items on it. Radiant powers of life, the coldest powers of undeath. Neither could thwart Aetheria's focused will as she wielded the power of the Origin to bring her wish to fruition. Within the chaotic miasma of warring forces, an elven body took shape. Each second of the ritual pushed on her an exhaustion equivalent to running a marathon, yet she maintained focus until everything dissipated and a purple-haired elf stood on the altar.

Werylin breathed in astonishment before running his trembling hands over his body. Shocked laughter erupted from his mouth.

"Put the pants on already, jeez," Aetheria said with a hint of affection.

"Why?" Werylin asked from a hoarse throat.

"Because I don't fancy seeing elf dong? I'm in a committed relationship these days." She gestured at the pants. "Not that you don't have a very impressive *wand*, but again—not on the menu."

The purple-haired elf laughed and complied. He pulled on a billowy white shirt to match the pants. "I meant, why did you go through all this work to resurrect me? How did you even summon me into a tower?"

"You offered me a good bit of help initially, so I decided to free you immediately. Then I kept meeting your grandchildren, children, and clan mates, and Karieth gave me the last bits I needed to assemble everything. A pretty special lady; she died trying to do what I just did."

Werylin looked shocked. "My children and *grandchildren* are still in the tower? Despite being bound so close to the tower, I never knew if they made it. Part of Oizys's lovely torture."

Arkaziel yawned and regarded the elf. "Oh, you are helpful, after all. Welcome to the party, Speaker of Creation, Dancer of Destruction. I am Arkaziel'aethiare'-anathemal'suriksyn'asuludar—"

"That's enough, Ark. No one will remember your full name."

Werylin held up a hand. "That is a StarMane, and it's talking to me, and it is half asleep on your shoulder..." The newly resurrected elf looked pallid for some reason.

"I get that you just resurrected, but those are all obvious statements. Which part is the question?" Aetheria did not hold back the sarcasm.

"I should heal him, just in case he went mad from the years of being undead," Arkaziel chimed in helpfully, and a pillar of light descended to engulf the elf. Goosebumps and shivers ran through the now-clothed elf that had nothing to do with magic.

"Why the revival? Why here? Where even are we? And how did you establish a friendship with a StarMane?" The former Imperator looked desperately confused.

"Oh. Well. This is the fiftieth floor of the Tower of Aetherius. We just broke through the Aetherial Veil, so no more training levels. Why here? Because you've got lots of reasons to hate Oizys, and the more, the merrier. Plus, I could use another voice of reason in this group. Arkaziel thinks the answer is just to eat everything in our path. As for the rest..."

Aetheria shrugged and dropped a large tent from her repository onto the frozen ground. "Let's talk over some food. I have an ambrosial fruit salad that should kickstart your cultivation and make you feel alive."

"Ambrosial fruit? Resurrection. The fiftieth floor..." The once-minstrel's purple eyes focused sharply on Aetheria and Arkaziel, and he laughed a little hysterically.

"You have Primordial Flames, are Tier Three, as is your companion, and you found my old equipment, even. Do you think I can even keep up with you? Even with ambrosial fruits?" For a former leader of elves, the newly restored Werylin seemed to have a shortage of confidence.

"Yeah, well, I may have infused you with Aether, too. I don't know if such a thing exists, but you're an Aetherial elf now. Eventually, you'll awaken the Flame of Aetherius in yourself, but I don't know how long that'll take. I imbued the tiniest of sparks in you so you wouldn't explode into a million pieces."

Werylin's purple eyes shone with moisture as he pondered how to express his gratitude. "My blade and words are at your disposal, Aetheria. Your cause will be mine." The elf seemed to ignore the potential of explosions.

"Cool, but you should have your own goals, too. Someday we'll be done with all this. It is just ten towers, after all." Aetheria grinned mischievously at the understatement of the year. "Maybe get your clan out of the tower and back

to Grief after we whoop Oizys?"

Werylin and Arkaziel laughed together.

The trio enjoyed Aetheria's ambrosia salad, but she kept putting off telling her tale to Werylin. She told the elf to eat. She would tell him the Etherfrost Asura's story soon enough.

Soon.

About the Author

Jamie Kojola is the author of the Odyssey of the Ethereal series, originally released on Royal Road. In her free time, she enjoys gardening, sewing, gaming, crafting, and playing D&D. Kojola lives in Minnesota with her two children, spouse, and three cats.